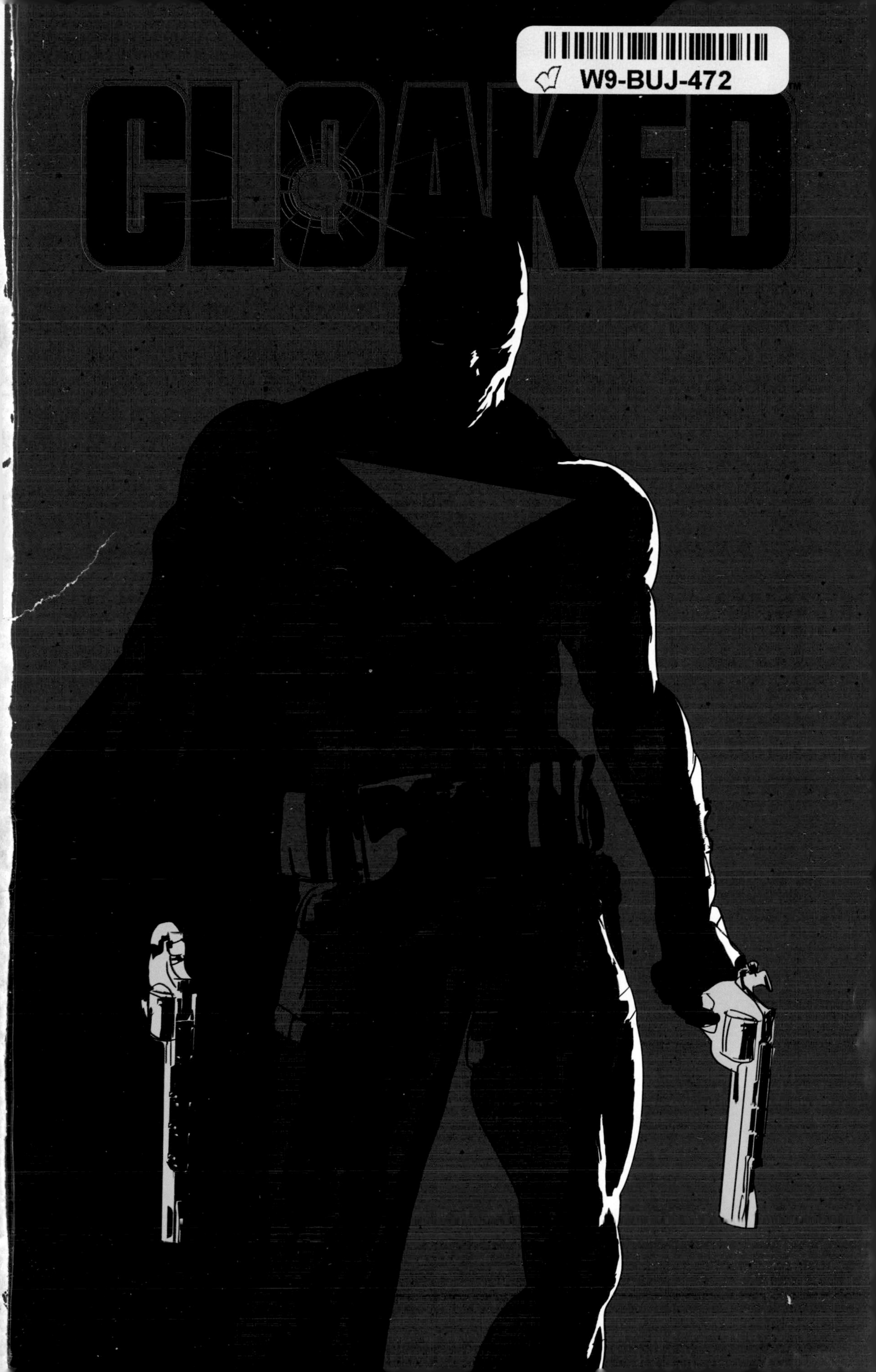
CLOAKED™

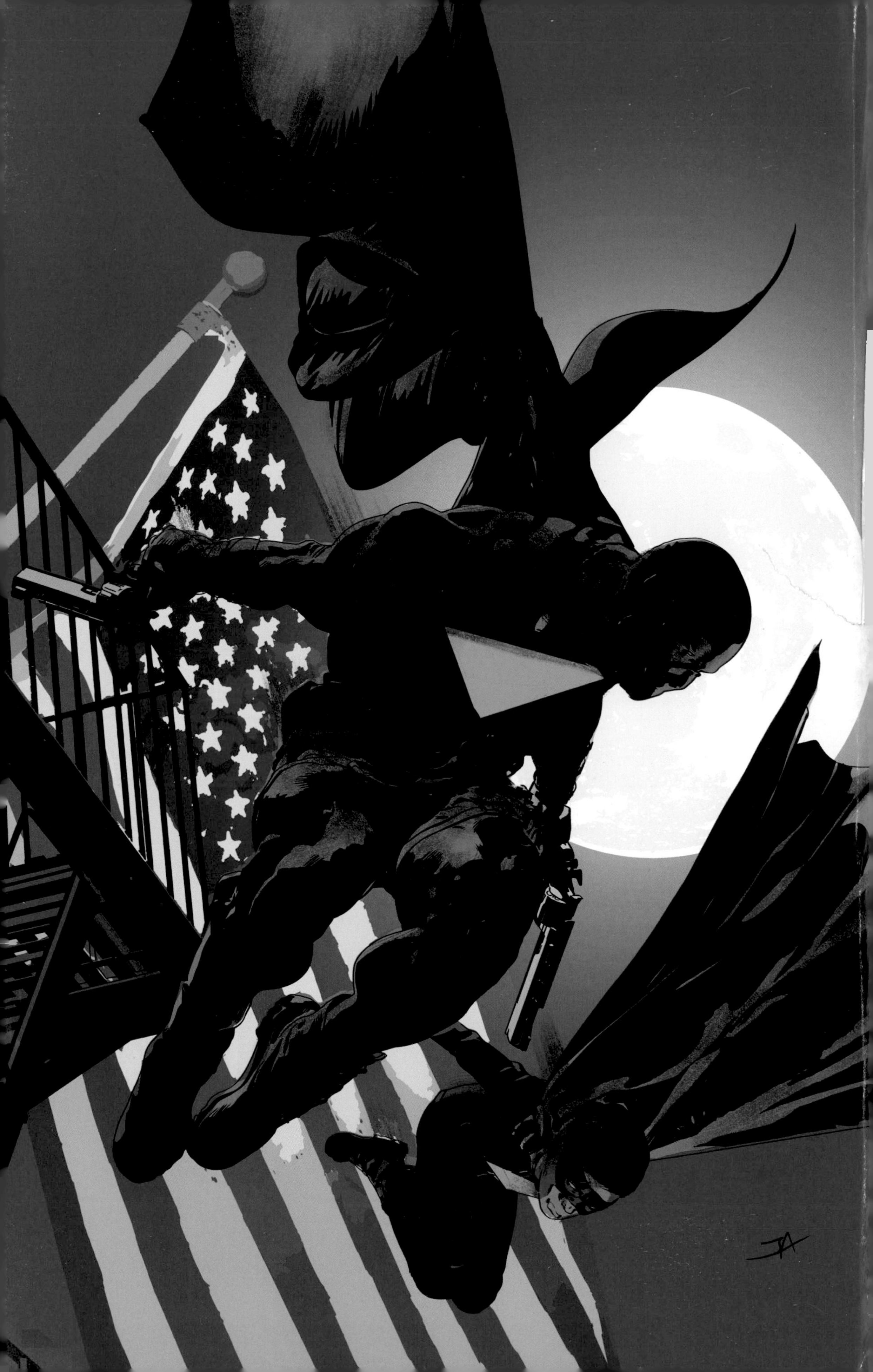

CLOAKED

STORY
MIKE RICHARDSON

ART AND COLORS
JORDI ARMENGOL

LETTERING
NATE PIEKOS of BLAMBOT

DARK HORSE BOOKS

PRESIDENT AND PUBLISHER
MIKE RICHARDSON

EDITORS
CHRIS WARNER AND **RANDY STRADLEY**

ASSOCIATE EDITOR
JENNY BLENK

DIGITAL ART TECHNICIAN
ANN GRAY

DESIGNER
SARAH TERRY

CLOAKED™

This volume collects issues one through four of the Dark Horse comic-book series *Cloaked*.

Dark Horse Books
A division of Dark Horse Comics LLC
10956 SE Main Street
Milwaukie, OR 97222

DarkHorse.com

International Licensing: (503) 905-2377
Comic Shop Locator Service: (888) 266-4226

First edition: July 2022
Ebook ISBN 978-1-50673-010-3
Trade Paperback ISBN 978-1-50673-009-7

1 3 5 7 9 10 8 6 4 2
Printed in China

FSC
www.fsc.org
MIX
Paper from
responsible sources
FSC® C169962

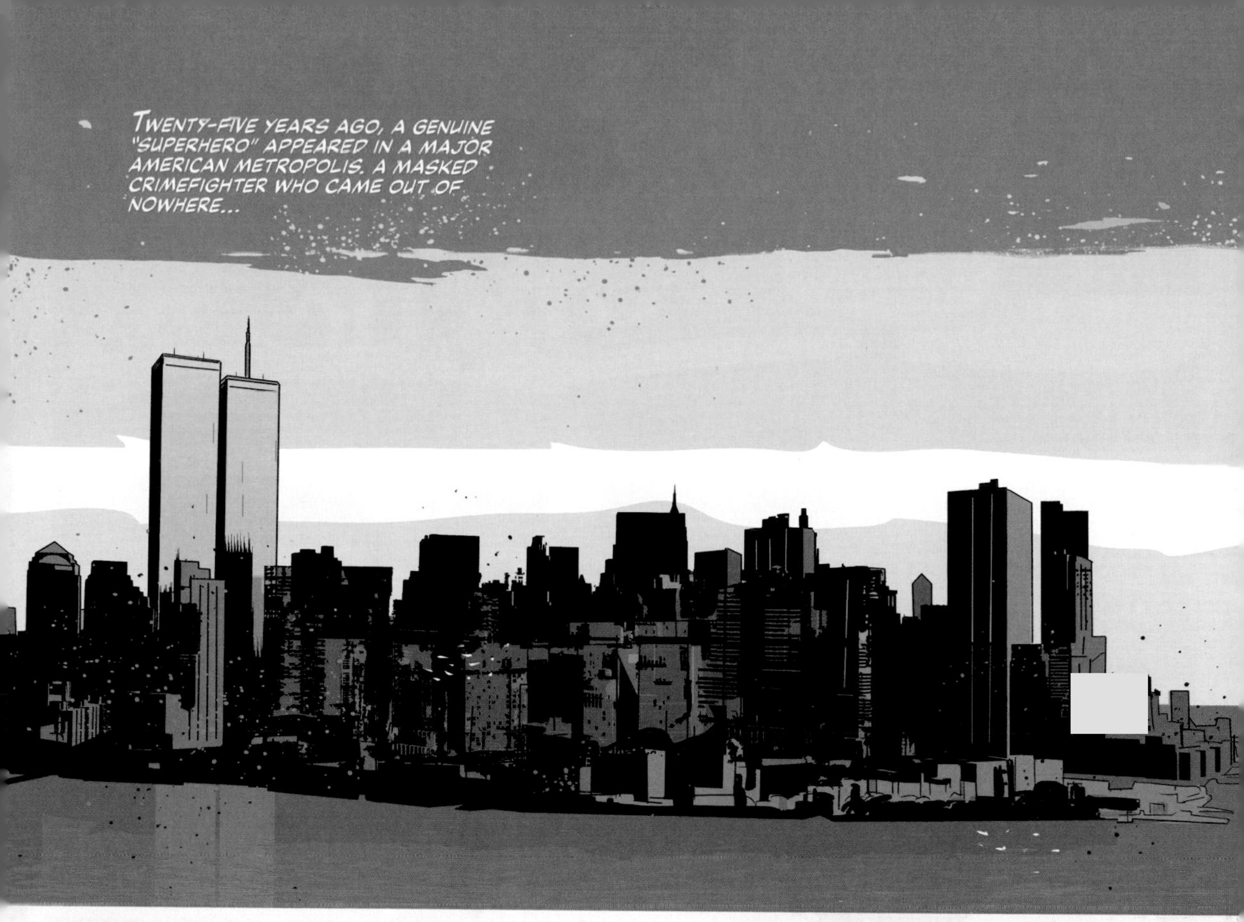
TWENTY-FIVE YEARS AGO, A GENUINE "SUPERHERO" APPEARED IN A MAJOR AMERICAN METROPOLIS. A MASKED CRIMEFIGHTER WHO CAME OUT OF NOWHERE...

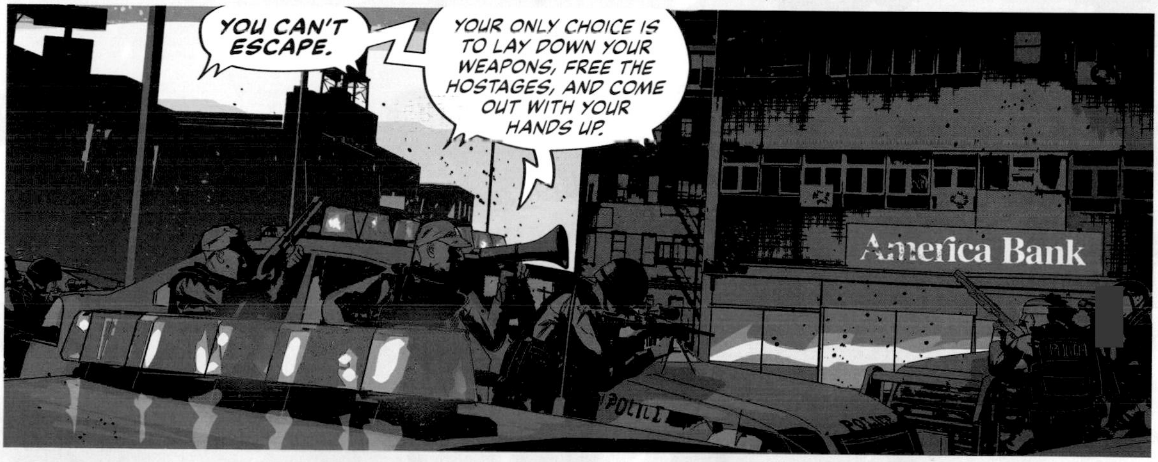
YOU CAN'T ESCAPE.
YOUR ONLY CHOICE IS TO LAY DOWN YOUR WEAPONS, FREE THE HOSTAGES, AND COME OUT WITH YOUR HANDS UP.
America Bank

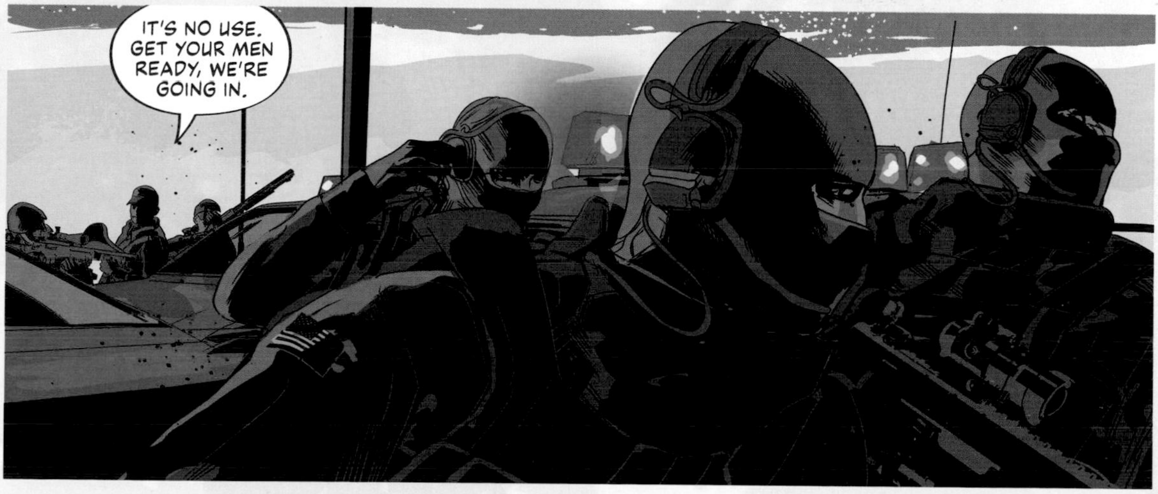
IT'S NO USE. GET YOUR MEN READY, WE'RE GOING IN.

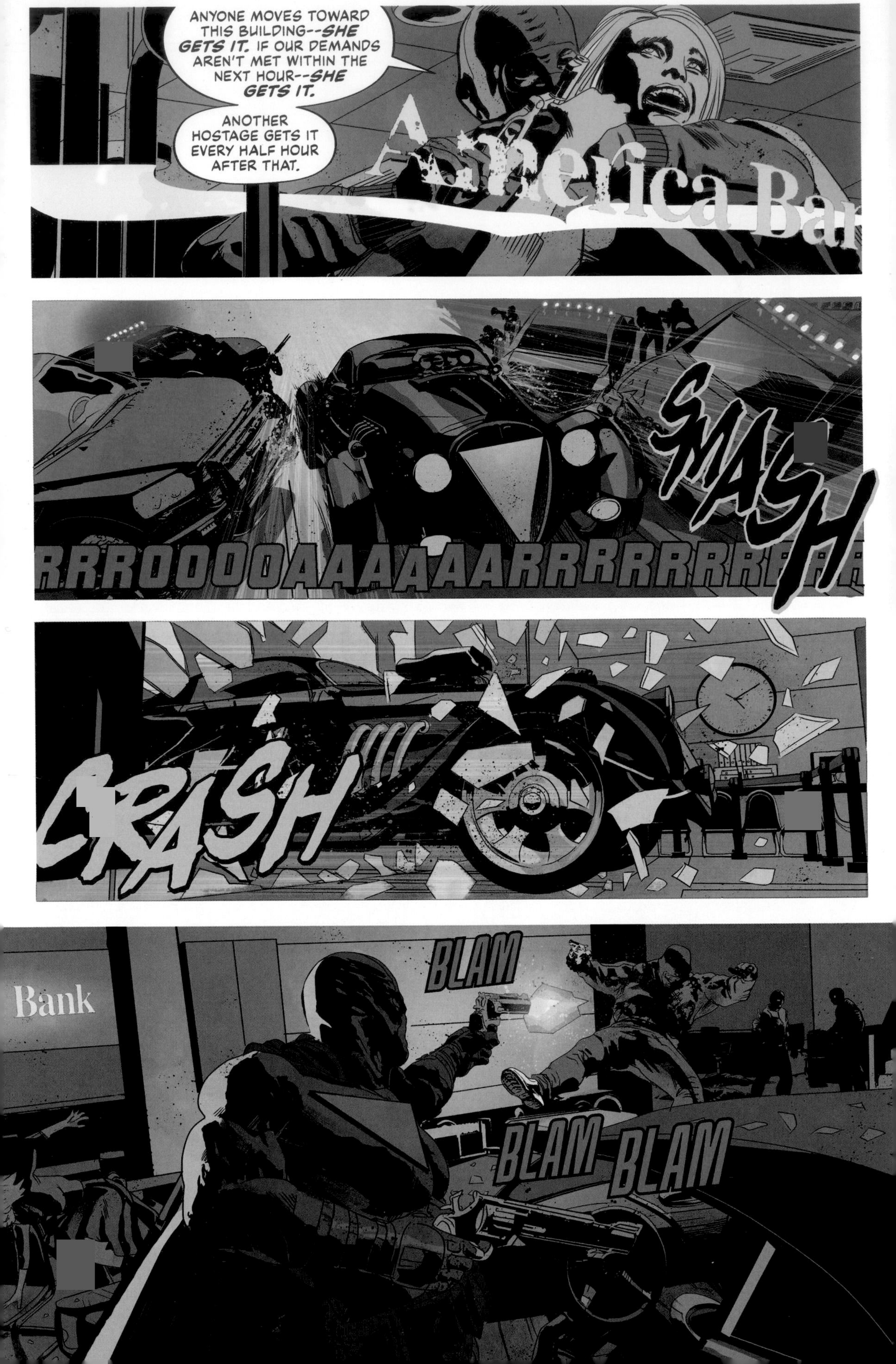
ANYONE MOVES TOWARD THIS BUILDING--*SHE GETS IT.* IF OUR DEMANDS AREN'T MET WITHIN THE NEXT HOUR--*SHE GETS IT.*
ANOTHER HOSTAGE GETS IT EVERY HALF HOUR AFTER THAT.
America Ba
SMASH
RRROOOOAAAAAARRRRRRRR
CRASH
Bank
BLAM
BLAM BLAM

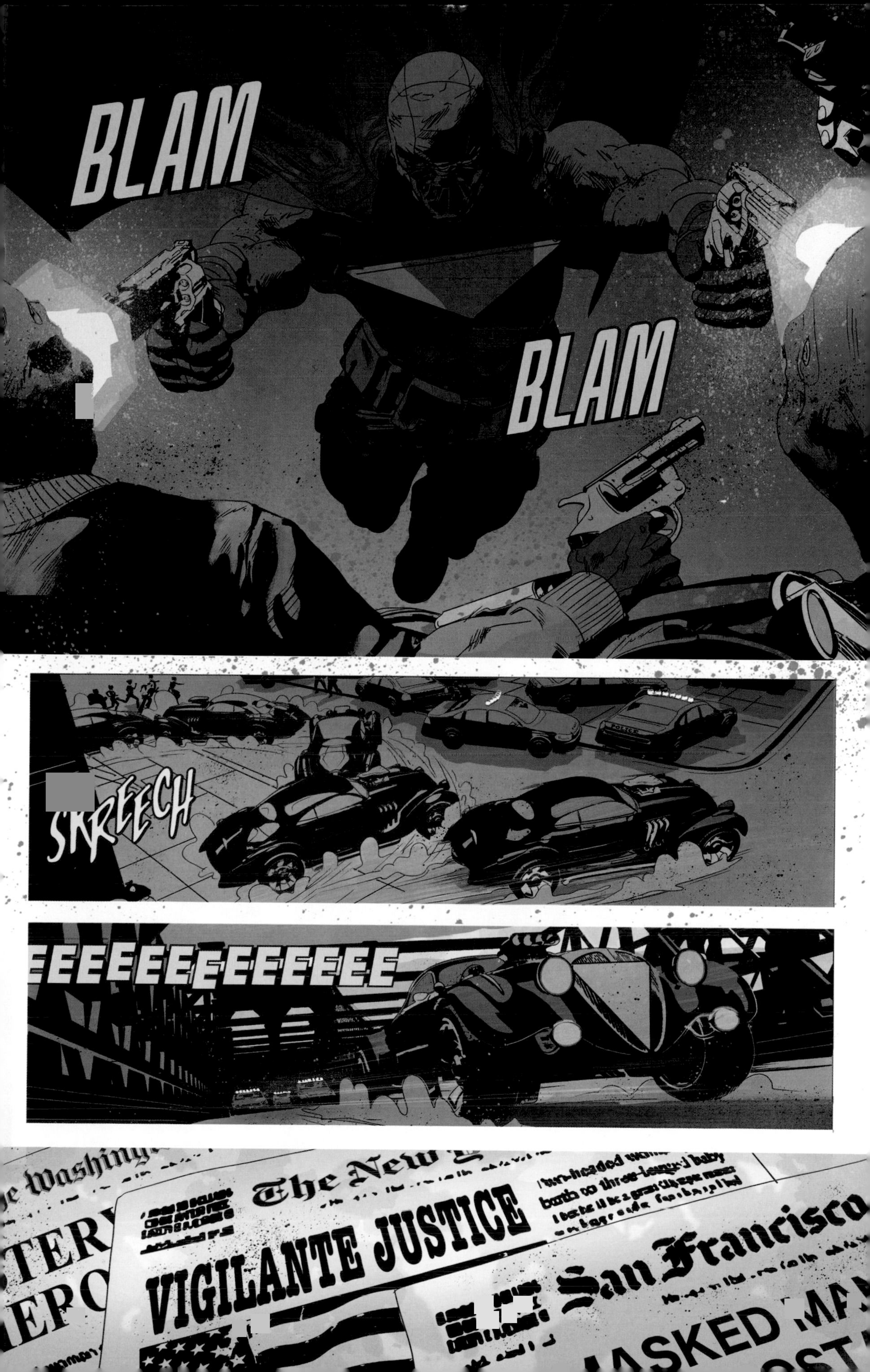
BLAM
BLAM
SKREECH
EEEEEEEEEEEE
VIGILANTE JUSTICE
San Francisco

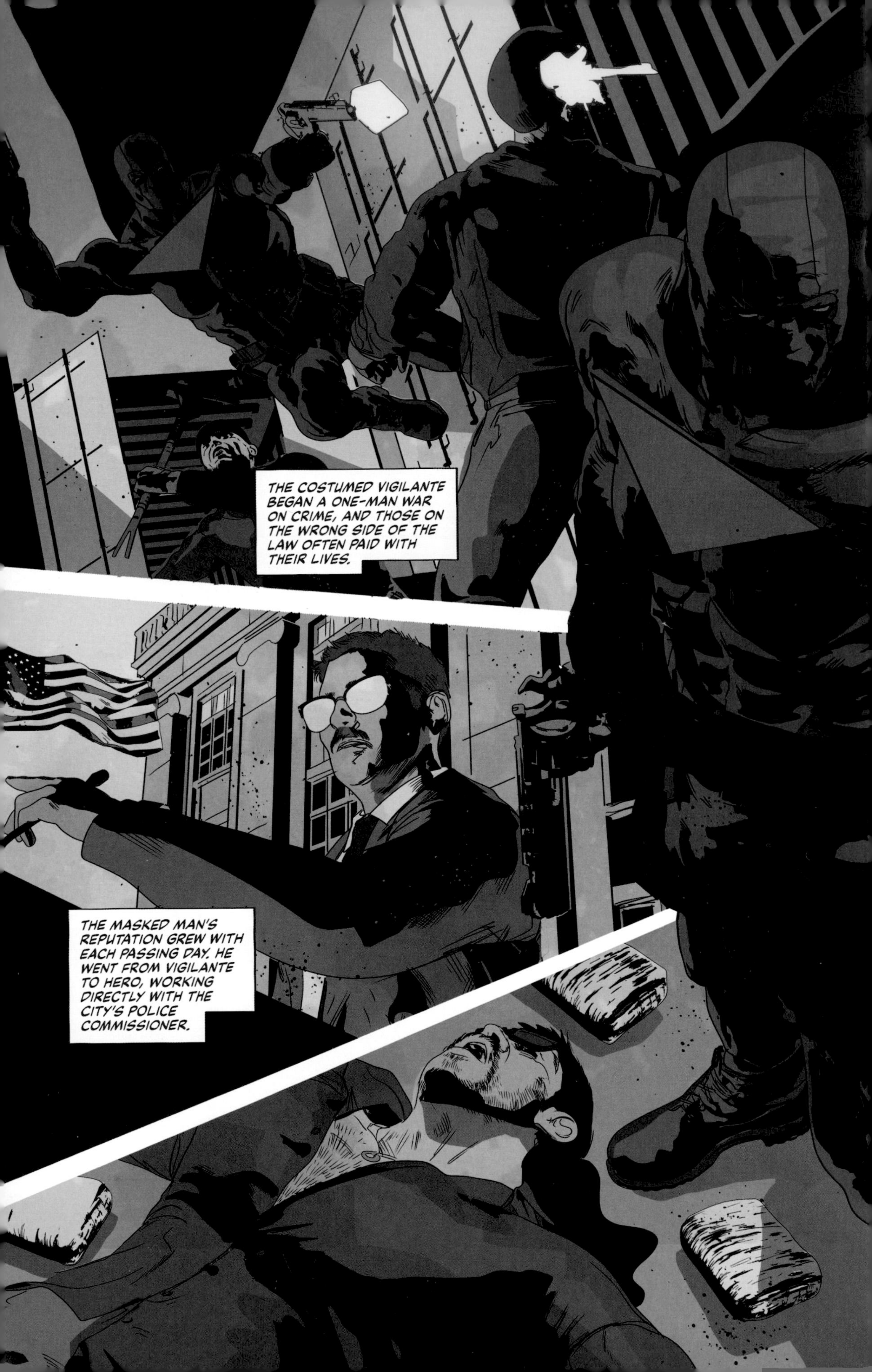
THE COSTUMED VIGILANTE BEGAN A ONE-MAN WAR ON CRIME, AND THOSE ON THE WRONG SIDE OF THE LAW OFTEN PAID WITH THEIR LIVES.
THE MASKED MAN'S REPUTATION GREW WITH EACH PASSING DAY. HE WENT FROM VIGILANTE TO HERO, WORKING DIRECTLY WITH THE CITY'S POLICE COMMISSIONER.

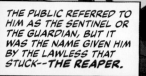

THE PUBLIC REFERRED TO HIM AS THE SENTINEL OR THE GUARDIAN, BUT IT WAS THE NAME GIVEN HIM BY THE LAWLESS THAT STUCK--**THE REAPER.**

TALES OF HIS AMAZING DEEDS SPREAD UNTIL IT WAS NO LONGER POSSIBLE TO SEPARATE FACT FROM FICTION. THE MASKED CRIMEFIGHTER BECAME A LIVING ICON...

...AND THEN HE DISAPPEARED.

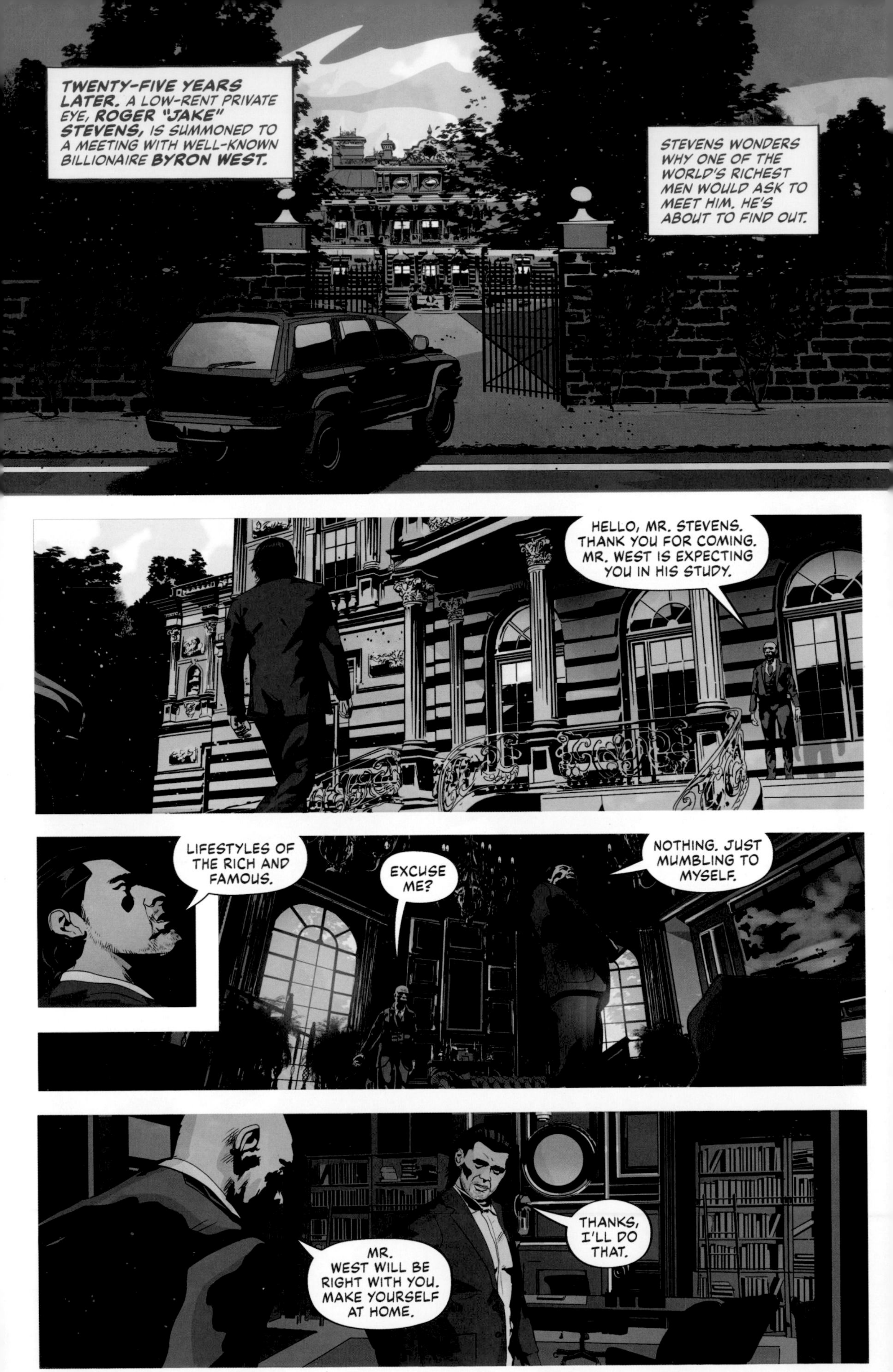
TWENTY-FIVE YEARS LATER. A LOW-RENT PRIVATE EYE, ROGER "JAKE" STEVENS, IS SUMMONED TO A MEETING WITH WELL-KNOWN BILLIONAIRE BYRON WEST.
STEVENS WONDERS WHY ONE OF THE WORLD'S RICHEST MEN WOULD ASK TO MEET HIM. HE'S ABOUT TO FIND OUT.
HELLO, MR. STEVENS. THANK YOU FOR COMING. MR. WEST IS EXPECTING YOU IN HIS STUDY.
LIFESTYLES OF THE RICH AND FAMOUS.
EXCUSE ME?
NOTHING. JUST MUMBLING TO MYSELF.
MR. WEST WILL BE RIGHT WITH YOU. MAKE YOURSELF AT HOME.
THANKS, I'LL DO THAT.

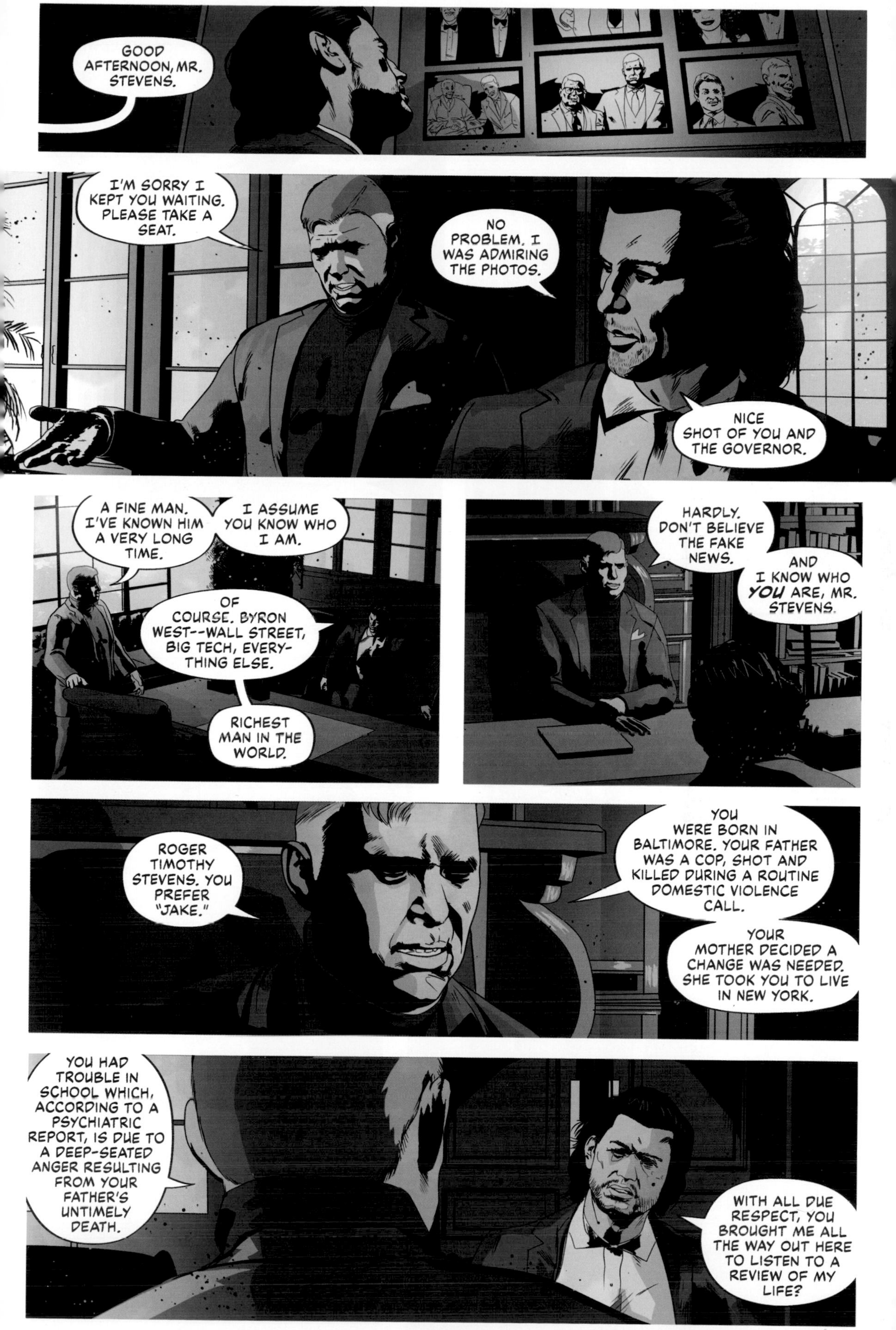
GOOD AFTERNOON, MR. STEVENS.
I'M SORRY I KEPT YOU WAITING. PLEASE TAKE A SEAT.
NO PROBLEM. I WAS ADMIRING THE PHOTOS.
NICE SHOT OF YOU AND THE GOVERNOR.
A FINE MAN. I'VE KNOWN HIM A VERY LONG TIME.
I ASSUME YOU KNOW WHO I AM.
OF COURSE. BYRON WEST--WALL STREET, BIG TECH, EVERYTHING ELSE.
RICHEST MAN IN THE WORLD.
HARDLY. DON'T BELIEVE THE FAKE NEWS.
AND I KNOW WHO *YOU* ARE, MR. STEVENS.
ROGER TIMOTHY STEVENS. YOU PREFER "JAKE."
YOU WERE BORN IN BALTIMORE. YOUR FATHER WAS A COP, SHOT AND KILLED DURING A ROUTINE DOMESTIC VIOLENCE CALL.
YOUR MOTHER DECIDED A CHANGE WAS NEEDED. SHE TOOK YOU TO LIVE IN NEW YORK.
YOU HAD TROUBLE IN SCHOOL WHICH, ACCORDING TO A PSYCHIATRIC REPORT, IS DUE TO A DEEP-SEATED ANGER RESULTING FROM YOUR FATHER'S UNTIMELY DEATH.
WITH ALL DUE RESPECT, YOU BROUGHT ME ALL THE WAY OUT HERE TO LISTEN TO A REVIEW OF MY LIFE?

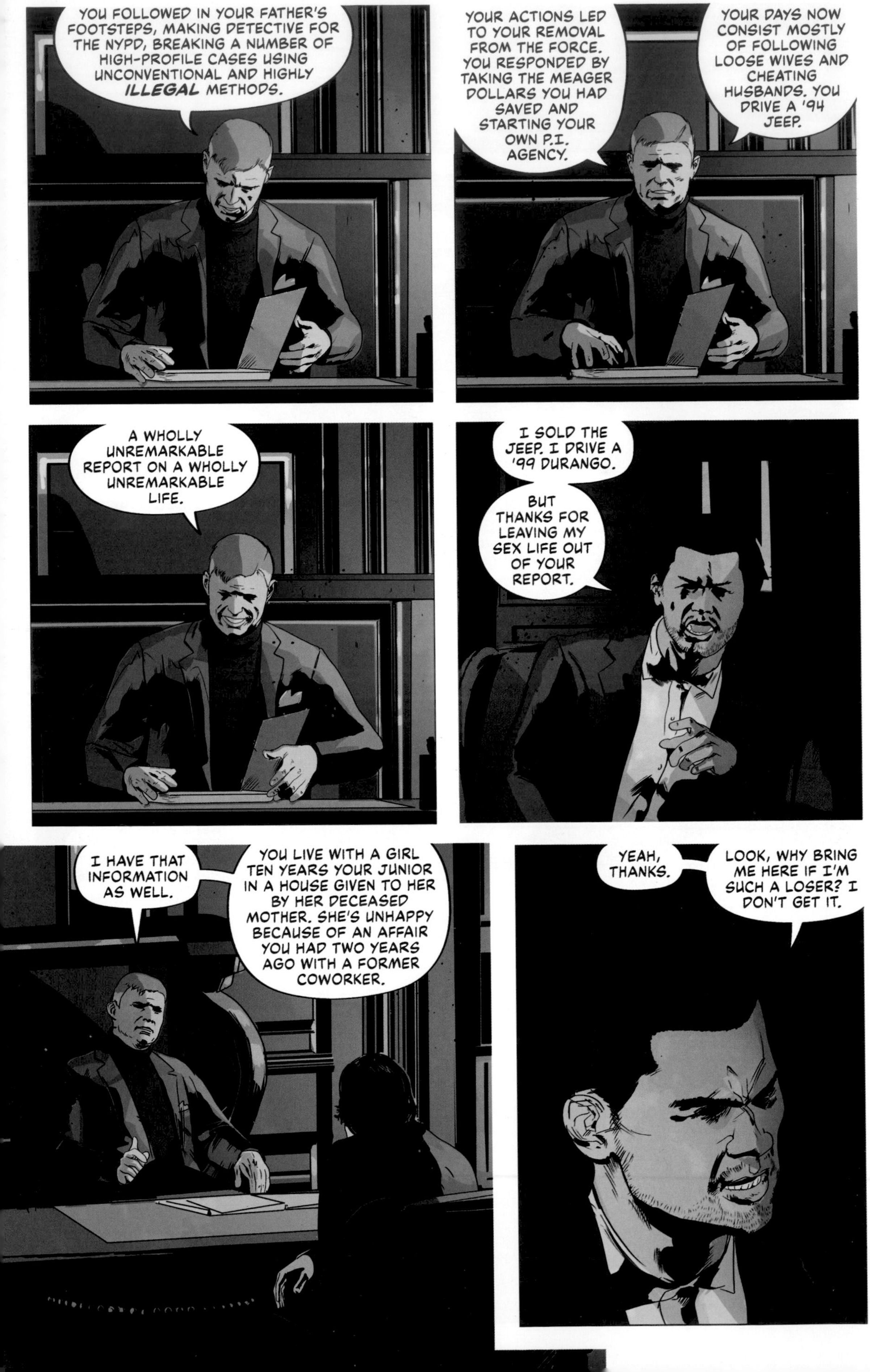
YOU FOLLOWED IN YOUR FATHER'S FOOTSTEPS, MAKING DETECTIVE FOR THE NYPD, BREAKING A NUMBER OF HIGH-PROFILE CASES USING UNCONVENTIONAL AND HIGHLY *ILLEGAL* METHODS.
YOUR ACTIONS LED TO YOUR REMOVAL FROM THE FORCE. YOU RESPONDED BY TAKING THE MEAGER DOLLARS YOU HAD SAVED AND STARTING YOUR OWN P.I. AGENCY.
YOUR DAYS NOW CONSIST MOSTLY OF FOLLOWING LOOSE WIVES AND CHEATING HUSBANDS. YOU DRIVE A '94 JEEP.
A WHOLLY UNREMARKABLE REPORT ON A WHOLLY UNREMARKABLE LIFE.
I SOLD THE JEEP. I DRIVE A '99 DURANGO.
BUT THANKS FOR LEAVING MY SEX LIFE OUT OF YOUR REPORT.
I HAVE THAT INFORMATION AS WELL.
YOU LIVE WITH A GIRL TEN YEARS YOUR JUNIOR IN A HOUSE GIVEN TO HER BY HER DECEASED MOTHER. SHE'S UNHAPPY BECAUSE OF AN AFFAIR YOU HAD TWO YEARS AGO WITH A FORMER COWORKER.
YEAH, THANKS.
LOOK, WHY BRING ME HERE IF I'M SUCH A LOSER? I DON'T GET IT.

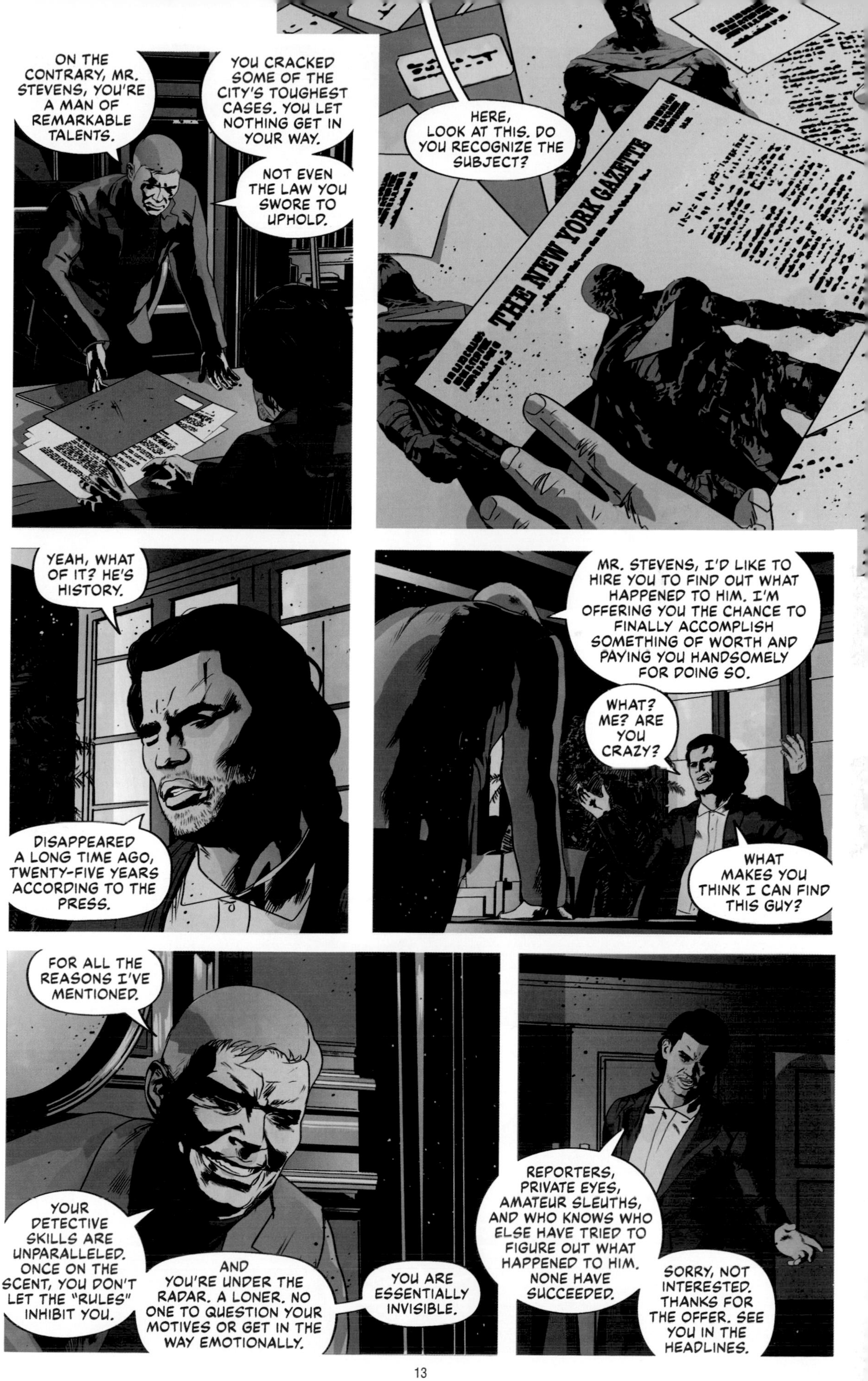
ON THE CONTRARY, MR. STEVENS, YOU'RE A MAN OF REMARKABLE TALENTS.
YOU CRACKED SOME OF THE CITY'S TOUGHEST CASES. YOU LET NOTHING GET IN YOUR WAY.
NOT EVEN THE LAW YOU SWORE TO UPHOLD.
HERE, LOOK AT THIS. DO YOU RECOGNIZE THE SUBJECT?
THE NEW YORK GAZETTE
YEAH, WHAT OF IT? HE'S HISTORY.
DISAPPEARED A LONG TIME AGO, TWENTY-FIVE YEARS ACCORDING TO THE PRESS.
MR. STEVENS, I'D LIKE TO HIRE YOU TO FIND OUT WHAT HAPPENED TO HIM. I'M OFFERING YOU THE CHANCE TO FINALLY ACCOMPLISH SOMETHING OF WORTH AND PAYING YOU HANDSOMELY FOR DOING SO.
WHAT? ME? ARE YOU CRAZY?
WHAT MAKES YOU THINK I CAN FIND THIS GUY?
FOR ALL THE REASONS I'VE MENTIONED.
YOUR DETECTIVE SKILLS ARE UNPARALLELED. ONCE ON THE SCENT, YOU DON'T LET THE "RULES" INHIBIT YOU.
AND YOU'RE UNDER THE RADAR. A LONER. NO ONE TO QUESTION YOUR MOTIVES OR GET IN THE WAY EMOTIONALLY.
YOU ARE ESSENTIALLY INVISIBLE.
REPORTERS, PRIVATE EYES, AMATEUR SLEUTHS, AND WHO KNOWS WHO ELSE HAVE TRIED TO FIGURE OUT WHAT HAPPENED TO HIM. NONE HAVE SUCCEEDED.
SORRY, NOT INTERESTED. THANKS FOR THE OFFER. SEE YOU IN THE HEADLINES.

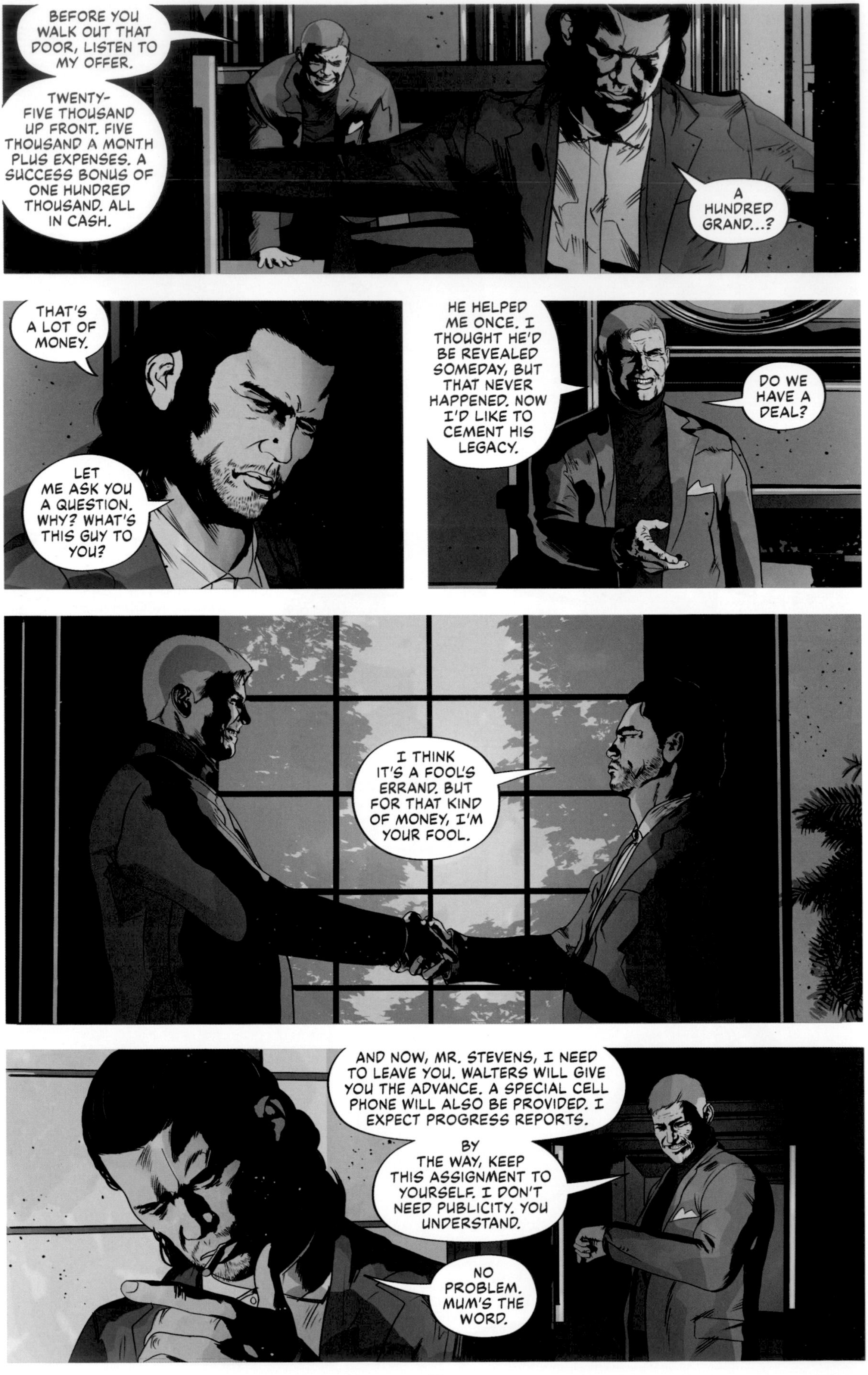
BEFORE YOU WALK OUT THAT DOOR, LISTEN TO MY OFFER.
TWENTY-FIVE THOUSAND UP FRONT. FIVE THOUSAND A MONTH PLUS EXPENSES. A SUCCESS BONUS OF ONE HUNDRED THOUSAND. ALL IN CASH.
A HUNDRED GRAND...?
THAT'S A LOT OF MONEY.
LET ME ASK YOU A QUESTION. WHY? WHAT'S THIS GUY TO YOU?
HE HELPED ME ONCE. I THOUGHT HE'D BE REVEALED SOMEDAY, BUT THAT NEVER HAPPENED. NOW I'D LIKE TO CEMENT HIS LEGACY.
DO WE HAVE A DEAL?
I THINK IT'S A FOOL'S ERRAND. BUT FOR THAT KIND OF MONEY, I'M YOUR FOOL.
AND NOW, MR. STEVENS, I NEED TO LEAVE YOU. WALTERS WILL GIVE YOU THE ADVANCE. A SPECIAL CELL PHONE WILL ALSO BE PROVIDED. I EXPECT PROGRESS REPORTS.
BY THE WAY, KEEP THIS ASSIGNMENT TO YOURSELF. I DON'T NEED PUBLICITY. YOU UNDERSTAND.
NO PROBLEM. MUM'S THE WORD.

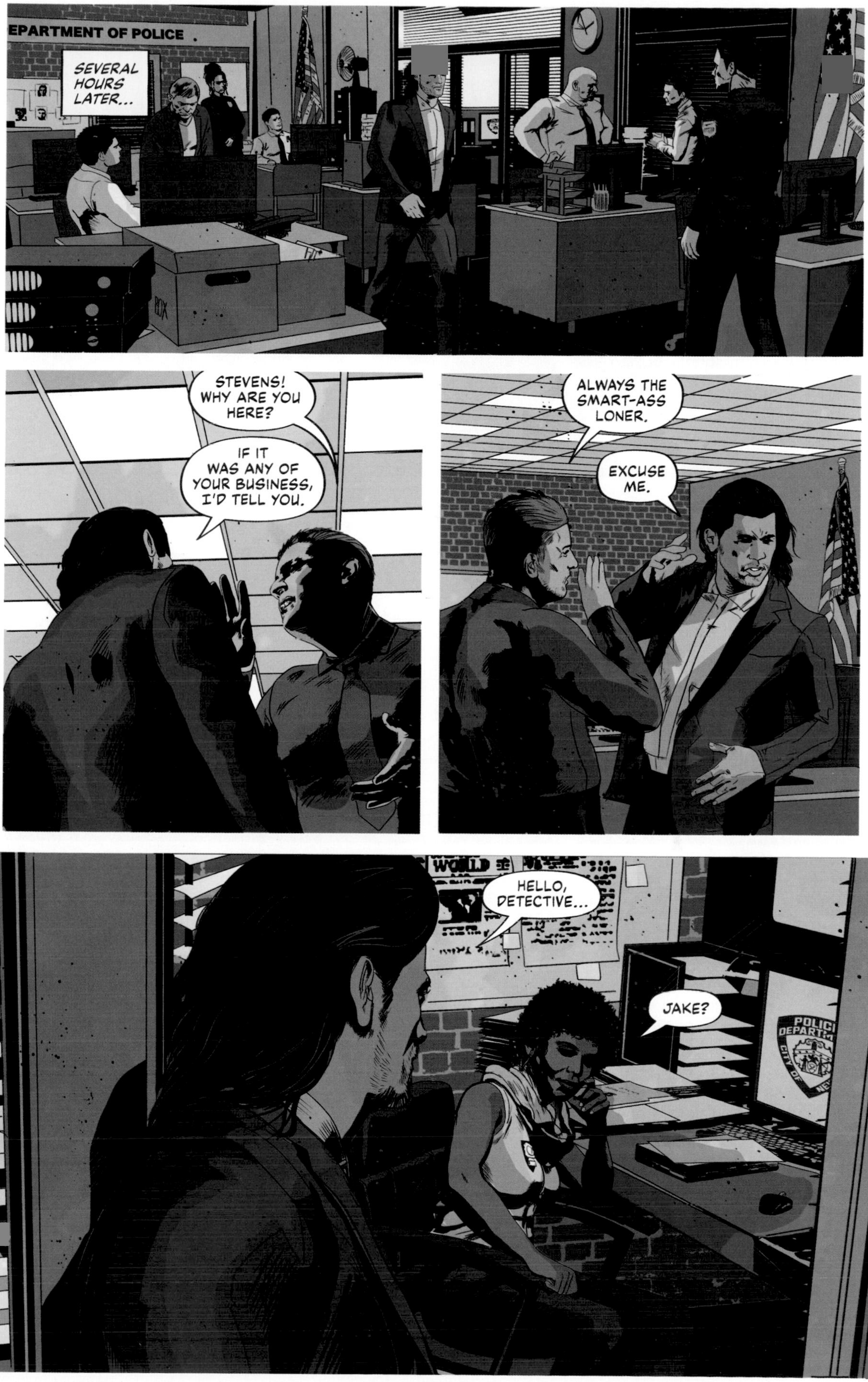
EPARTMENT OF POLICE
SEVERAL HOURS LATER...
STEVENS! WHY ARE YOU HERE?
IF IT WAS ANY OF YOUR BUSINESS, I'D TELL YOU.
ALWAYS THE SMART-ASS LONER.
EXCUSE ME.
HELLO, DETECTIVE...
JAKE?

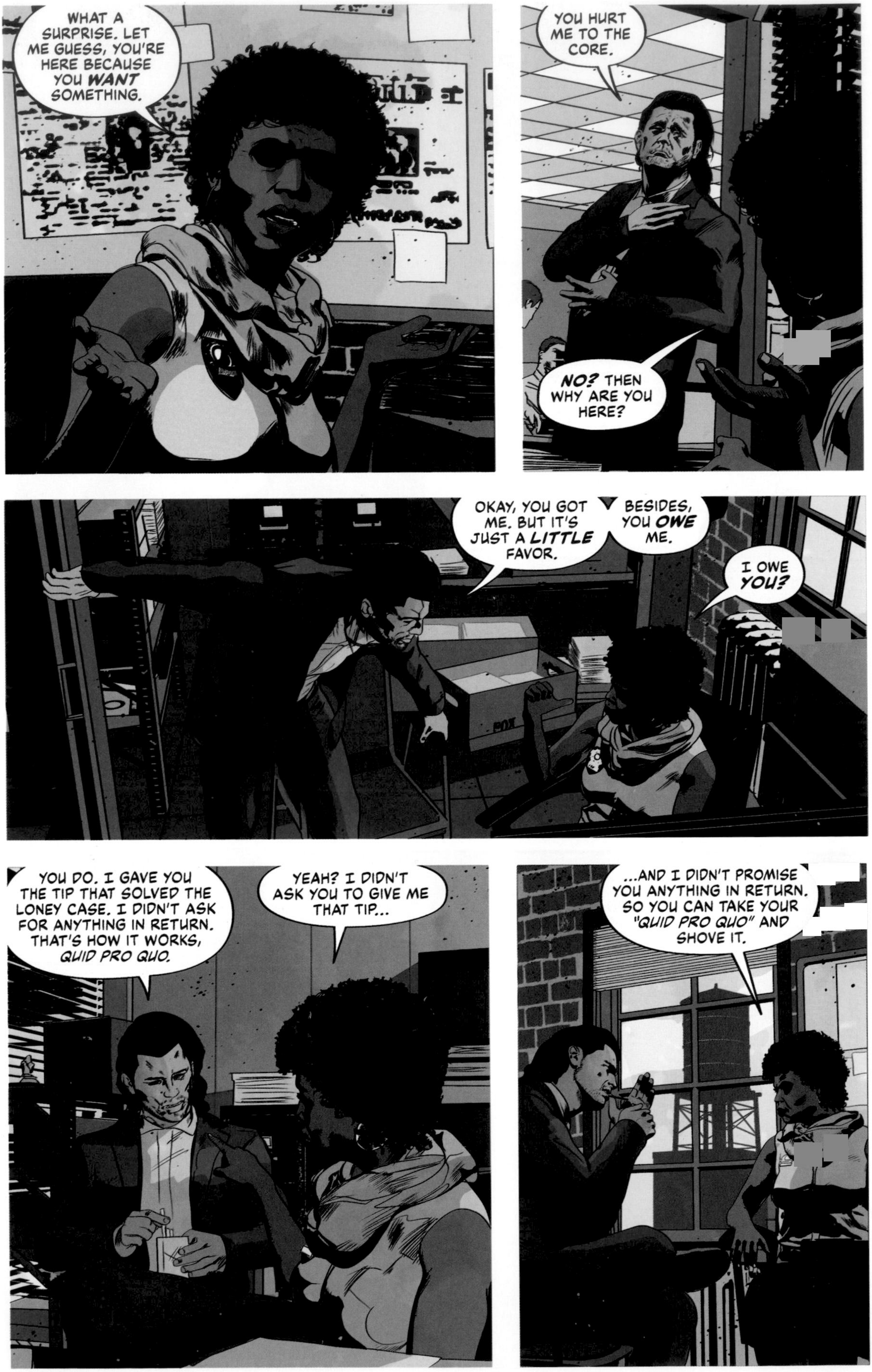
WHAT A SURPRISE. LET ME GUESS, YOU'RE HERE BECAUSE YOU *WANT* SOMETHING.
YOU HURT ME TO THE CORE.
NO? THEN WHY ARE YOU HERE?
OKAY, YOU GOT ME. BUT IT'S JUST A *LITTLE* FAVOR.
BESIDES, YOU *OWE* ME.
I OWE *YOU?*
YOU DO. I GAVE YOU THE TIP THAT SOLVED THE LONEY CASE. I DIDN'T ASK FOR ANYTHING IN RETURN. THAT'S HOW IT WORKS, *QUID PRO QUO.*
YEAH? I DIDN'T ASK YOU TO GIVE ME THAT TIP...
...AND I DIDN'T PROMISE YOU ANYTHING IN RETURN. SO YOU CAN TAKE YOUR "*QUID PRO QUO*" AND SHOVE IT.

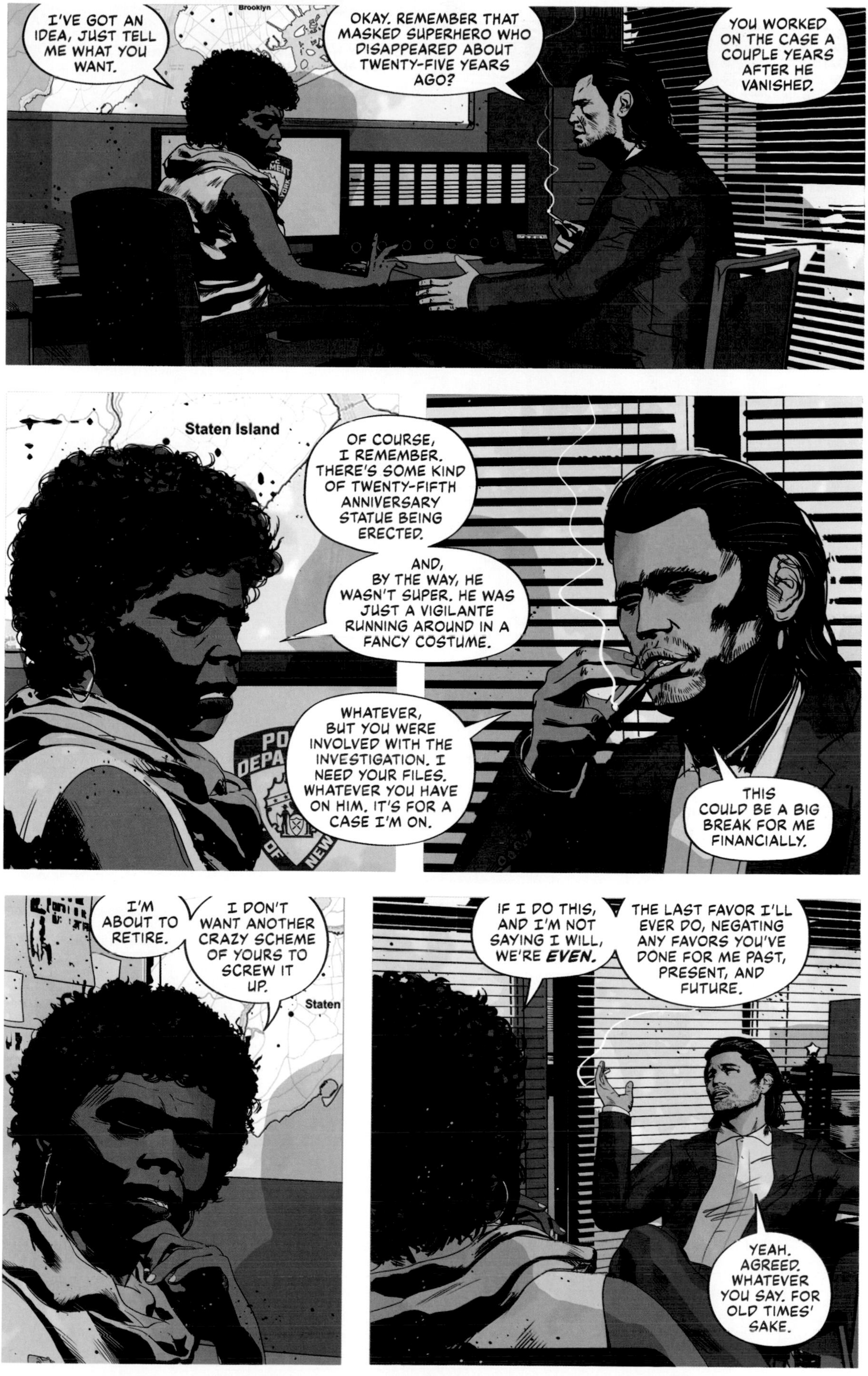
Brooklyn
I'VE GOT AN IDEA, JUST TELL ME WHAT YOU WANT.
OKAY. REMEMBER THAT MASKED SUPERHERO WHO DISAPPEARED ABOUT TWENTY-FIVE YEARS AGO?
YOU WORKED ON THE CASE A COUPLE YEARS AFTER HE VANISHED.
Staten Island
OF COURSE, I REMEMBER. THERE'S SOME KIND OF TWENTY-FIFTH ANNIVERSARY STATUE BEING ERECTED.
AND, BY THE WAY, HE WASN'T SUPER. HE WAS JUST A VIGILANTE RUNNING AROUND IN A FANCY COSTUME.
WHATEVER, BUT YOU WERE INVOLVED WITH THE INVESTIGATION. I NEED YOUR FILES. WHATEVER YOU HAVE ON HIM. IT'S FOR A CASE I'M ON.
THIS COULD BE A BIG BREAK FOR ME FINANCIALLY.
I'M ABOUT TO RETIRE.
I DON'T WANT ANOTHER CRAZY SCHEME OF YOURS TO SCREW IT UP.
Staten
IF I DO THIS, AND I'M NOT SAYING I WILL, WE'RE *EVEN.*
THE LAST FAVOR I'LL EVER DO, NEGATING ANY FAVORS YOU'VE DONE FOR ME PAST, PRESENT, AND FUTURE.
YEAH. AGREED. WHATEVER YOU SAY. FOR OLD TIMES' SAKE.

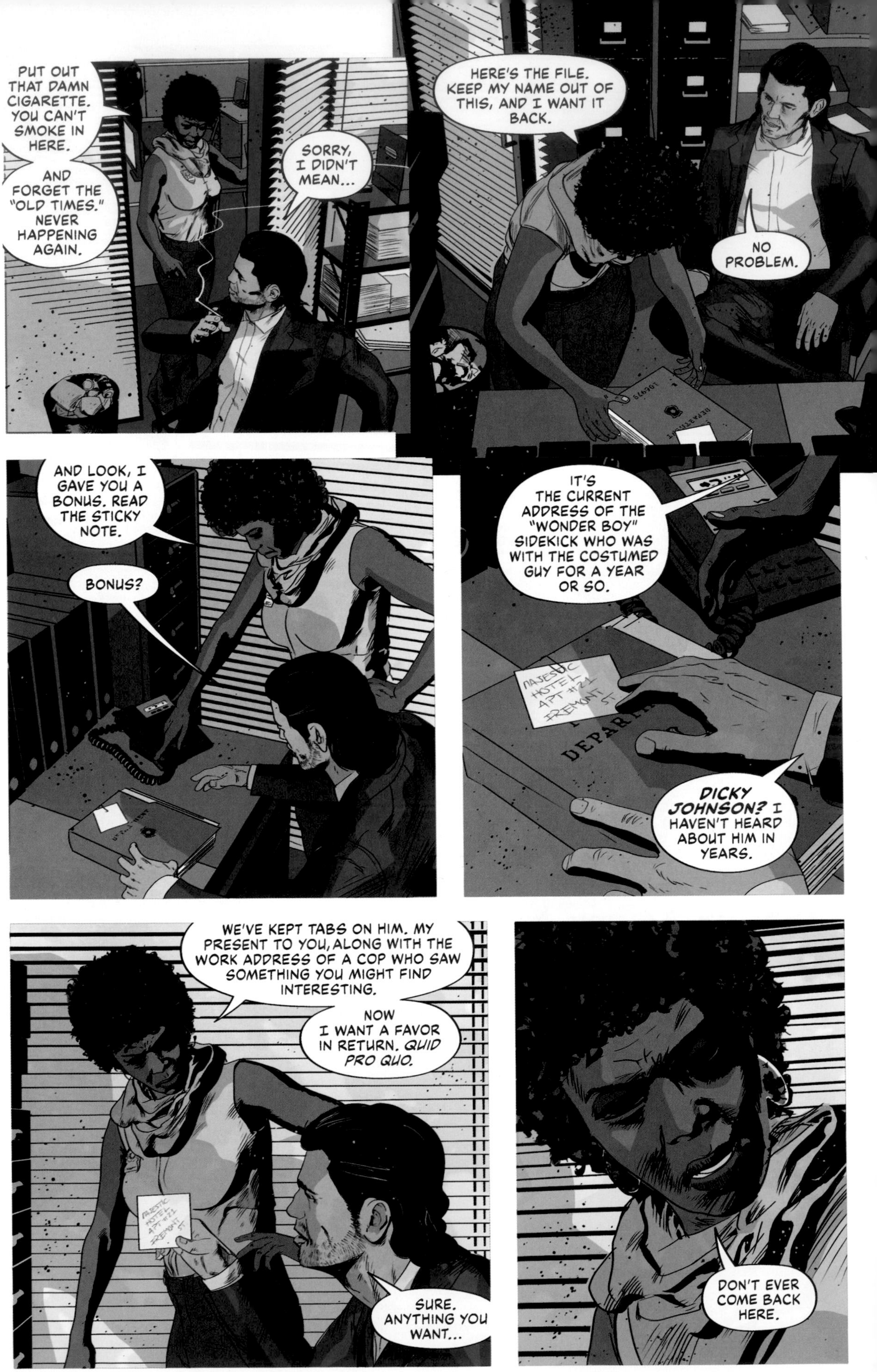
PUT OUT THAT DAMN CIGARETTE. YOU CAN'T SMOKE IN HERE.
AND FORGET THE "OLD TIMES." NEVER HAPPENING AGAIN.
SORRY, I DIDN'T MEAN...
HERE'S THE FILE. KEEP MY NAME OUT OF THIS, AND I WANT IT BACK.
NO PROBLEM.
AND LOOK, I GAVE YOU A BONUS. READ THE STICKY NOTE.
BONUS?
IT'S THE CURRENT ADDRESS OF THE "WONDER BOY" SIDEKICK WHO WAS WITH THE COSTUMED GUY FOR A YEAR OR SO.
MAJESTIC HOTEL APT #21 FREMONT ST.
DEPARTMENT
DICKY JOHNSON? I HAVEN'T HEARD ABOUT HIM IN YEARS.
WE'VE KEPT TABS ON HIM. MY PRESENT TO YOU, ALONG WITH THE WORK ADDRESS OF A COP WHO SAW SOMETHING YOU MIGHT FIND INTERESTING.
NOW I WANT A FAVOR IN RETURN. QUID PRO QUO.
SURE. ANYTHING YOU WANT...
DON'T EVER COME BACK HERE.

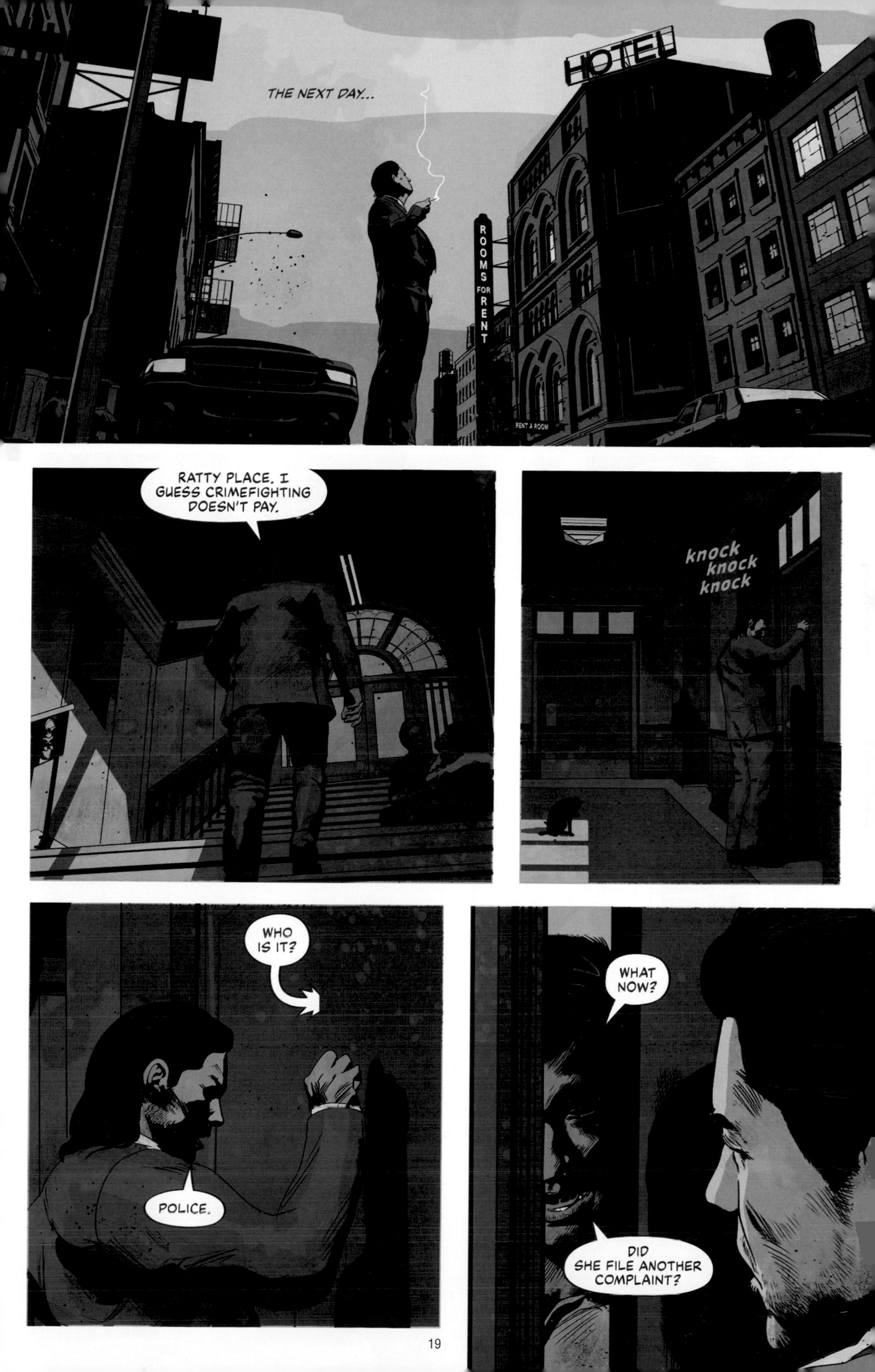
THE NEXT DAY...
HOTEL
ROOMS FOR RENT
RENT A ROOM
RATTY PLACE. I GUESS CRIMEFIGHTING DOESN'T PAY.
knock knock knock
WHO IS IT?
POLICE.
WHAT NOW?
DID SHE FILE ANOTHER COMPLAINT?

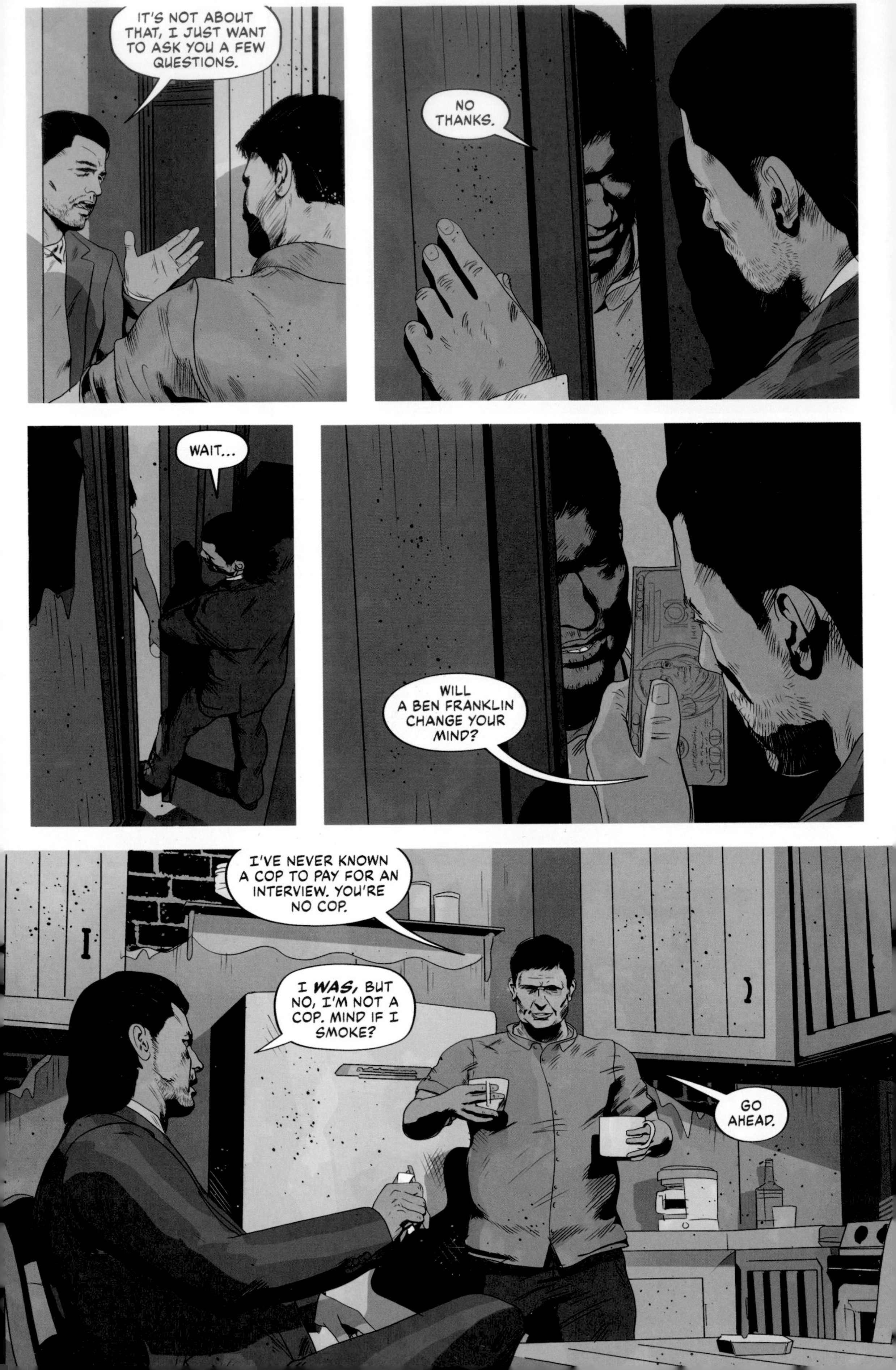
IT'S NOT ABOUT THAT, I JUST WANT TO ASK YOU A FEW QUESTIONS.
NO THANKS.
WAIT...
WILL A BEN FRANKLIN CHANGE YOUR MIND?
I'VE NEVER KNOWN A COP TO PAY FOR AN INTERVIEW. YOU'RE NO COP.
I *WAS,* BUT NO, I'M NOT A COP. MIND IF I SMOKE?
GO AHEAD.

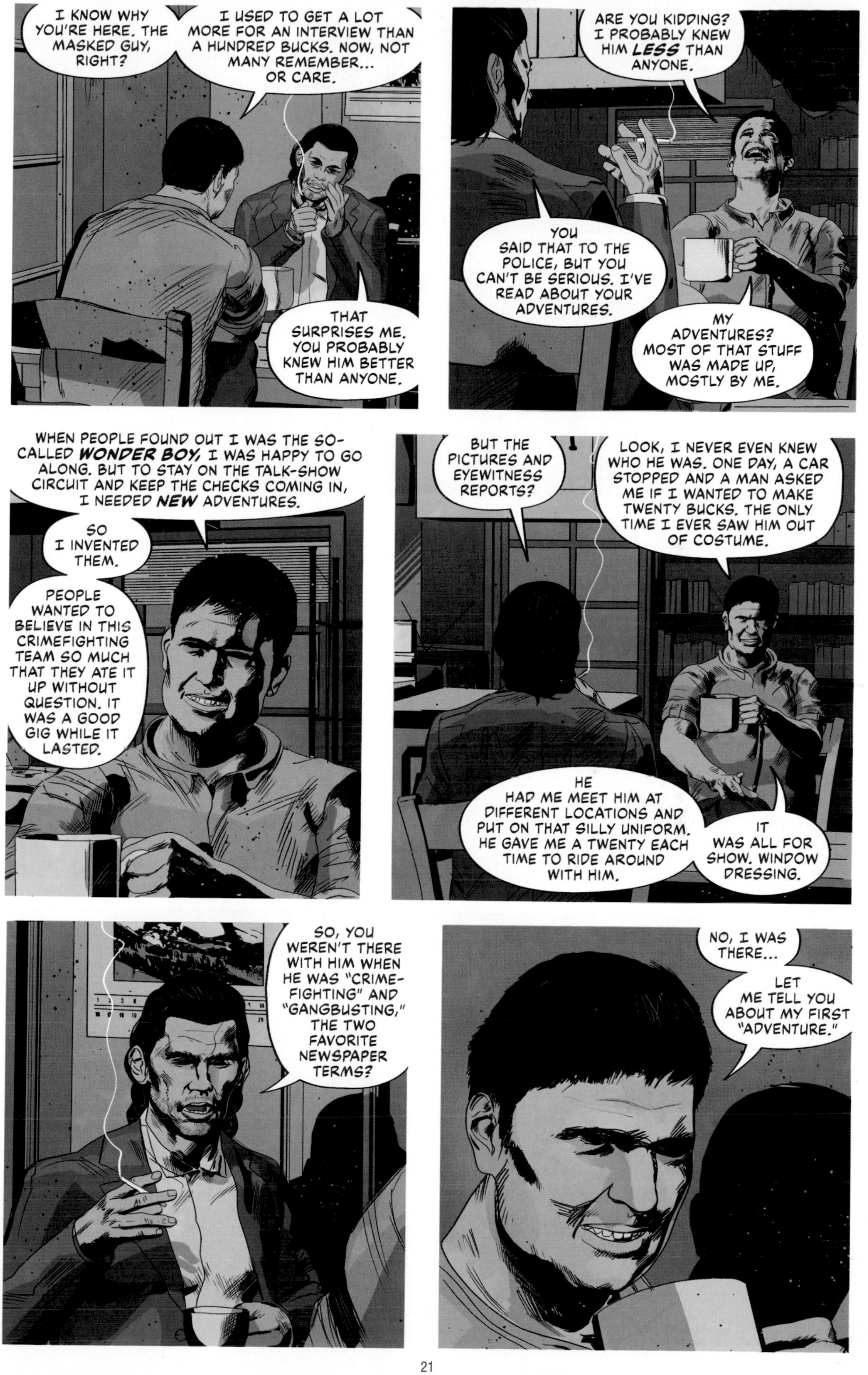

I KNOW WHY YOU'RE HERE. THE MASKED GUY, RIGHT?
I USED TO GET A LOT MORE FOR AN INTERVIEW THAN A HUNDRED BUCKS. NOW, NOT MANY REMEMBER... OR CARE.
THAT SURPRISES ME. YOU PROBABLY KNEW HIM BETTER THAN ANYONE.
ARE YOU KIDDING? I PROBABLY KNEW HIM *LESS* THAN ANYONE.
YOU SAID THAT TO THE POLICE, BUT YOU CAN'T BE SERIOUS. I'VE READ ABOUT YOUR ADVENTURES.
MY ADVENTURES? MOST OF THAT STUFF WAS MADE UP, MOSTLY BY ME.
WHEN PEOPLE FOUND OUT I WAS THE SO-CALLED ***WONDER BOY,*** I WAS HAPPY TO GO ALONG. BUT TO STAY ON THE TALK-SHOW CIRCUIT AND KEEP THE CHECKS COMING IN, I NEEDED ***NEW*** ADVENTURES.
SO I INVENTED THEM.
PEOPLE WANTED TO BELIEVE IN THIS CRIMEFIGHTING TEAM SO MUCH THAT THEY ATE IT UP WITHOUT QUESTION. IT WAS A GOOD GIG WHILE IT LASTED.
BUT THE PICTURES AND EYEWITNESS REPORTS?
LOOK, I NEVER EVEN KNEW WHO HE WAS. ONE DAY, A CAR STOPPED AND A MAN ASKED ME IF I WANTED TO MAKE TWENTY BUCKS. THE ONLY TIME I EVER SAW HIM OUT OF COSTUME.
HE HAD ME MEET HIM AT DIFFERENT LOCATIONS AND PUT ON THAT SILLY UNIFORM. HE GAVE ME A TWENTY EACH TIME TO RIDE AROUND WITH HIM.
IT WAS ALL FOR SHOW. WINDOW DRESSING.
SO, YOU WEREN'T THERE WITH HIM WHEN HE WAS "CRIME-FIGHTING" AND "GANGBUSTING," THE TWO FAVORITE NEWSPAPER TERMS?
NO, I WAS THERE...
LET ME TELL YOU ABOUT MY FIRST "ADVENTURE."

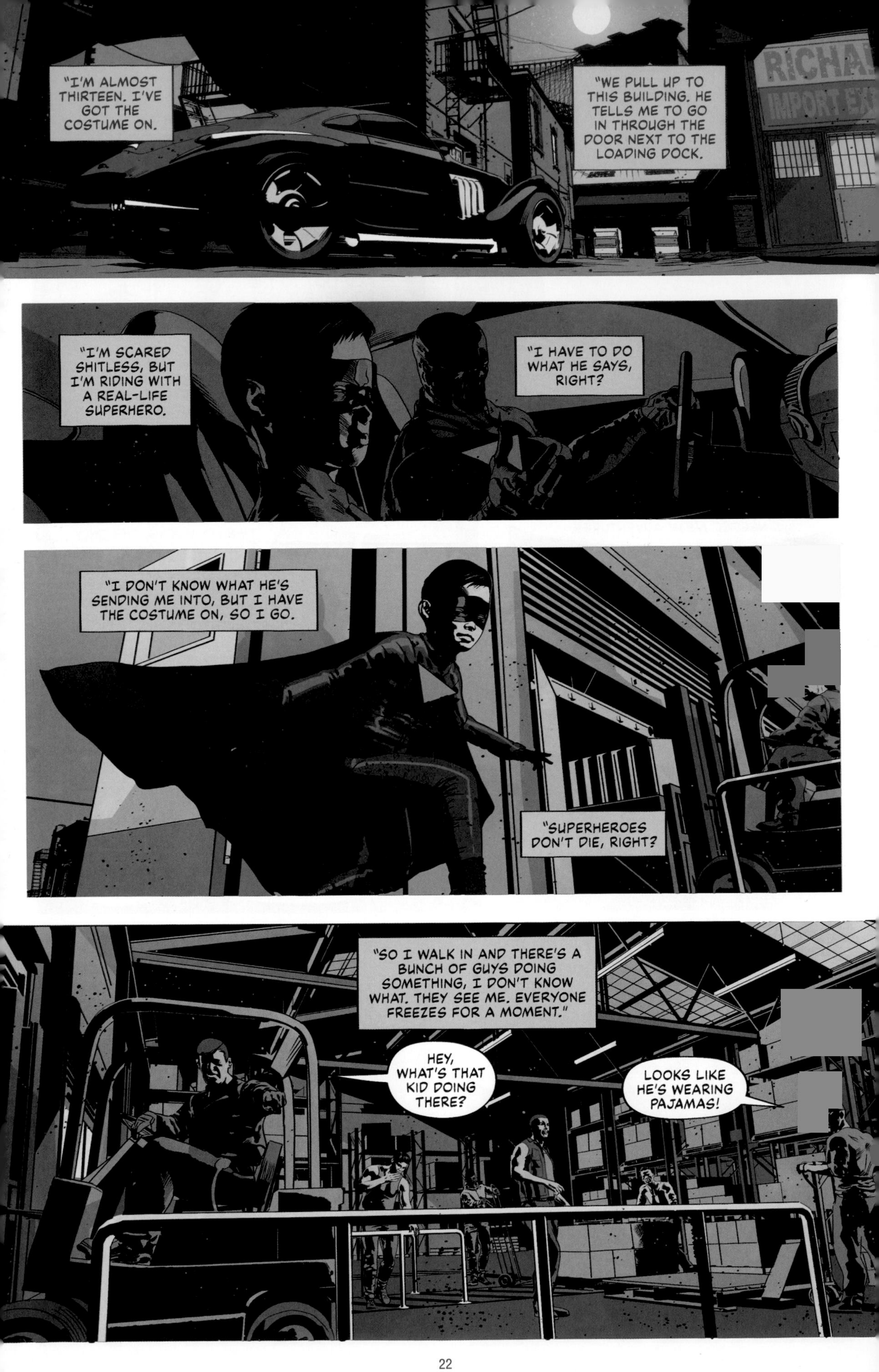
"I'M ALMOST THIRTEEN. I'VE GOT THE COSTUME ON.
"WE PULL UP TO THIS BUILDING. HE TELLS ME TO GO IN THROUGH THE DOOR NEXT TO THE LOADING DOCK.
"I'M SCARED SHITLESS, BUT I'M RIDING WITH A REAL-LIFE SUPERHERO.
"I HAVE TO DO WHAT HE SAYS, RIGHT?
"I DON'T KNOW WHAT HE'S SENDING ME INTO, BUT I HAVE THE COSTUME ON, SO I GO.
"SUPERHEROES DON'T DIE, RIGHT?
"SO I WALK IN AND THERE'S A BUNCH OF GUYS DOING SOMETHING, I DON'T KNOW WHAT. THEY SEE ME. EVERYONE FREEZES FOR A MOMENT."
HEY, WHAT'S THAT KID DOING THERE?
LOOKS LIKE HE'S WEARING PAJAMAS!

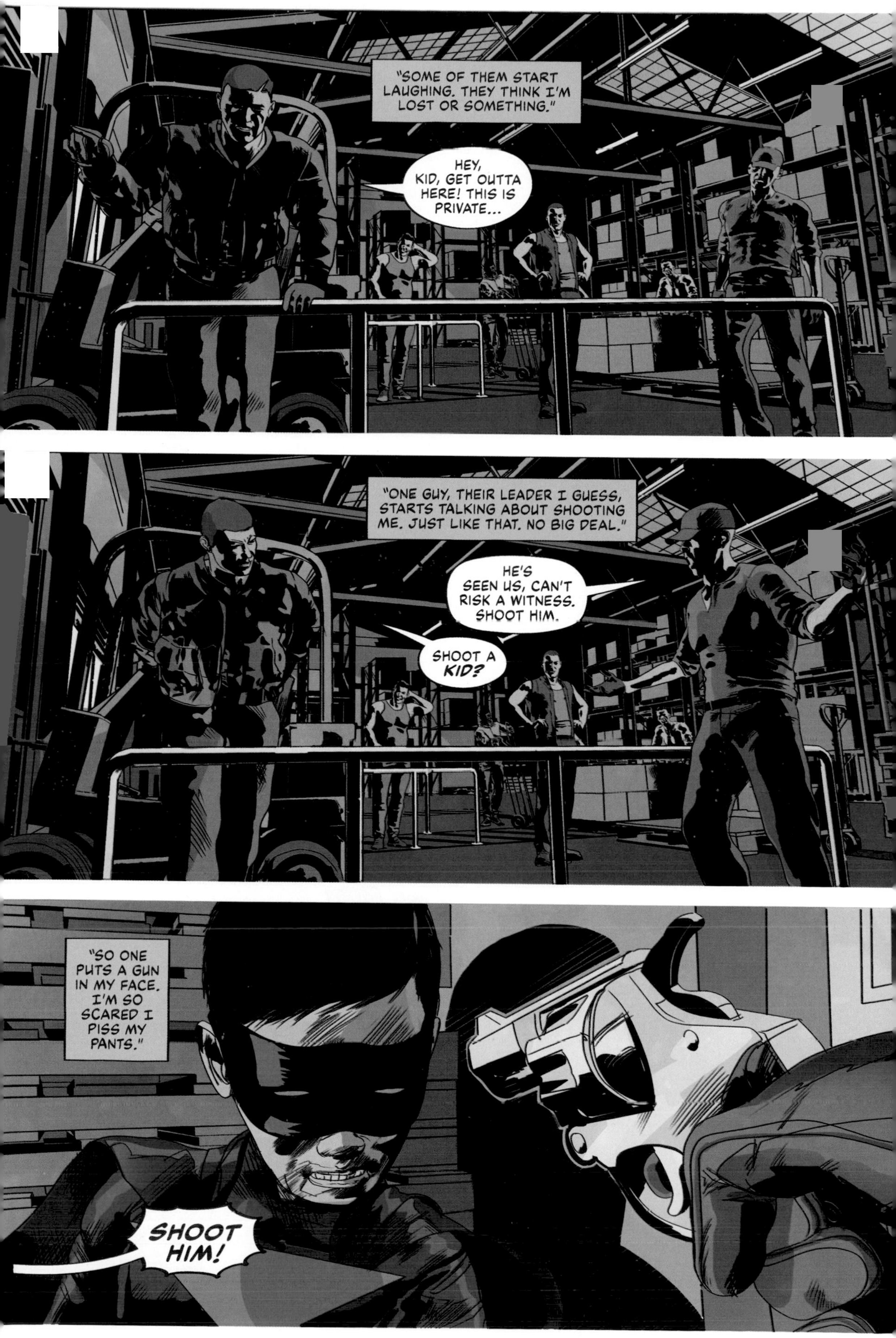
"SOME OF THEM START LAUGHING. THEY THINK I'M LOST OR SOMETHING."
HEY, KID, GET OUTTA HERE! THIS IS PRIVATE...
"ONE GUY, THEIR LEADER I GUESS, STARTS TALKING ABOUT SHOOTING ME. JUST LIKE THAT. NO BIG DEAL."
HE'S SEEN US, CAN'T RISK A WITNESS. SHOOT HIM.
SHOOT A *KID?*
"SO ONE PUTS A GUN IN MY FACE. I'M SO SCARED I PISS MY PANTS."
SHOOT HIM!

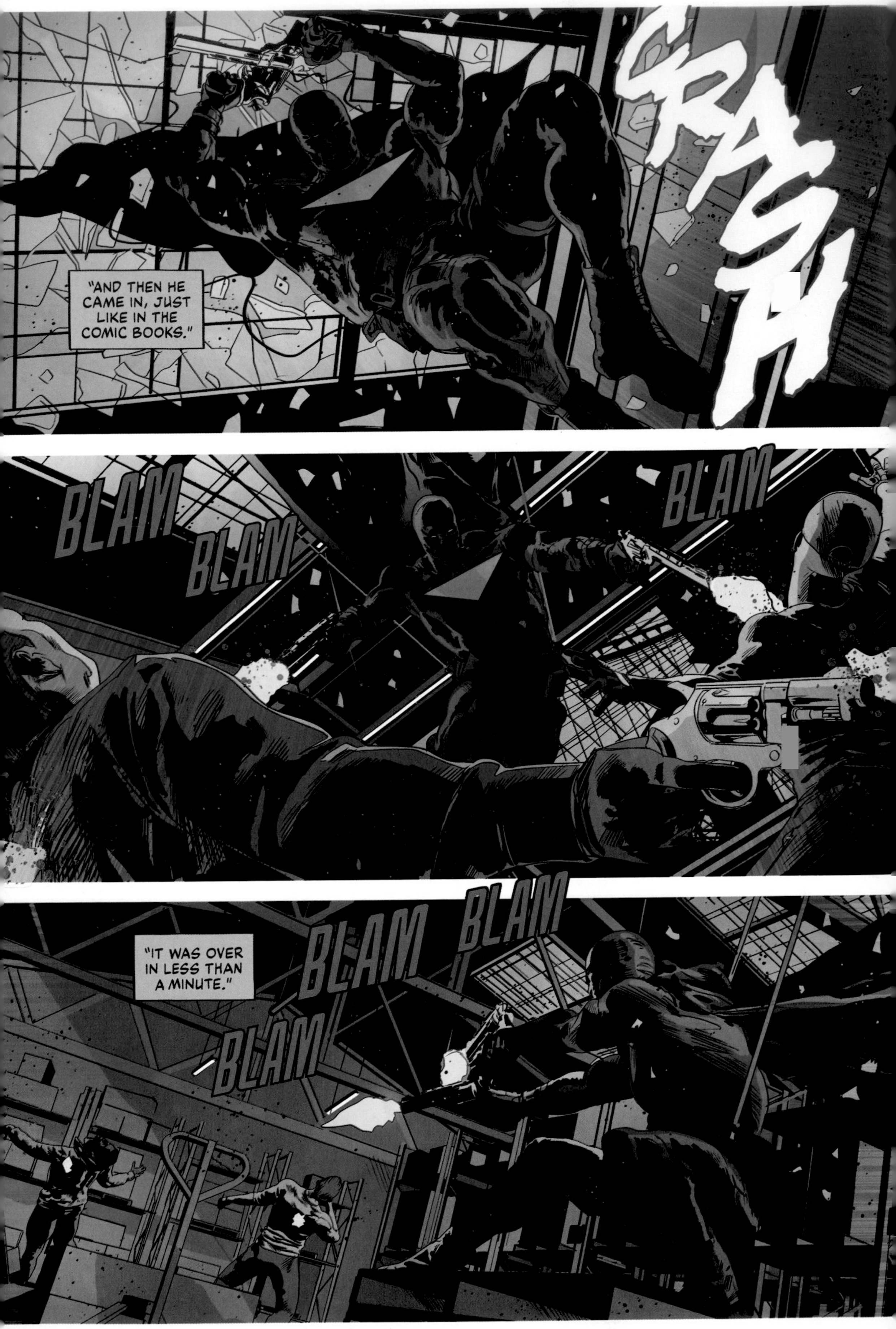

"AND THEN HE CAME IN, JUST LIKE IN THE COMIC BOOKS."
CRASH
BLAM
BLAM
BLAM
"IT WAS OVER IN LESS THAN A MINUTE."
BLAM
BLAM
BLAM

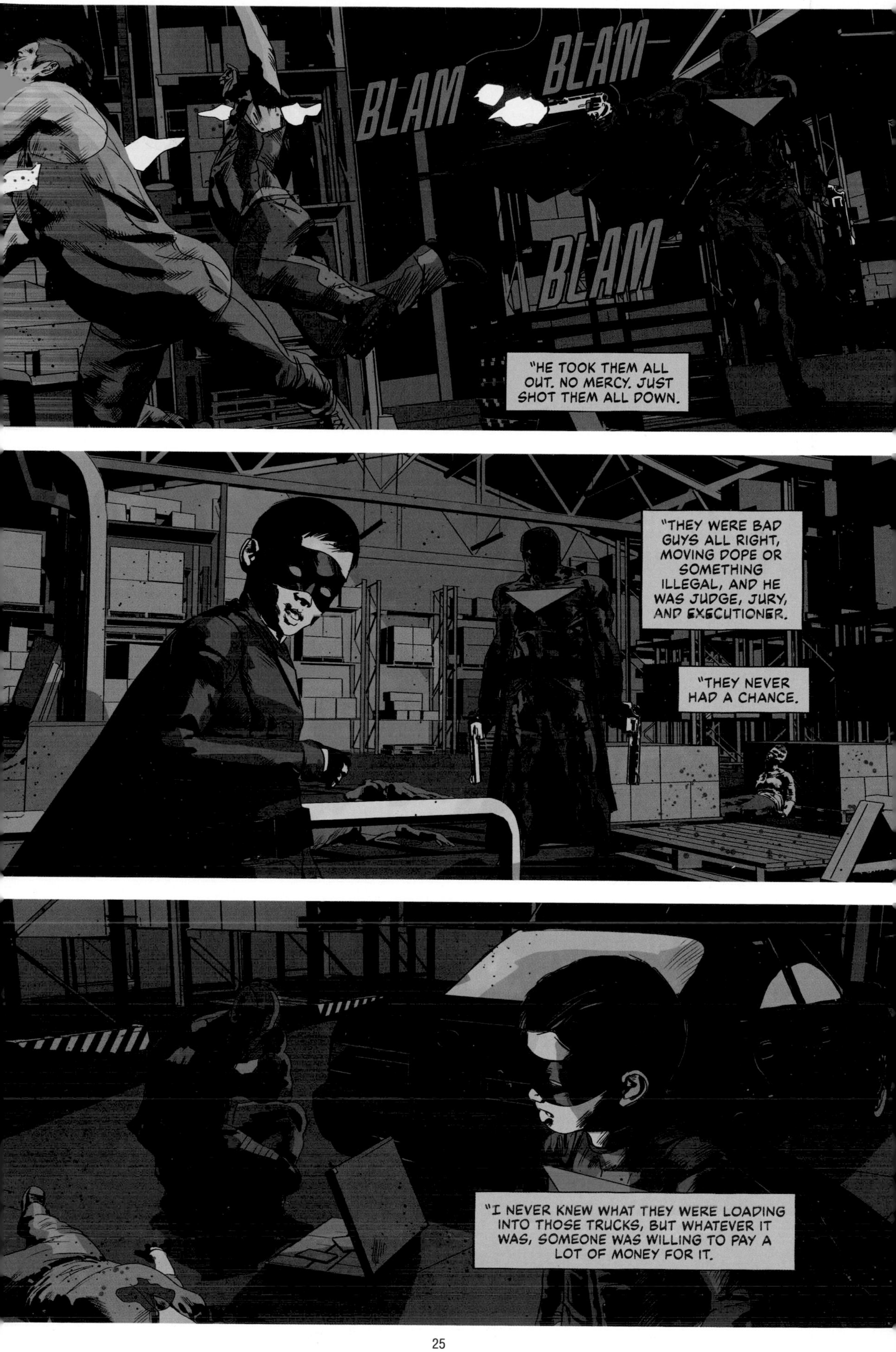
BLAM
BLAM
BLAM
"HE TOOK THEM ALL OUT. NO MERCY. JUST SHOT THEM ALL DOWN.
"THEY WERE BAD GUYS ALL RIGHT, MOVING DOPE OR SOMETHING ILLEGAL, AND HE WAS JUDGE, JURY, AND EXECUTIONER.
"THEY NEVER HAD A CHANCE.
"I NEVER KNEW WHAT THEY WERE LOADING INTO THOSE TRUCKS, BUT WHATEVER IT WAS, SOMEONE WAS WILLING TO PAY A LOT OF MONEY FOR IT.

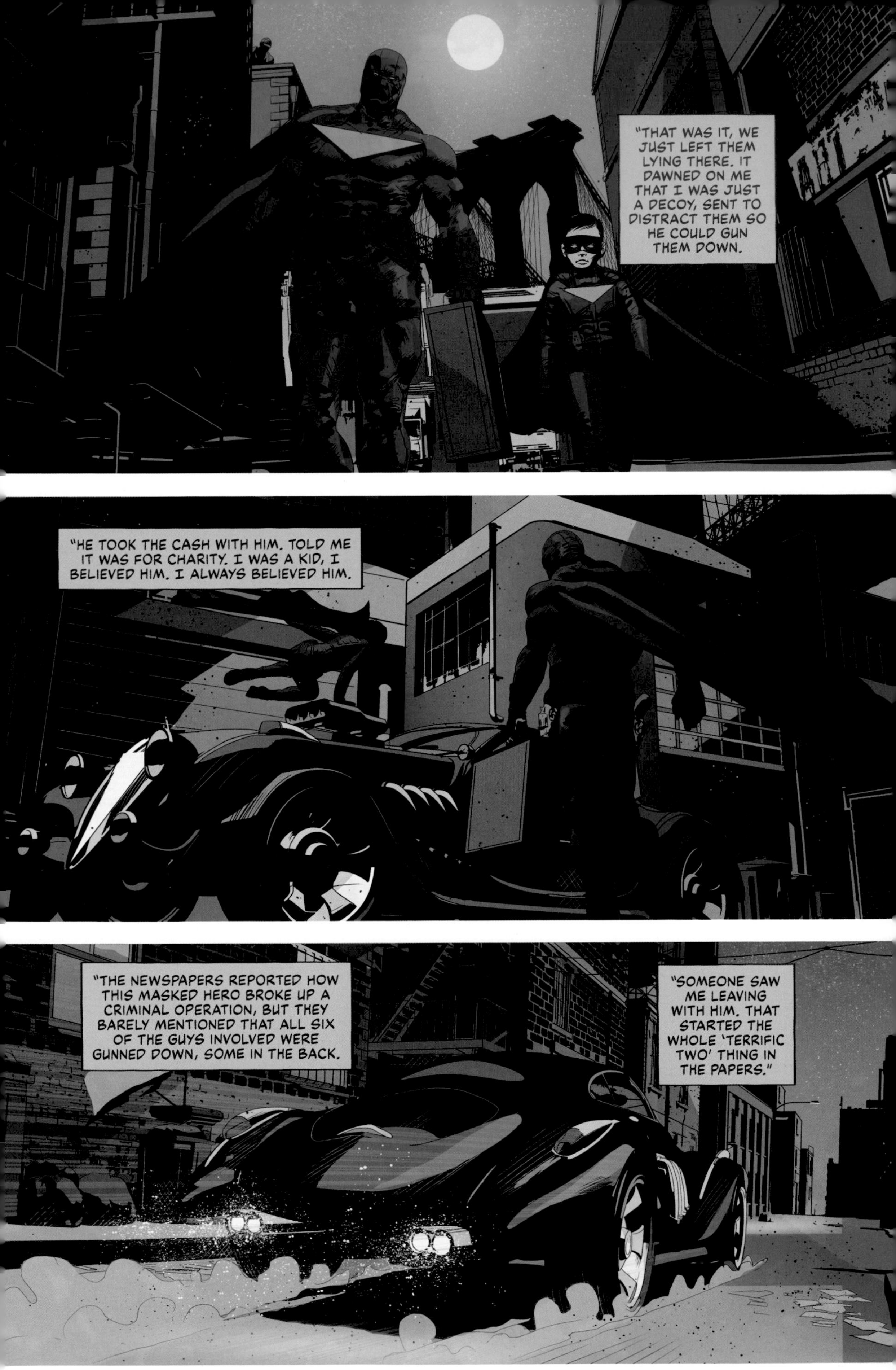
"THAT WAS IT, WE JUST LEFT THEM LYING THERE. IT DAWNED ON ME THAT I WAS JUST A DECOY, SENT TO DISTRACT THEM SO HE COULD GUN THEM DOWN.
"HE TOOK THE CASH WITH HIM. TOLD ME IT WAS FOR CHARITY. I WAS A KID, I BELIEVED HIM. I ALWAYS BELIEVED HIM.
"THE NEWSPAPERS REPORTED HOW THIS MASKED HERO BROKE UP A CRIMINAL OPERATION, BUT THEY BARELY MENTIONED THAT ALL SIX OF THE GUYS INVOLVED WERE GUNNED DOWN, SOME IN THE BACK.
"SOMEONE SAW ME LEAVING WITH HIM. THAT STARTED THE WHOLE 'TERRIFIC TWO' THING IN THE PAPERS."

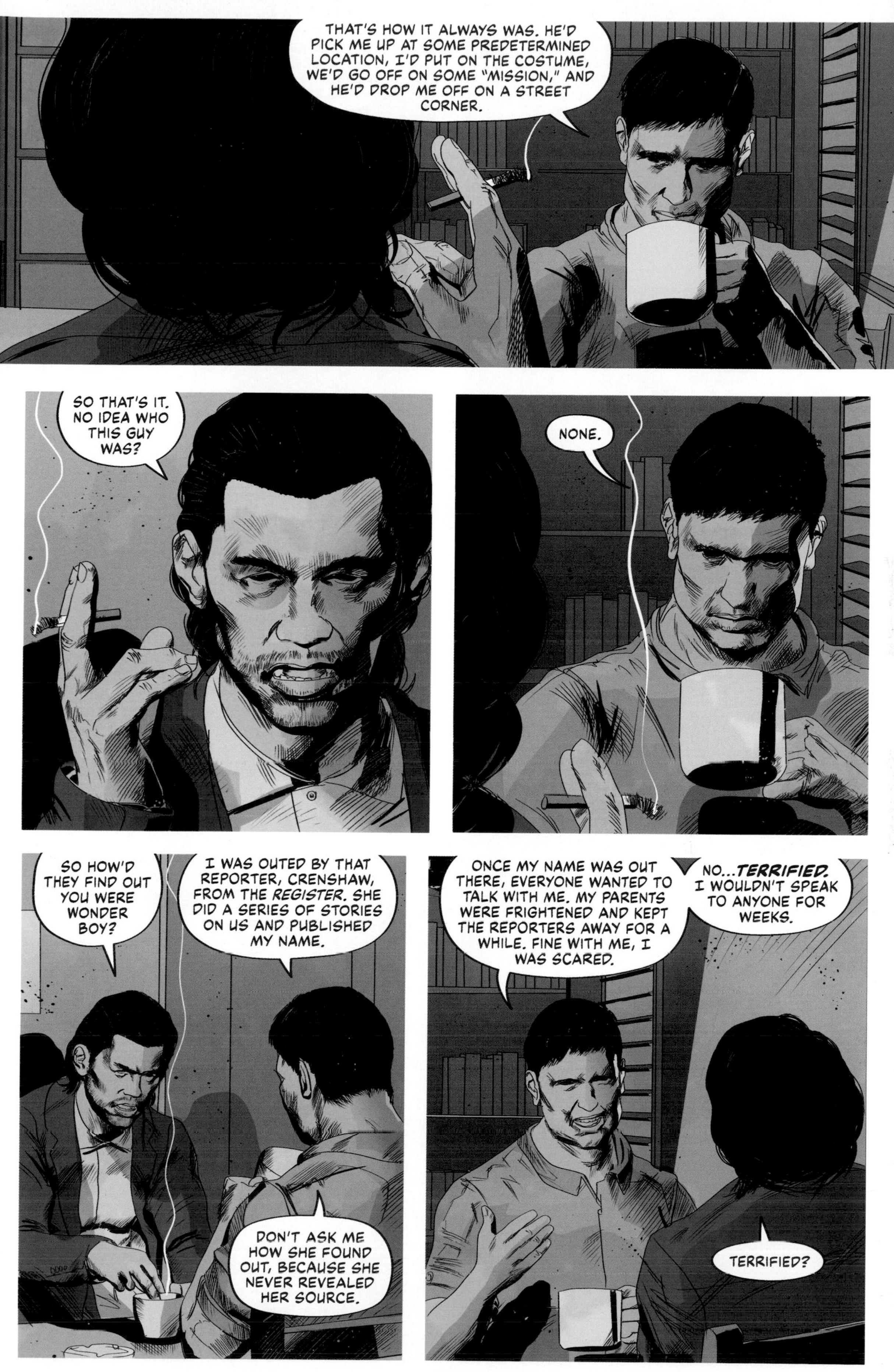
THAT'S HOW IT ALWAYS WAS. HE'D PICK ME UP AT SOME PREDETERMINED LOCATION, I'D PUT ON THE COSTUME, WE'D GO OFF ON SOME "MISSION," AND HE'D DROP ME OFF ON A STREET CORNER.
SO THAT'S IT. NO IDEA WHO THIS GUY WAS?
NONE.
SO HOW'D THEY FIND OUT YOU WERE WONDER BOY?
I WAS OUTED BY THAT REPORTER, CRENSHAW, FROM THE *REGISTER*. SHE DID A SERIES OF STORIES ON US AND PUBLISHED MY NAME.
DON'T ASK ME HOW SHE FOUND OUT, BECAUSE SHE NEVER REVEALED HER SOURCE.
ONCE MY NAME WAS OUT THERE, EVERYONE WANTED TO TALK WITH ME. MY PARENTS WERE FRIGHTENED AND KEPT THE REPORTERS AWAY FOR A WHILE. FINE WITH ME, I WAS SCARED.
TERRIFIED?
NO...***TERRIFIED.*** I WOULDN'T SPEAK TO ANYONE FOR WEEKS.

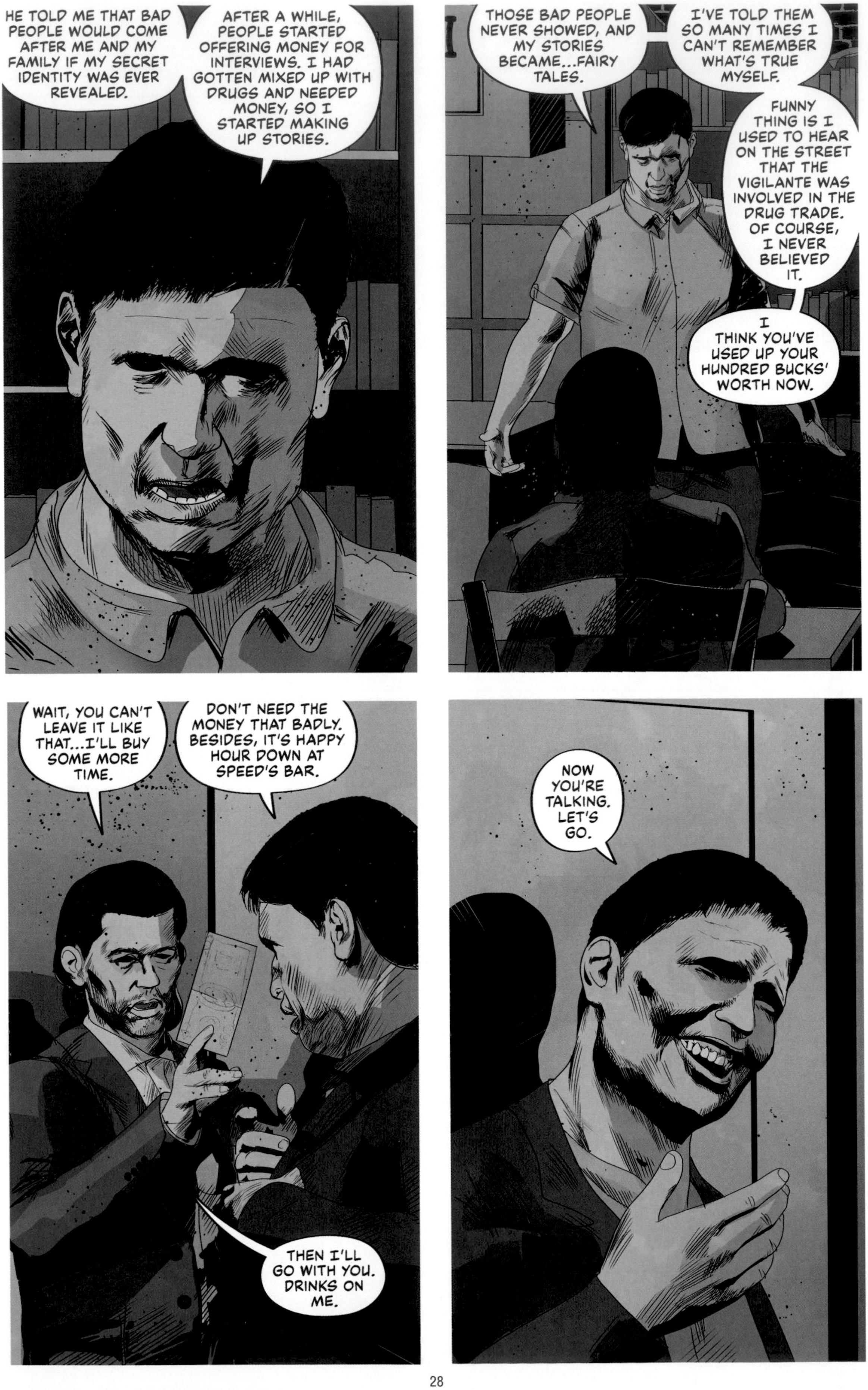
HE TOLD ME THAT BAD PEOPLE WOULD COME AFTER ME AND MY FAMILY IF MY SECRET IDENTITY WAS EVER REVEALED.
AFTER A WHILE, PEOPLE STARTED OFFERING MONEY FOR INTERVIEWS. I HAD GOTTEN MIXED UP WITH DRUGS AND NEEDED MONEY, SO I STARTED MAKING UP STORIES.
THOSE BAD PEOPLE NEVER SHOWED, AND MY STORIES BECAME...FAIRY TALES.
I'VE TOLD THEM SO MANY TIMES I CAN'T REMEMBER WHAT'S TRUE MYSELF.
FUNNY THING IS I USED TO HEAR ON THE STREET THAT THE VIGILANTE WAS INVOLVED IN THE DRUG TRADE. OF COURSE, I NEVER BELIEVED IT.
I THINK YOU'VE USED UP YOUR HUNDRED BUCKS' WORTH NOW.
WAIT, YOU CAN'T LEAVE IT LIKE THAT...I'LL BUY SOME MORE TIME.
DON'T NEED THE MONEY THAT BADLY. BESIDES, IT'S HAPPY HOUR DOWN AT SPEED'S BAR.
THEN I'LL GO WITH YOU. DRINKS ON ME.
NOW YOU'RE TALKING. LET'S GO.

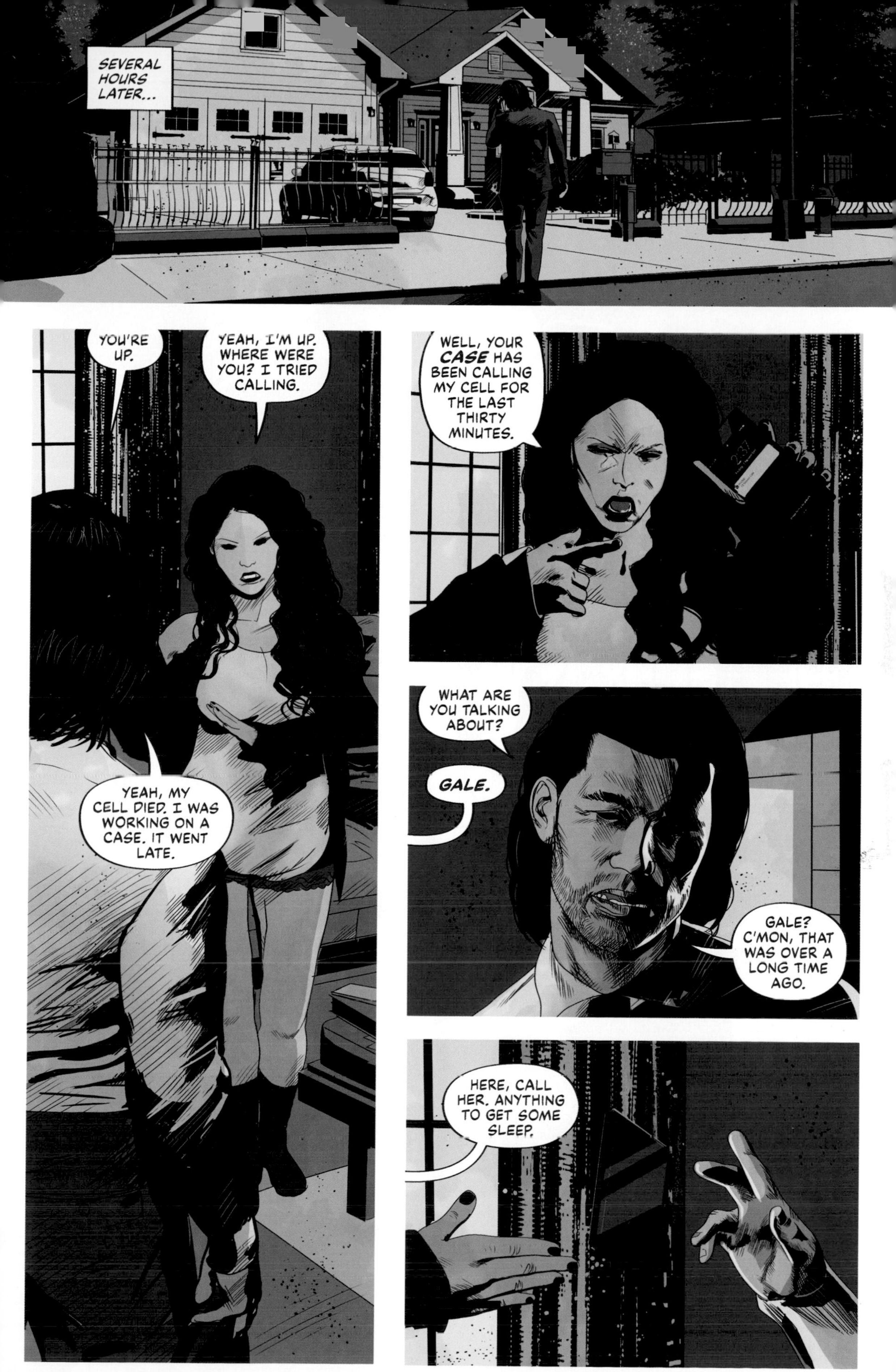
SEVERAL HOURS LATER...
YOU'RE UP.
YEAH, I'M UP. WHERE WERE YOU? I TRIED CALLING.
YEAH, MY CELL DIED. I WAS WORKING ON A CASE. IT WENT LATE.
WELL, YOUR CASE HAS BEEN CALLING MY CELL FOR THE LAST THIRTY MINUTES.
WHAT ARE YOU TALKING ABOUT?
GALE.
GALE? C'MON, THAT WAS OVER A LONG TIME AGO.
HERE, CALL HER. ANYTHING TO GET SOME SLEEP.

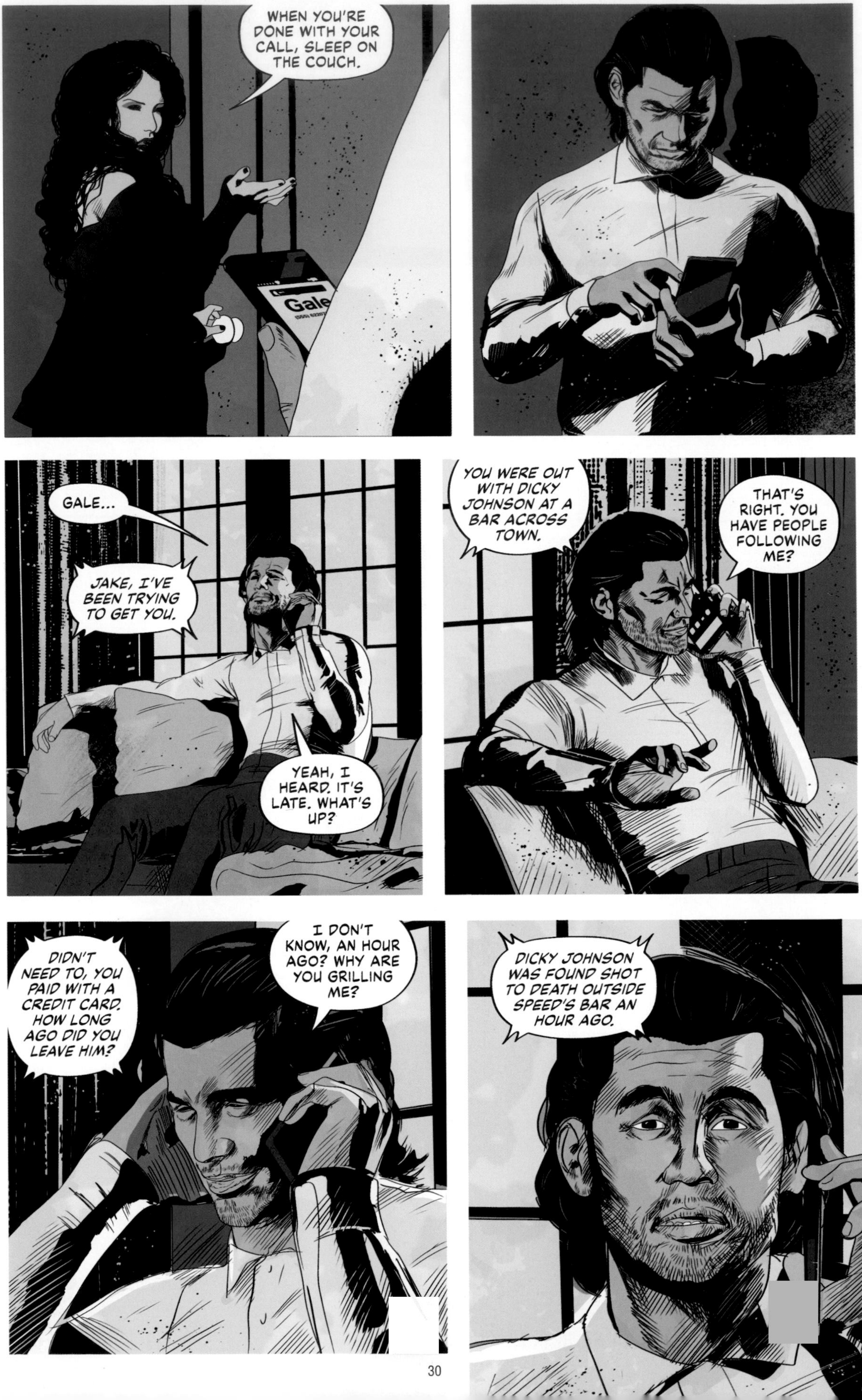
WHEN YOU'RE DONE WITH YOUR CALL, SLEEP ON THE COUCH.
GALE...
JAKE, I'VE BEEN TRYING TO GET YOU.
YEAH, I HEARD. IT'S LATE. WHAT'S UP?
YOU WERE OUT WITH DICKY JOHNSON AT A BAR ACROSS TOWN.
THAT'S RIGHT. YOU HAVE PEOPLE FOLLOWING ME?
DIDN'T NEED TO, YOU PAID WITH A CREDIT CARD. HOW LONG AGO DID YOU LEAVE HIM?
I DON'T KNOW, AN HOUR AGO? WHY ARE YOU GRILLING ME?
DICKY JOHNSON WAS FOUND SHOT TO DEATH OUTSIDE SPEED'S BAR AN HOUR AGO.

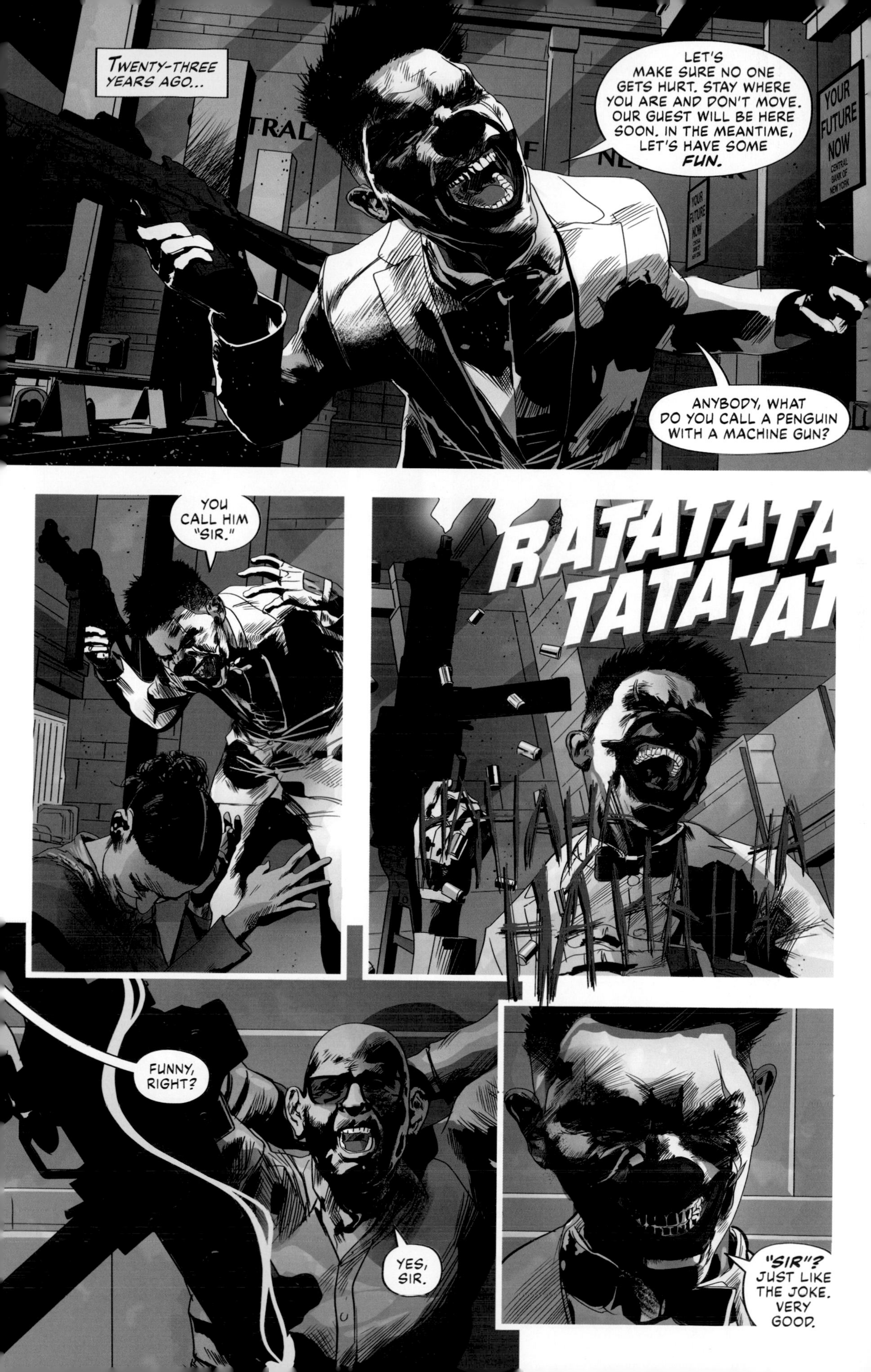
TWENTY-THREE YEARS AGO...
LET'S MAKE SURE NO ONE GETS HURT. STAY WHERE YOU ARE AND DON'T MOVE. OUR GUEST WILL BE HERE SOON. IN THE MEANTIME, LET'S HAVE SOME FUN.
YOUR FUTURE NOW
CENTRAL BANK OF NEW YORK
ANYBODY, WHAT DO YOU CALL A PENGUIN WITH A MACHINE GUN?
YOU CALL HIM "SIR."
RATATATA
TATATAT
FUNNY, RIGHT?
YES, SIR.
"SIR"? JUST LIKE THE JOKE. VERY GOOD.

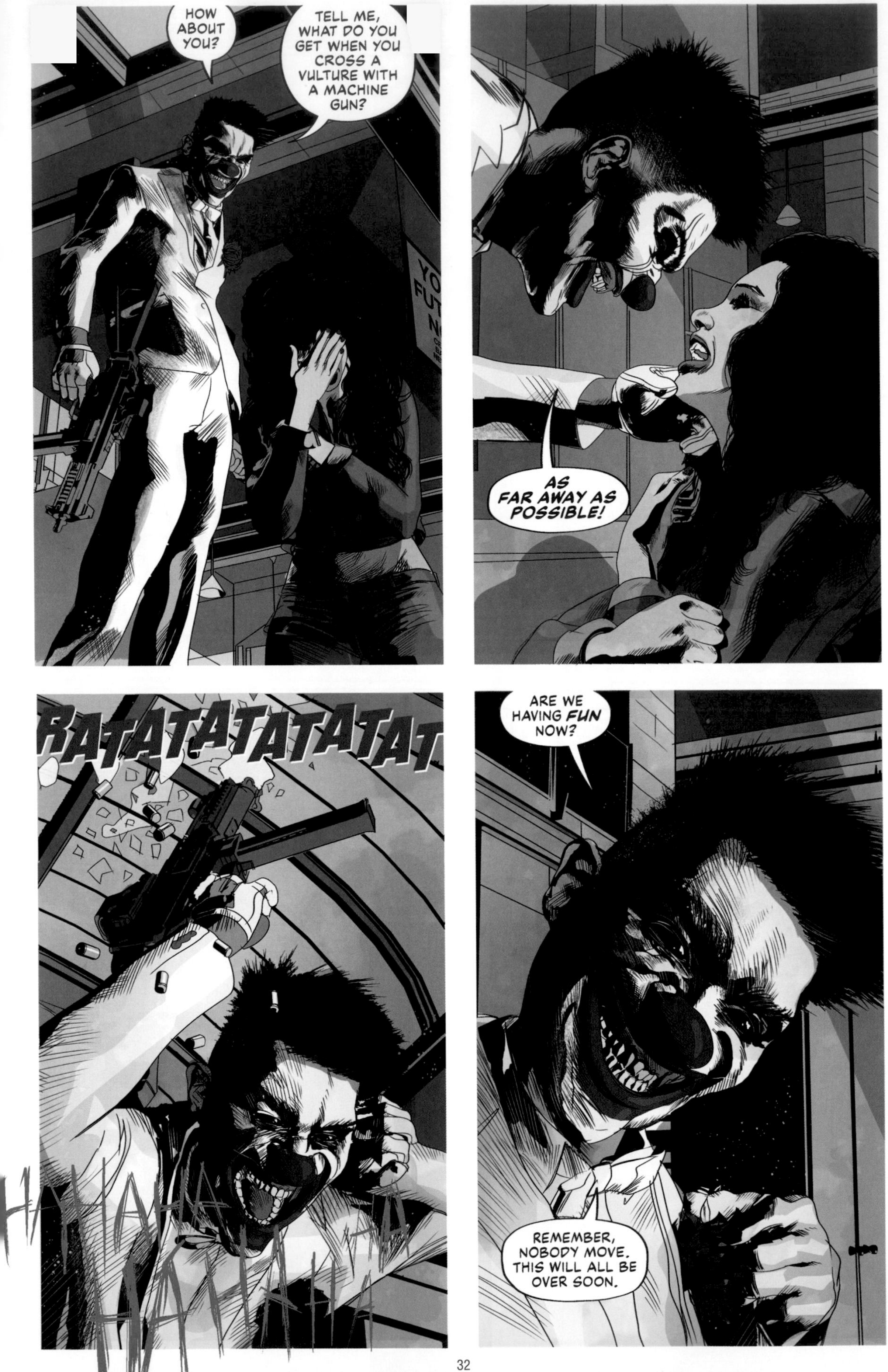
HOW ABOUT YOU?
TELL ME, WHAT DO YOU GET WHEN YOU CROSS A VULTURE WITH A MACHINE GUN?
AS FAR AWAY AS POSSIBLE!
RATATATATATAT
ARE WE HAVING *FUN* NOW?
REMEMBER, NOBODY MOVE. THIS WILL ALL BE OVER SOON.

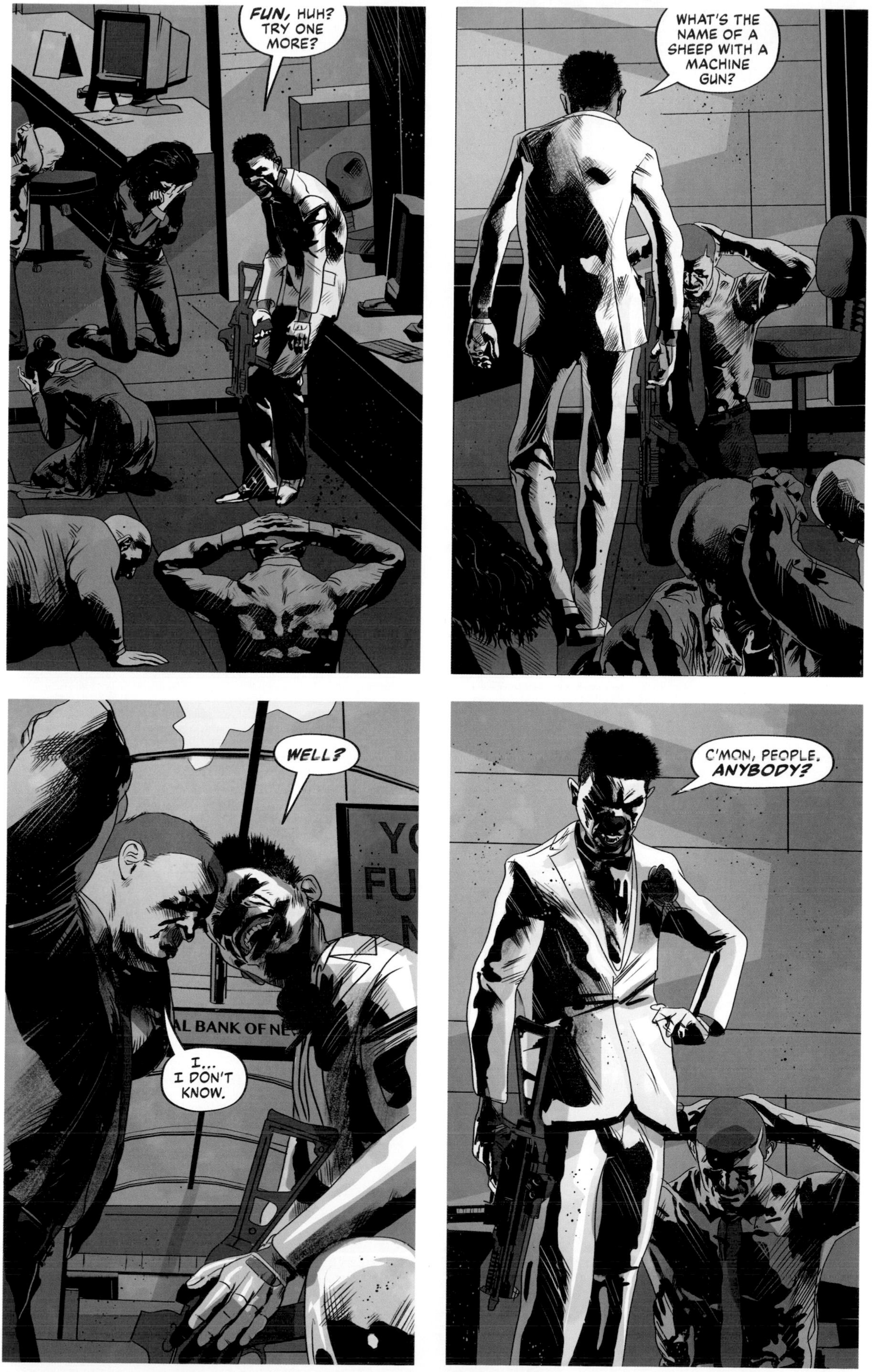
FUN, HUH? TRY ONE MORE?
WHAT'S THE NAME OF A SHEEP WITH A MACHINE GUN?
WELL?
YO FU N
AL BANK OF NE
I... I DON'T KNOW.
C'MON, PEOPLE. ANYBODY?

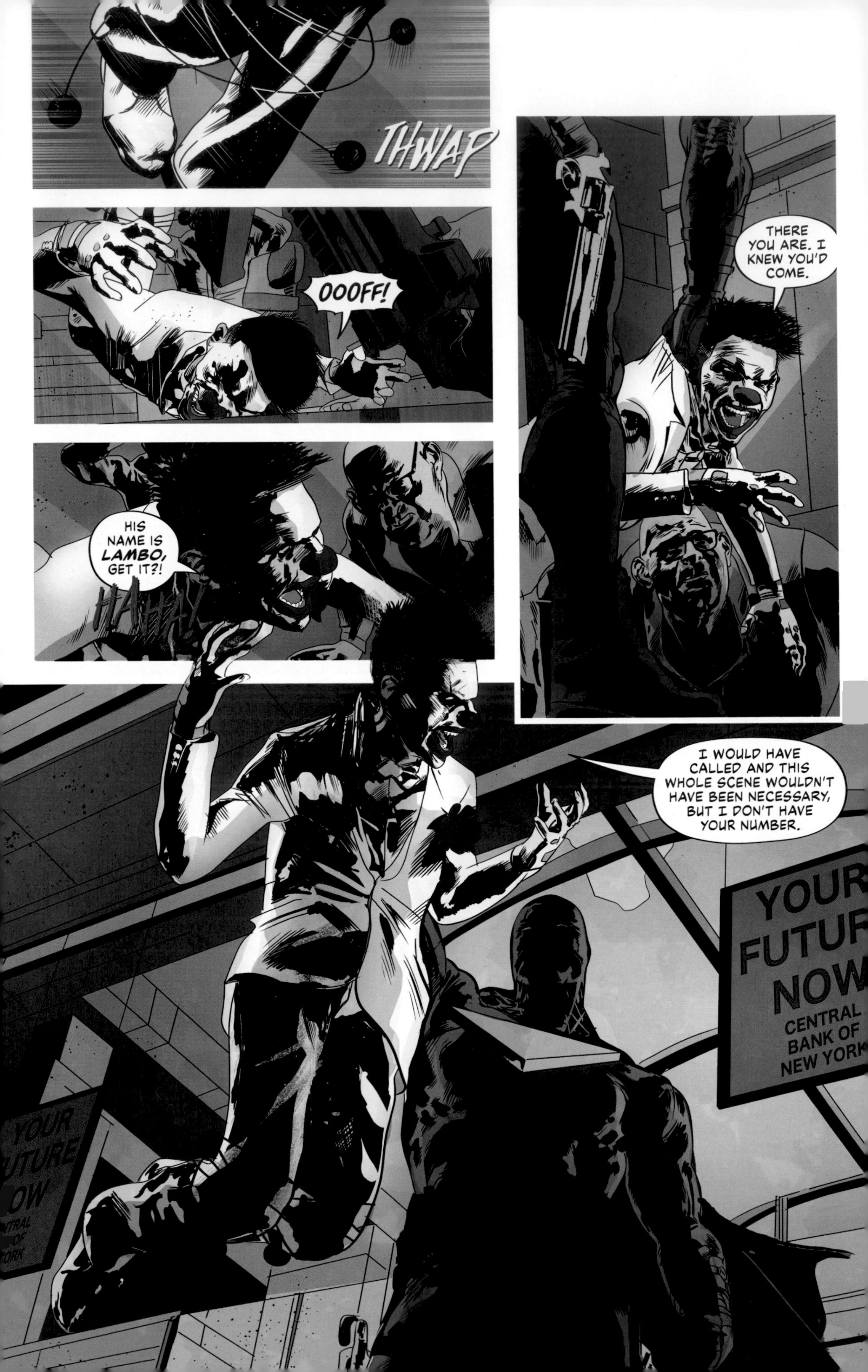
THWAP
OOOFF!
HIS NAME IS LAMBO, GET IT?!
HA HA!
THERE YOU ARE. I KNEW YOU'D COME.
I WOULD HAVE CALLED AND THIS WHOLE SCENE WOULDN'T HAVE BEEN NECESSARY, BUT I DON'T HAVE YOUR NUMBER.
YOUR FUTUR NOW CENTRAL BANK OF NEW YORK
YOUR UTURE OW NTRAL OF ORK

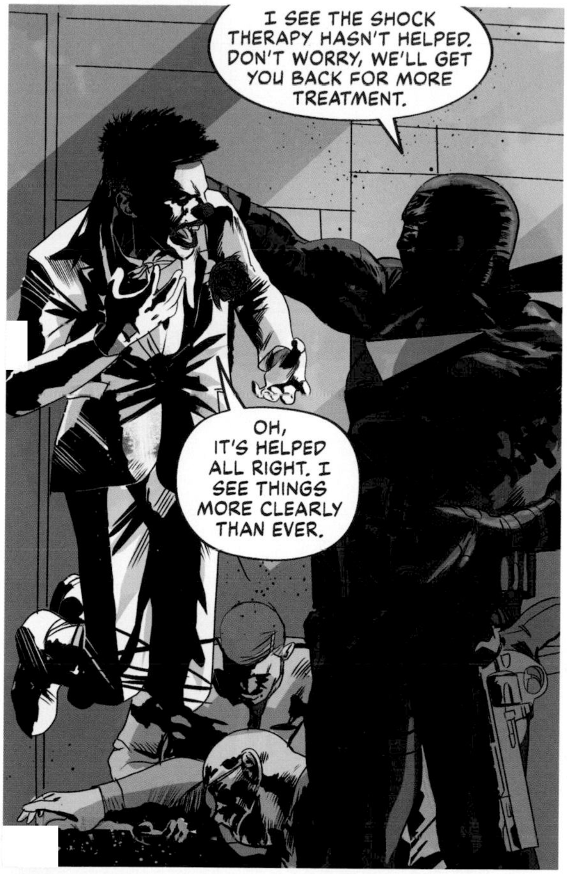
I SEE THE SHOCK THERAPY HASN'T HELPED. DON'T WORRY, WE'LL GET YOU BACK FOR MORE TREATMENT.
OH, IT'S HELPED ALL RIGHT. I SEE THINGS MORE CLEARLY THAN EVER.

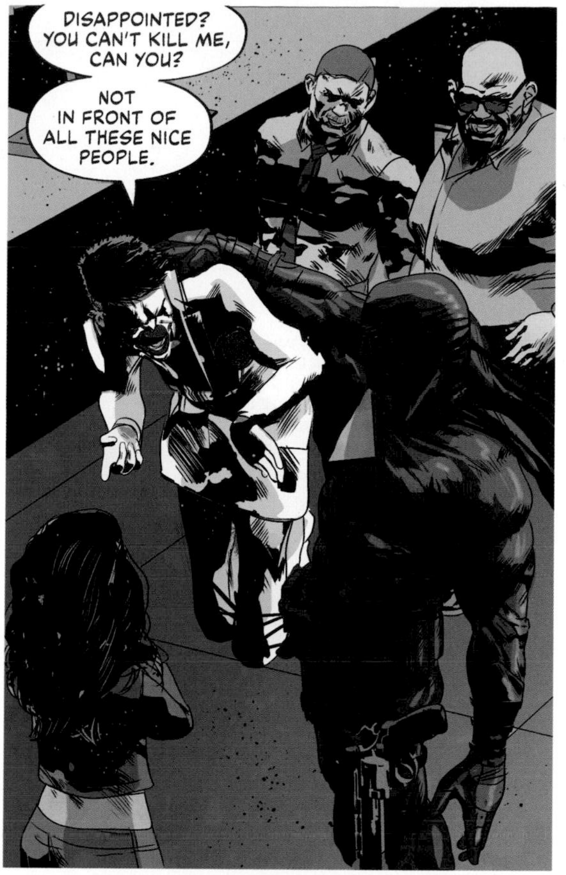
DISAPPOINTED? YOU CAN'T KILL ME, CAN YOU?
NOT IN FRONT OF ALL THESE NICE PEOPLE.

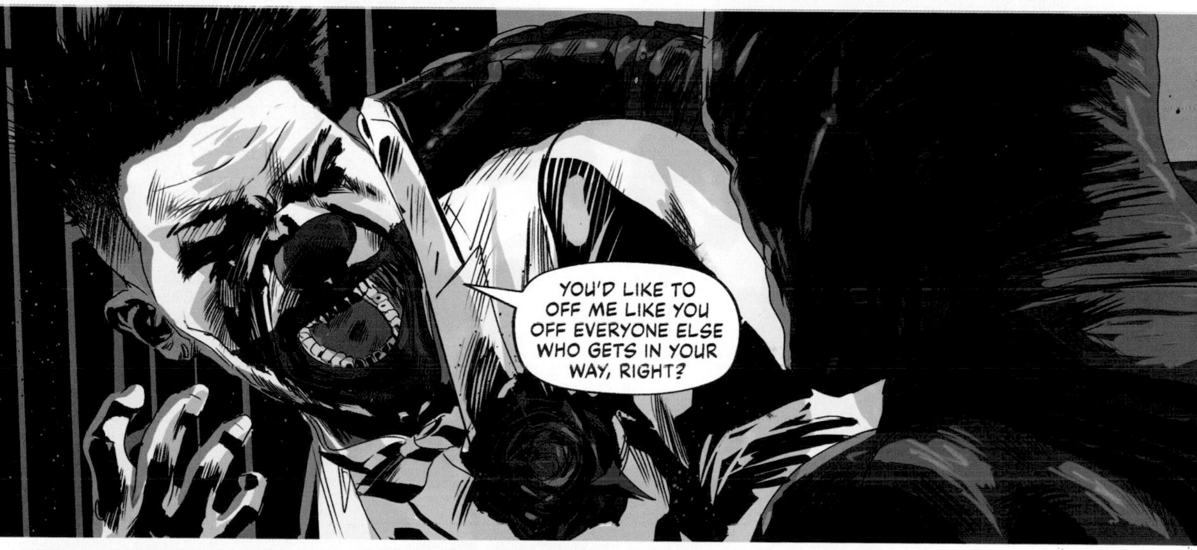
YOU'D LIKE TO OFF ME LIKE YOU OFF EVERYONE ELSE WHO GETS IN YOUR WAY, RIGHT?

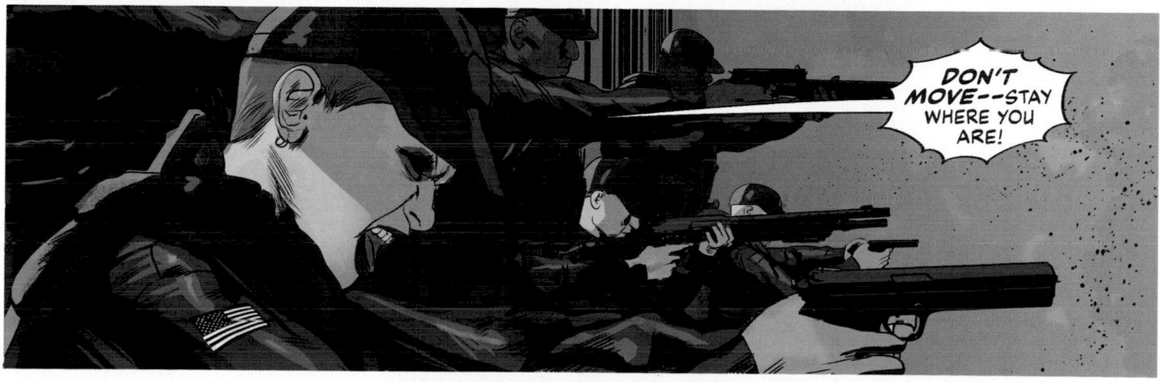
DON'T MOVE--STAY WHERE YOU ARE!

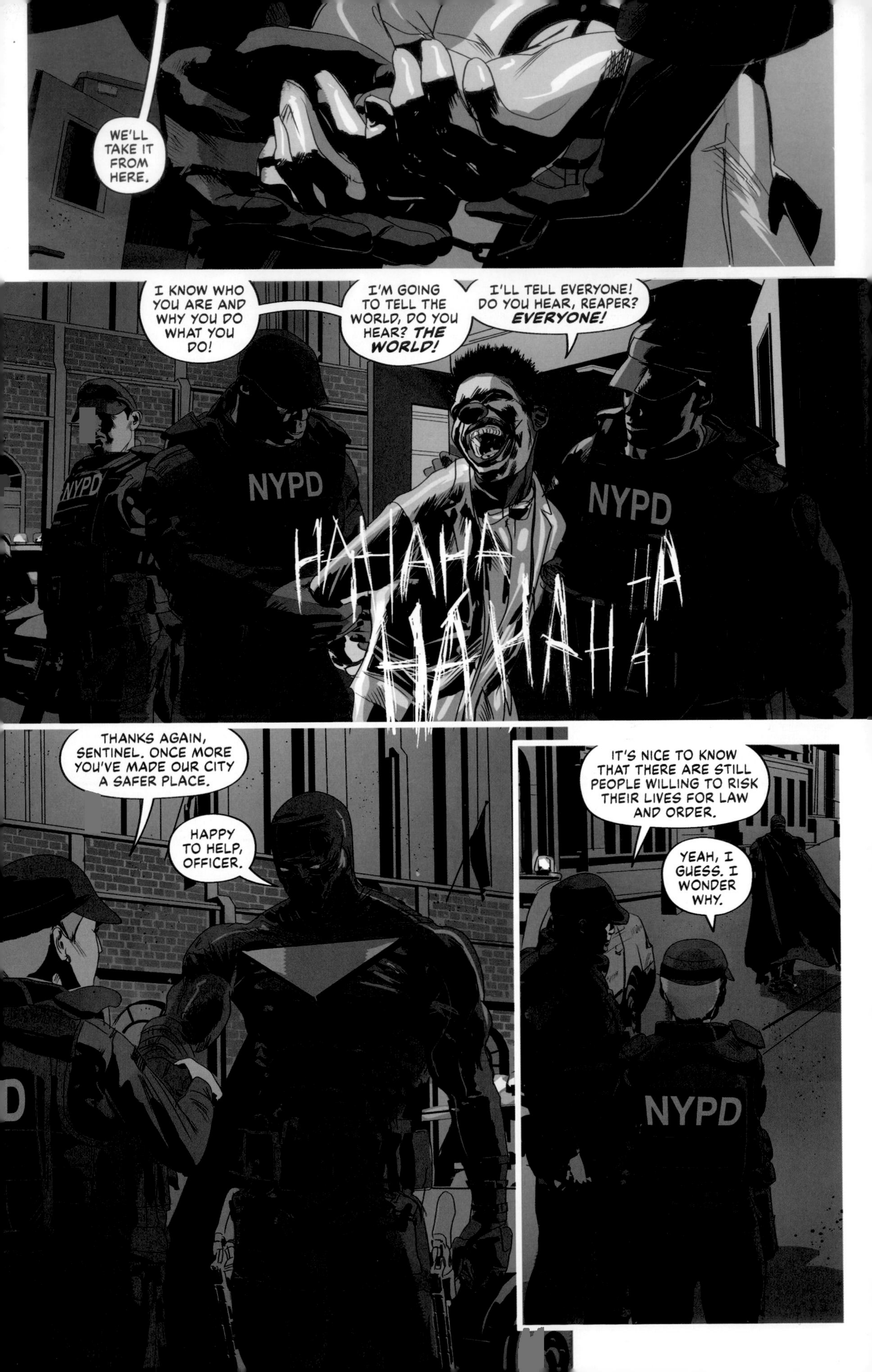
WE'LL TAKE IT FROM HERE.
I KNOW WHO YOU ARE AND WHY YOU DO WHAT YOU DO!
I'M GOING TO TELL THE WORLD, DO YOU HEAR? *THE WORLD!*
I'LL TELL EVERYONE! DO YOU HEAR, REAPER? *EVERYONE!*
HAHAHA HA
HAHAHAHA
THANKS AGAIN, SENTINEL. ONCE MORE YOU'VE MADE OUR CITY A SAFER PLACE.
HAPPY TO HELP, OFFICER.
IT'S NICE TO KNOW THAT THERE ARE STILL PEOPLE WILLING TO RISK THEIR LIVES FOR LAW AND ORDER.
YEAH, I GUESS. I WONDER WHY.

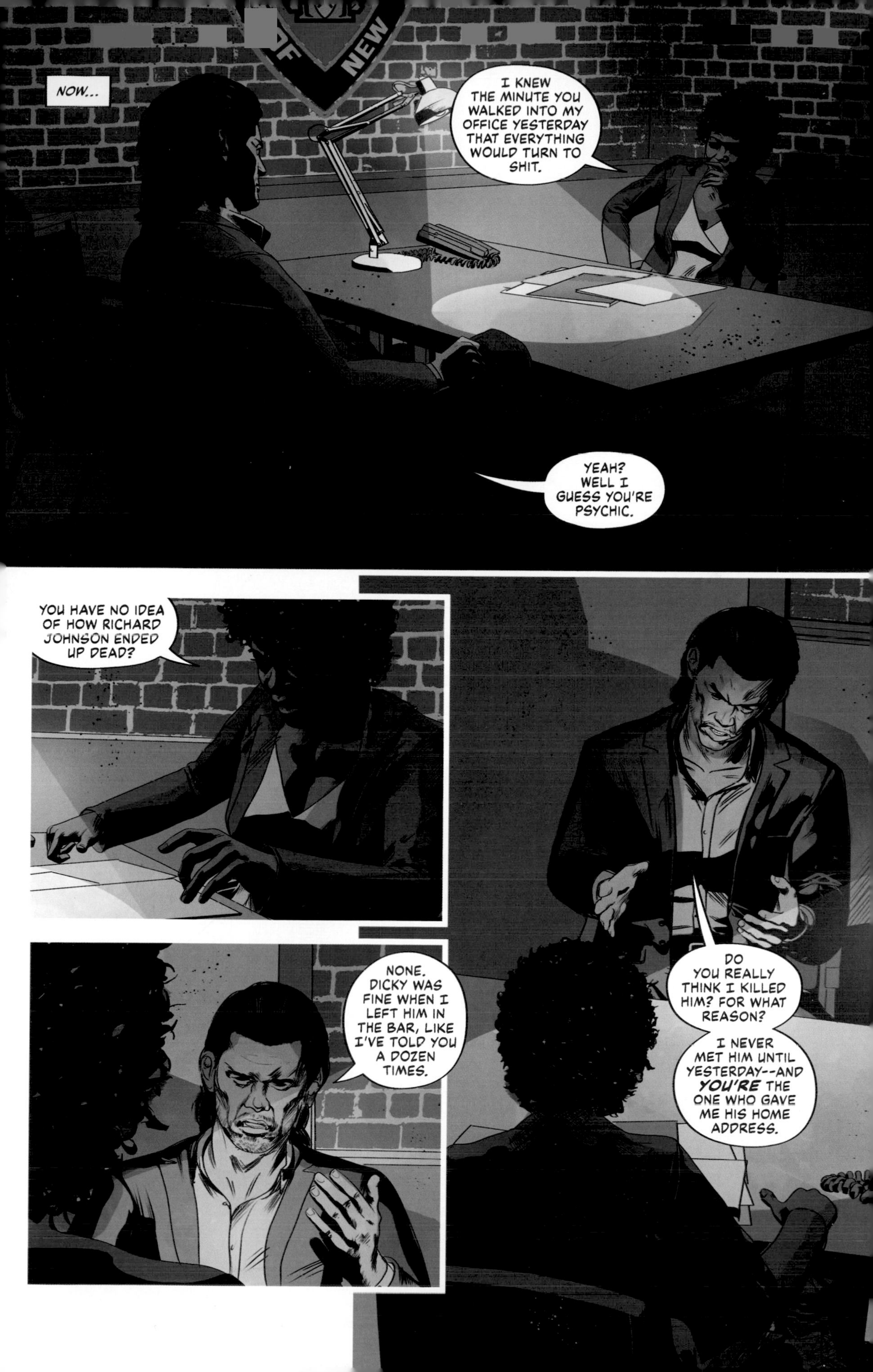
NOW...
I KNEW THE MINUTE YOU WALKED INTO MY OFFICE YESTERDAY THAT EVERYTHING WOULD TURN TO SHIT.
YEAH? WELL I GUESS YOU'RE PSYCHIC.
YOU HAVE NO IDEA OF HOW RICHARD JOHNSON ENDED UP DEAD?
NONE. DICKY WAS FINE WHEN I LEFT HIM IN THE BAR, LIKE I'VE TOLD YOU A DOZEN TIMES.
DO YOU REALLY THINK I KILLED HIM? FOR WHAT REASON?
I NEVER MET HIM UNTIL YESTERDAY--AND *YOU'RE* THE ONE WHO GAVE ME HIS HOME ADDRESS.

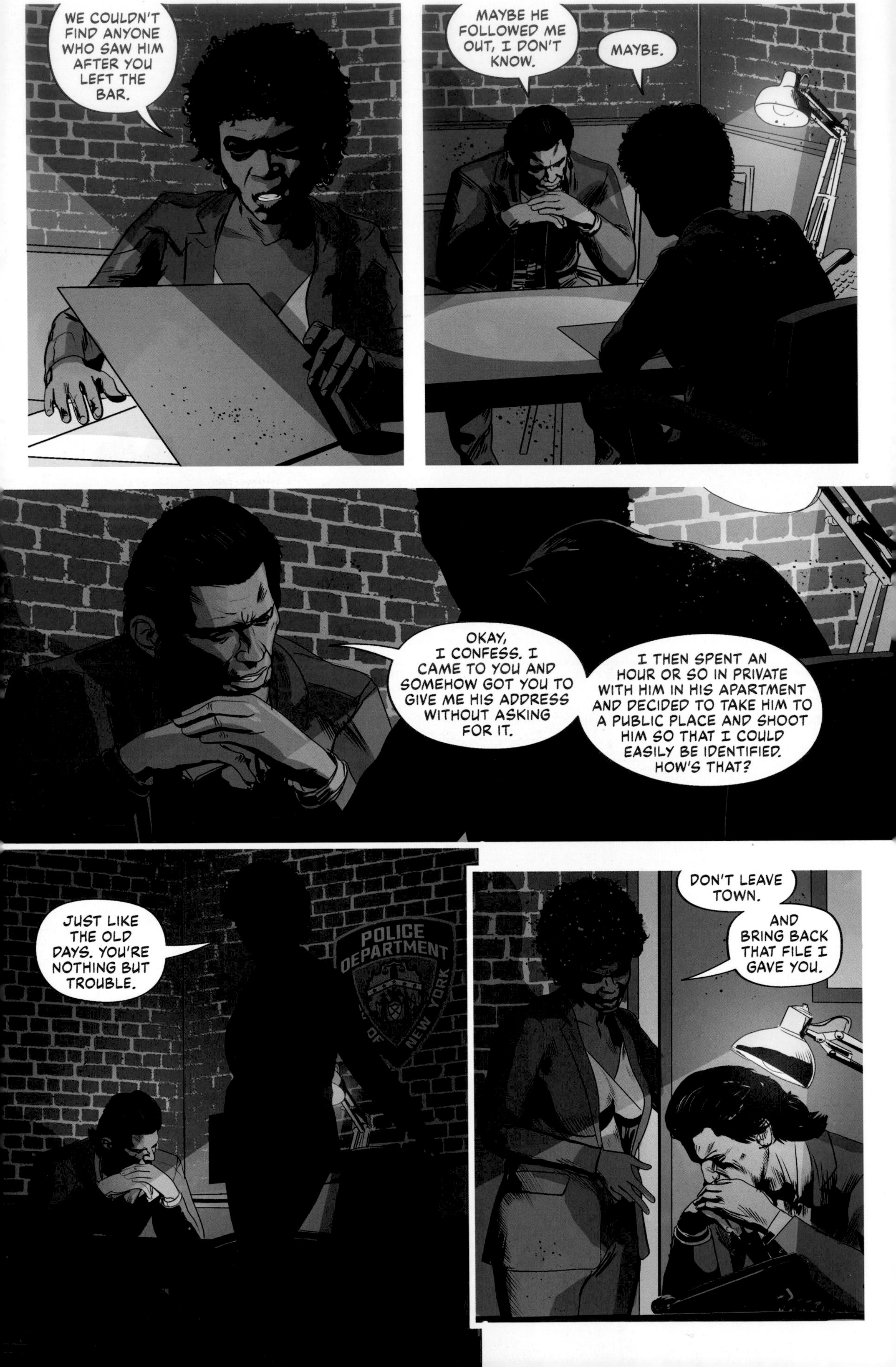
WE COULDN'T FIND ANYONE WHO SAW HIM AFTER YOU LEFT THE BAR.
MAYBE HE FOLLOWED ME OUT, I DON'T KNOW.
MAYBE.
OKAY, I CONFESS. I CAME TO YOU AND SOMEHOW GOT YOU TO GIVE ME HIS ADDRESS WITHOUT ASKING FOR IT.
I THEN SPENT AN HOUR OR SO IN PRIVATE WITH HIM IN HIS APARTMENT AND DECIDED TO TAKE HIM TO A PUBLIC PLACE AND SHOOT HIM SO THAT I COULD EASILY BE IDENTIFIED. HOW'S THAT?
JUST LIKE THE OLD DAYS. YOU'RE NOTHING BUT TROUBLE.
POLICE DEPARTMENT
DON'T LEAVE TOWN.
AND BRING BACK THAT FILE I GAVE YOU.

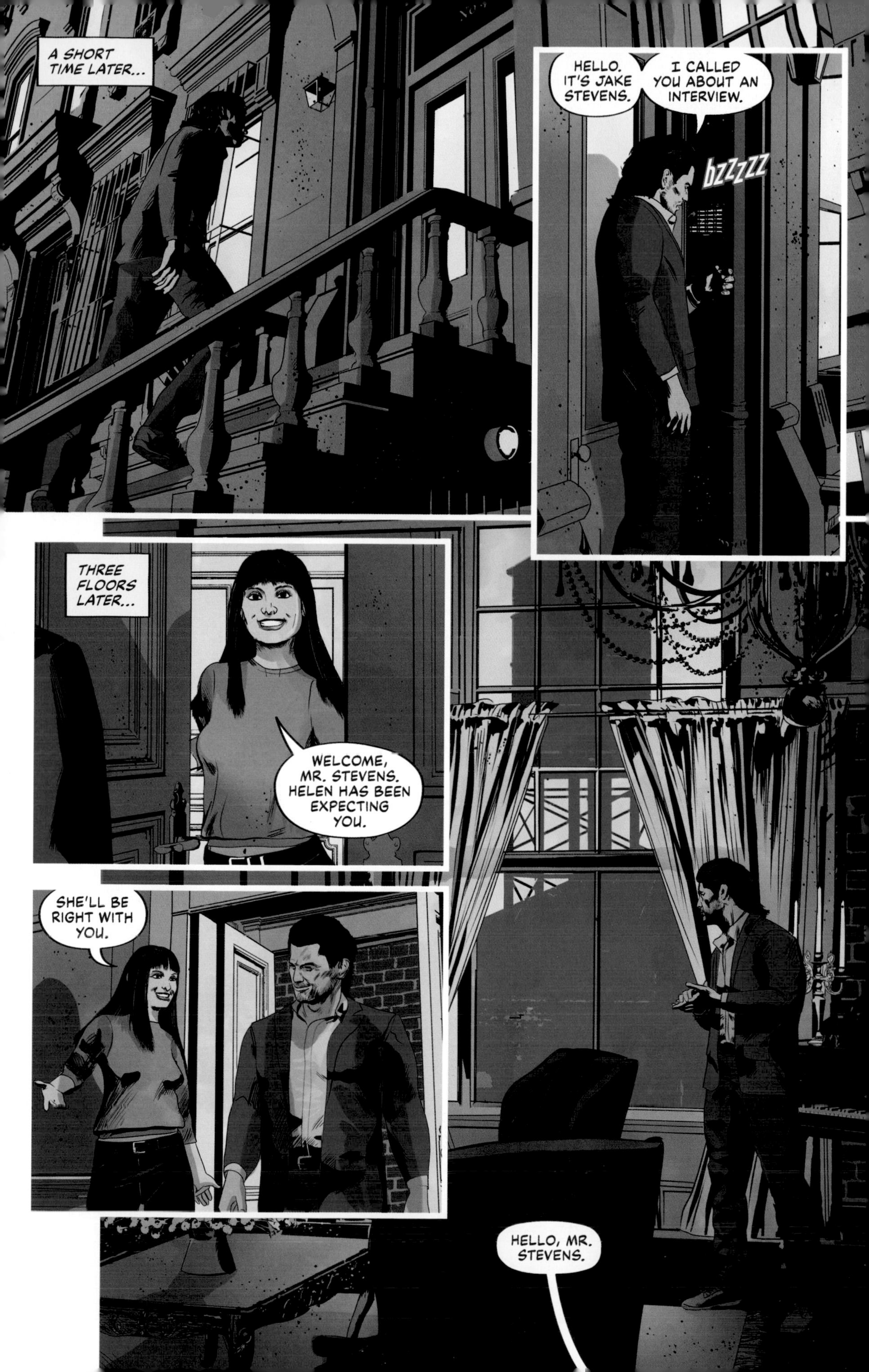

A SHORT TIME LATER...
HELLO. IT'S JAKE STEVENS.
I CALLED YOU ABOUT AN INTERVIEW.
bzzzzz
THREE FLOORS LATER...
WELCOME, MR. STEVENS. HELEN HAS BEEN EXPECTING YOU.
SHE'LL BE RIGHT WITH YOU.
HELLO, MR. STEVENS.

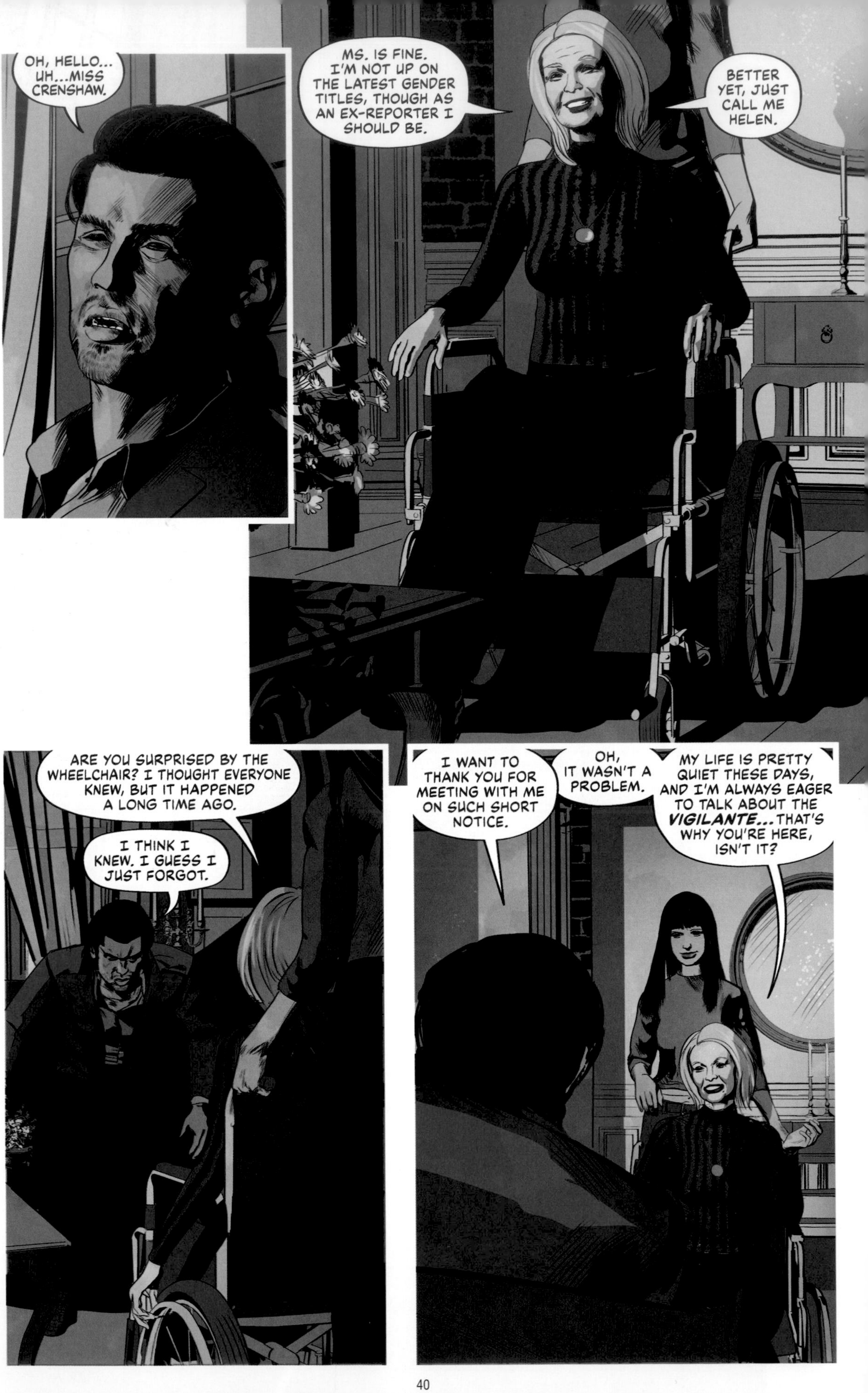
OH, HELLO... UH...MISS CRENSHAW.
MS. IS FINE. I'M NOT UP ON THE LATEST GENDER TITLES, THOUGH AS AN EX-REPORTER I SHOULD BE.
BETTER YET, JUST CALL ME HELEN.
ARE YOU SURPRISED BY THE WHEELCHAIR? I THOUGHT EVERYONE KNEW, BUT IT HAPPENED A LONG TIME AGO.
I THINK I KNEW. I GUESS I JUST FORGOT.
I WANT TO THANK YOU FOR MEETING WITH ME ON SUCH SHORT NOTICE.
OH, IT WASN'T A PROBLEM.
MY LIFE IS PRETTY QUIET THESE DAYS, AND I'M ALWAYS EAGER TO TALK ABOUT THE *VIGILANTE*... THAT'S WHY YOU'RE HERE, ISN'T IT?

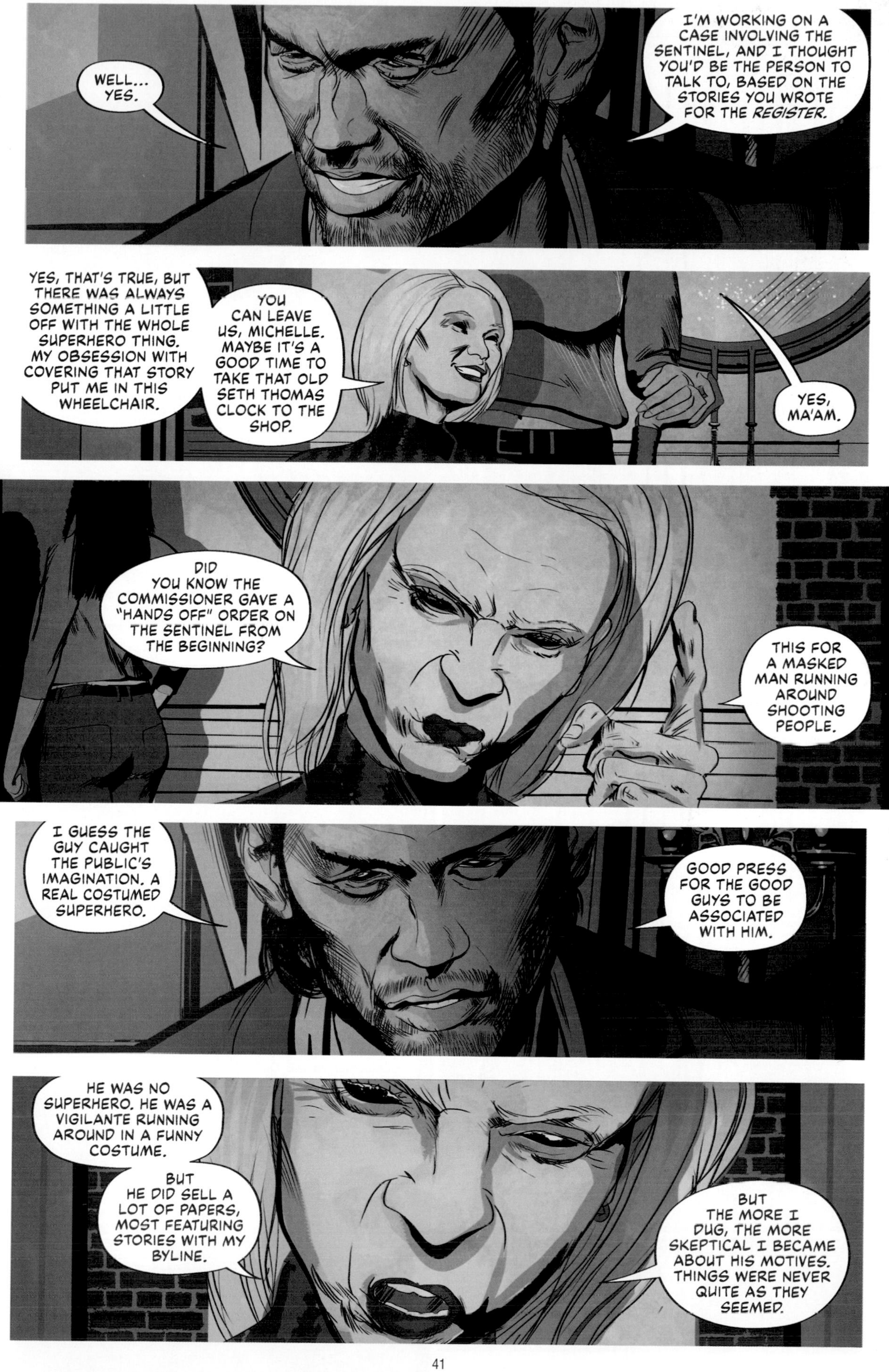
WELL... YES.
I'M WORKING ON A CASE INVOLVING THE SENTINEL, AND I THOUGHT YOU'D BE THE PERSON TO TALK TO, BASED ON THE STORIES YOU WROTE FOR THE *REGISTER.*
YES, THAT'S TRUE, BUT THERE WAS ALWAYS SOMETHING A LITTLE OFF WITH THE WHOLE SUPERHERO THING. MY OBSESSION WITH COVERING THAT STORY PUT ME IN THIS WHEELCHAIR.
YOU CAN LEAVE US, MICHELLE. MAYBE IT'S A GOOD TIME TO TAKE THAT OLD SETH THOMAS CLOCK TO THE SHOP.
YES, MA'AM.
DID YOU KNOW THE COMMISSIONER GAVE A "HANDS OFF" ORDER ON THE SENTINEL FROM THE BEGINNING?
THIS FOR A MASKED MAN RUNNING AROUND SHOOTING PEOPLE.
I GUESS THE GUY CAUGHT THE PUBLIC'S IMAGINATION. A REAL COSTUMED SUPERHERO.
GOOD PRESS FOR THE GOOD GUYS TO BE ASSOCIATED WITH HIM.
HE WAS NO SUPERHERO. HE WAS A VIGILANTE RUNNING AROUND IN A FUNNY COSTUME.
BUT HE DID SELL A LOT OF PAPERS, MOST FEATURING STORIES WITH MY BYLINE.
BUT THE MORE I DUG, THE MORE SKEPTICAL I BECAME ABOUT HIS MOTIVES. THINGS WERE NEVER QUITE AS THEY SEEMED.

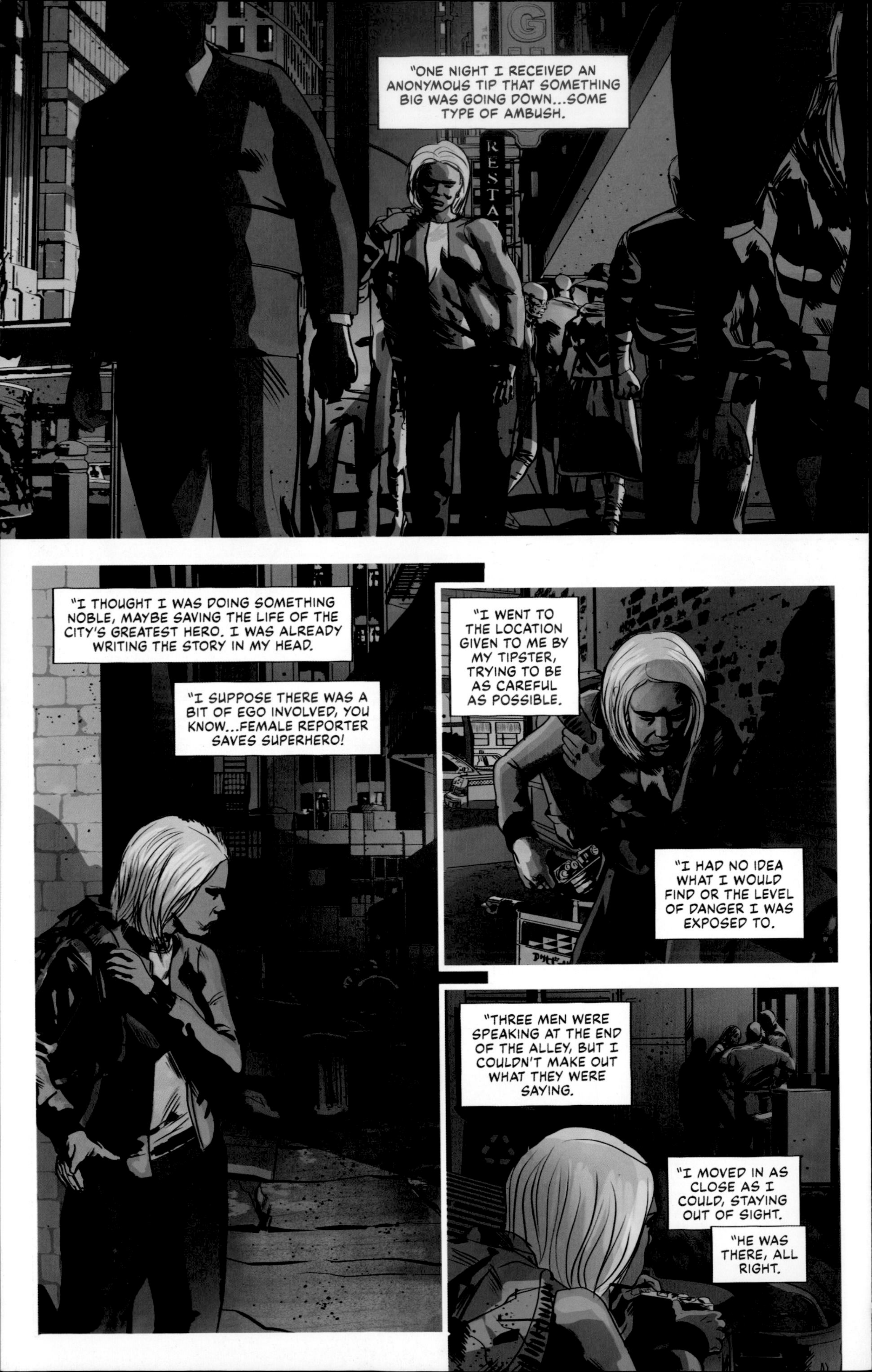
"ONE NIGHT I RECEIVED AN ANONYMOUS TIP THAT SOMETHING BIG WAS GOING DOWN...SOME TYPE OF AMBUSH.
"I THOUGHT I WAS DOING SOMETHING NOBLE, MAYBE SAVING THE LIFE OF THE CITY'S GREATEST HERO. I WAS ALREADY WRITING THE STORY IN MY HEAD.
"I SUPPOSE THERE WAS A BIT OF EGO INVOLVED, YOU KNOW...FEMALE REPORTER SAVES SUPERHERO!
"I WENT TO THE LOCATION GIVEN TO ME BY MY TIPSTER, TRYING TO BE AS CAREFUL AS POSSIBLE.
"I HAD NO IDEA WHAT I WOULD FIND OR THE LEVEL OF DANGER I WAS EXPOSED TO.
"THREE MEN WERE SPEAKING AT THE END OF THE ALLEY, BUT I COULDN'T MAKE OUT WHAT THEY WERE SAYING.
"I MOVED IN AS CLOSE AS I COULD, STAYING OUT OF SIGHT.
"HE WAS THERE, ALL RIGHT.

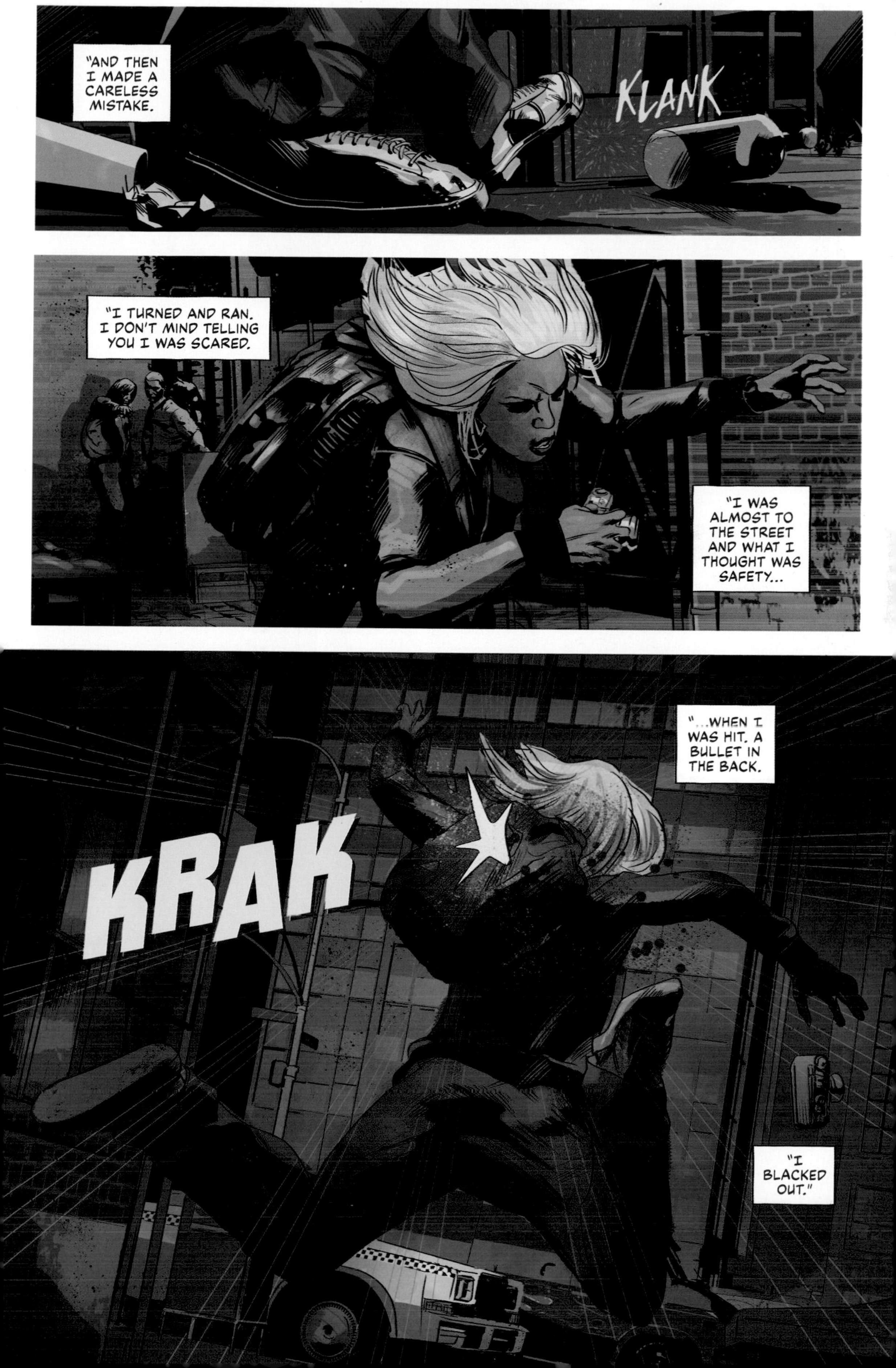
"AND THEN I MADE A CARELESS MISTAKE.
KLANK
"I TURNED AND RAN. I DON'T MIND TELLING YOU I WAS SCARED.
"I WAS ALMOST TO THE STREET AND WHAT I THOUGHT WAS SAFETY...
"...WHEN I WAS HIT. A BULLET IN THE BACK.
KRAK
"I BLACKED OUT."

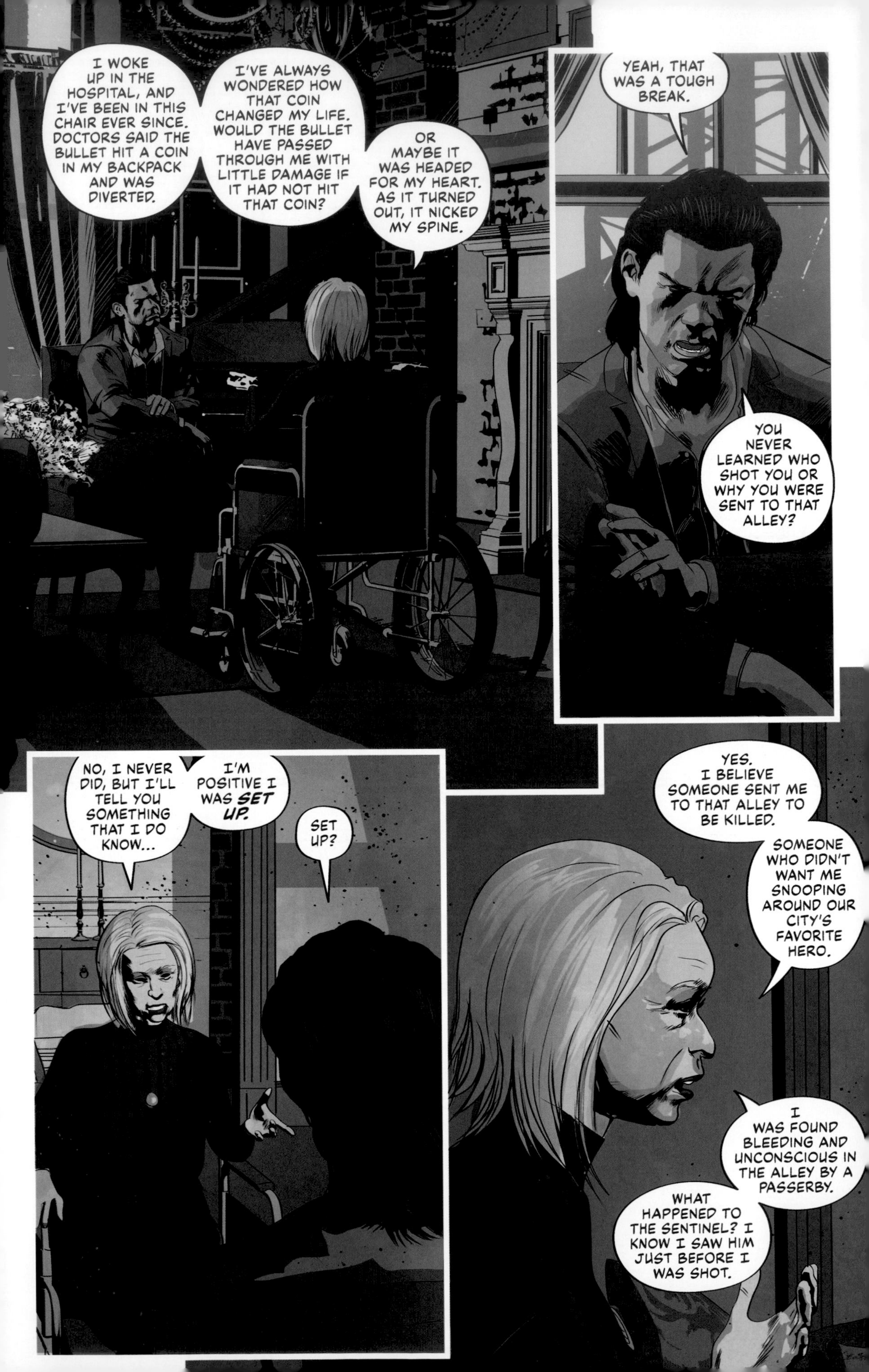
I WOKE UP IN THE HOSPITAL, AND I'VE BEEN IN THIS CHAIR EVER SINCE. DOCTORS SAID THE BULLET HIT A COIN IN MY BACKPACK AND WAS DIVERTED.
I'VE ALWAYS WONDERED HOW THAT COIN CHANGED MY LIFE. WOULD THE BULLET HAVE PASSED THROUGH ME WITH LITTLE DAMAGE IF IT HAD NOT HIT THAT COIN?
OR MAYBE IT WAS HEADED FOR MY HEART. AS IT TURNED OUT, IT NICKED MY SPINE.
YEAH, THAT WAS A TOUGH BREAK.
YOU NEVER LEARNED WHO SHOT YOU OR WHY YOU WERE SENT TO THAT ALLEY?
NO, I NEVER DID, BUT I'LL TELL YOU SOMETHING THAT I DO KNOW...
I'M POSITIVE I WAS SET UP.
SET UP?
YES. I BELIEVE SOMEONE SENT ME TO THAT ALLEY TO BE KILLED.
SOMEONE WHO DIDN'T WANT ME SNOOPING AROUND OUR CITY'S FAVORITE HERO.
I WAS FOUND BLEEDING AND UNCONSCIOUS IN THE ALLEY BY A PASSERBY.
WHAT HAPPENED TO THE SENTINEL? I KNOW I SAW HIM JUST BEFORE I WAS SHOT.

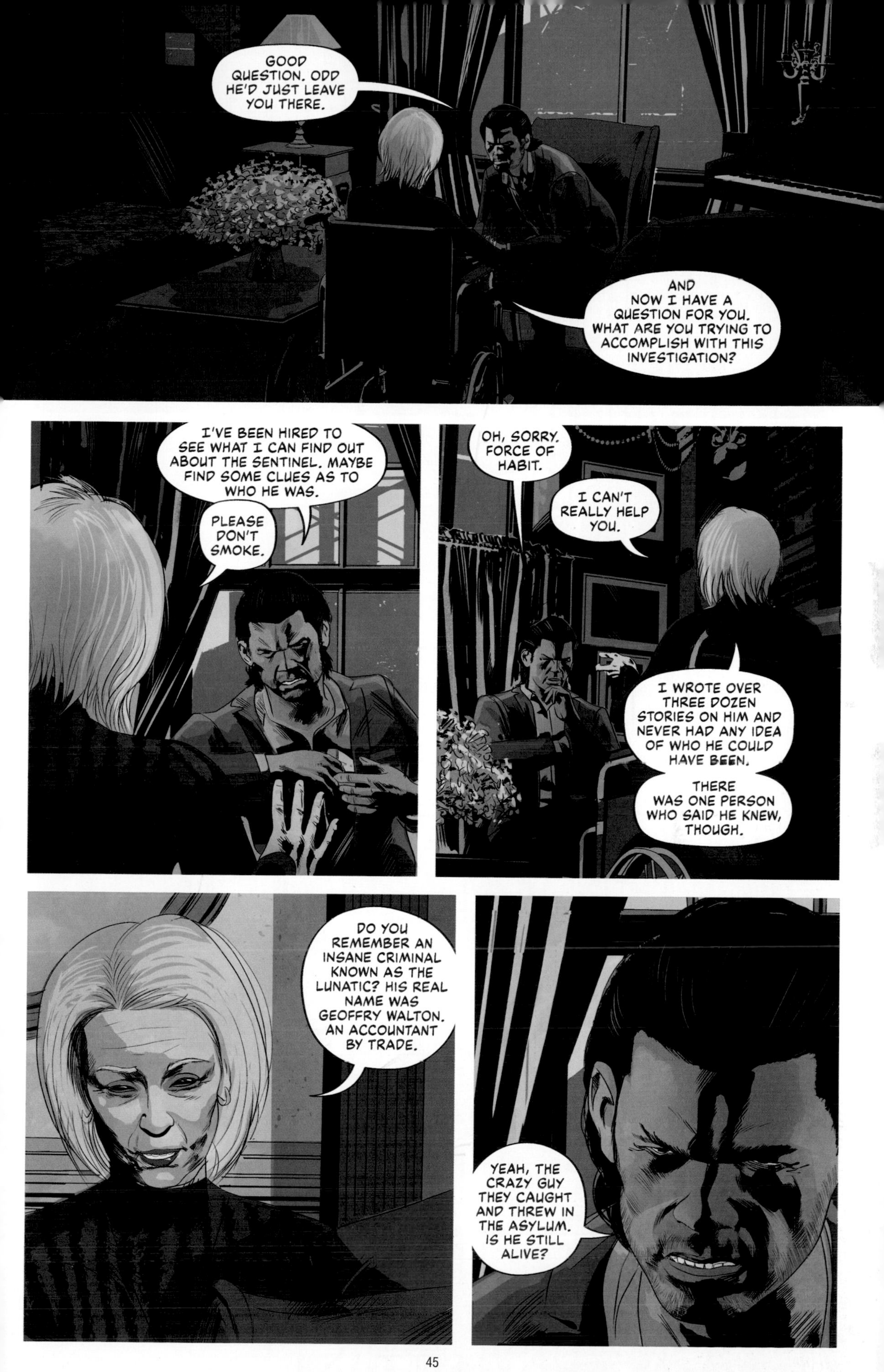
GOOD QUESTION. ODD HE'D JUST LEAVE YOU THERE.
AND NOW I HAVE A QUESTION FOR YOU. WHAT ARE YOU TRYING TO ACCOMPLISH WITH THIS INVESTIGATION?
I'VE BEEN HIRED TO SEE WHAT I CAN FIND OUT ABOUT THE SENTINEL. MAYBE FIND SOME CLUES AS TO WHO HE WAS.
PLEASE DON'T SMOKE.
OH, SORRY. FORCE OF HABIT.
I CAN'T REALLY HELP YOU.
I WROTE OVER THREE DOZEN STORIES ON HIM AND NEVER HAD ANY IDEA OF WHO HE COULD HAVE BEEN.
THERE WAS ONE PERSON WHO SAID HE KNEW, THOUGH.
DO YOU REMEMBER AN INSANE CRIMINAL KNOWN AS THE LUNATIC? HIS REAL NAME WAS GEOFFRY WALTON. AN ACCOUNTANT BY TRADE.
YEAH, THE CRAZY GUY THEY CAUGHT AND THREW IN THE ASYLUM. IS HE STILL ALIVE?

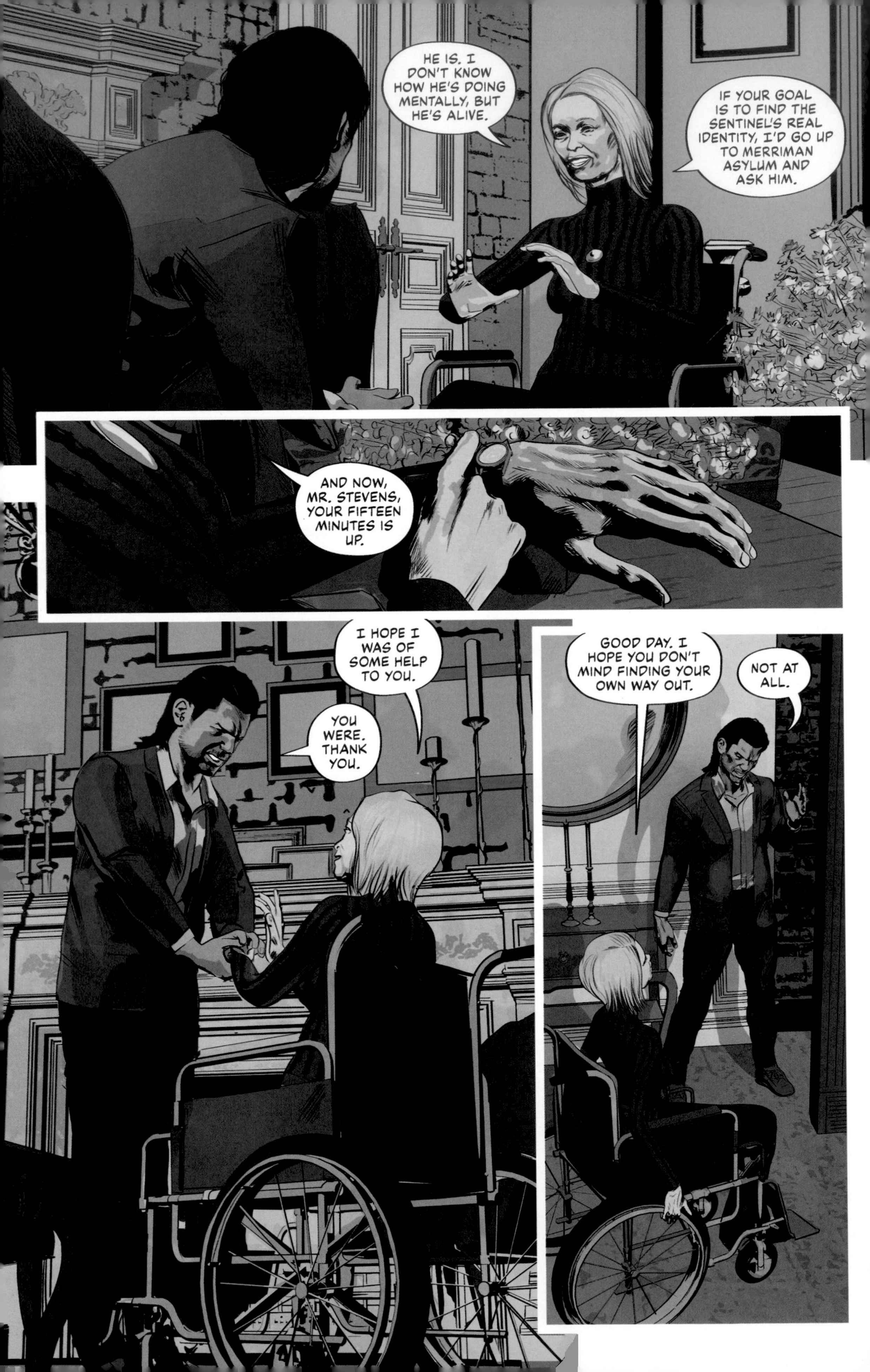
HE IS. I DON'T KNOW HOW HE'S DOING MENTALLY, BUT HE'S ALIVE.
IF YOUR GOAL IS TO FIND THE SENTINEL'S REAL IDENTITY, I'D GO UP TO MERRIMAN ASYLUM AND ASK HIM.
AND NOW, MR. STEVENS, YOUR FIFTEEN MINUTES IS UP.
I HOPE I WAS OF SOME HELP TO YOU.
YOU WERE. THANK YOU.
GOOD DAY. I HOPE YOU DON'T MIND FINDING YOUR OWN WAY OUT.
NOT AT ALL.

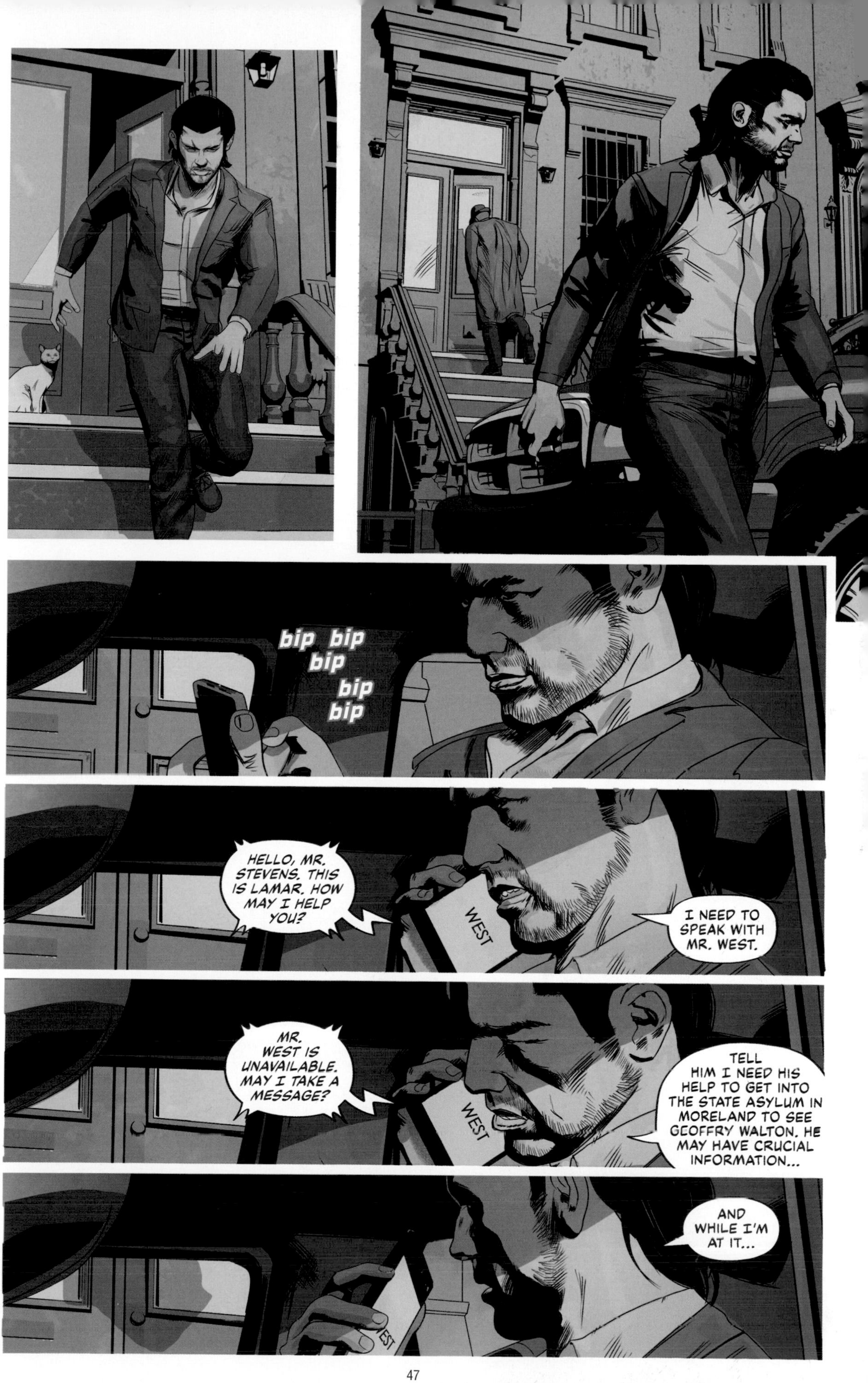
bip bip bip bip bip
HELLO, MR. STEVENS. THIS IS LAMAR. HOW MAY I HELP YOU?
WEST
I NEED TO SPEAK WITH MR. WEST.
MR. WEST IS UNAVAILABLE. MAY I TAKE A MESSAGE?
WEST
TELL HIM I NEED HIS HELP TO GET INTO THE STATE ASYLUM IN MORELAND TO SEE GEOFFRY WALTON. HE MAY HAVE CRUCIAL INFORMATION...
AND WHILE I'M AT IT...
EST

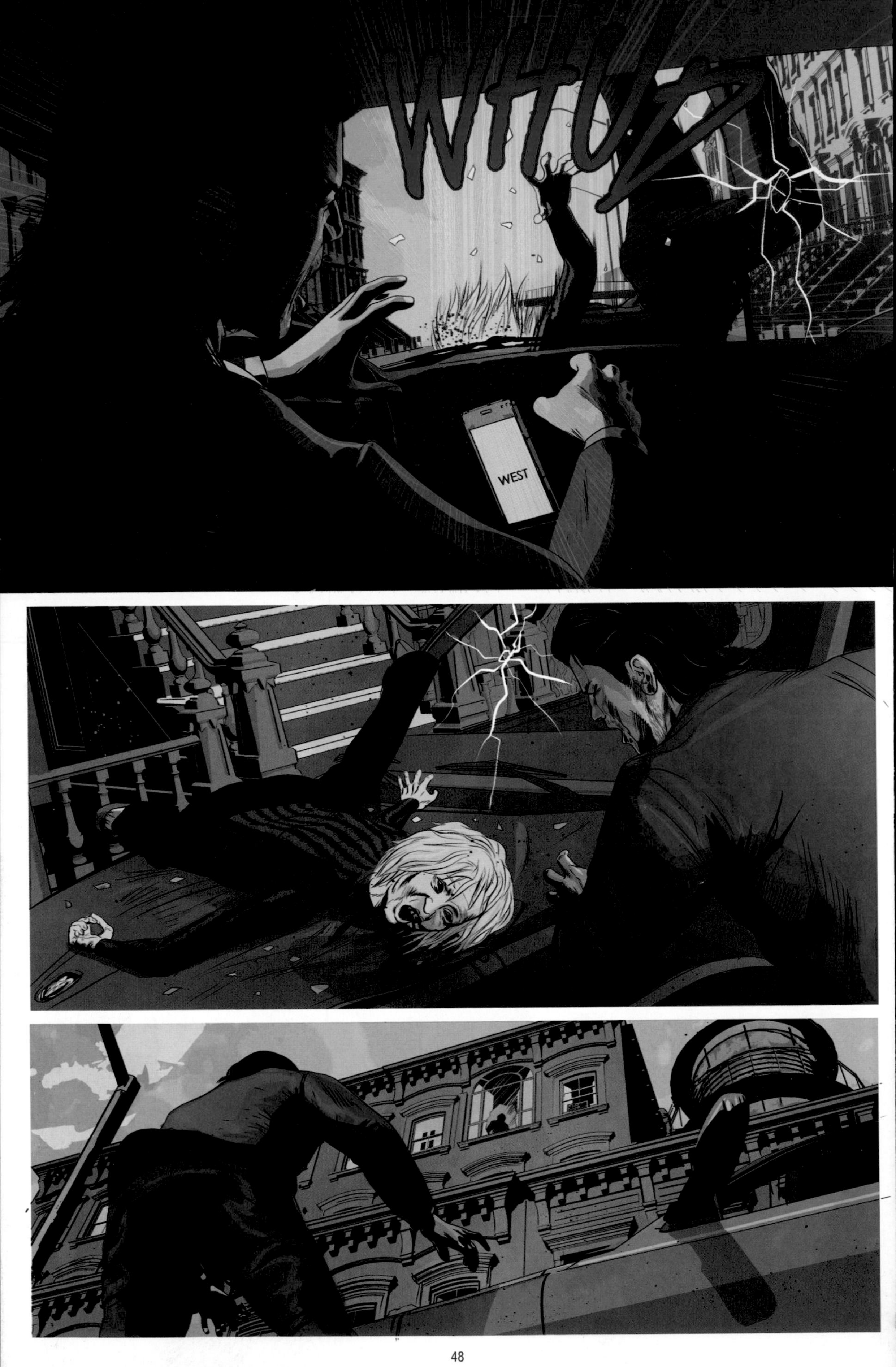
WHUD
WEST

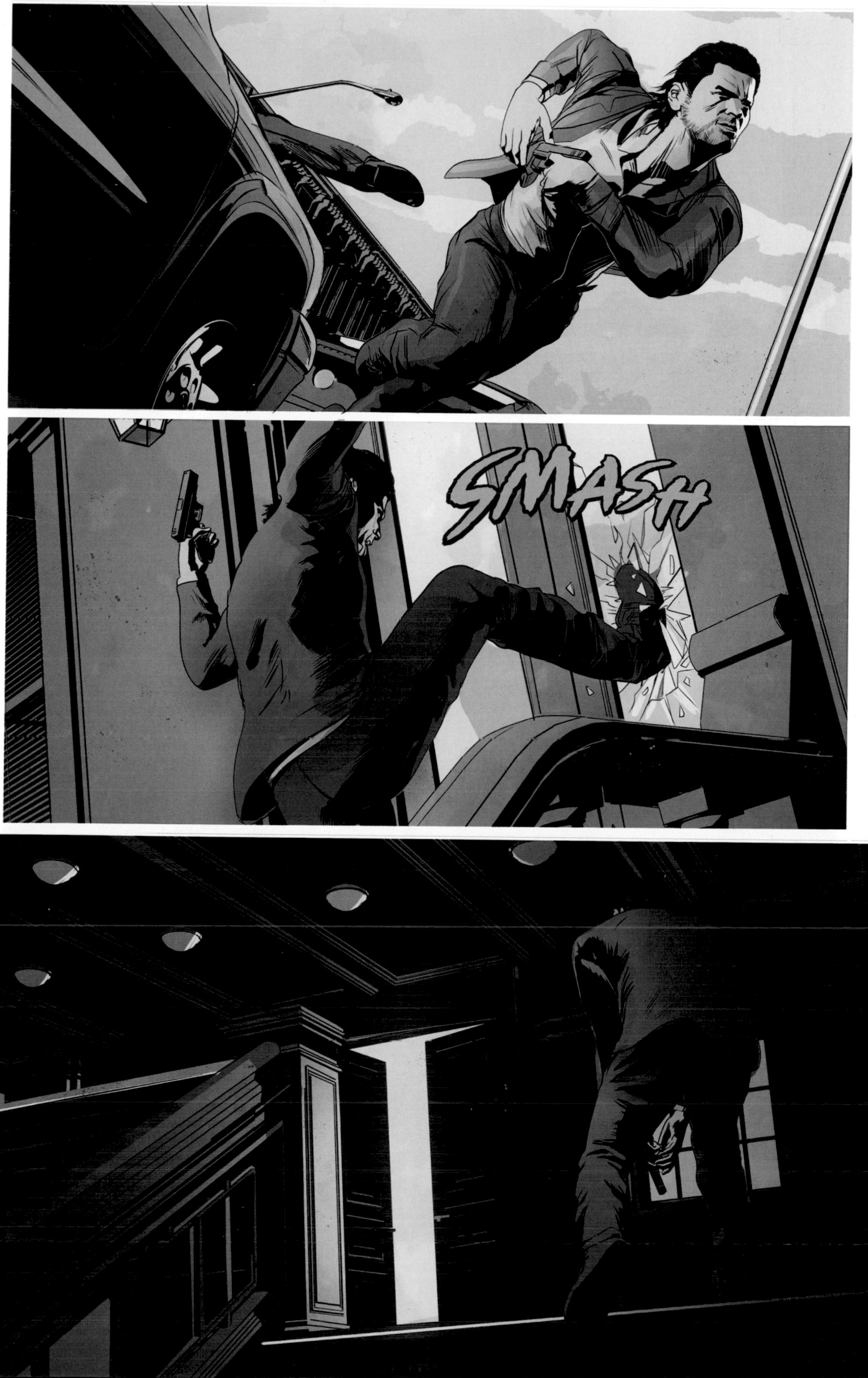
SMASH

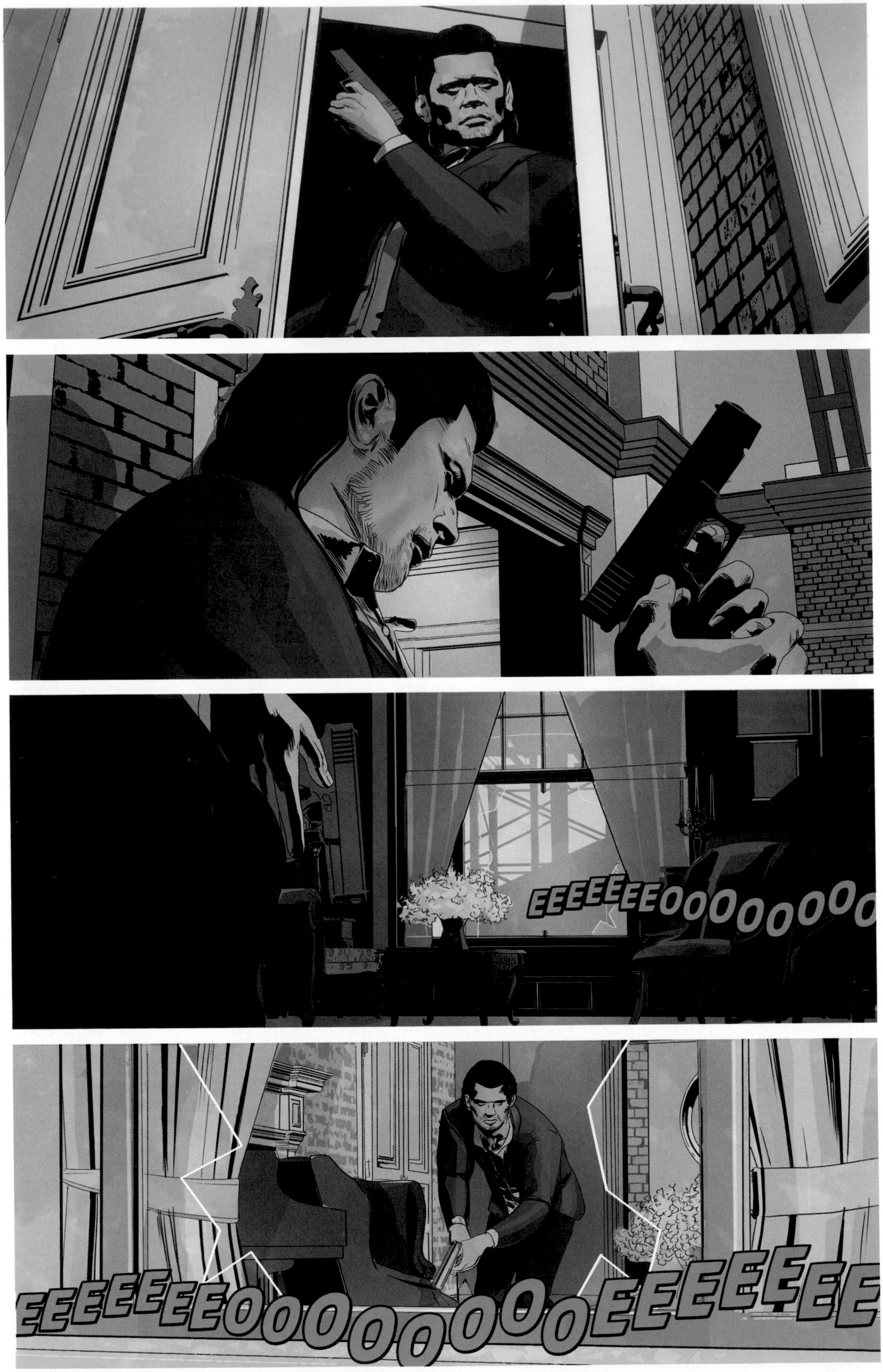

EEEEEEEOOOOOOOOO
EEEEEEEEOOOOOOOOOEEEEEEEE

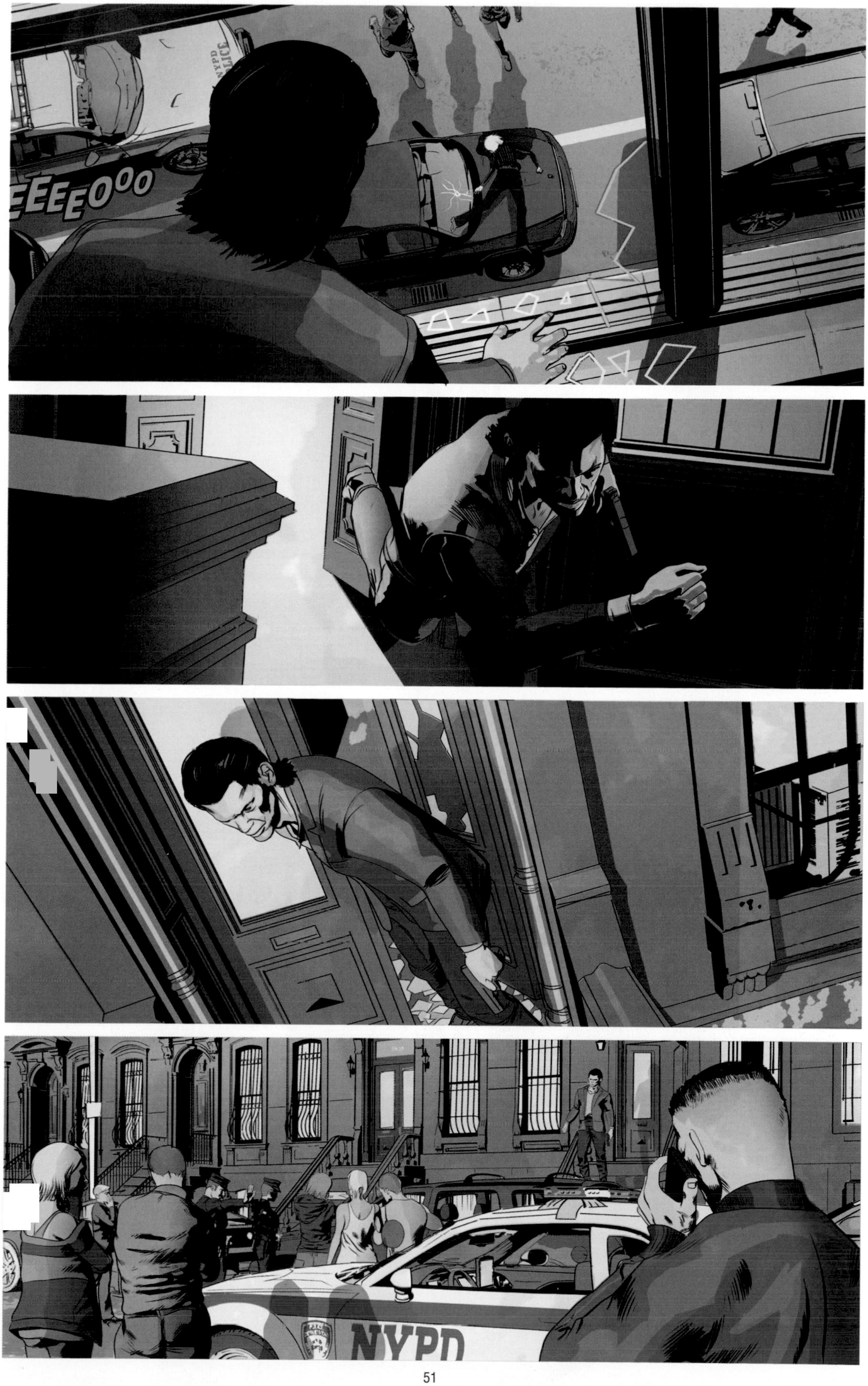
EEEEOOO
NYPD

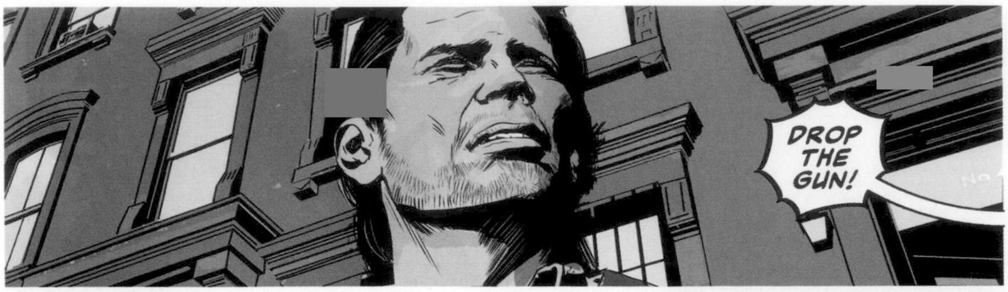
DROP THE GUN!

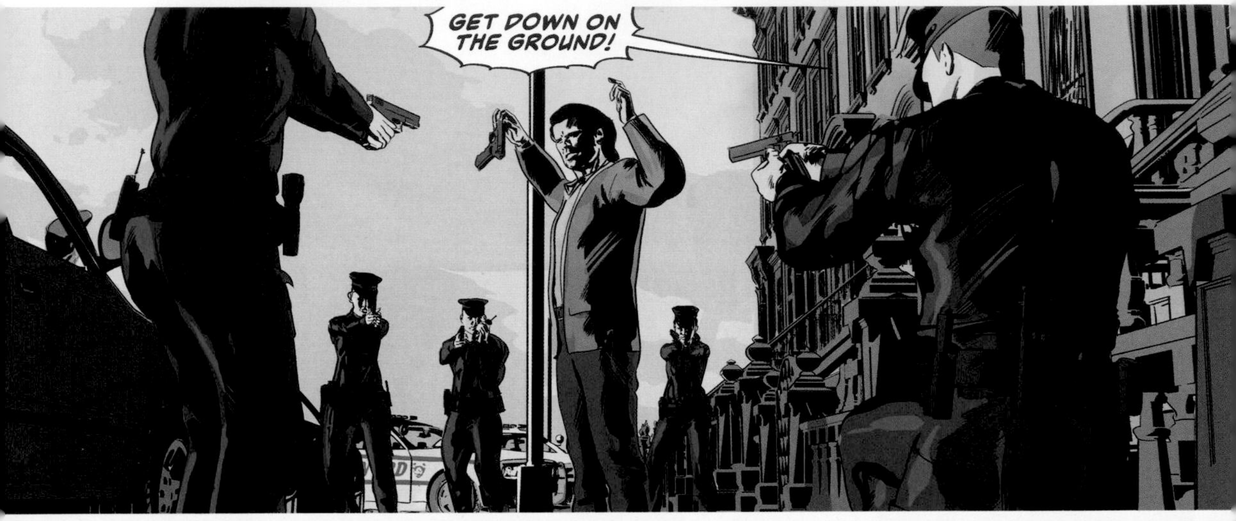
GET DOWN ON THE GROUND!

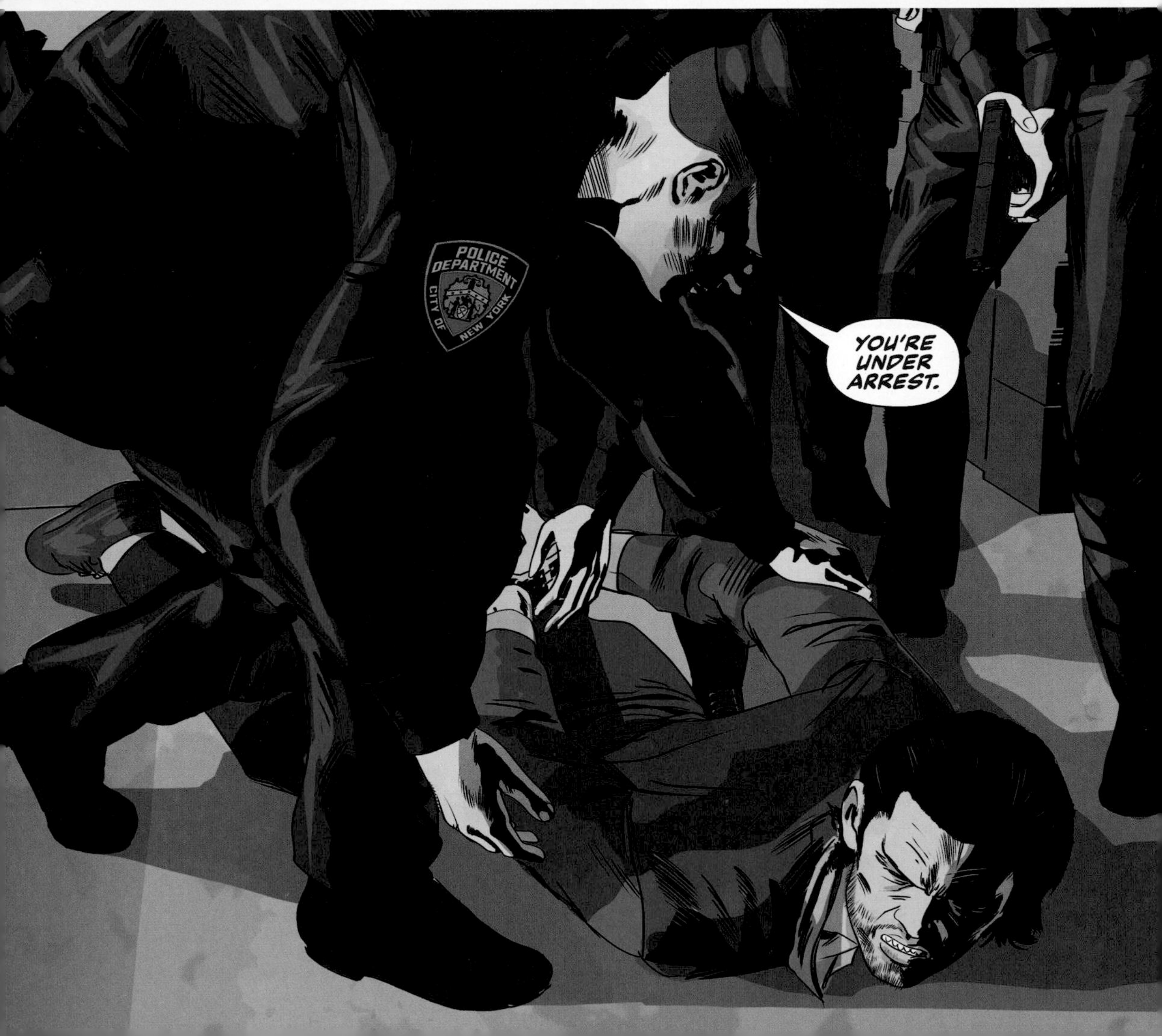
YOU'RE UNDER ARREST.

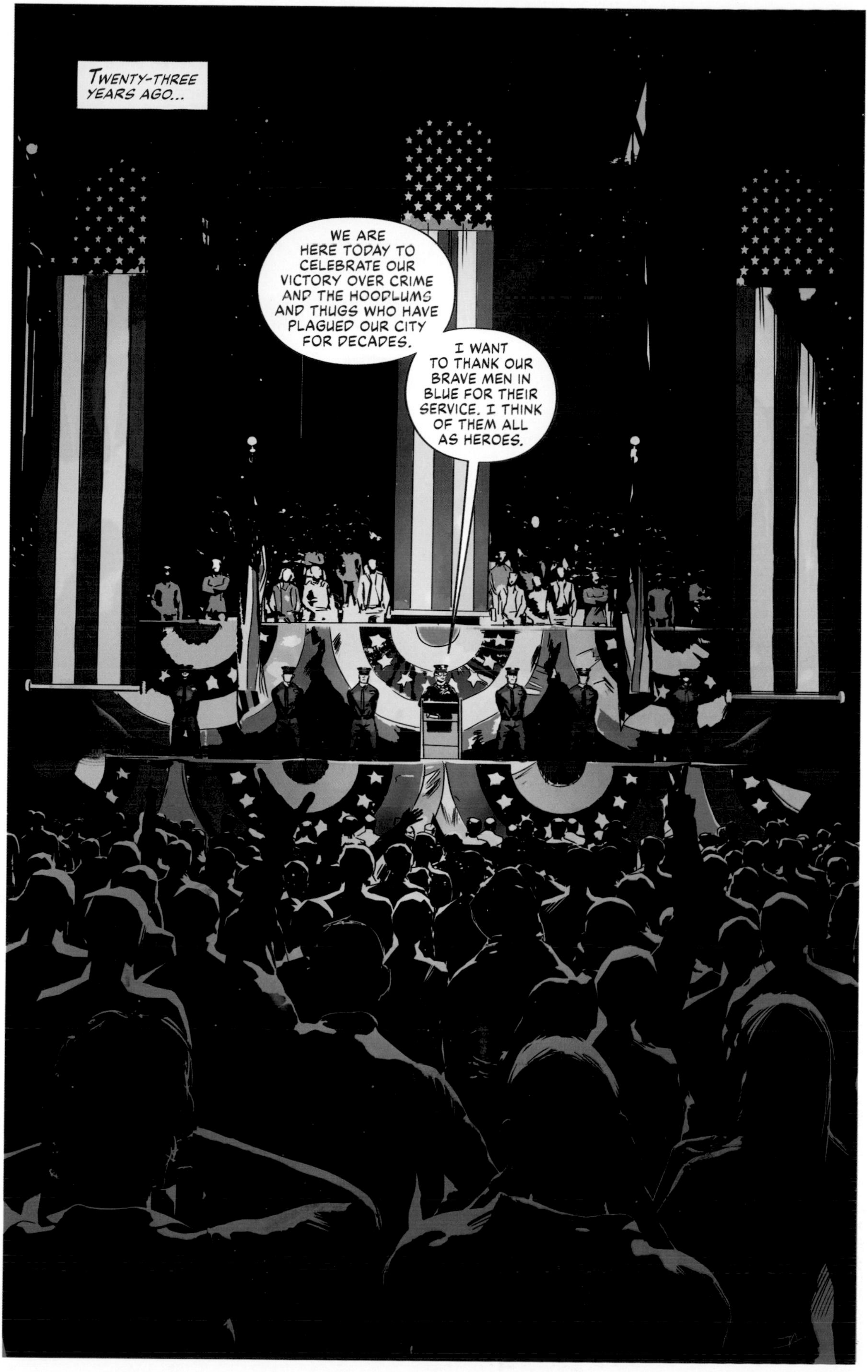
TWENTY-THREE YEARS AGO...
WE ARE HERE TODAY TO CELEBRATE OUR VICTORY OVER CRIME AND THE HOODLUMS AND THUGS WHO HAVE PLAGUED OUR CITY FOR DECADES.
I WANT TO THANK OUR BRAVE MEN IN BLUE FOR THEIR SERVICE. I THINK OF THEM ALL AS HEROES.

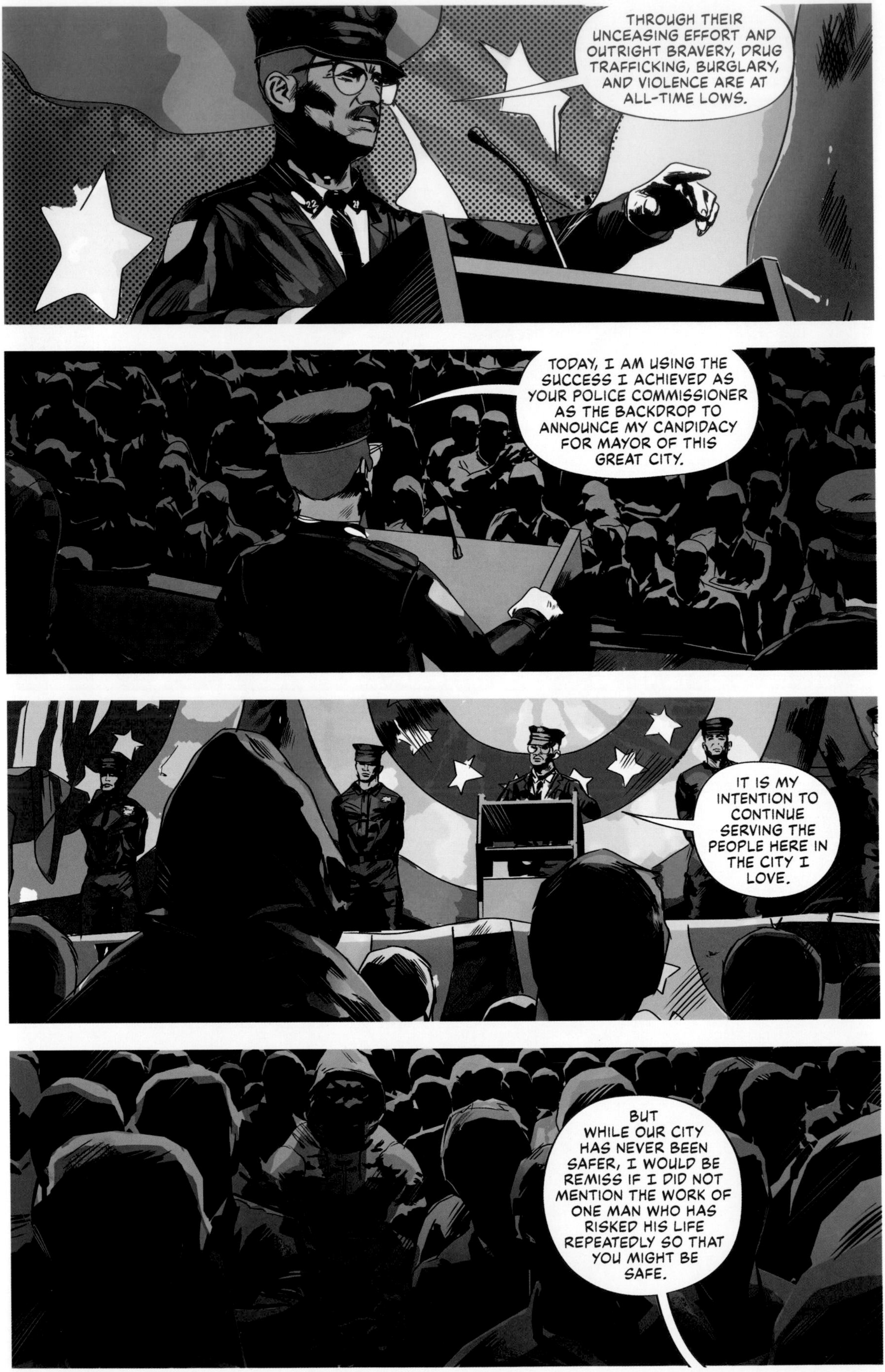
THROUGH THEIR UNCEASING EFFORT AND OUTRIGHT BRAVERY, DRUG TRAFFICKING, BURGLARY, AND VIOLENCE ARE AT ALL-TIME LOWS.
TODAY, I AM USING THE SUCCESS I ACHIEVED AS YOUR POLICE COMMISSIONER AS THE BACKDROP TO ANNOUNCE MY CANDIDACY FOR MAYOR OF THIS GREAT CITY.
IT IS MY INTENTION TO CONTINUE SERVING THE PEOPLE HERE IN THE CITY I LOVE.
BUT WHILE OUR CITY HAS NEVER BEEN SAFER, I WOULD BE REMISS IF I DID NOT MENTION THE WORK OF ONE MAN WHO HAS RISKED HIS LIFE REPEATEDLY SO THAT YOU MIGHT BE SAFE.

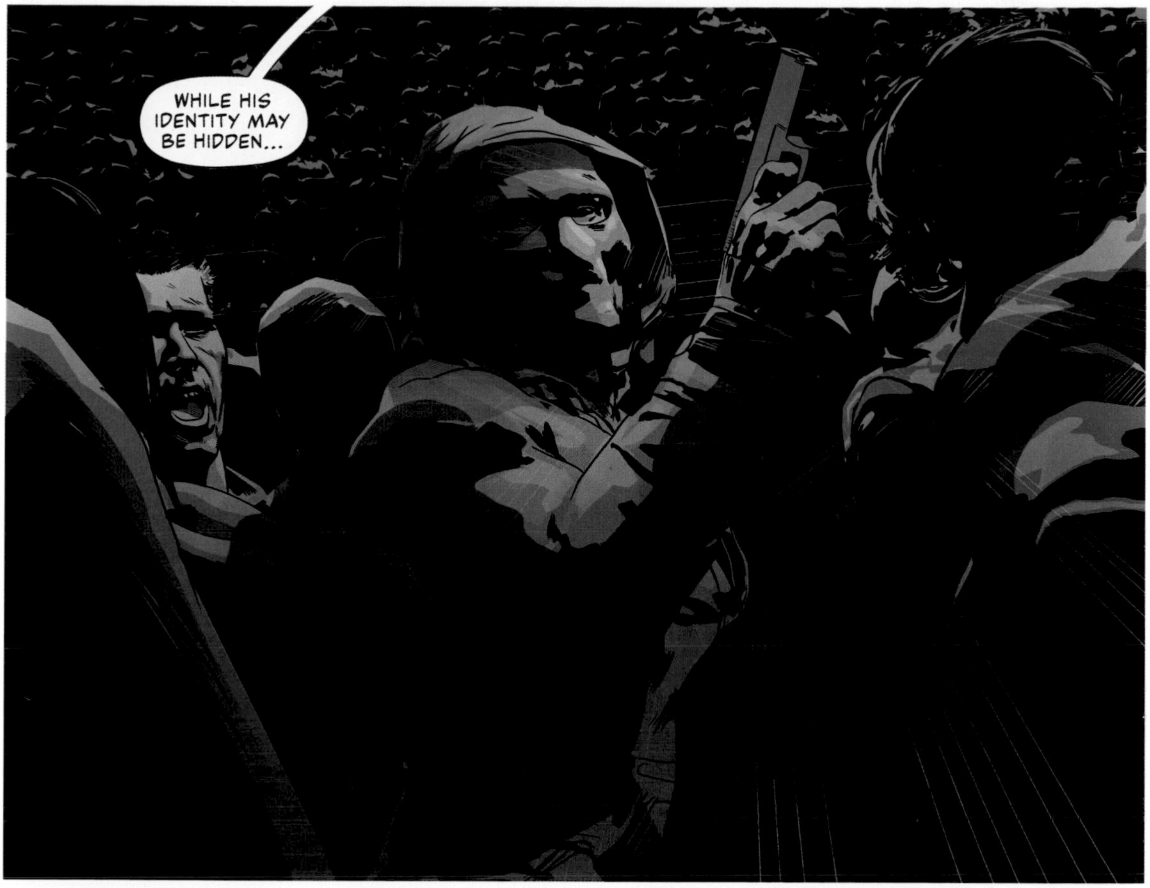
WHILE HIS IDENTITY MAY BE HIDDEN...

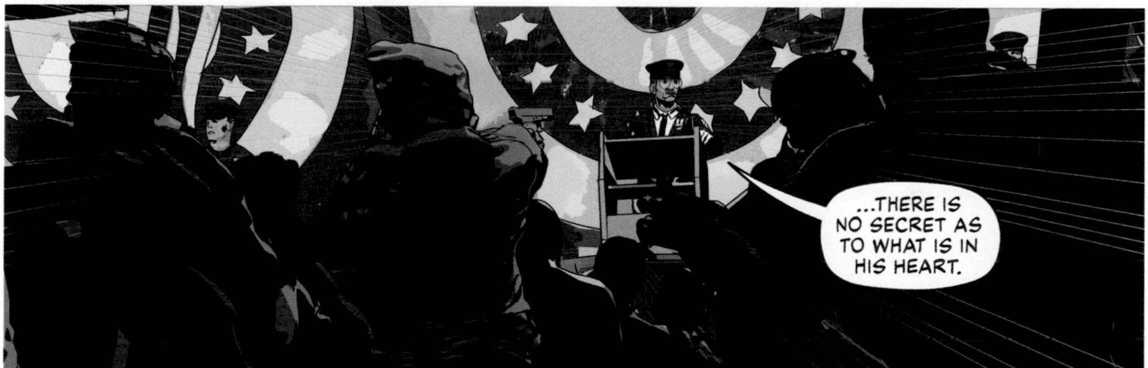
...THERE IS NO SECRET AS TO WHAT IS IN HIS HEART.

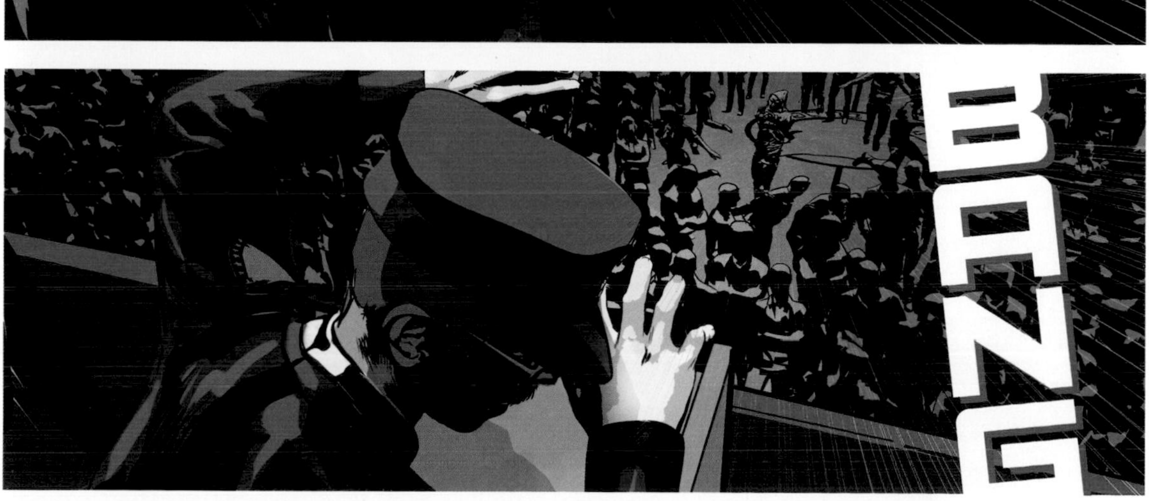
BANG

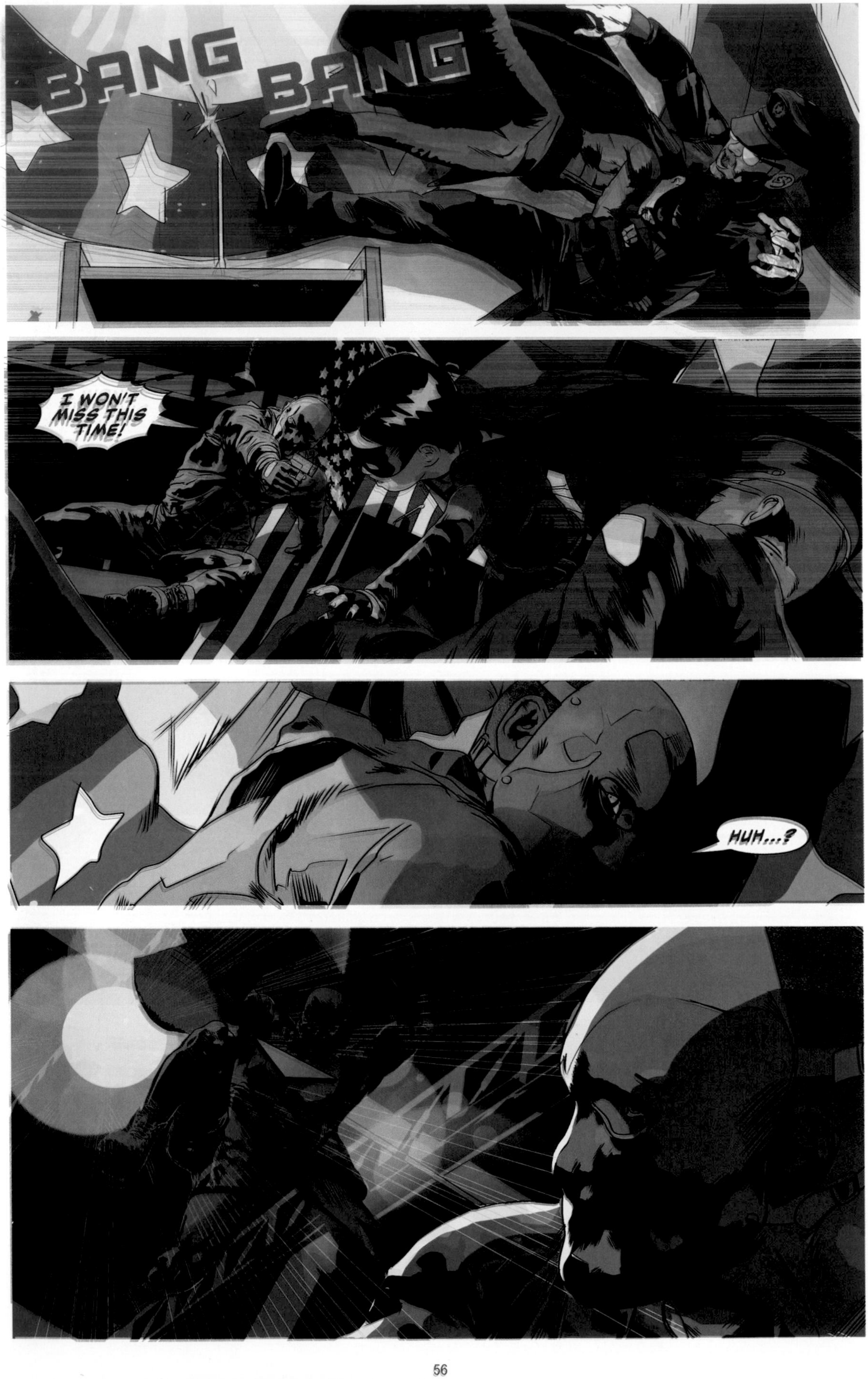
BANG
BANG
I WON'T MISS THIS TIME!
HUH...?

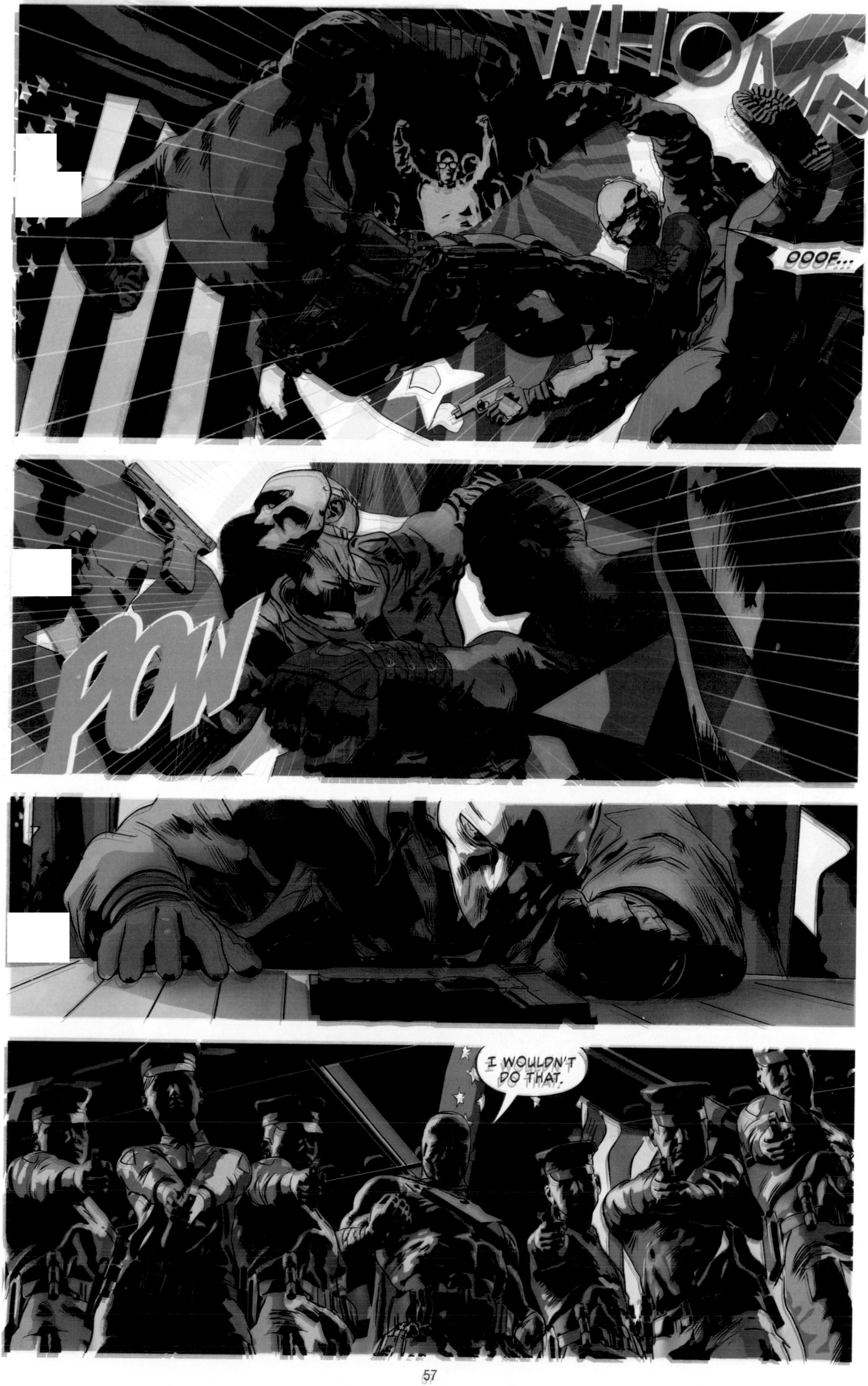
WHOMP
OOOF...
POW
I WOULDN'T DO THAT.

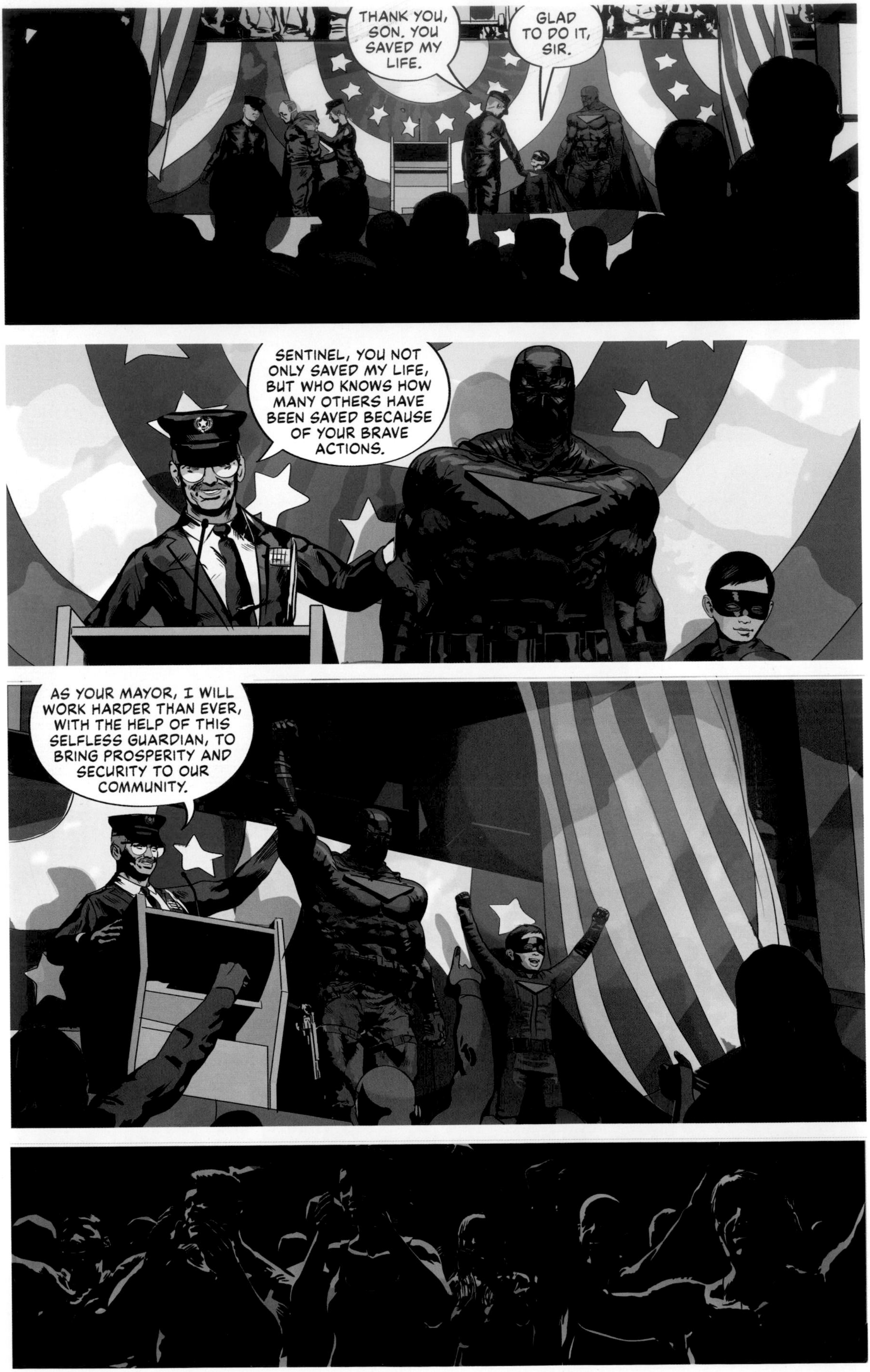
THANK YOU, SON. YOU SAVED MY LIFE.
GLAD TO DO IT, SIR.
SENTINEL, YOU NOT ONLY SAVED MY LIFE, BUT WHO KNOWS HOW MANY OTHERS HAVE BEEN SAVED BECAUSE OF YOUR BRAVE ACTIONS.
AS YOUR MAYOR, I WILL WORK HARDER THAN EVER, WITH THE HELP OF THIS SELFLESS GUARDIAN, TO BRING PROSPERITY AND SECURITY TO OUR COMMUNITY.

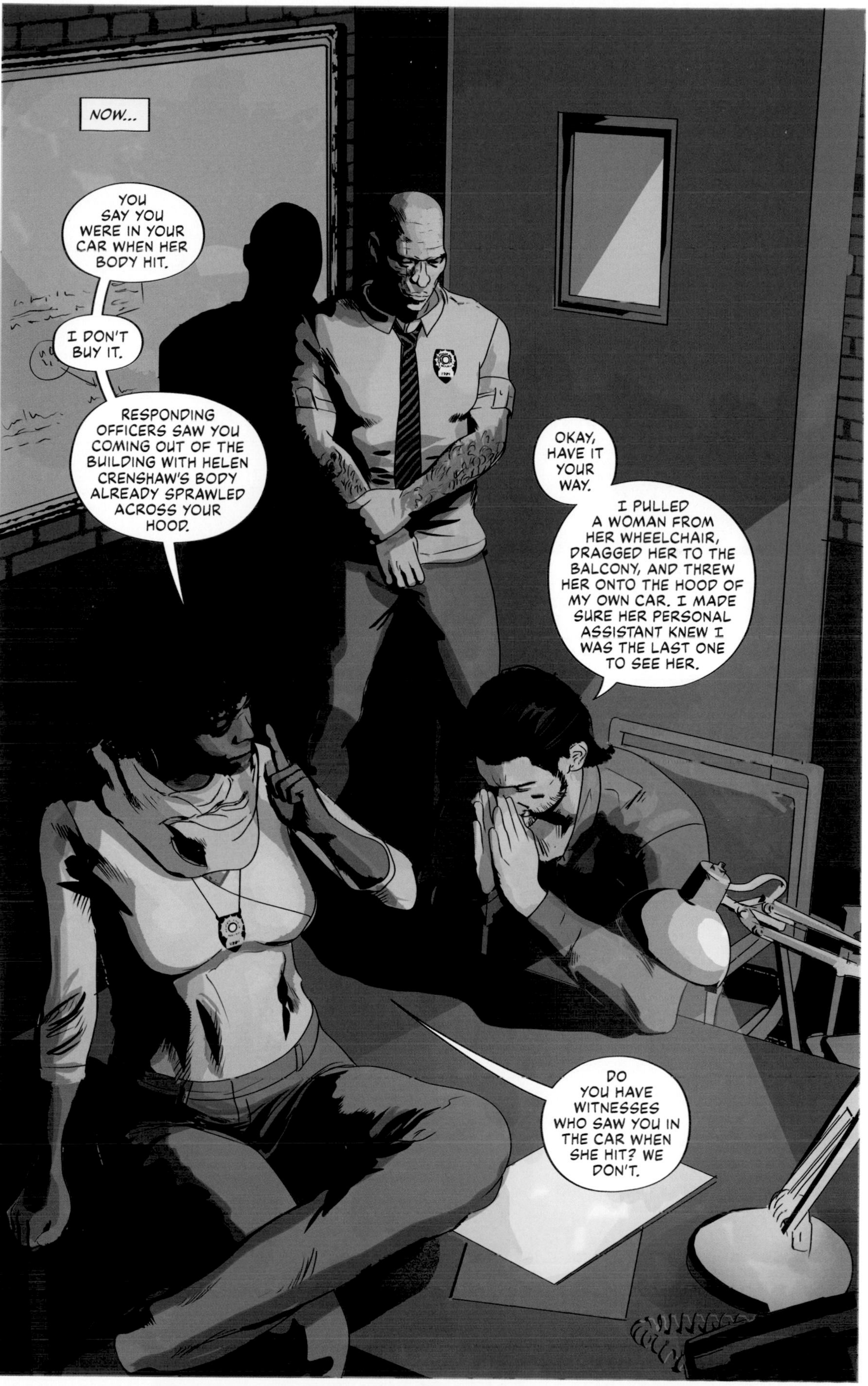
NOW...
YOU SAY YOU WERE IN YOUR CAR WHEN HER BODY HIT.
I DON'T BUY IT.
RESPONDING OFFICERS SAW YOU COMING OUT OF THE BUILDING WITH HELEN CRENSHAW'S BODY ALREADY SPRAWLED ACROSS YOUR HOOD.
OKAY, HAVE IT YOUR WAY.
I PULLED A WOMAN FROM HER WHEELCHAIR, DRAGGED HER TO THE BALCONY, AND THREW HER ONTO THE HOOD OF MY OWN CAR. I MADE SURE HER PERSONAL ASSISTANT KNEW I WAS THE LAST ONE TO SEE HER.
DO YOU HAVE WITNESSES WHO SAW YOU IN THE CAR WHEN SHE HIT? WE DON'T.

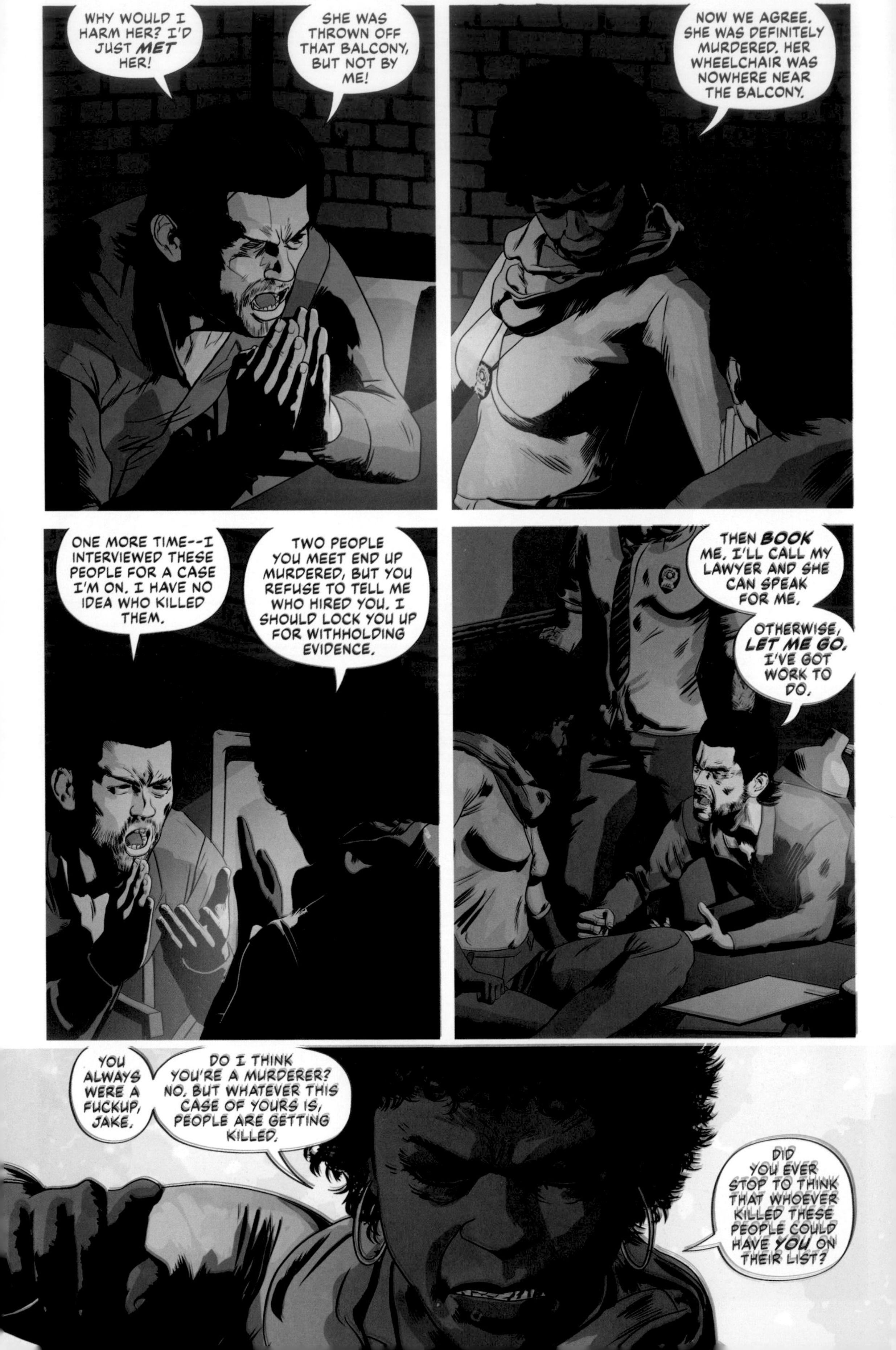
WHY WOULD I HARM HER? I'D JUST MET HER!
SHE WAS THROWN OFF THAT BALCONY, BUT NOT BY ME!
NOW WE AGREE. SHE WAS DEFINITELY MURDERED. HER WHEELCHAIR WAS NOWHERE NEAR THE BALCONY.
ONE MORE TIME--I INTERVIEWED THESE PEOPLE FOR A CASE I'M ON. I HAVE NO IDEA WHO KILLED THEM.
TWO PEOPLE YOU MEET END UP MURDERED, BUT YOU REFUSE TO TELL ME WHO HIRED YOU. I SHOULD LOCK YOU UP FOR WITHHOLDING EVIDENCE.
THEN BOOK ME. I'LL CALL MY LAWYER AND SHE CAN SPEAK FOR ME.
OTHERWISE, LET ME GO. I'VE GOT WORK TO DO.
YOU ALWAYS WERE A FUCKUP, JAKE.
DO I THINK YOU'RE A MURDERER? NO. BUT WHATEVER THIS CASE OF YOURS IS, PEOPLE ARE GETTING KILLED.
DID YOU EVER STOP TO THINK THAT WHOEVER KILLED THESE PEOPLE COULD HAVE YOU ON THEIR LIST?

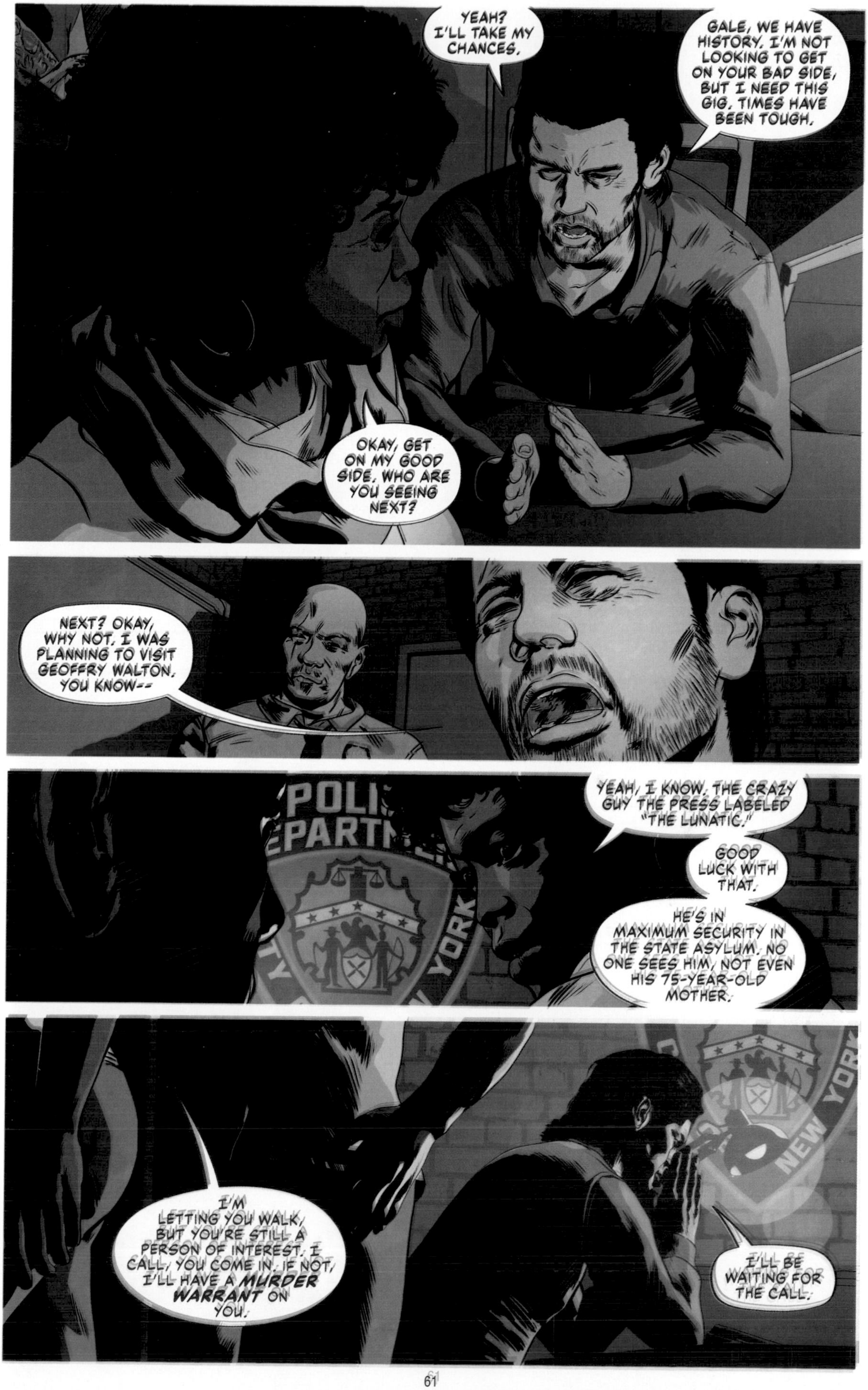

YEAH? I'LL TAKE MY CHANCES.
GALE, WE HAVE HISTORY. I'M NOT LOOKING TO GET ON YOUR BAD SIDE, BUT I NEED THIS GIG. TIMES HAVE BEEN TOUGH.
OKAY, GET ON MY GOOD SIDE. WHO ARE YOU SEEING NEXT?
NEXT? OKAY, WHY NOT. I WAS PLANNING TO VISIT GEOFFRY WALTON, YOU KNOW--
YEAH, I KNOW. THE CRAZY GUY THE PRESS LABELED "THE LUNATIC."
GOOD LUCK WITH THAT.
HE'S IN MAXIMUM SECURITY IN THE STATE ASYLUM. NO ONE SEES HIM, NOT EVEN HIS 75-YEAR-OLD MOTHER.
I'M LETTING YOU WALK, BUT YOU'RE STILL A PERSON OF INTEREST. I CALL, YOU COME IN. IF NOT, I'LL HAVE A MURDER WARRANT ON YOU.
I'LL BE WAITING FOR THE CALL.

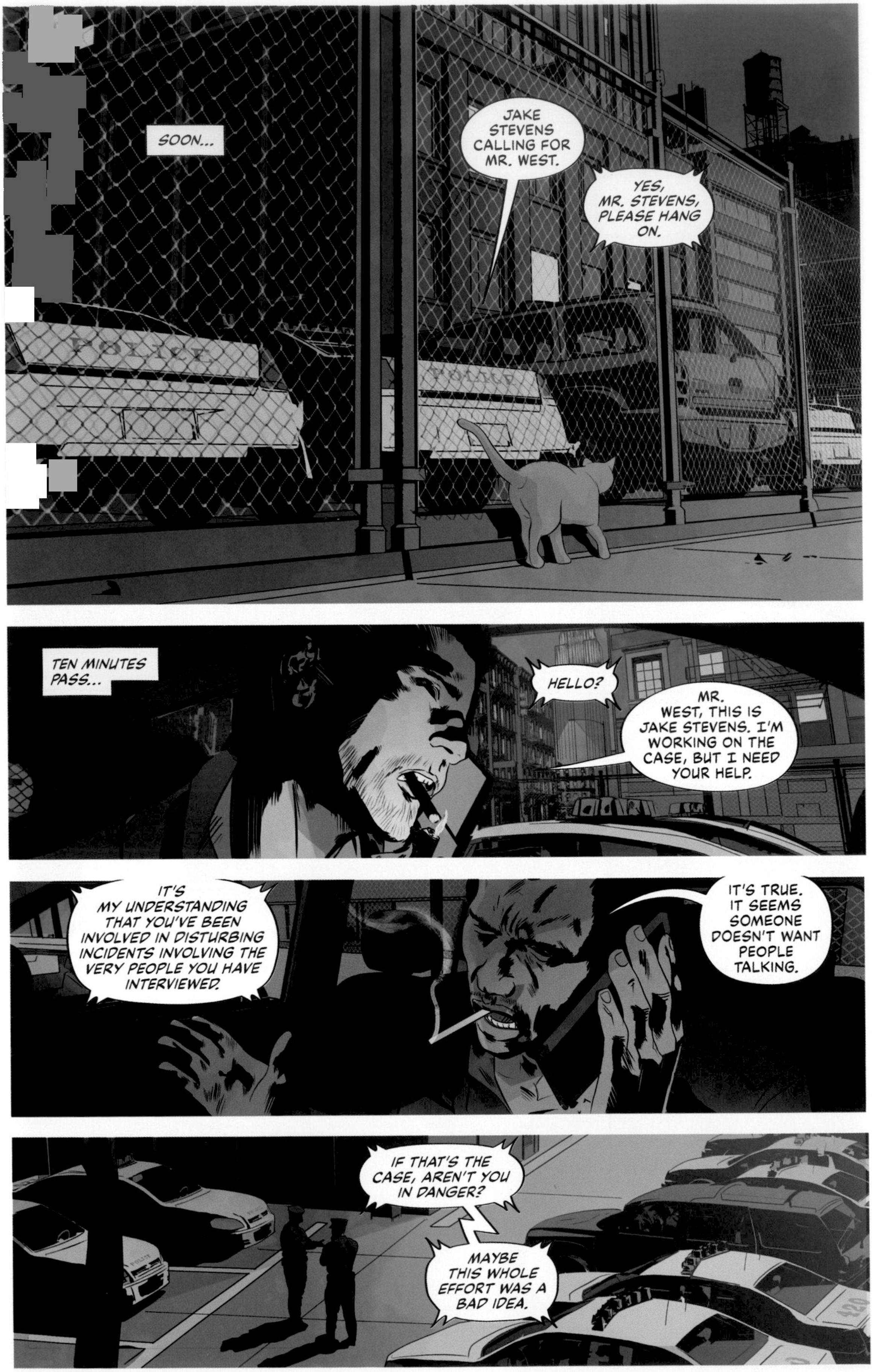
SOON...
JAKE STEVENS CALLING FOR MR. WEST.
YES, MR. STEVENS, PLEASE HANG ON.
POLICE
TEN MINUTES PASS...
HELLO?
MR. WEST, THIS IS JAKE STEVENS. I'M WORKING ON THE CASE, BUT I NEED YOUR HELP.
IT'S MY UNDERSTANDING THAT YOU'VE BEEN INVOLVED IN DISTURBING INCIDENTS INVOLVING THE VERY PEOPLE YOU HAVE INTERVIEWED.
IT'S TRUE. IT SEEMS SOMEONE DOESN'T WANT PEOPLE TALKING.
IF THAT'S THE CASE, AREN'T YOU IN DANGER?
MAYBE THIS WHOLE EFFORT WAS A BAD IDEA.

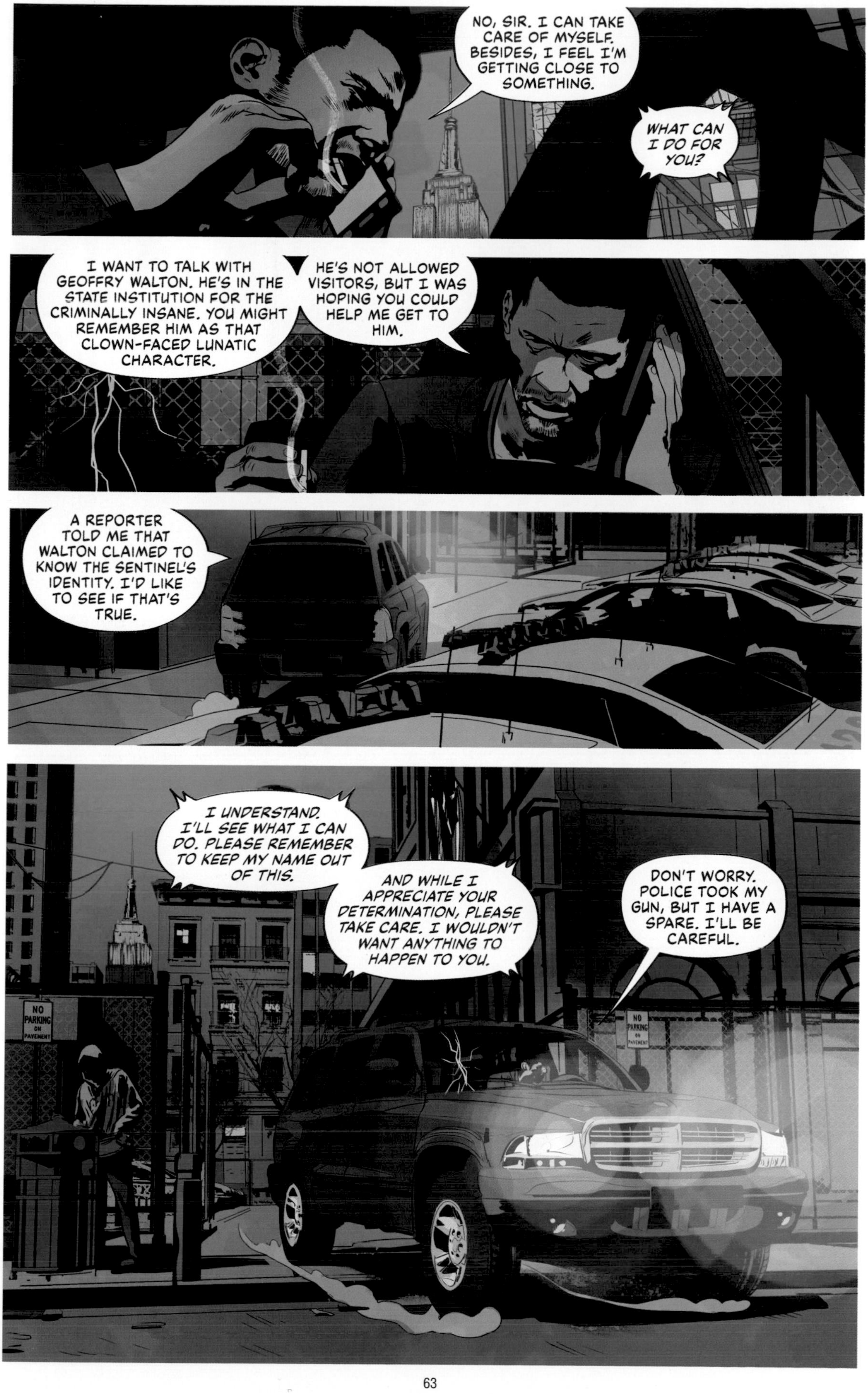
NO, SIR. I CAN TAKE CARE OF MYSELF. BESIDES, I FEEL I'M GETTING CLOSE TO SOMETHING.
WHAT CAN I DO FOR YOU?
I WANT TO TALK WITH GEOFFRY WALTON. HE'S IN THE STATE INSTITUTION FOR THE CRIMINALLY INSANE. YOU MIGHT REMEMBER HIM AS THAT CLOWN-FACED LUNATIC CHARACTER.
HE'S NOT ALLOWED VISITORS, BUT I WAS HOPING YOU COULD HELP ME GET TO HIM.
A REPORTER TOLD ME THAT WALTON CLAIMED TO KNOW THE SENTINEL'S IDENTITY. I'D LIKE TO SEE IF THAT'S TRUE.
I UNDERSTAND. I'LL SEE WHAT I CAN DO. PLEASE REMEMBER TO KEEP MY NAME OUT OF THIS.
AND WHILE I APPRECIATE YOUR DETERMINATION, PLEASE TAKE CARE. I WOULDN'T WANT ANYTHING TO HAPPEN TO YOU.
DON'T WORRY. POLICE TOOK MY GUN, BUT I HAVE A SPARE. I'LL BE CAREFUL.
NO PARKING ON PAVEMENT
NO PARKING ON PAVEMENT

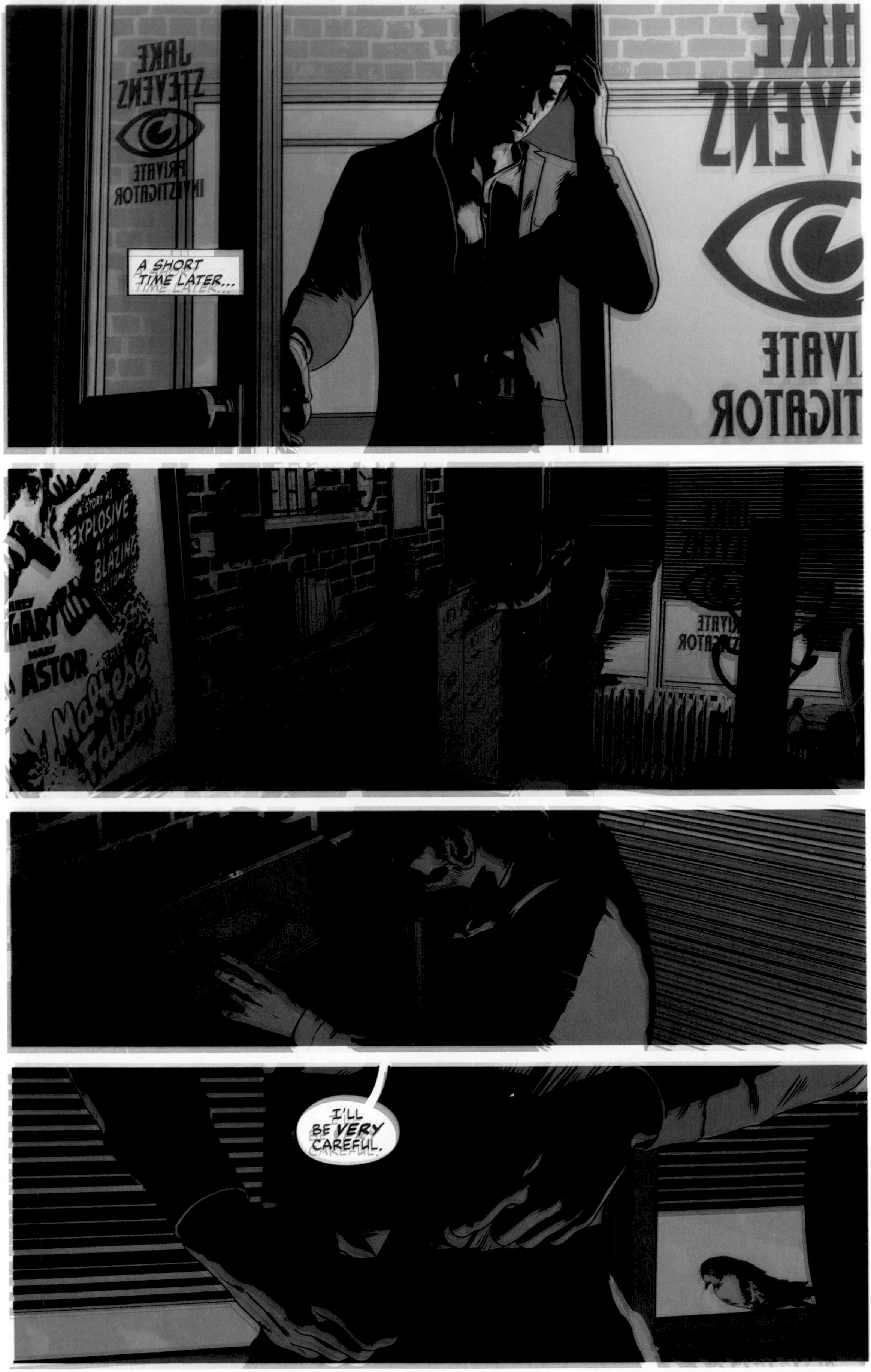
A SHORT TIME LATER...
A STORY AS EXPLOSIVE AS HIS BLAZING AUTOMATICS
ASTOR
I'LL BE VERY CAREFUL.

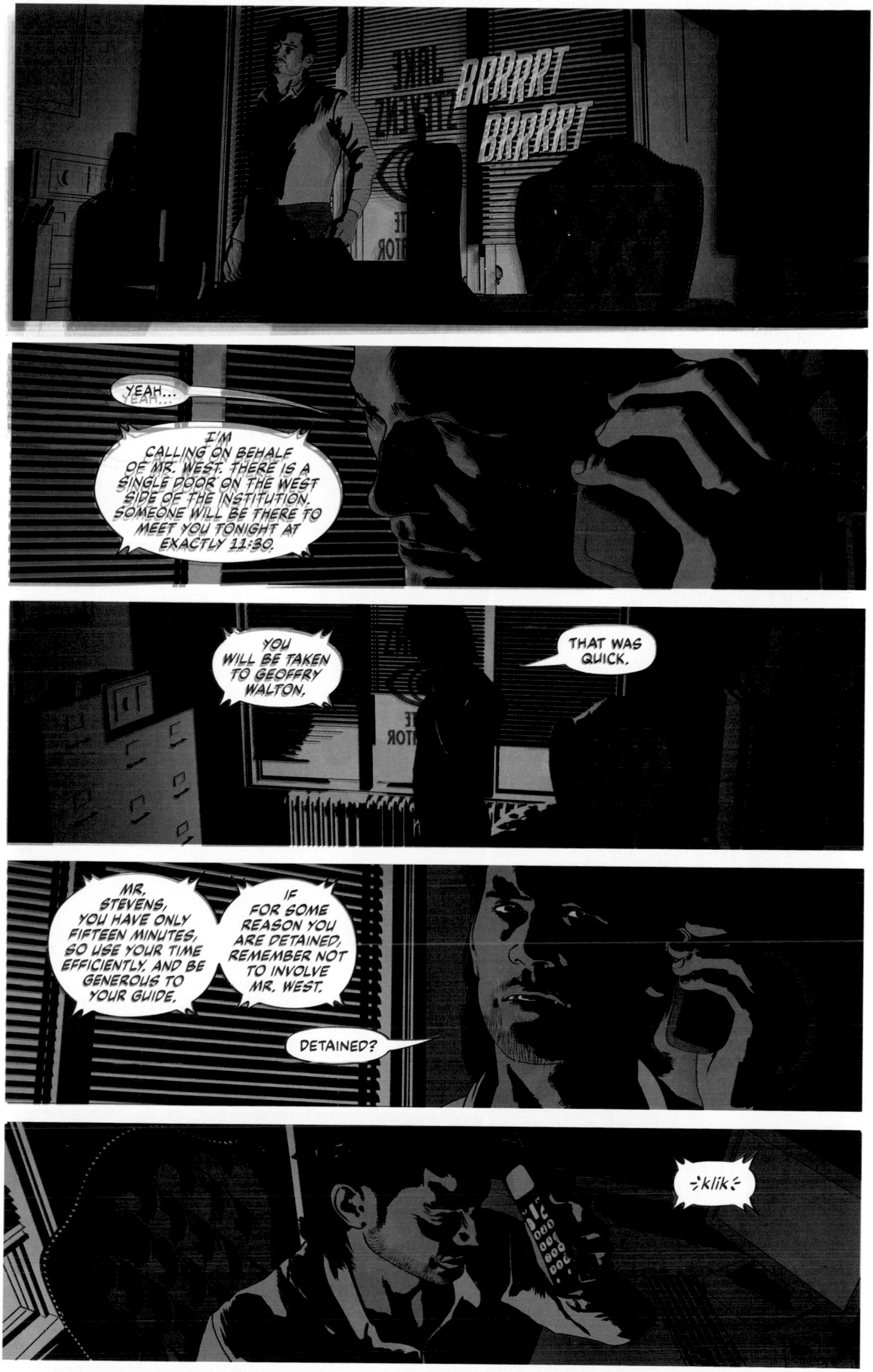
BRRRRT
BRRRRT
YEAH...
I'M CALLING ON BEHALF OF MR. WEST. THERE IS A SINGLE DOOR ON THE WEST SIDE OF THE INSTITUTION. SOMEONE WILL BE THERE TO MEET YOU TONIGHT AT EXACTLY 11:30.
YOU WILL BE TAKEN TO GEOFFRY WALTON.
THAT WAS QUICK.
MR. STEVENS, YOU HAVE ONLY FIFTEEN MINUTES, SO USE YOUR TIME EFFICIENTLY. AND BE GENEROUS TO YOUR GUIDE.
IF FOR SOME REASON YOU ARE DETAINED, REMEMBER NOT TO INVOLVE MR. WEST.
DETAINED?
klik

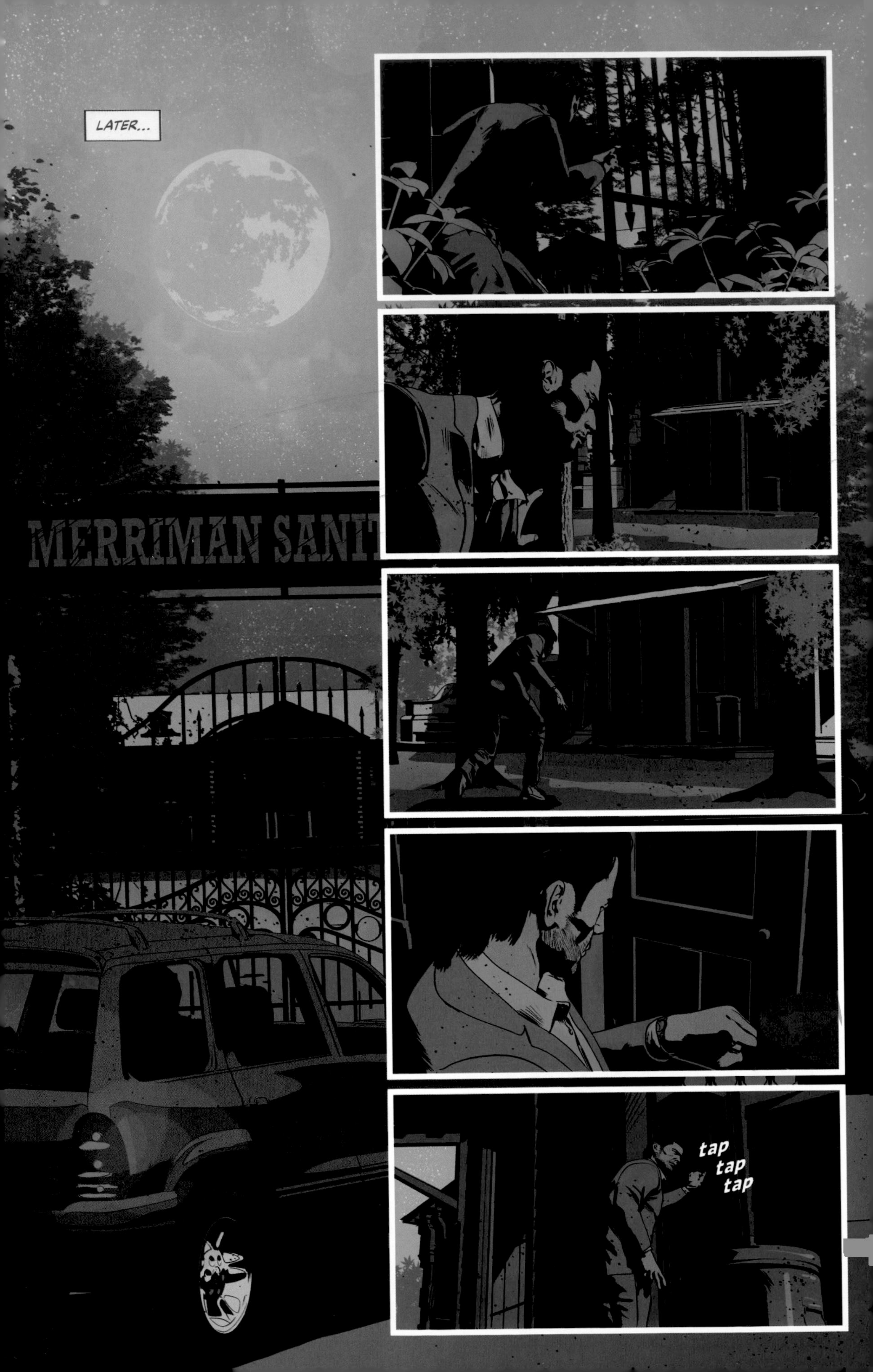
LATER...
MERRIMAN SANIT
tap
tap
tap

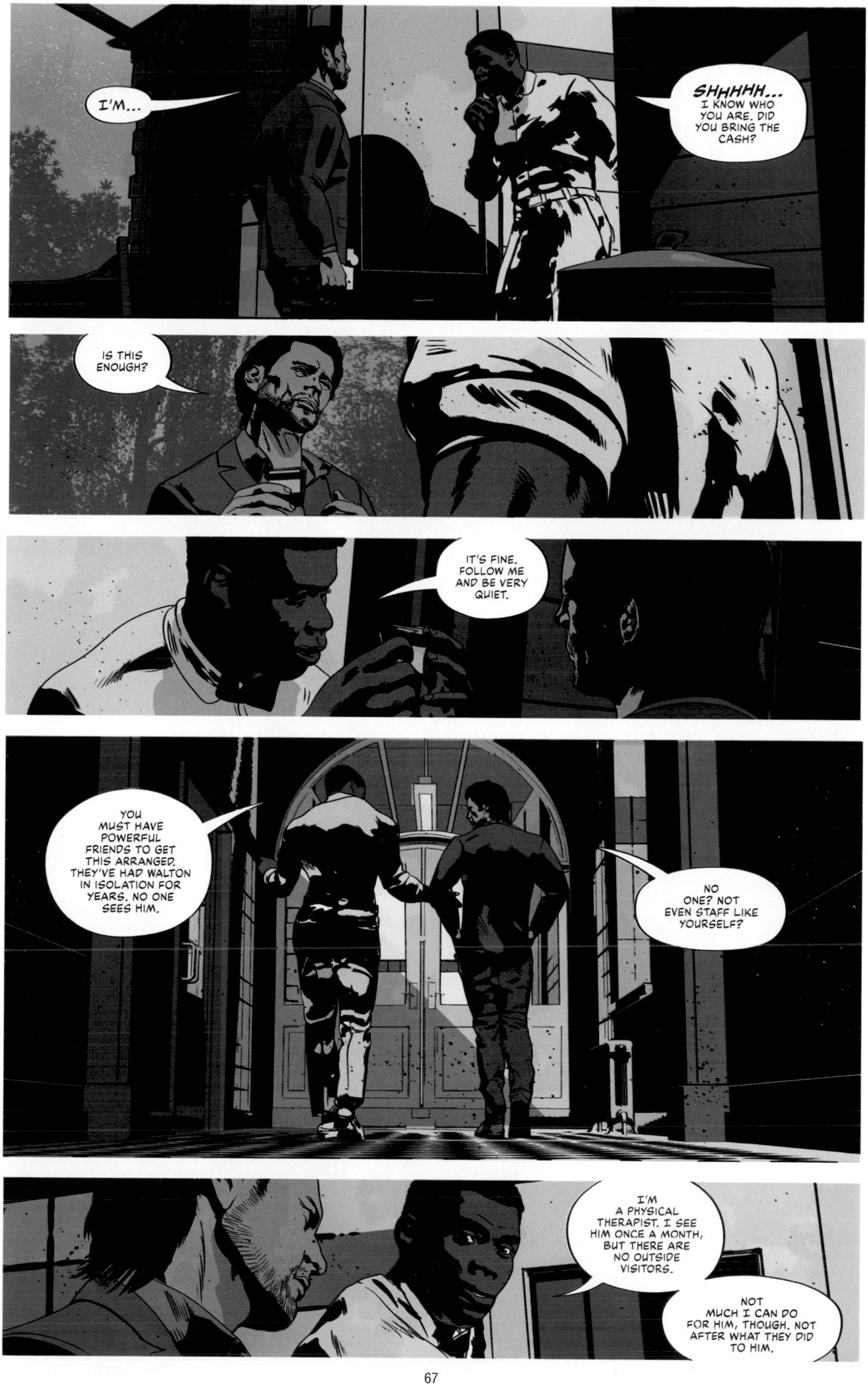
I'M...
SHHHHH... I KNOW WHO YOU ARE. DID YOU BRING THE CASH?
IS THIS ENOUGH?
IT'S FINE. FOLLOW ME AND BE VERY QUIET.
YOU MUST HAVE POWERFUL FRIENDS TO GET THIS ARRANGED. THEY'VE HAD WALTON IN ISOLATION FOR YEARS. NO ONE SEES HIM.
NO ONE? NOT EVEN STAFF LIKE YOURSELF?
I'M A PHYSICAL THERAPIST. I SEE HIM ONCE A MONTH, BUT THERE ARE NO OUTSIDE VISITORS.
NOT MUCH I CAN DO FOR HIM, THOUGH. NOT AFTER WHAT THEY DID TO HIM.

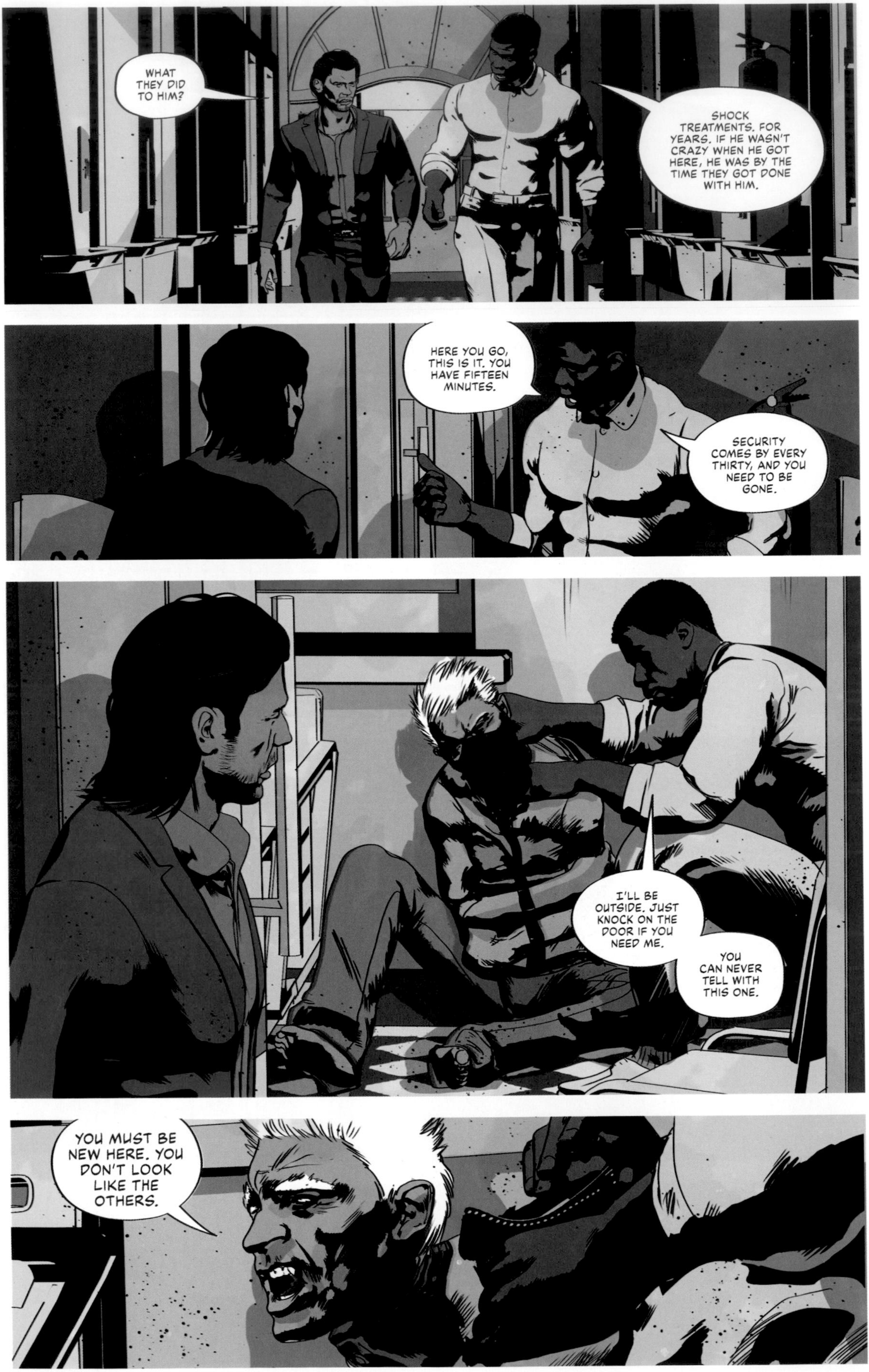
WHAT THEY DID TO HIM?
SHOCK TREATMENTS. FOR YEARS. IF HE WASN'T CRAZY WHEN HE GOT HERE, HE WAS BY THE TIME THEY GOT DONE WITH HIM.
HERE YOU GO, THIS IS IT. YOU HAVE FIFTEEN MINUTES.
SECURITY COMES BY EVERY THIRTY, AND YOU NEED TO BE GONE.
I'LL BE OUTSIDE. JUST KNOCK ON THE DOOR IF YOU NEED ME.
YOU CAN NEVER TELL WITH THIS ONE.
YOU MUST BE NEW HERE. YOU DON'T LOOK LIKE THE OTHERS.

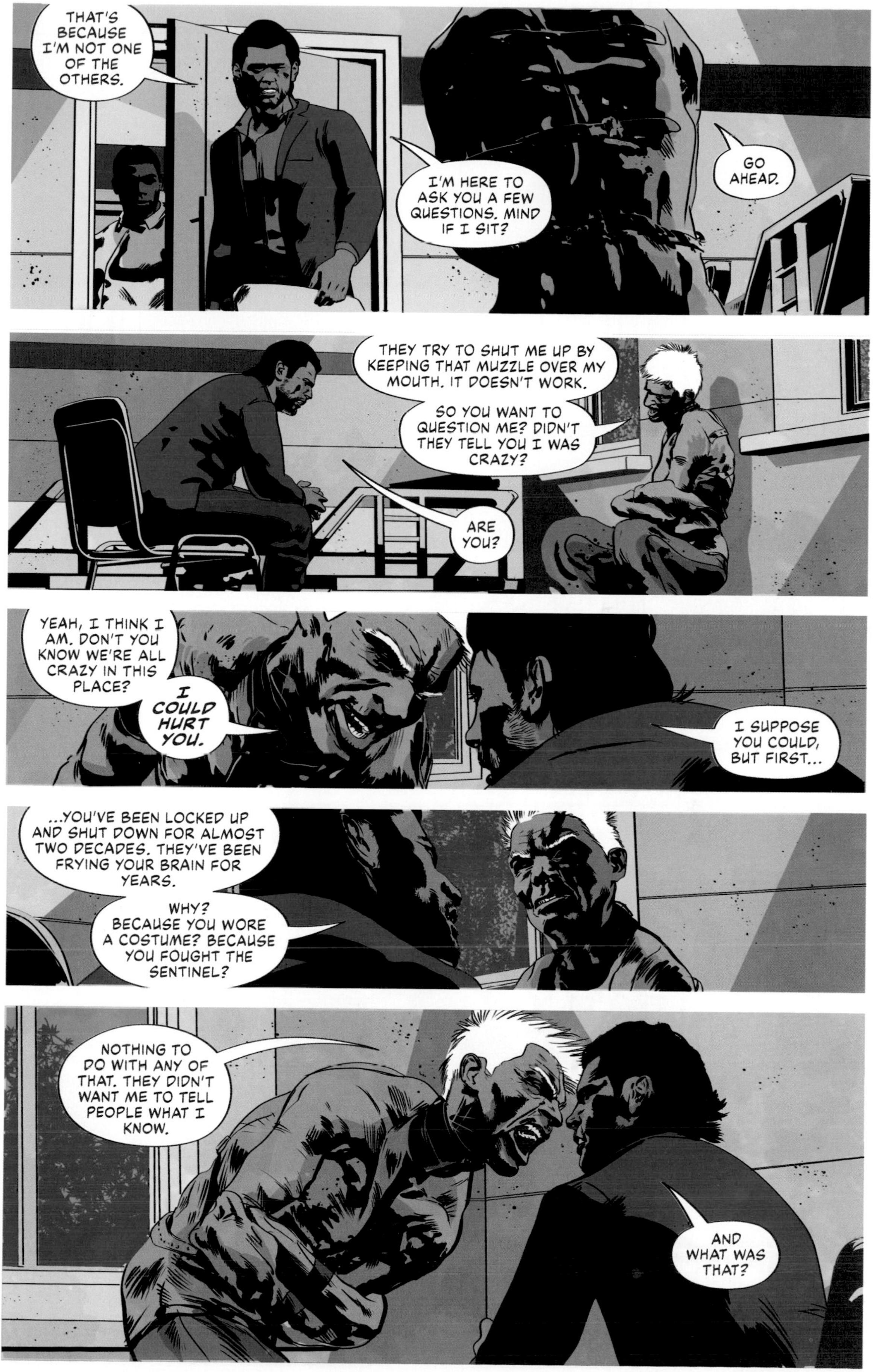
THAT'S BECAUSE I'M NOT ONE OF THE OTHERS.
I'M HERE TO ASK YOU A FEW QUESTIONS. MIND IF I SIT?
GO AHEAD.
THEY TRY TO SHUT ME UP BY KEEPING THAT MUZZLE OVER MY MOUTH. IT DOESN'T WORK.
SO YOU WANT TO QUESTION ME? DIDN'T THEY TELL YOU I WAS CRAZY?
ARE YOU?
YEAH, I THINK I AM. DON'T YOU KNOW WE'RE ALL CRAZY IN THIS PLACE?
I COULD HURT YOU.
I SUPPOSE YOU COULD, BUT FIRST...
...YOU'VE BEEN LOCKED UP AND SHUT DOWN FOR ALMOST TWO DECADES. THEY'VE BEEN FRYING YOUR BRAIN FOR YEARS.
WHY? BECAUSE YOU WORE A COSTUME? BECAUSE YOU FOUGHT THE SENTINEL?
NOTHING TO DO WITH ANY OF THAT. THEY DIDN'T WANT ME TO TELL PEOPLE WHAT I KNOW.
AND WHAT WAS THAT?

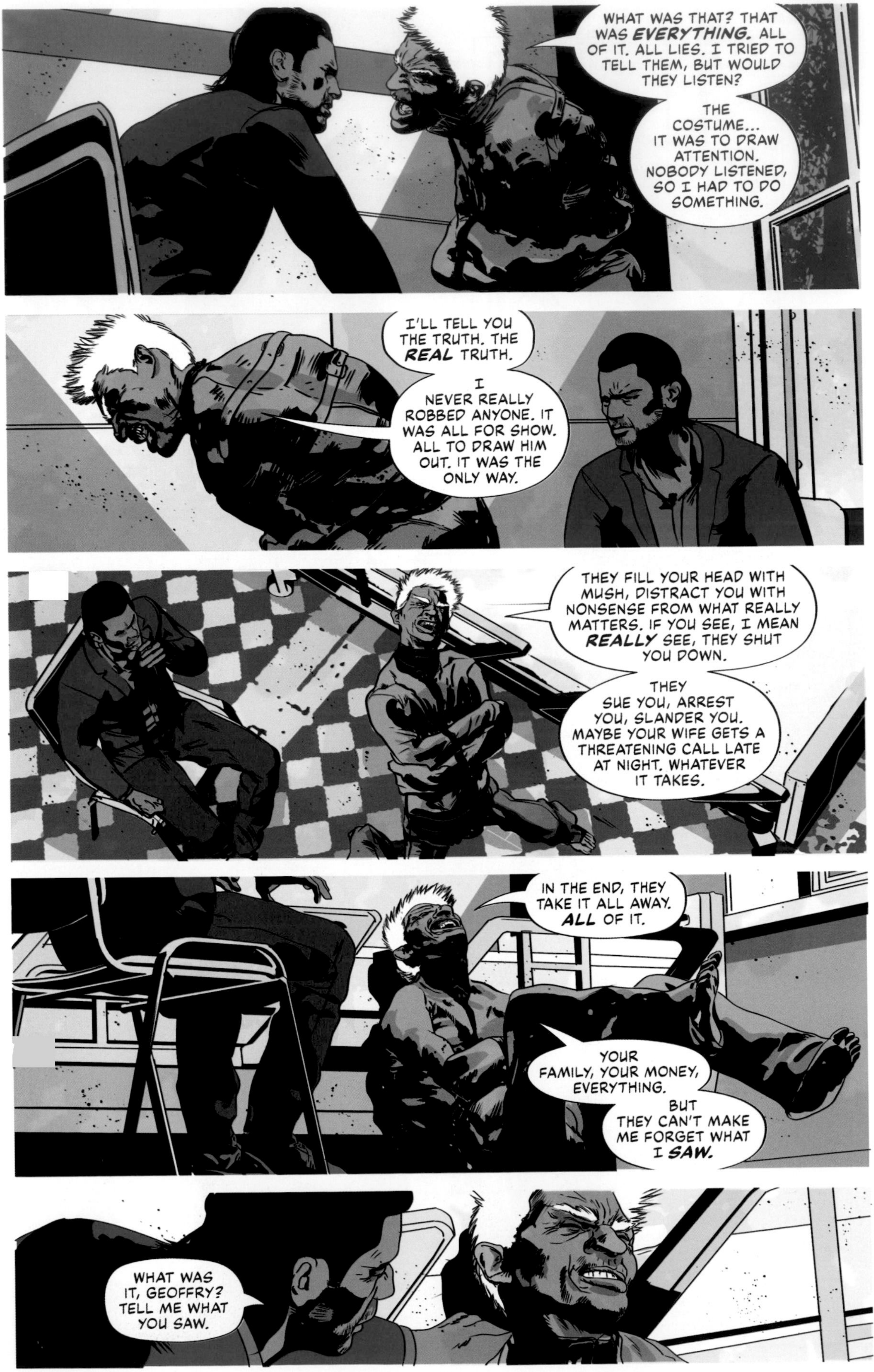
WHAT WAS THAT? THAT WAS EVERYTHING. ALL OF IT. ALL LIES. I TRIED TO TELL THEM, BUT WOULD THEY LISTEN?
THE COSTUME... IT WAS TO DRAW ATTENTION. NOBODY LISTENED, SO I HAD TO DO SOMETHING.
I'LL TELL YOU THE TRUTH. THE REAL TRUTH.
I NEVER REALLY ROBBED ANYONE. IT WAS ALL FOR SHOW. ALL TO DRAW HIM OUT. IT WAS THE ONLY WAY.
THEY FILL YOUR HEAD WITH MUSH, DISTRACT YOU WITH NONSENSE FROM WHAT REALLY MATTERS. IF YOU SEE, I MEAN REALLY SEE, THEY SHUT YOU DOWN.
THEY SUE YOU, ARREST YOU, SLANDER YOU. MAYBE YOUR WIFE GETS A THREATENING CALL LATE AT NIGHT. WHATEVER IT TAKES.
IN THE END, THEY TAKE IT ALL AWAY. ALL OF IT.
YOUR FAMILY, YOUR MONEY, EVERYTHING.
BUT THEY CAN'T MAKE ME FORGET WHAT I SAW.
WHAT WAS IT, GEOFFRY? TELL ME WHAT YOU SAW.

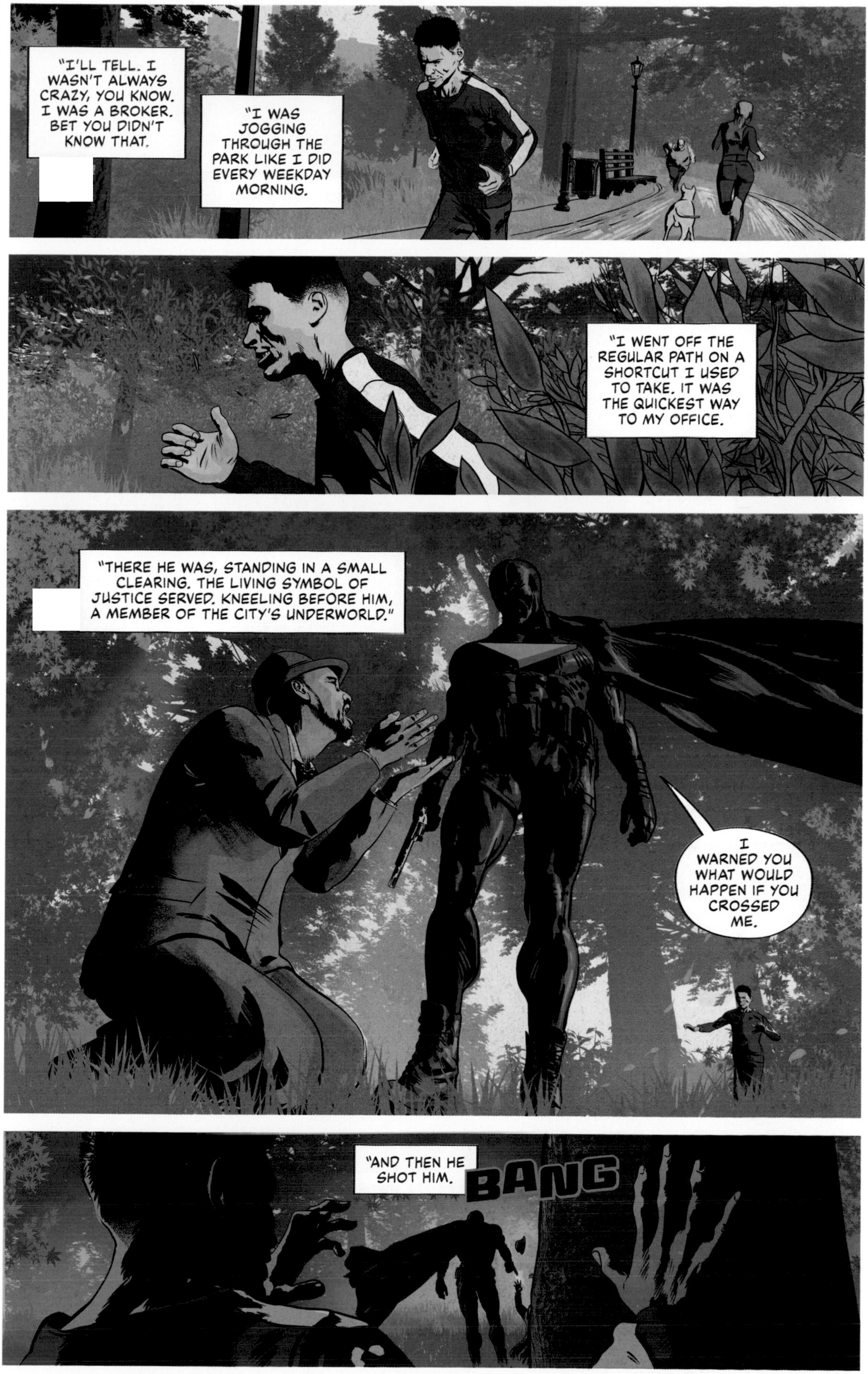
"I'LL TELL. I WASN'T ALWAYS CRAZY, YOU KNOW. I WAS A BROKER. BET YOU DIDN'T KNOW THAT.
"I WAS JOGGING THROUGH THE PARK LIKE I DID EVERY WEEKDAY MORNING.
"I WENT OFF THE REGULAR PATH ON A SHORTCUT I USED TO TAKE. IT WAS THE QUICKEST WAY TO MY OFFICE.
"THERE HE WAS, STANDING IN A SMALL CLEARING. THE LIVING SYMBOL OF JUSTICE SERVED. KNEELING BEFORE HIM, A MEMBER OF THE CITY'S UNDERWORLD."
I WARNED YOU WHAT WOULD HAPPEN IF YOU CROSSED ME.
"AND THEN HE SHOT HIM.
BANG

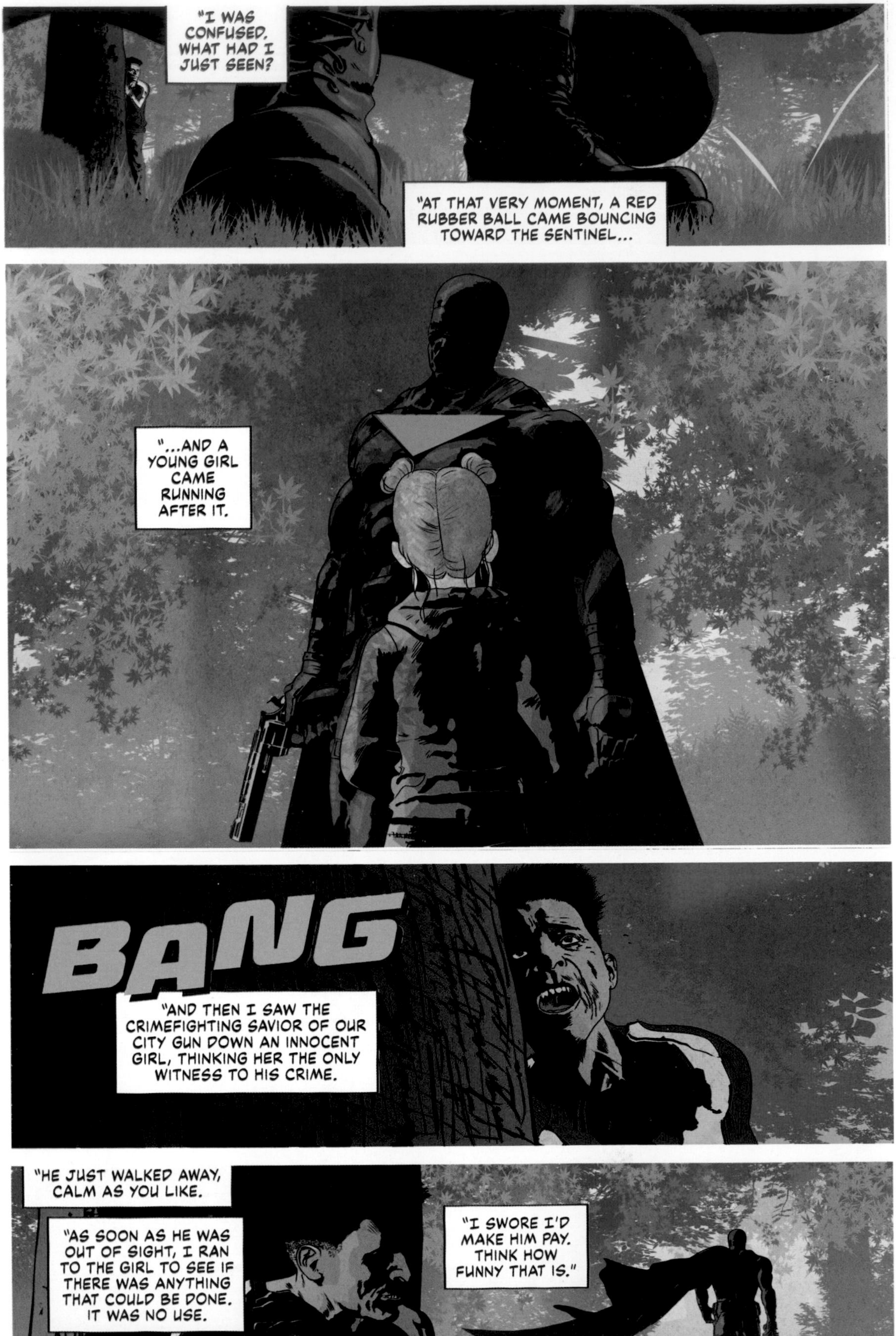

"I WAS CONFUSED. WHAT HAD I JUST SEEN?
"AT THAT VERY MOMENT, A RED RUBBER BALL CAME BOUNCING TOWARD THE SENTINEL...
"...AND A YOUNG GIRL CAME RUNNING AFTER IT.
BANG
"AND THEN I SAW THE CRIMEFIGHTING SAVIOR OF OUR CITY GUN DOWN AN INNOCENT GIRL, THINKING HER THE ONLY WITNESS TO HIS CRIME.
"HE JUST WALKED AWAY, CALM AS YOU LIKE.
"AS SOON AS HE WAS OUT OF SIGHT, I RAN TO THE GIRL TO SEE IF THERE WAS ANYTHING THAT COULD BE DONE. IT WAS NO USE.
"I SWORE I'D MAKE HIM PAY. THINK HOW FUNNY THAT IS."

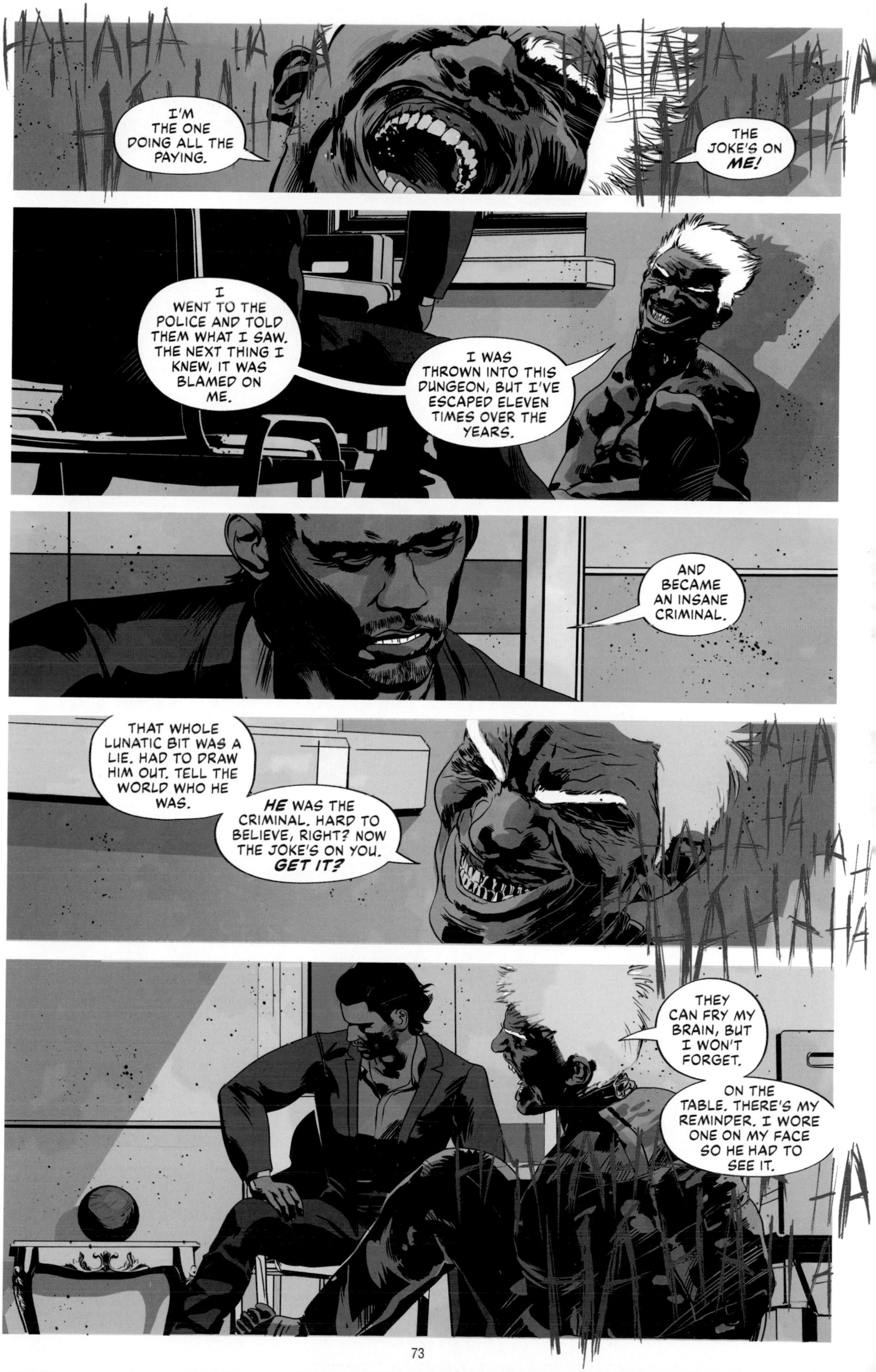
I'M THE ONE DOING ALL THE PAYING.
THE JOKE'S ON **ME!**
I WENT TO THE POLICE AND TOLD THEM WHAT I SAW. THE NEXT THING I KNEW, IT WAS BLAMED ON ME.
I WAS THROWN INTO THIS DUNGEON, BUT I'VE ESCAPED ELEVEN TIMES OVER THE YEARS.
AND BECAME AN INSANE CRIMINAL.
THAT WHOLE LUNATIC BIT WAS A LIE. HAD TO DRAW HIM OUT. TELL THE WORLD WHO HE WAS.
HE WAS THE CRIMINAL. HARD TO BELIEVE, RIGHT? NOW THE JOKE'S ON YOU. ***GET IT?***
THEY CAN FRY MY BRAIN, BUT I WON'T FORGET.
ON THE TABLE. THERE'S MY REMINDER. I WORE ONE ON MY FACE SO HE HAD TO SEE IT.

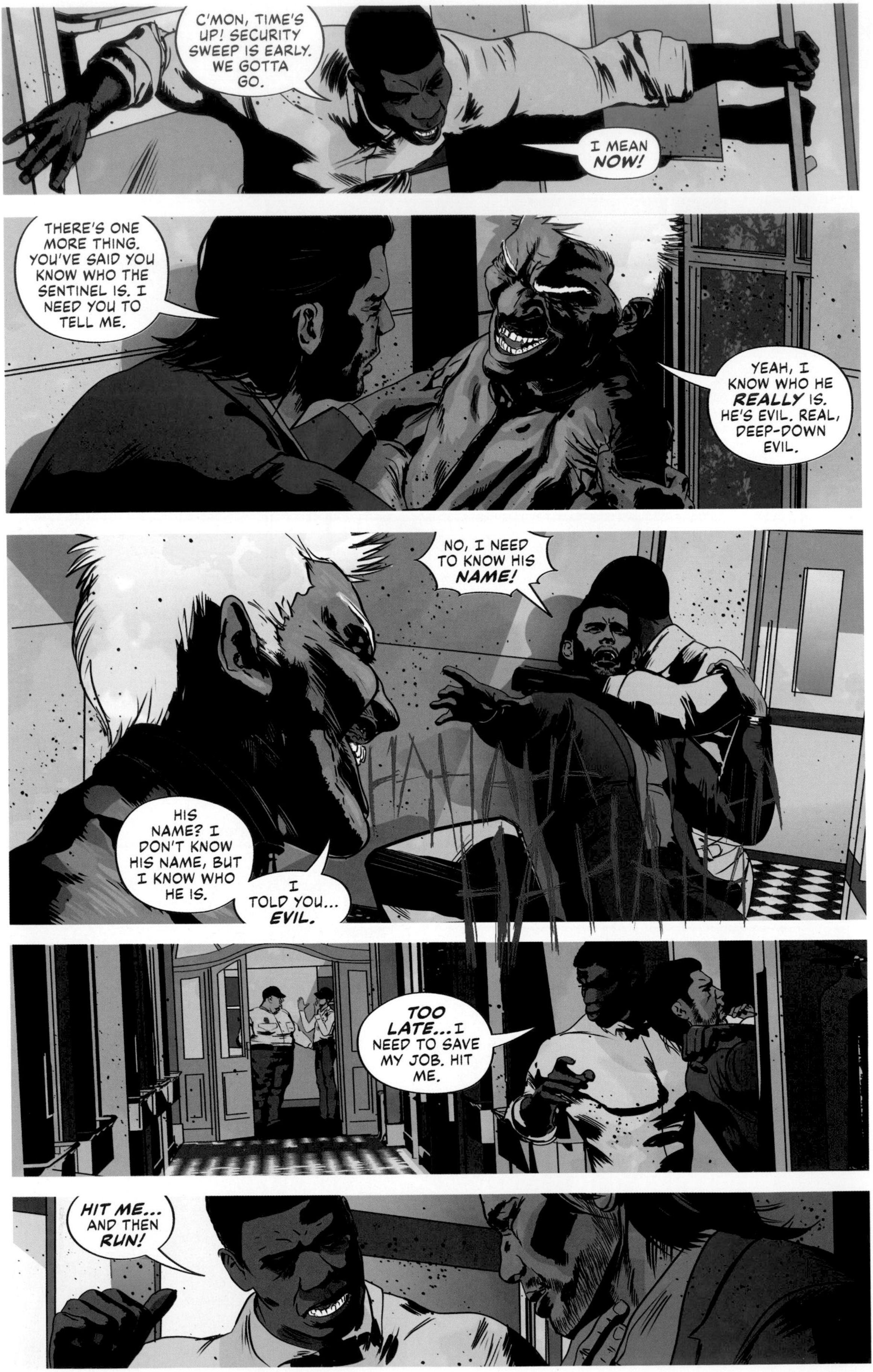
C'MON, TIME'S UP! SECURITY SWEEP IS EARLY. WE GOTTA GO.
I MEAN NOW!
THERE'S ONE MORE THING. YOU'VE SAID YOU KNOW WHO THE SENTINEL IS. I NEED YOU TO TELL ME.
YEAH, I KNOW WHO HE REALLY IS. HE'S EVIL. REAL, DEEP-DOWN EVIL.
NO, I NEED TO KNOW HIS NAME!
HIS NAME? I DON'T KNOW HIS NAME, BUT I KNOW WHO HE IS.
I TOLD YOU... EVIL.
TOO LATE... I NEED TO SAVE MY JOB. HIT ME.
HIT ME... AND THEN RUN!

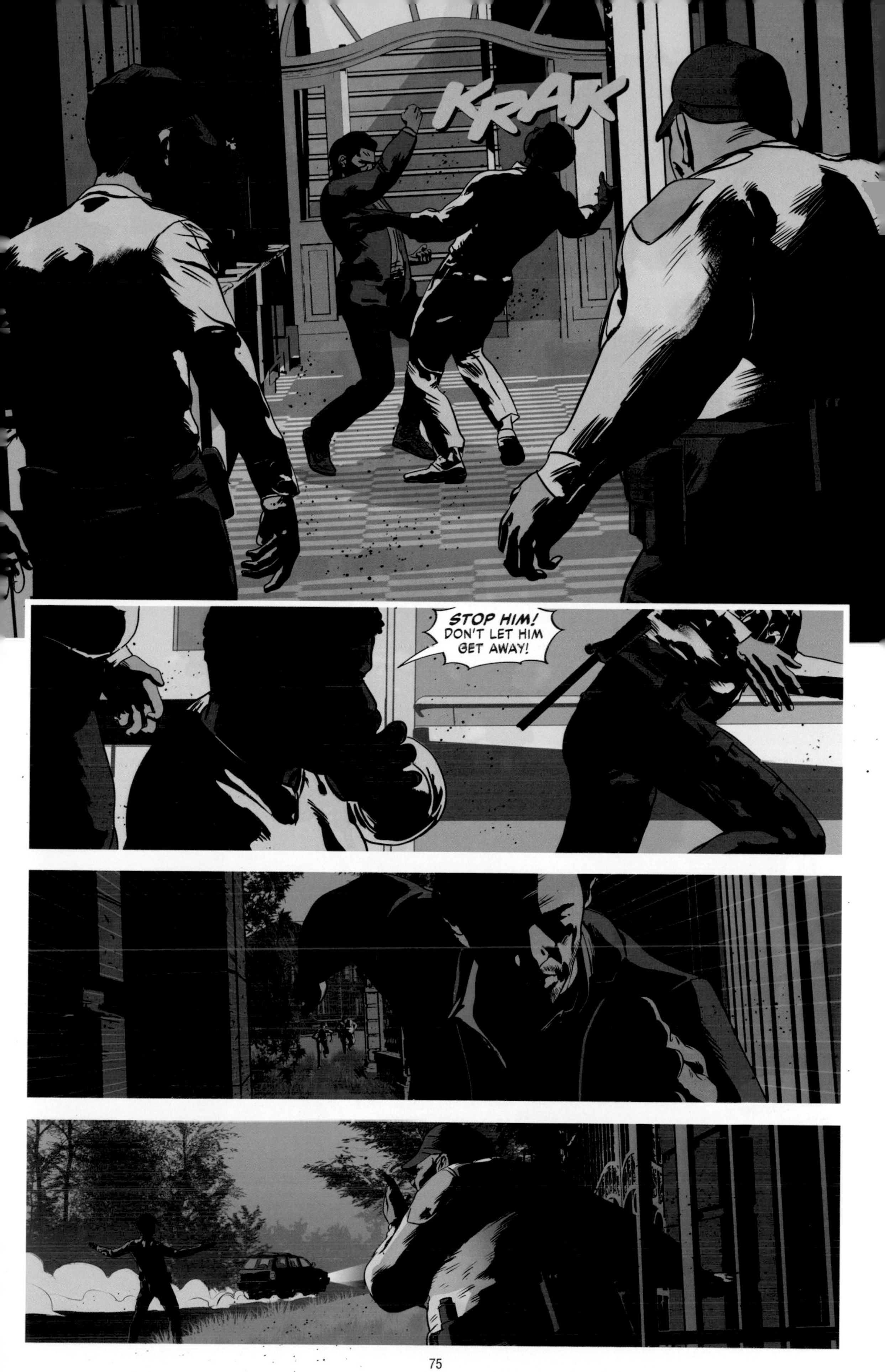
KRAK
STOP HIM! DON'T LET HIM GET AWAY!

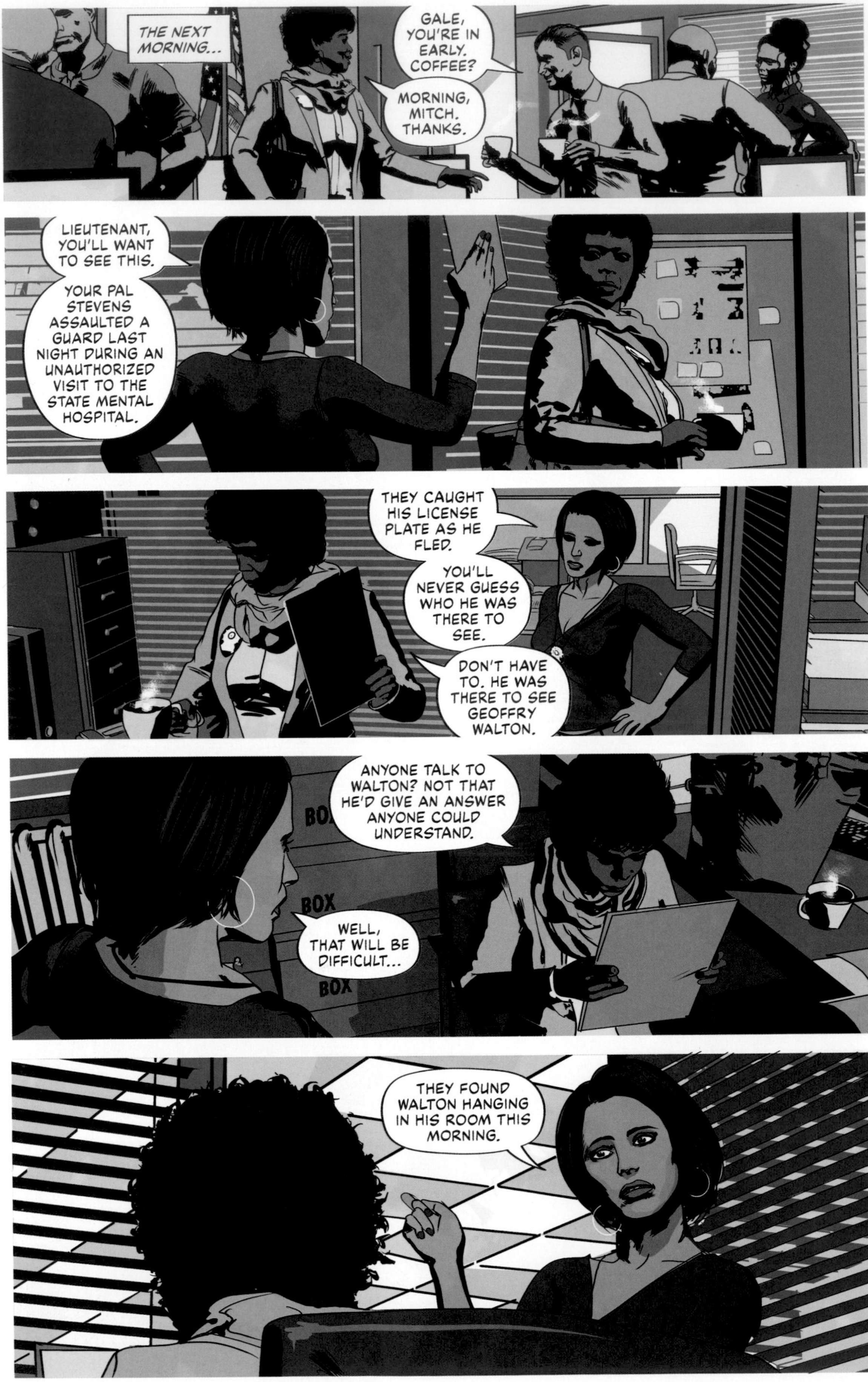
THE NEXT MORNING...
GALE, YOU'RE IN EARLY. COFFEE?
MORNING, MITCH. THANKS.
LIEUTENANT, YOU'LL WANT TO SEE THIS.
YOUR PAL STEVENS ASSAULTED A GUARD LAST NIGHT DURING AN UNAUTHORIZED VISIT TO THE STATE MENTAL HOSPITAL.
THEY CAUGHT HIS LICENSE PLATE AS HE FLED.
YOU'LL NEVER GUESS WHO HE WAS THERE TO SEE.
DON'T HAVE TO. HE WAS THERE TO SEE GEOFFRY WALTON.
ANYONE TALK TO WALTON? NOT THAT HE'D GIVE AN ANSWER ANYONE COULD UNDERSTAND.
BOX
BOX
WELL, THAT WILL BE DIFFICULT...
BOX
THEY FOUND WALTON HANGING IN HIS ROOM THIS MORNING.

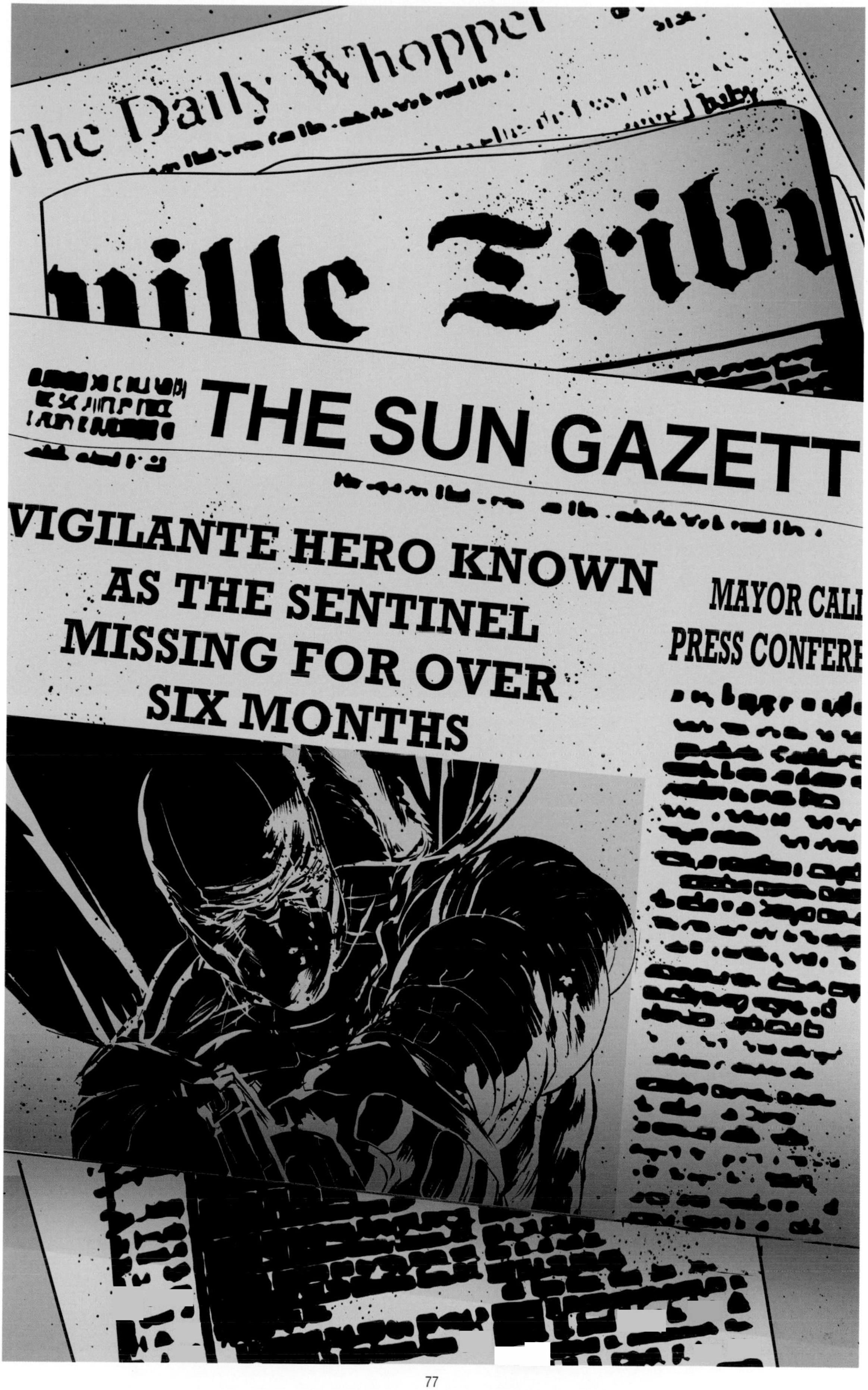

The Daily Whopper
THE SUN GAZETT
VIGILANTE HERO KNOWN AS THE SENTINEL MISSING FOR OVER SIX MONTHS
MAYOR CALL
PRESS CONFERE

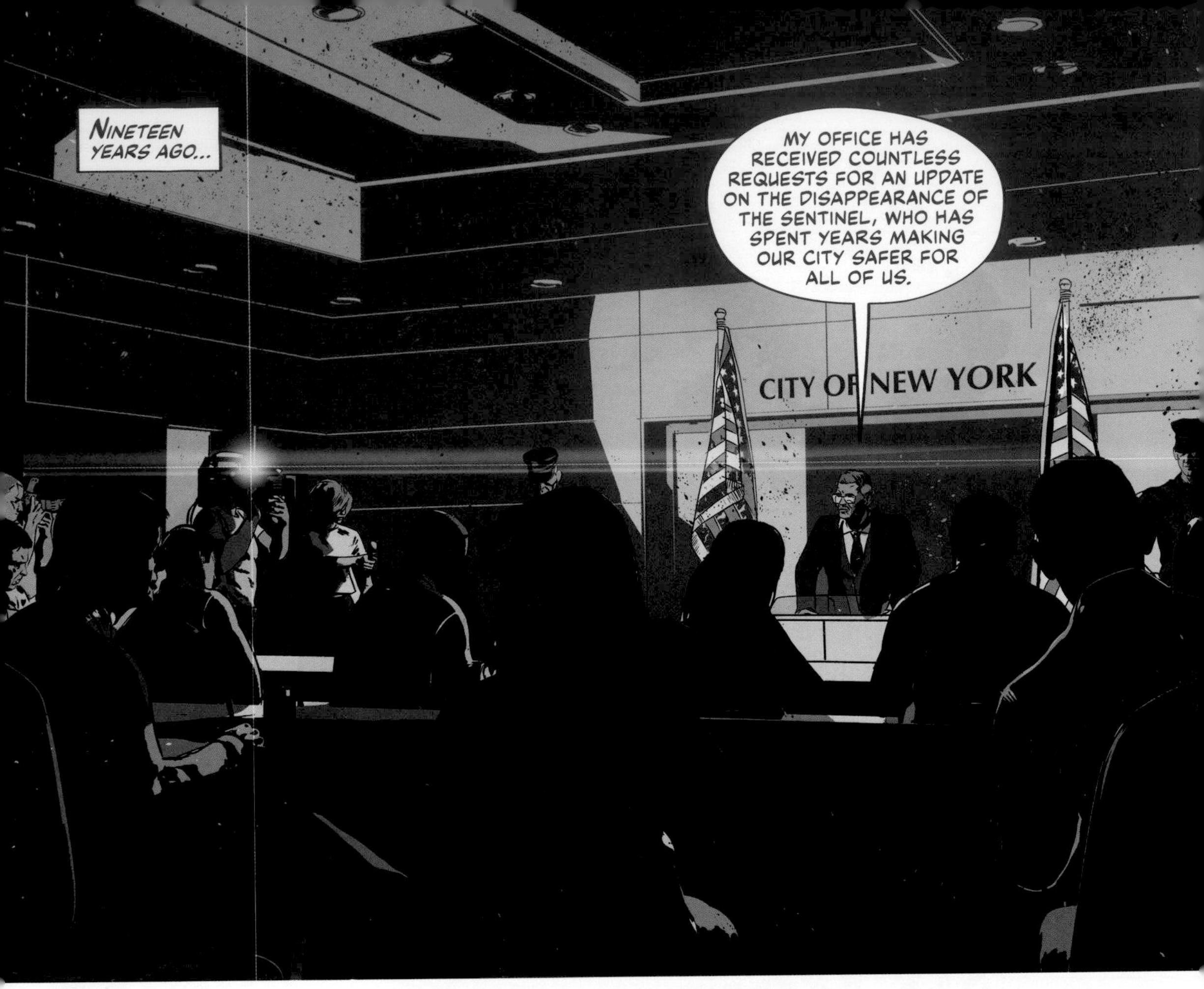
NINETEEN YEARS AGO...
MY OFFICE HAS RECEIVED COUNTLESS REQUESTS FOR AN UPDATE ON THE DISAPPEARANCE OF THE SENTINEL, WHO HAS SPENT YEARS MAKING OUR CITY SAFER FOR ALL OF US.
CITY OF NEW YORK

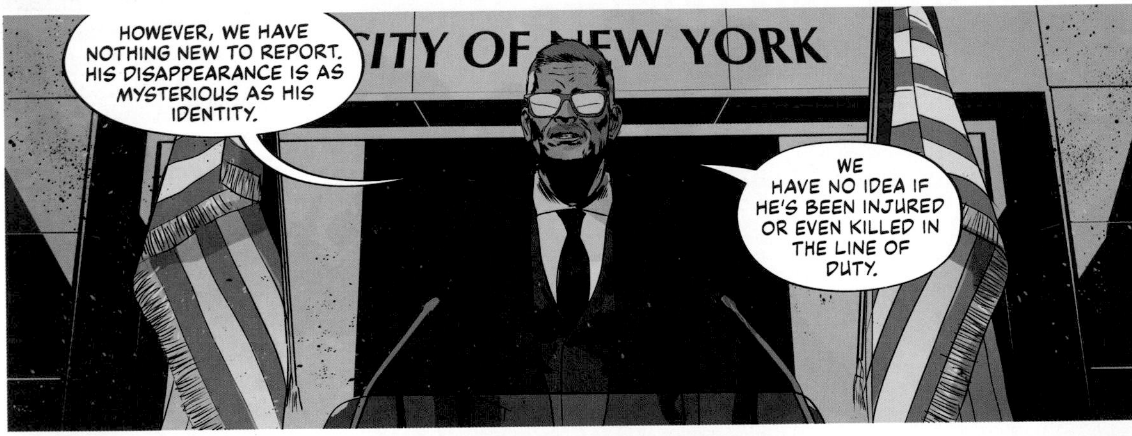
HOWEVER, WE HAVE NOTHING NEW TO REPORT. HIS DISAPPEARANCE IS AS MYSTERIOUS AS HIS IDENTITY.
WE HAVE NO IDEA IF HE'S BEEN INJURED OR EVEN KILLED IN THE LINE OF DUTY.

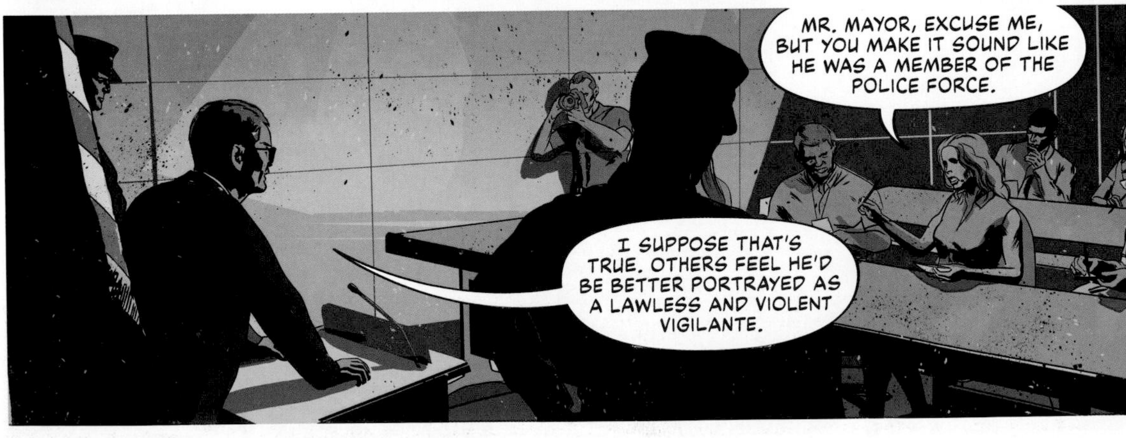
MR. MAYOR, EXCUSE ME, BUT YOU MAKE IT SOUND LIKE HE WAS A MEMBER OF THE POLICE FORCE.
I SUPPOSE THAT'S TRUE. OTHERS FEEL HE'D BE BETTER PORTRAYED AS A LAWLESS AND VIOLENT VIGILANTE.

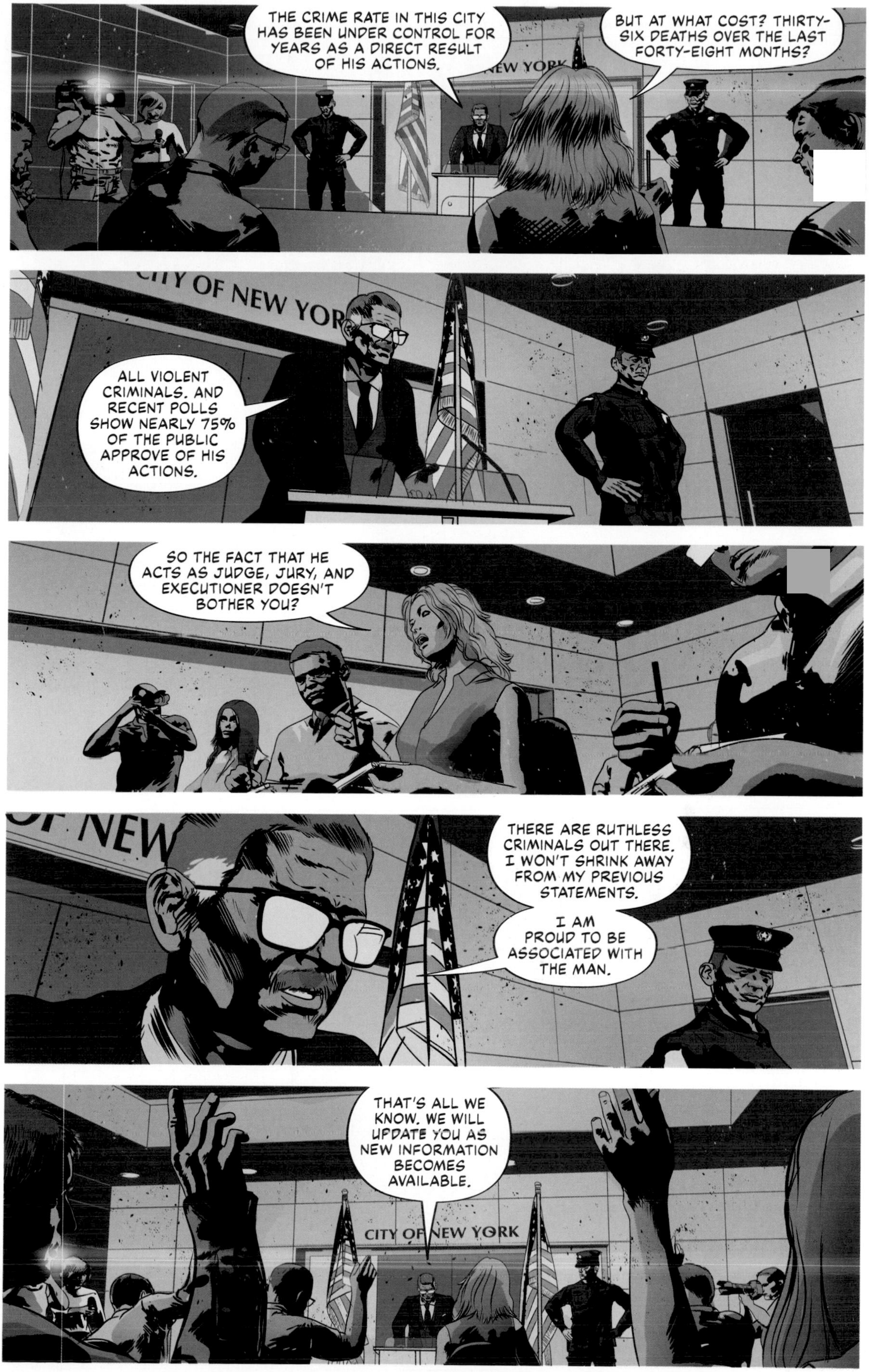
THE CRIME RATE IN THIS CITY HAS BEEN UNDER CONTROL FOR YEARS AS A DIRECT RESULT OF HIS ACTIONS.
BUT AT WHAT COST? THIRTY-SIX DEATHS OVER THE LAST FORTY-EIGHT MONTHS?
NEW YORK
CITY OF NEW YOR
ALL VIOLENT CRIMINALS. AND RECENT POLLS SHOW NEARLY 75% OF THE PUBLIC APPROVE OF HIS ACTIONS.
SO THE FACT THAT HE ACTS AS JUDGE, JURY, AND EXECUTIONER DOESN'T BOTHER YOU?
OF NEW
THERE ARE RUTHLESS CRIMINALS OUT THERE. I WON'T SHRINK AWAY FROM MY PREVIOUS STATEMENTS.
I AM PROUD TO BE ASSOCIATED WITH THE MAN.
THAT'S ALL WE KNOW. WE WILL UPDATE YOU AS NEW INFORMATION BECOMES AVAILABLE.
CITY OF NEW YORK

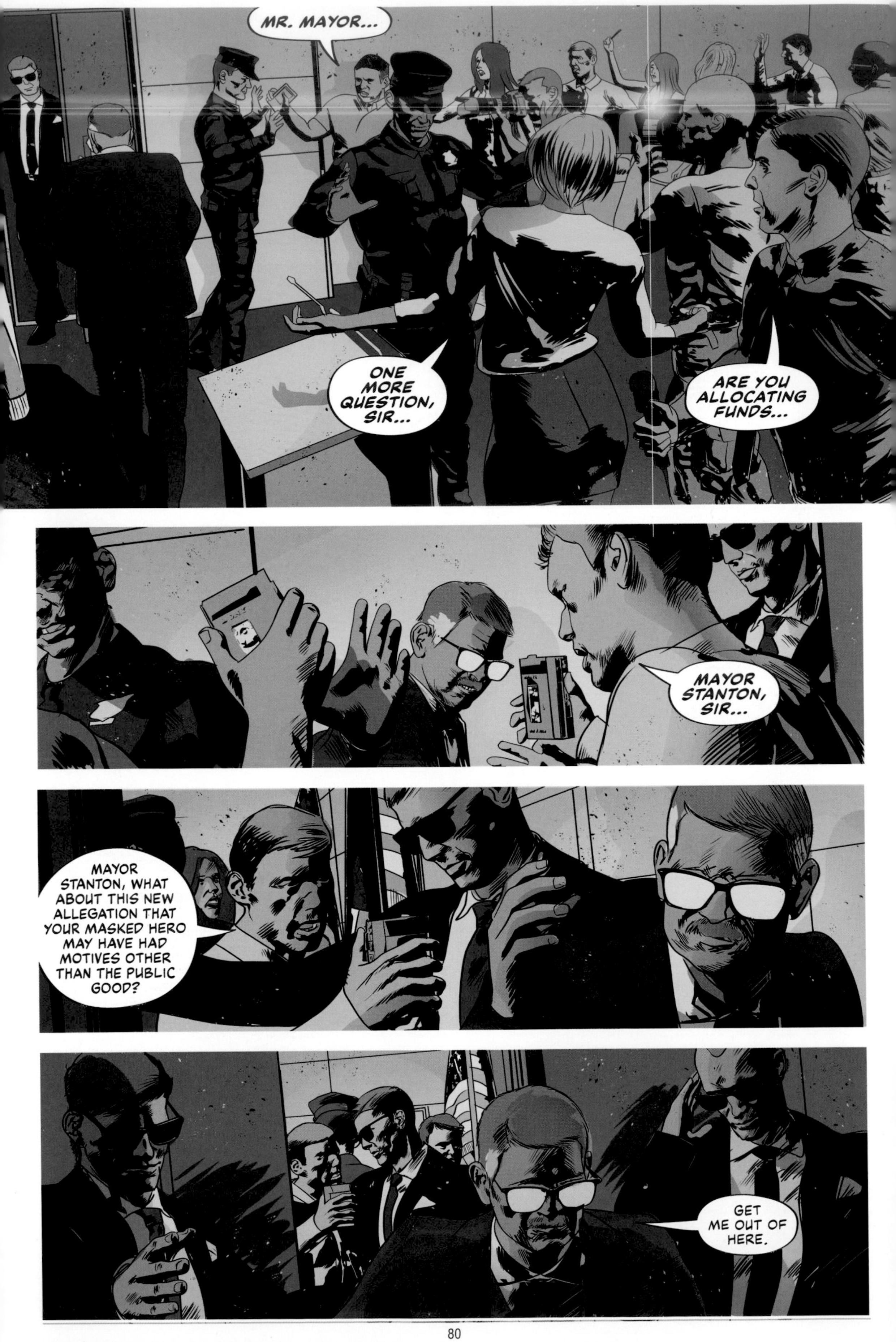
MR. MAYOR...
ONE MORE QUESTION, SIR...
ARE YOU ALLOCATING FUNDS...
MAYOR STANTON, SIR...
MAYOR STANTON, WHAT ABOUT THIS NEW ALLEGATION THAT YOUR MASKED HERO MAY HAVE HAD MOTIVES OTHER THAN THE PUBLIC GOOD?
GET ME OUT OF HERE.

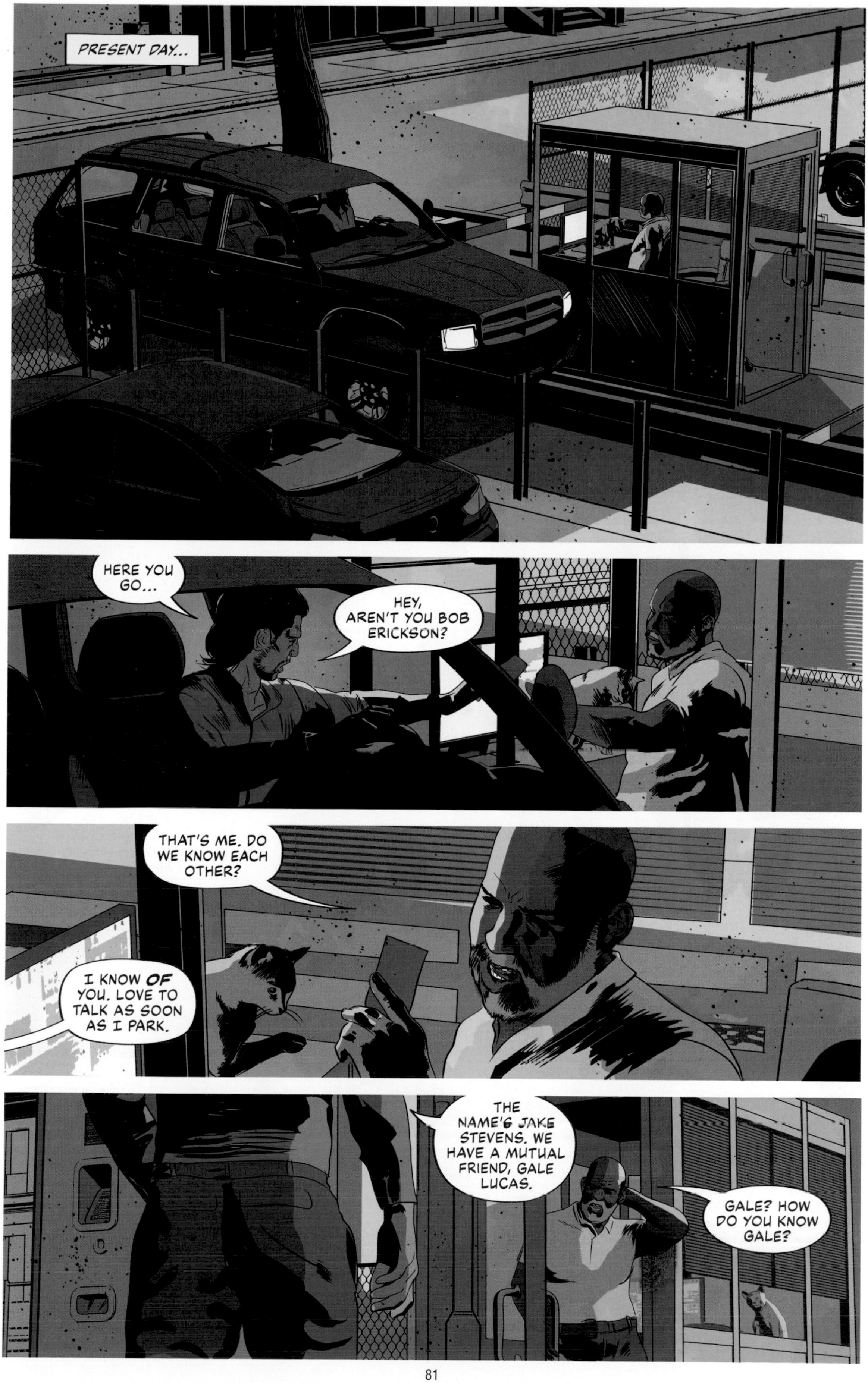
PRESENT DAY...
HERE YOU GO...
HEY, AREN'T YOU BOB ERICKSON?
THAT'S ME. DO WE KNOW EACH OTHER?
I KNOW *OF* YOU. LOVE TO TALK AS SOON AS I PARK.
THE NAME'S JAKE STEVENS. WE HAVE A MUTUAL FRIEND, GALE LUCAS.
GALE? HOW DO YOU KNOW GALE?

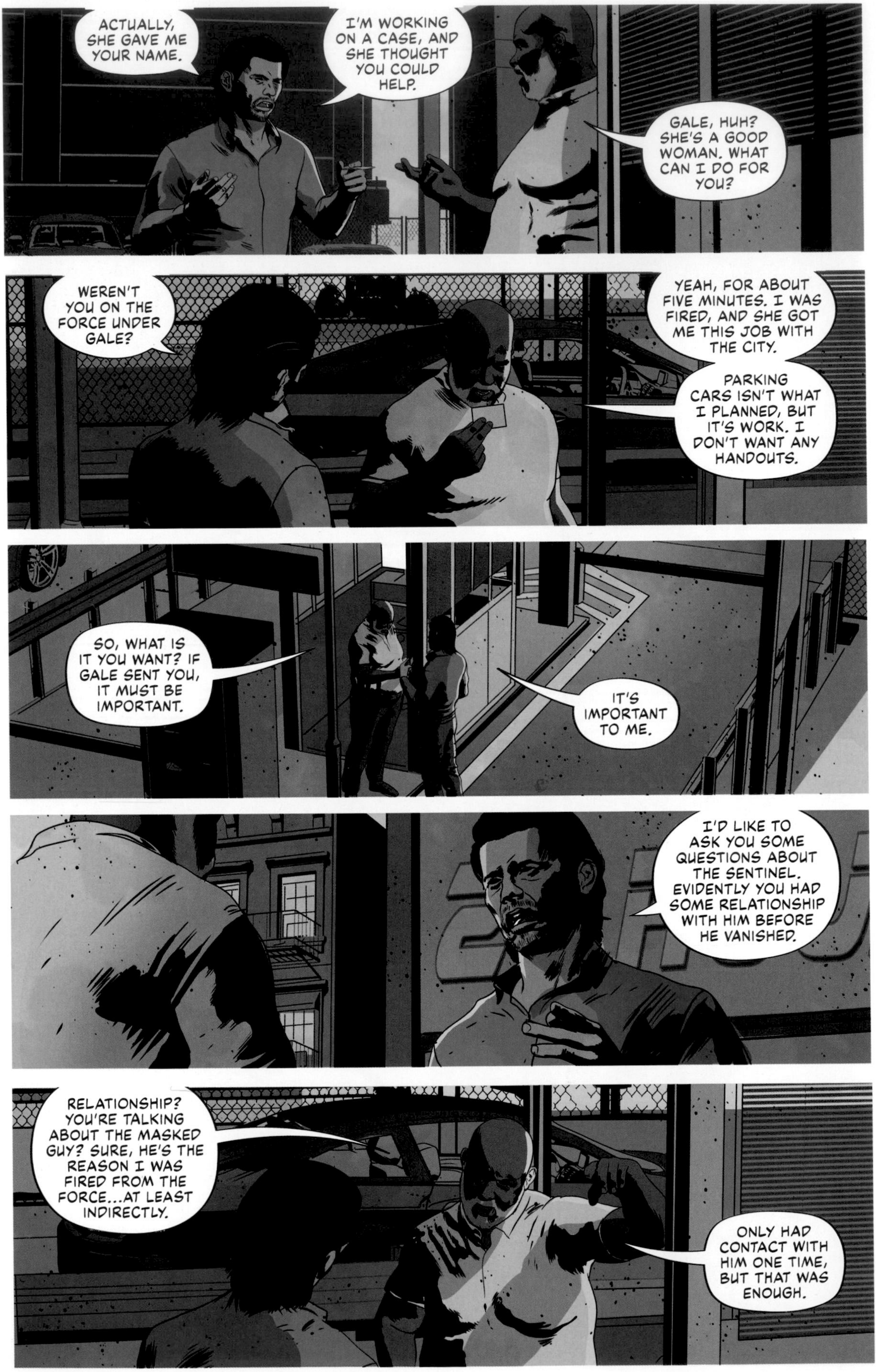
ACTUALLY, SHE GAVE ME YOUR NAME.
I'M WORKING ON A CASE, AND SHE THOUGHT YOU COULD HELP.
GALE, HUH? SHE'S A GOOD WOMAN. WHAT CAN I DO FOR YOU?
WEREN'T YOU ON THE FORCE UNDER GALE?
YEAH, FOR ABOUT FIVE MINUTES. I WAS FIRED, AND SHE GOT ME THIS JOB WITH THE CITY.
PARKING CARS ISN'T WHAT I PLANNED, BUT IT'S WORK. I DON'T WANT ANY HANDOUTS.
SO, WHAT IS IT YOU WANT? IF GALE SENT YOU, IT MUST BE IMPORTANT.
IT'S IMPORTANT TO ME.
I'D LIKE TO ASK YOU SOME QUESTIONS ABOUT THE SENTINEL. EVIDENTLY YOU HAD SOME RELATIONSHIP WITH HIM BEFORE HE VANISHED.
RELATIONSHIP? YOU'RE TALKING ABOUT THE MASKED GUY? SURE, HE'S THE REASON I WAS FIRED FROM THE FORCE...AT LEAST INDIRECTLY.
ONLY HAD CONTACT WITH HIM ONE TIME, BUT THAT WAS ENOUGH.

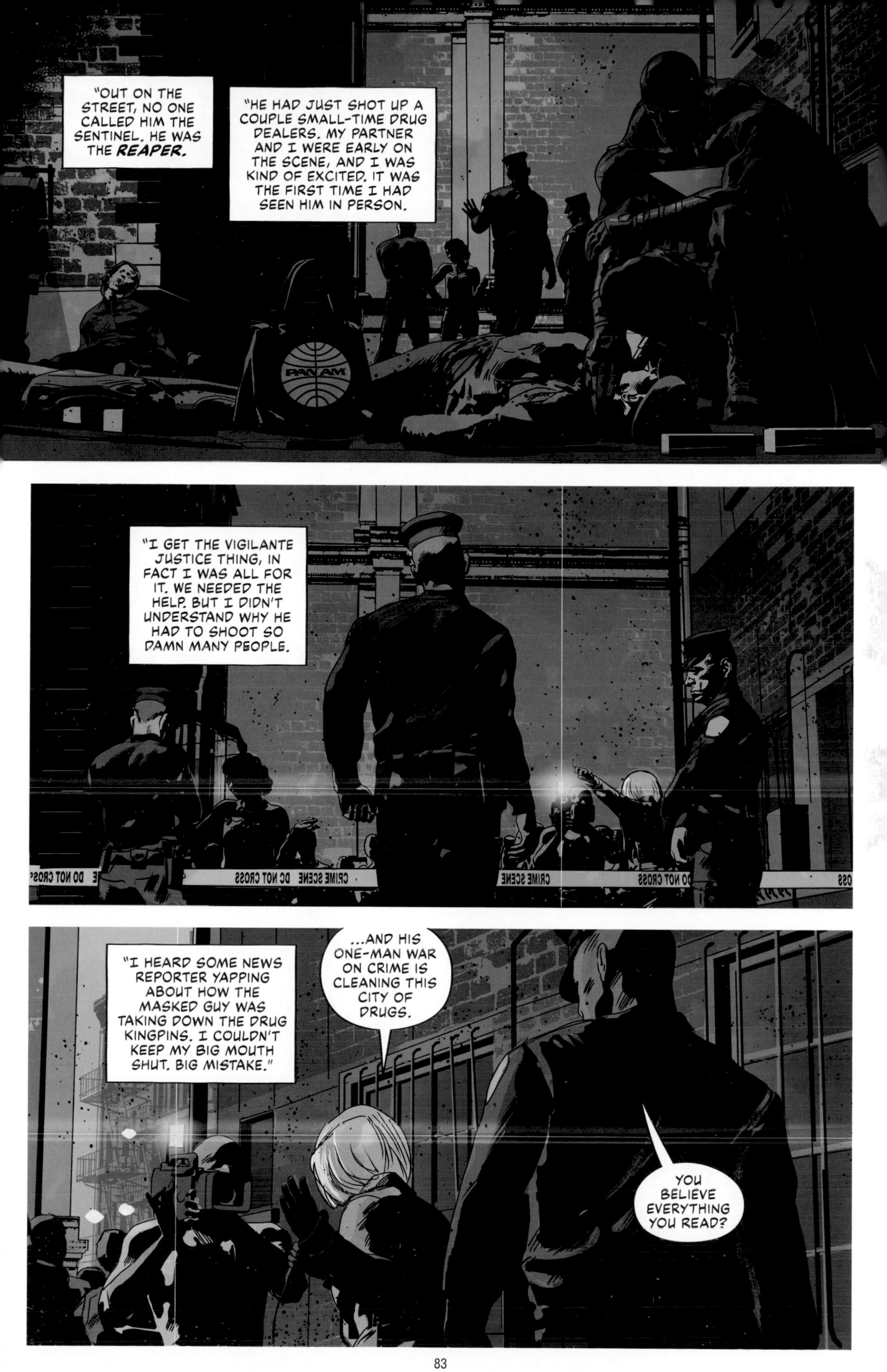
"OUT ON THE STREET, NO ONE CALLED HIM THE SENTINEL. HE WAS THE *REAPER.*
"HE HAD JUST SHOT UP A COUPLE SMALL-TIME DRUG DEALERS. MY PARTNER AND I WERE EARLY ON THE SCENE, AND I WAS KIND OF EXCITED. IT WAS THE FIRST TIME I HAD SEEN HIM IN PERSON.
PAN AM
"I GET THE VIGILANTE JUSTICE THING, IN FACT I WAS ALL FOR IT. WE NEEDED THE HELP. BUT I DIDN'T UNDERSTAND WHY HE HAD TO SHOOT SO DAMN MANY PEOPLE.
DO NOT CROSS
CRIME SCENE DO NOT CROSS
CRIME SCENE
DO NOT CROSS
"I HEARD SOME NEWS REPORTER YAPPING ABOUT HOW THE MASKED GUY WAS TAKING DOWN THE DRUG KINGPINS. I COULDN'T KEEP MY BIG MOUTH SHUT. BIG MISTAKE."
...AND HIS ONE-MAN WAR ON CRIME IS CLEANING THIS CITY OF DRUGS.
YOU BELIEVE EVERYTHING YOU READ?

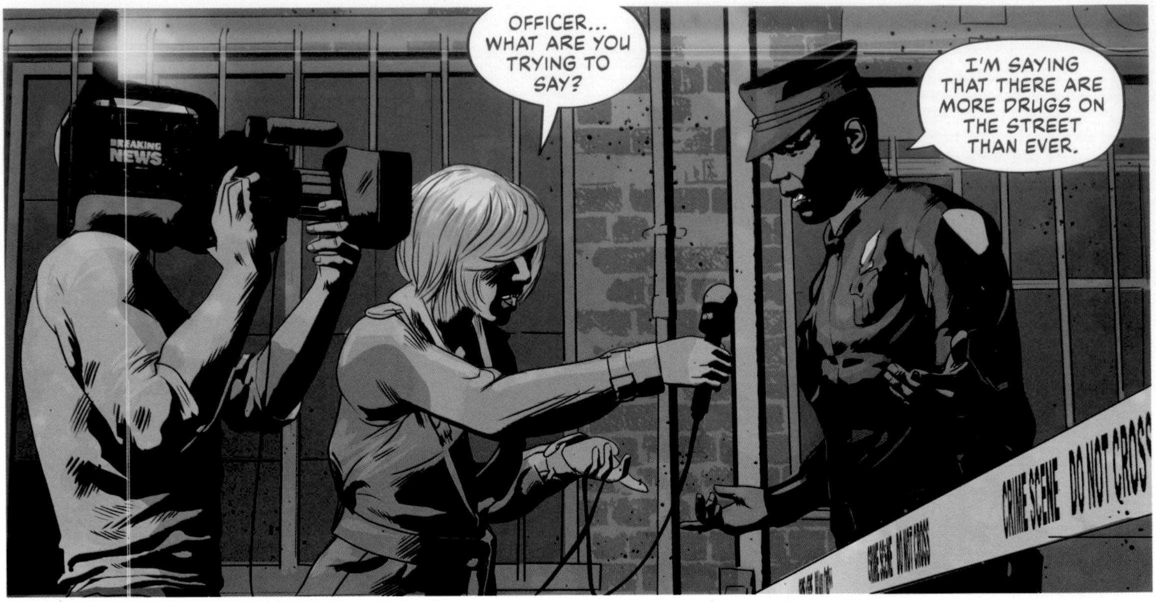
BREAKING NEWS
OFFICER... WHAT ARE YOU TRYING TO SAY?
I'M SAYING THAT THERE ARE MORE DRUGS ON THE STREET THAN EVER.
CRIME SCENE DO NOT CROSS

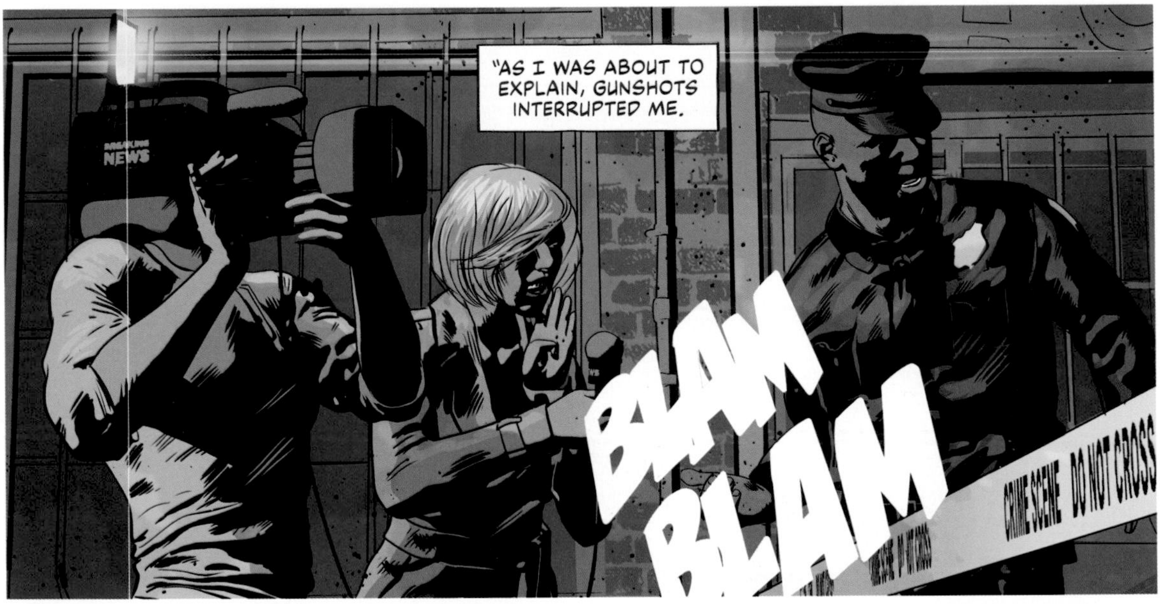
"AS I WAS ABOUT TO EXPLAIN, GUNSHOTS INTERRUPTED ME.
BREAKING NEWS
BLAM
BLAM
CRIME SCENE DO NOT CROSS

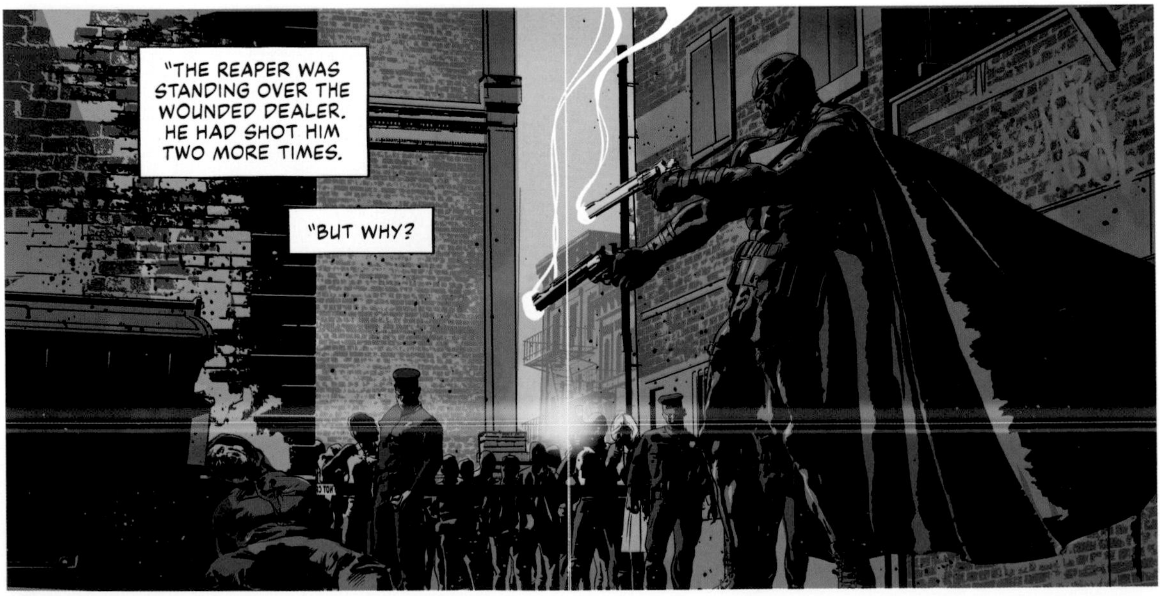
"THE REAPER WAS STANDING OVER THE WOUNDED DEALER. HE HAD SHOT HIM TWO MORE TIMES.
"BUT WHY?

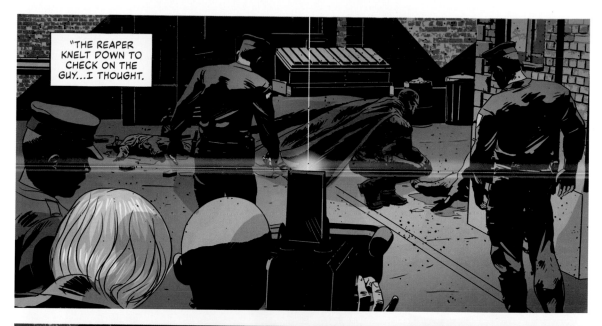

"THE REAPER KNELT DOWN TO CHECK ON THE GUY...I THOUGHT.

"WHEN HE STOOD UP, A GUN WAS LYING BY THE GUY'S HAND.

"I'LL TELL YOU LIKE I TOLD EVERYONE ELSE--THERE WAS NOTHING ON THE GROUND BEFORE THE REAPER KNELT DOWN."

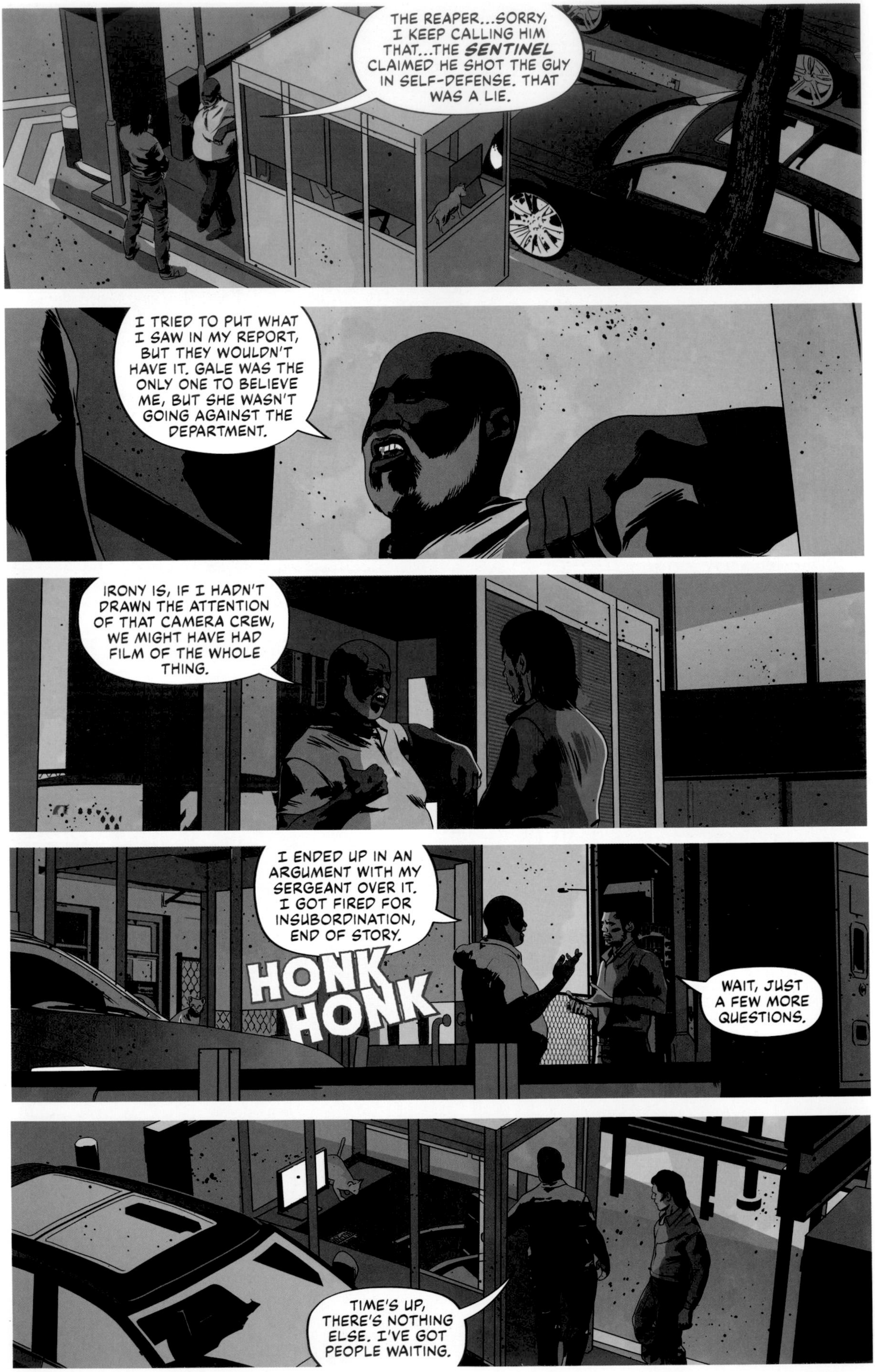
THE REAPER...SORRY, I KEEP CALLING HIM THAT...THE SENTINEL CLAIMED HE SHOT THE GUY IN SELF-DEFENSE. THAT WAS A LIE.
I TRIED TO PUT WHAT I SAW IN MY REPORT, BUT THEY WOULDN'T HAVE IT. GALE WAS THE ONLY ONE TO BELIEVE ME, BUT SHE WASN'T GOING AGAINST THE DEPARTMENT.
IRONY IS, IF I HADN'T DRAWN THE ATTENTION OF THAT CAMERA CREW, WE MIGHT HAVE HAD FILM OF THE WHOLE THING.
I ENDED UP IN AN ARGUMENT WITH MY SERGEANT OVER IT. I GOT FIRED FOR INSUBORDINATION, END OF STORY.
HONK HONK
WAIT, JUST A FEW MORE QUESTIONS.
TIME'S UP, THERE'S NOTHING ELSE. I'VE GOT PEOPLE WAITING.

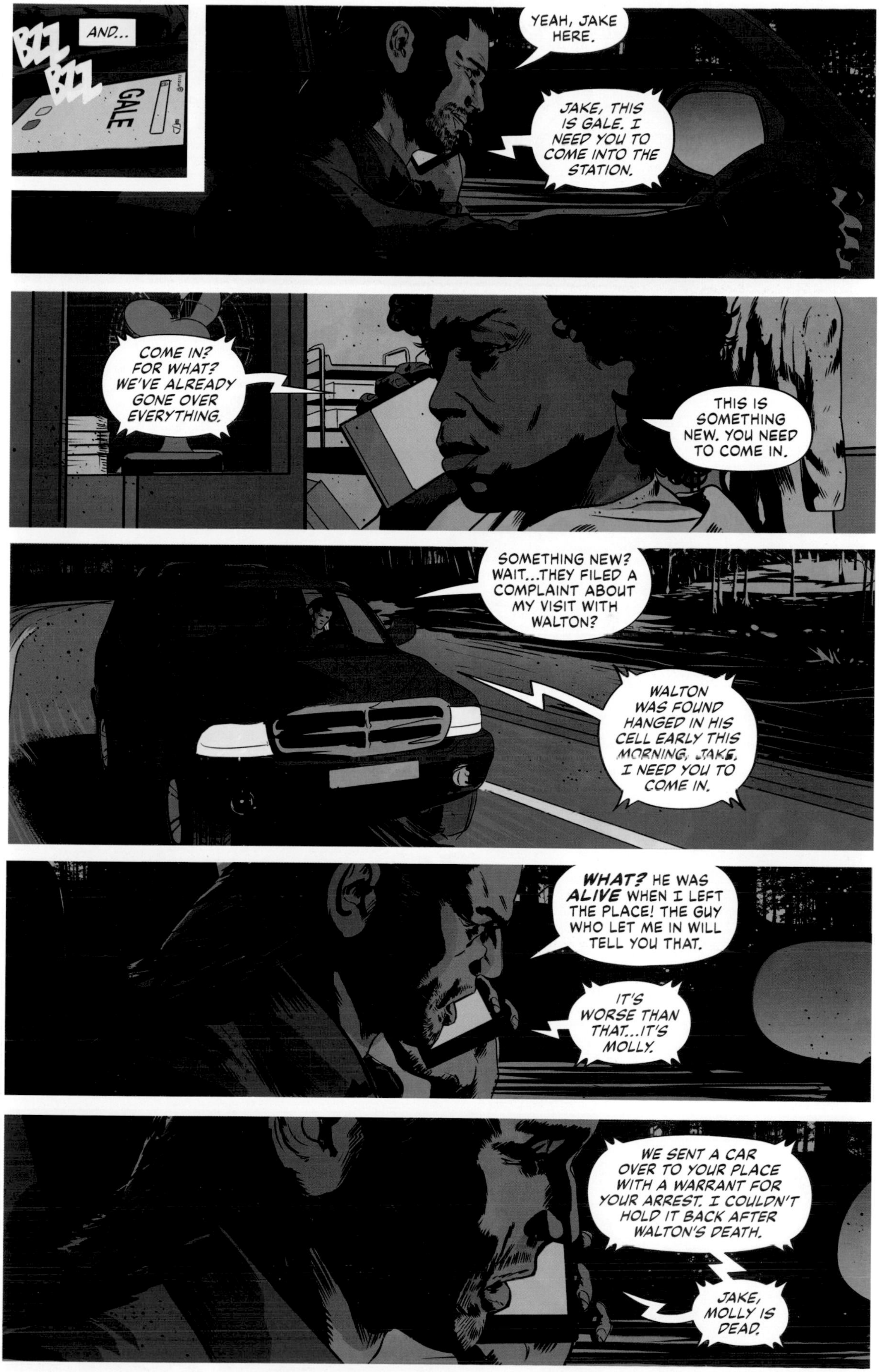
BZZ BZZ
AND...
GALE
YEAH, JAKE HERE.
JAKE, THIS IS GALE. I NEED YOU TO COME INTO THE STATION.
COME IN? FOR WHAT? WE'VE ALREADY GONE OVER EVERYTHING.
THIS IS SOMETHING NEW. YOU NEED TO COME IN.
SOMETHING NEW? WAIT...THEY FILED A COMPLAINT ABOUT MY VISIT WITH WALTON?
WALTON WAS FOUND HANGED IN HIS CELL EARLY THIS MORNING, JAKE. I NEED YOU TO COME IN.
WHAT? HE WAS ALIVE WHEN I LEFT THE PLACE! THE GUY WHO LET ME IN WILL TELL YOU THAT.
IT'S WORSE THAN THAT...IT'S MOLLY.
WE SENT A CAR OVER TO YOUR PLACE WITH A WARRANT FOR YOUR ARREST. I COULDN'T HOLD IT BACK AFTER WALTON'S DEATH.
JAKE, MOLLY IS DEAD.

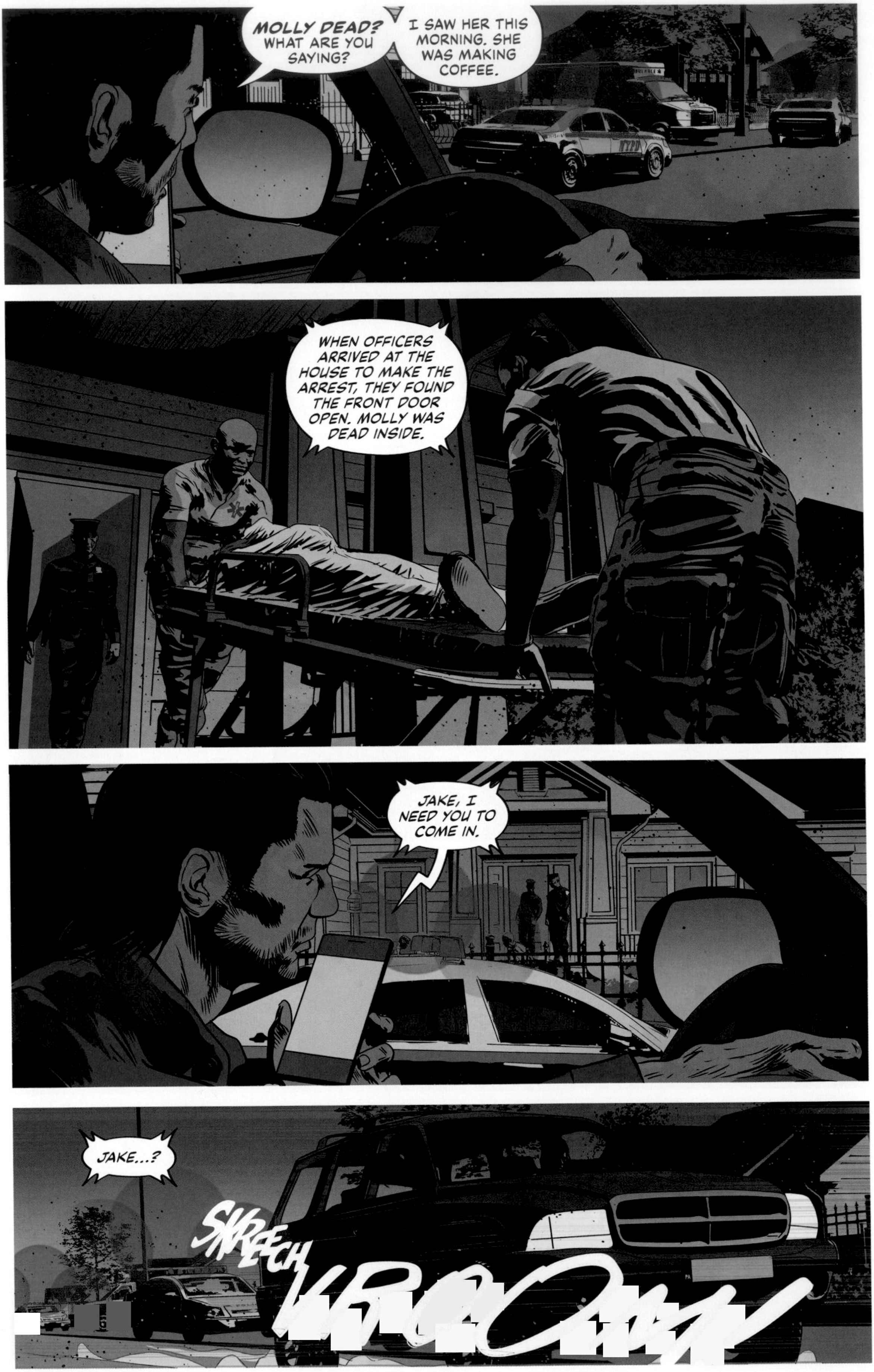
MOLLY DEAD? WHAT ARE YOU SAYING?
I SAW HER THIS MORNING. SHE WAS MAKING COFFEE.
WHEN OFFICERS ARRIVED AT THE HOUSE TO MAKE THE ARREST, THEY FOUND THE FRONT DOOR OPEN. MOLLY WAS DEAD INSIDE.
JAKE, I NEED YOU TO COME IN.
JAKE...?
SKREECH

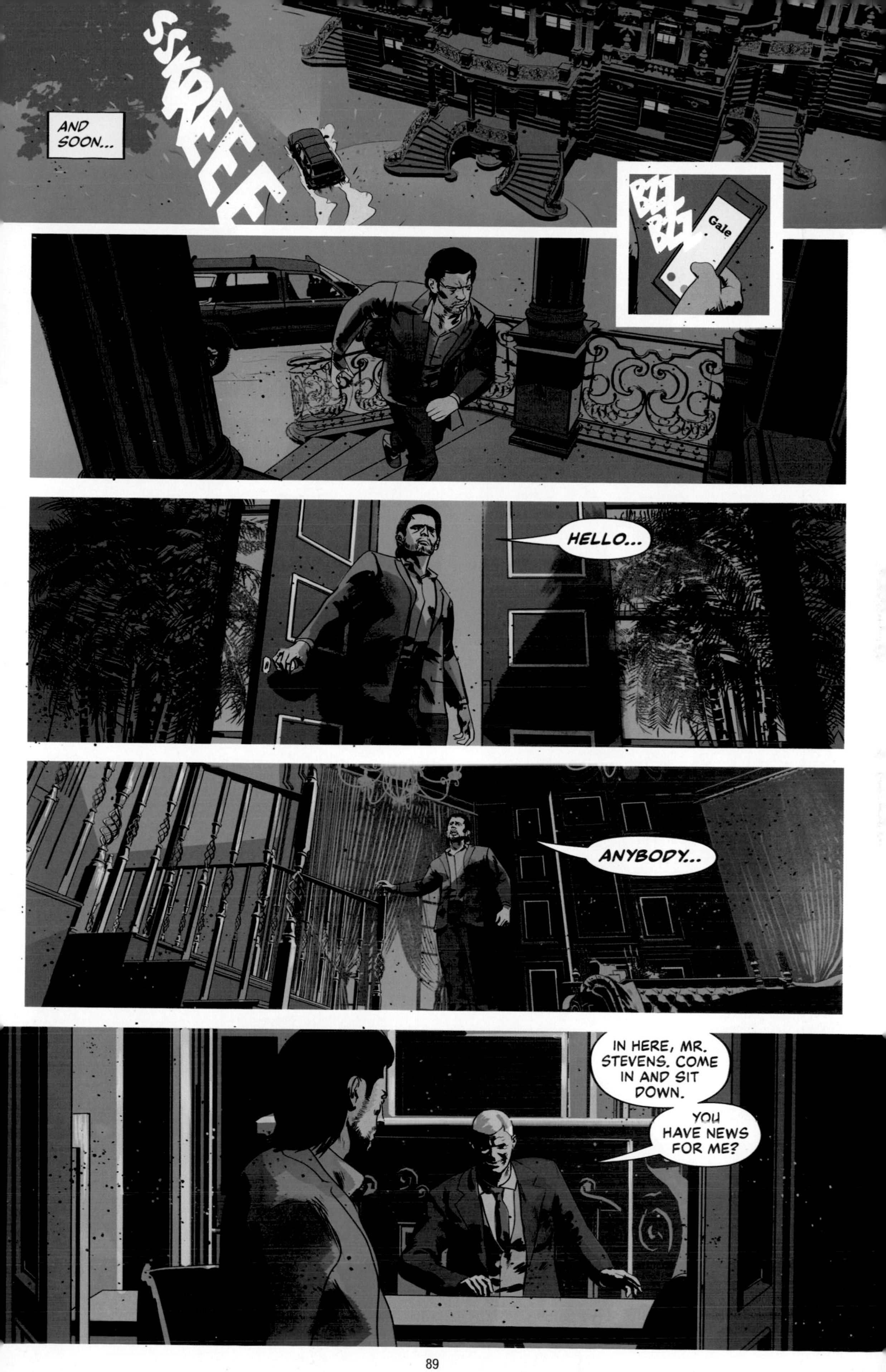
AND SOON...
SSKREEE
BZZ BZZ
Gale
HELLO...
ANYBODY...
IN HERE, MR. STEVENS. COME IN AND SIT DOWN.
YOU HAVE NEWS FOR ME?

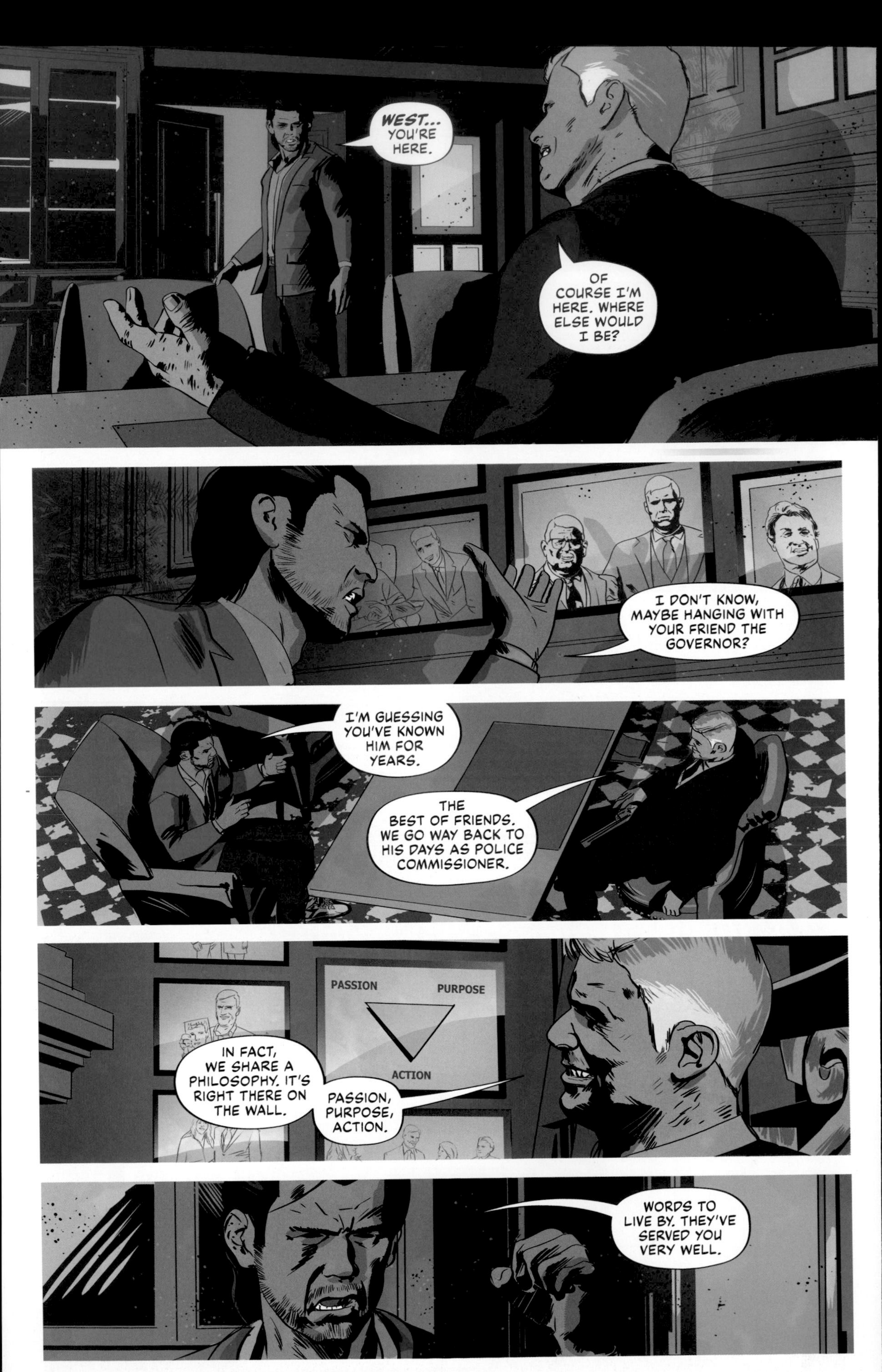
WEST... YOU'RE HERE.
OF COURSE I'M HERE. WHERE ELSE WOULD I BE?
I DON'T KNOW, MAYBE HANGING WITH YOUR FRIEND THE GOVERNOR?
I'M GUESSING YOU'VE KNOWN HIM FOR YEARS.
THE BEST OF FRIENDS. WE GO WAY BACK TO HIS DAYS AS POLICE COMMISSIONER.
PASSION
PURPOSE
ACTION
IN FACT, WE SHARE A PHILOSOPHY. IT'S RIGHT THERE ON THE WALL.
PASSION, PURPOSE, ACTION.
WORDS TO LIVE BY. THEY'VE SERVED YOU VERY WELL.

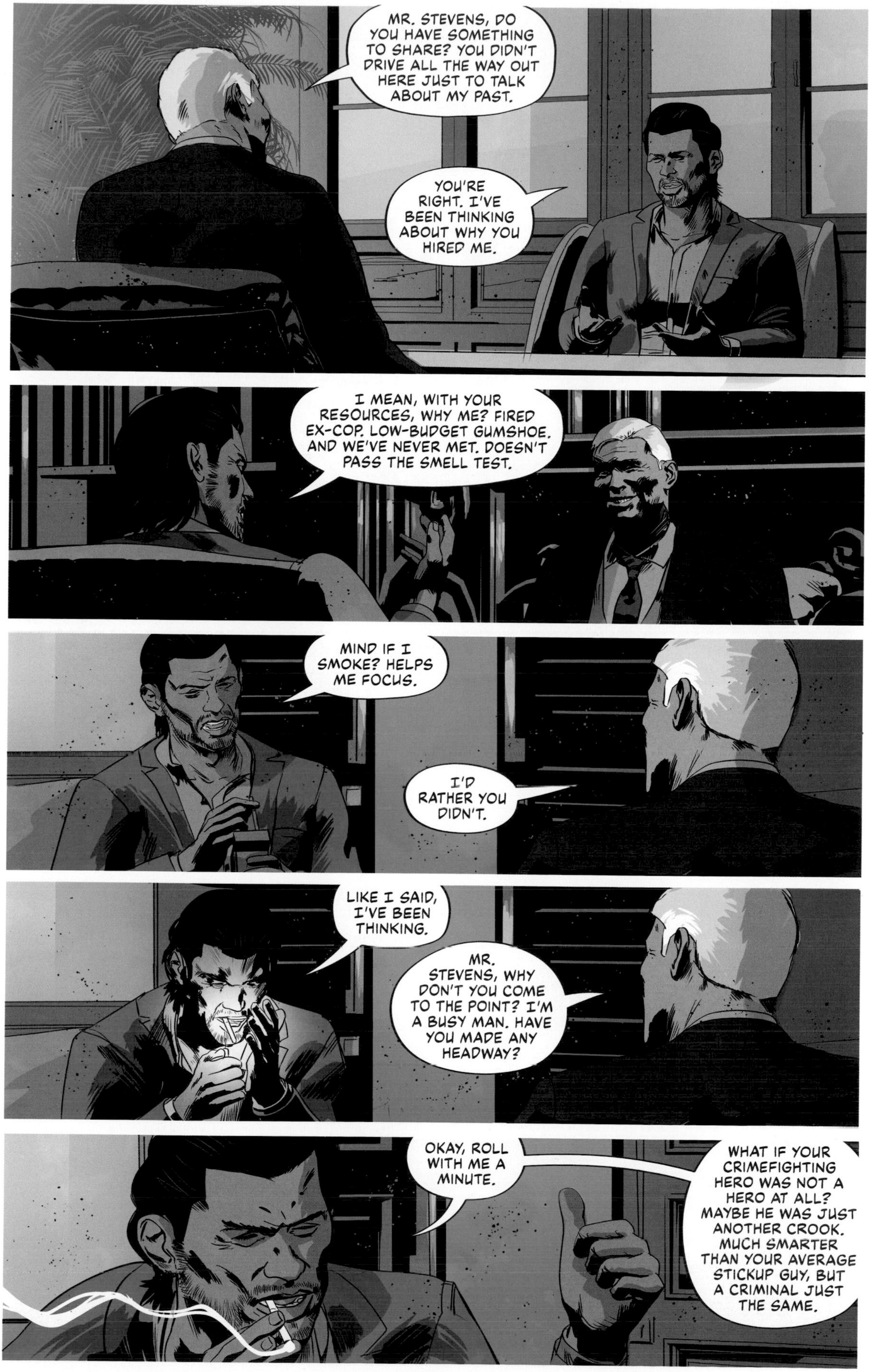
MR. STEVENS, DO YOU HAVE SOMETHING TO SHARE? YOU DIDN'T DRIVE ALL THE WAY OUT HERE JUST TO TALK ABOUT MY PAST.
YOU'RE RIGHT. I'VE BEEN THINKING ABOUT WHY YOU HIRED ME.
I MEAN, WITH YOUR RESOURCES, WHY ME? FIRED EX-COP. LOW-BUDGET GUMSHOE. AND WE'VE NEVER MET. DOESN'T PASS THE SMELL TEST.
MIND IF I SMOKE? HELPS ME FOCUS.
I'D RATHER YOU DIDN'T.
LIKE I SAID, I'VE BEEN THINKING.
MR. STEVENS, WHY DON'T YOU COME TO THE POINT? I'M A BUSY MAN. HAVE YOU MADE ANY HEADWAY?
OKAY, ROLL WITH ME A MINUTE.
WHAT IF YOUR CRIMEFIGHTING HERO WAS NOT A HERO AT ALL? MAYBE HE WAS JUST ANOTHER CROOK. MUCH SMARTER THAN YOUR AVERAGE STICKUP GUY, BUT A CRIMINAL JUST THE SAME.

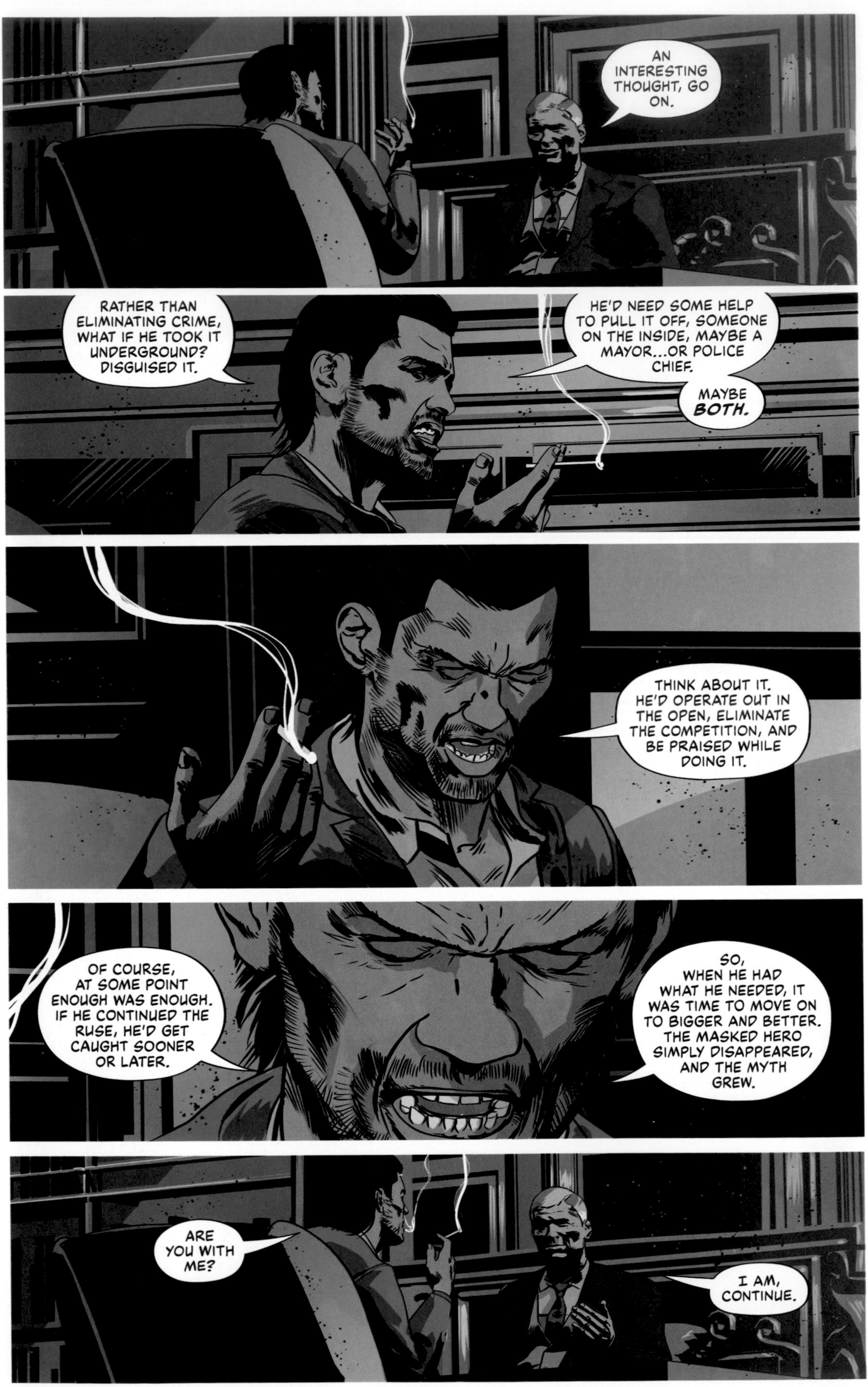
AN INTERESTING THOUGHT, GO ON.
RATHER THAN ELIMINATING CRIME, WHAT IF HE TOOK IT UNDERGROUND? DISGUISED IT.
HE'D NEED SOME HELP TO PULL IT OFF, SOMEONE ON THE INSIDE, MAYBE A MAYOR...OR POLICE CHIEF.
MAYBE *BOTH.*
THINK ABOUT IT. HE'D OPERATE OUT IN THE OPEN, ELIMINATE THE COMPETITION, AND BE PRAISED WHILE DOING IT.
OF COURSE, AT SOME POINT ENOUGH WAS ENOUGH. IF HE CONTINUED THE RUSE, HE'D GET CAUGHT SOONER OR LATER.
SO, WHEN HE HAD WHAT HE NEEDED, IT WAS TIME TO MOVE ON TO BIGGER AND BETTER. THE MASKED HERO SIMPLY DISAPPEARED, AND THE MYTH GREW.
ARE YOU WITH ME?
I AM, CONTINUE.

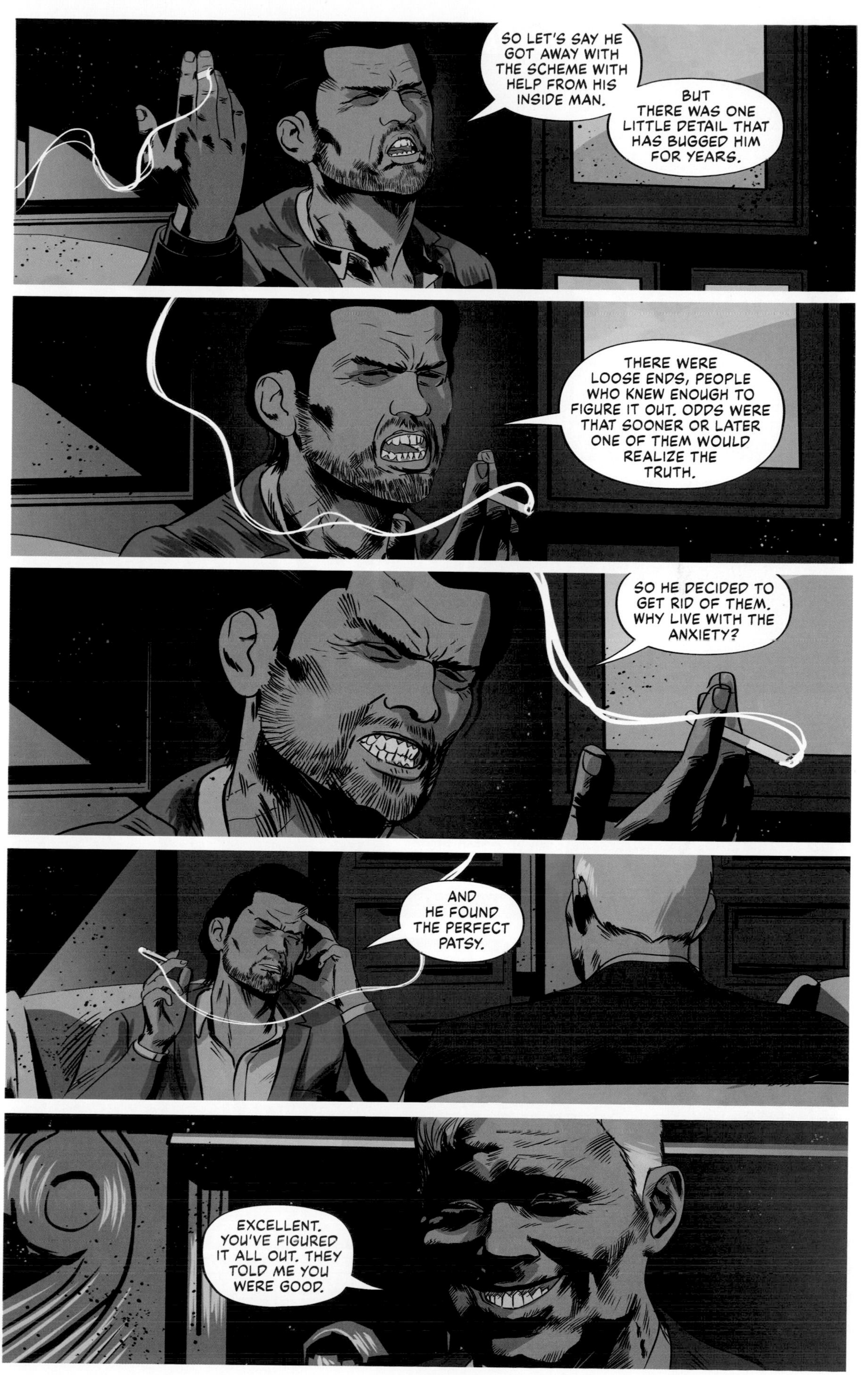
SO LET'S SAY HE GOT AWAY WITH THE SCHEME WITH HELP FROM HIS INSIDE MAN.
BUT THERE WAS ONE LITTLE DETAIL THAT HAS BUGGED HIM FOR YEARS.
THERE WERE LOOSE ENDS, PEOPLE WHO KNEW ENOUGH TO FIGURE IT OUT. ODDS WERE THAT SOONER OR LATER ONE OF THEM WOULD REALIZE THE TRUTH.
SO HE DECIDED TO GET RID OF THEM. WHY LIVE WITH THE ANXIETY?
AND HE FOUND THE PERFECT PATSY.
EXCELLENT. YOU'VE FIGURED IT ALL OUT. THEY TOLD ME YOU WERE GOOD.

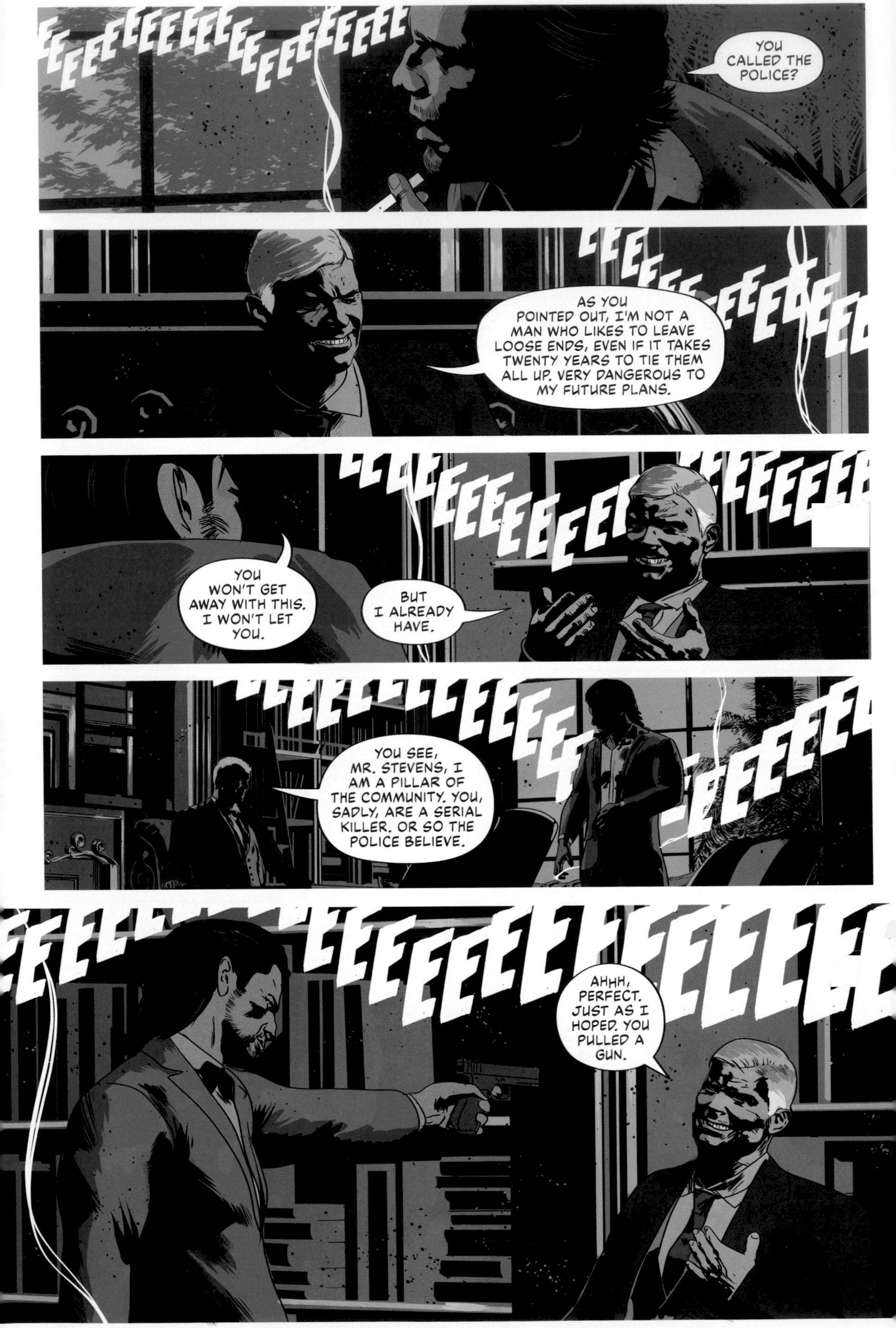
EEEEEEEEEEEEEEEEEE
YOU CALLED THE POLICE?
AS YOU POINTED OUT, I'M NOT A MAN WHO LIKES TO LEAVE LOOSE ENDS, EVEN IF IT TAKES TWENTY YEARS TO TIE THEM ALL UP. VERY DANGEROUS TO MY FUTURE PLANS.
YOU WON'T GET AWAY WITH THIS. I WON'T LET YOU.
BUT I ALREADY HAVE.
YOU SEE, MR. STEVENS, I AM A PILLAR OF THE COMMUNITY. YOU, SADLY, ARE A SERIAL KILLER. OR SO THE POLICE BELIEVE.
AHHH, PERFECT. JUST AS I HOPED. YOU PULLED A GUN.

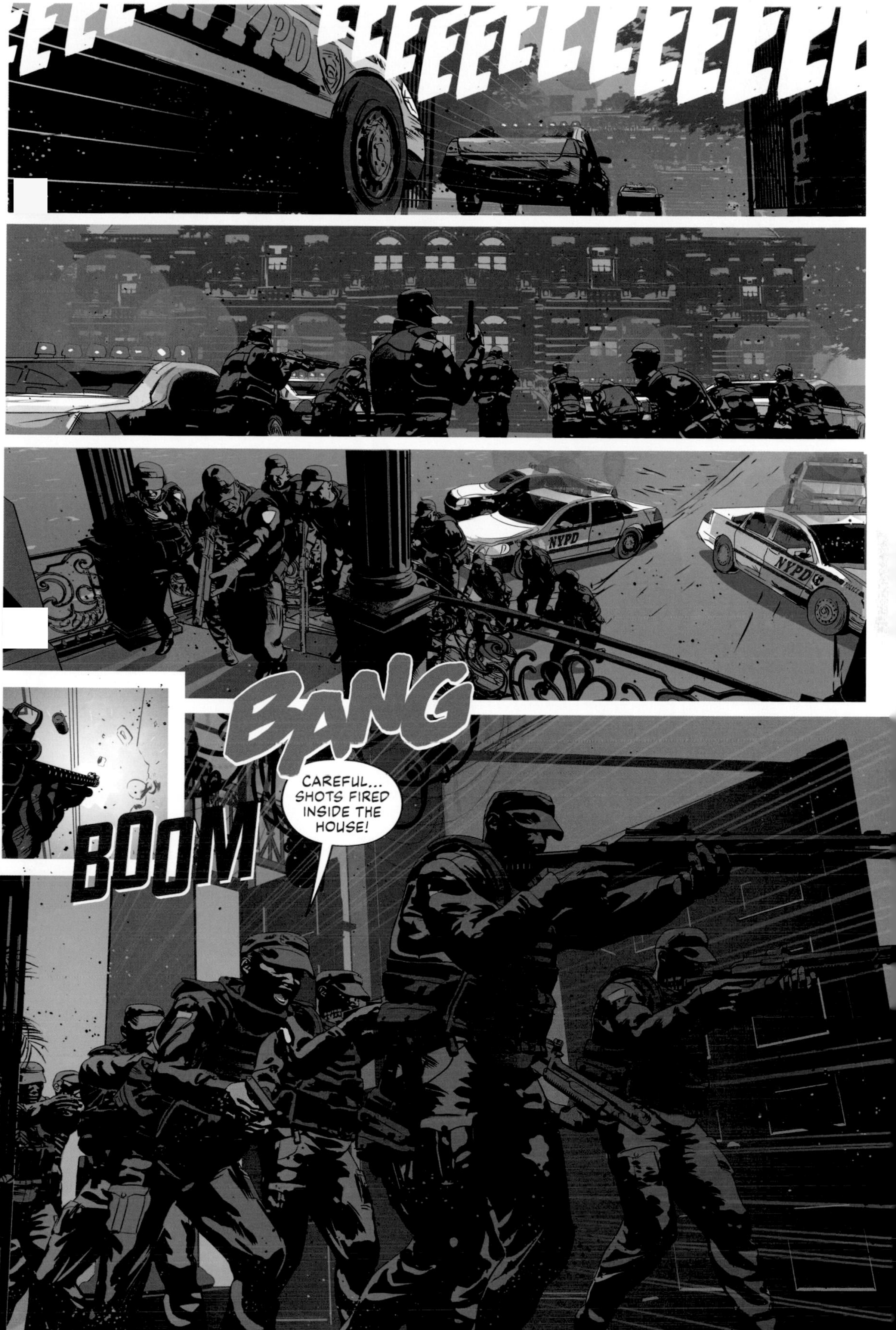
EEEEEEEEEEEEEEE
NYPD
BANG
BOOM
CAREFUL... SHOTS FIRED INSIDE THE HOUSE!

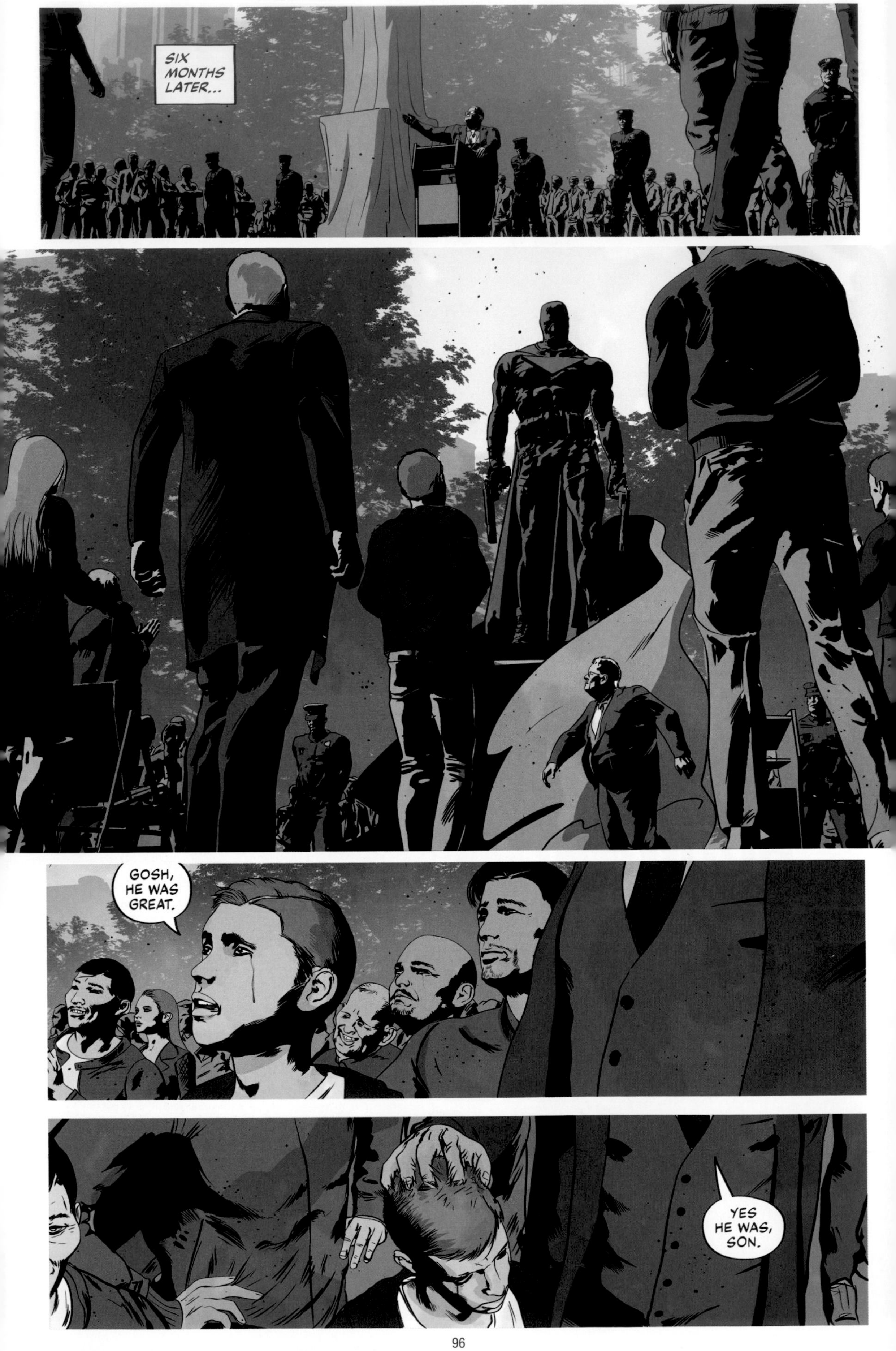
SIX MONTHS LATER...
GOSH, HE WAS GREAT.
YES HE WAS, SON.

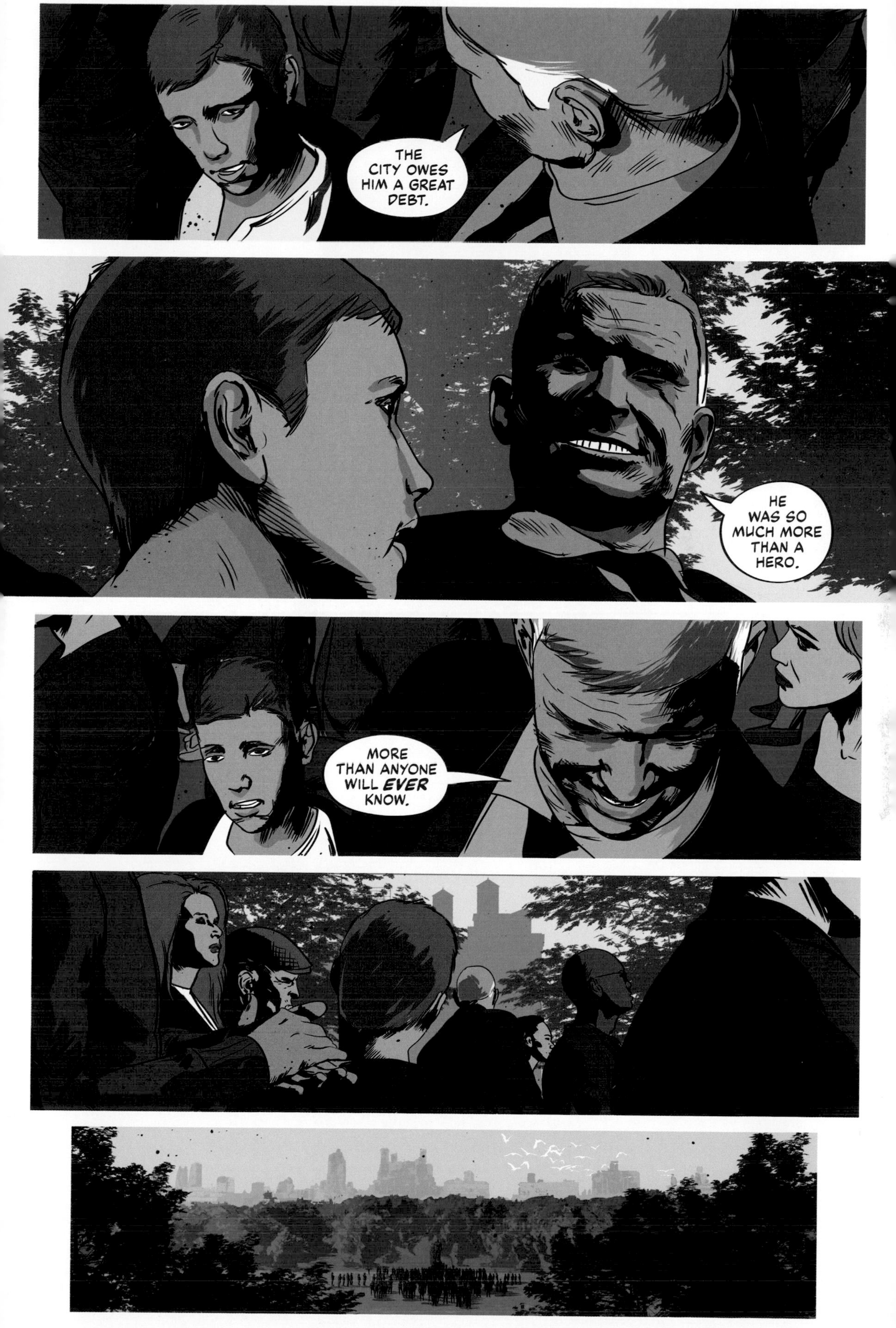
THE CITY OWES HIM A GREAT DEBT.
HE WAS SO MUCH MORE THAN A HERO.
MORE THAN ANYONE WILL *EVER* KNOW.

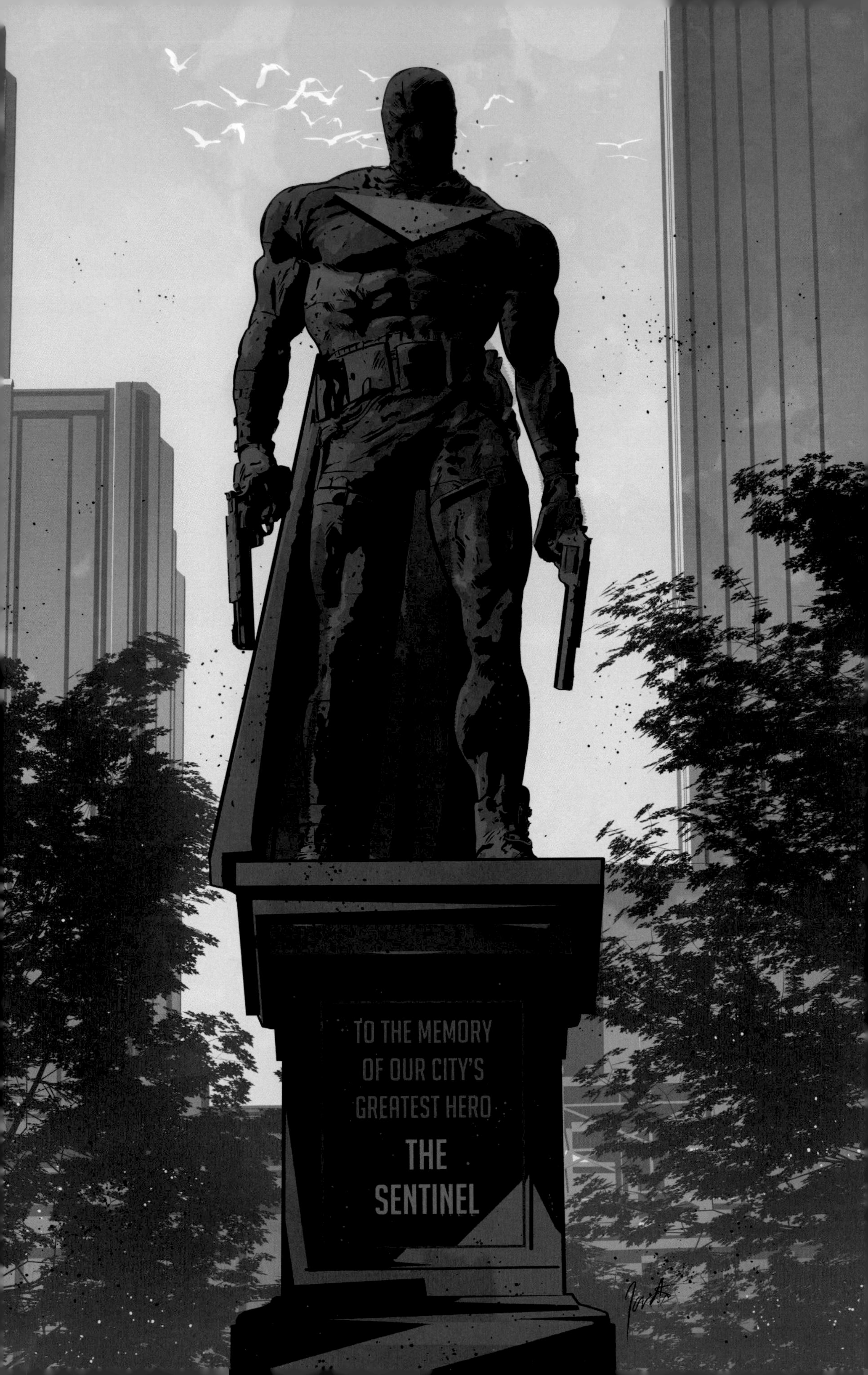
TO THE MEMORY
OF OUR CITY'S
GREATEST HERO
THE
SENTINEL

GALLERY

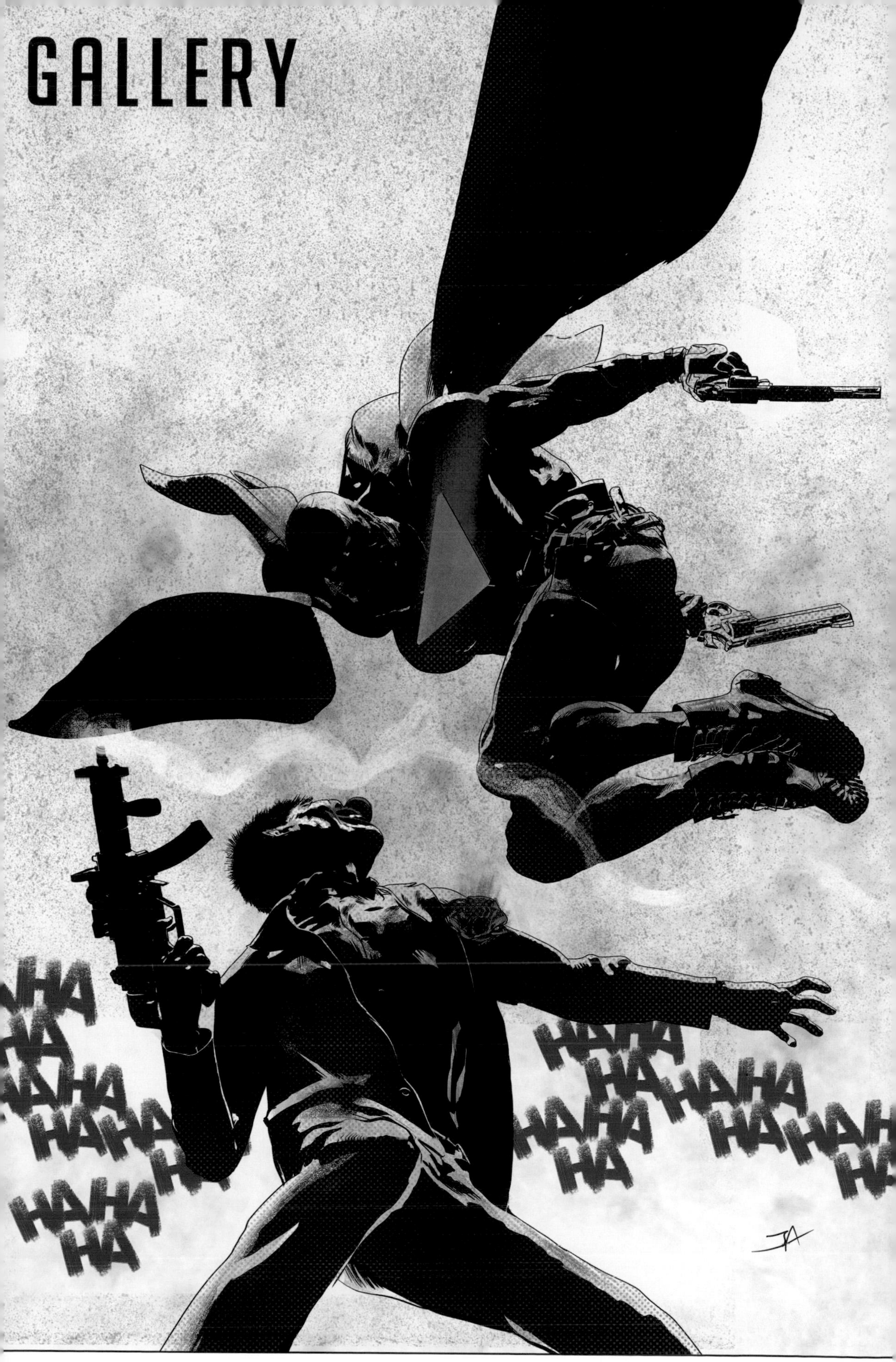
HAHA
HA
HAHA
HAHA
HA
HAHA
HA
HAHA
HA
HAHA
HAHA
HA
HAHA
HA

COVER ART FROM *CLOAKED* #3

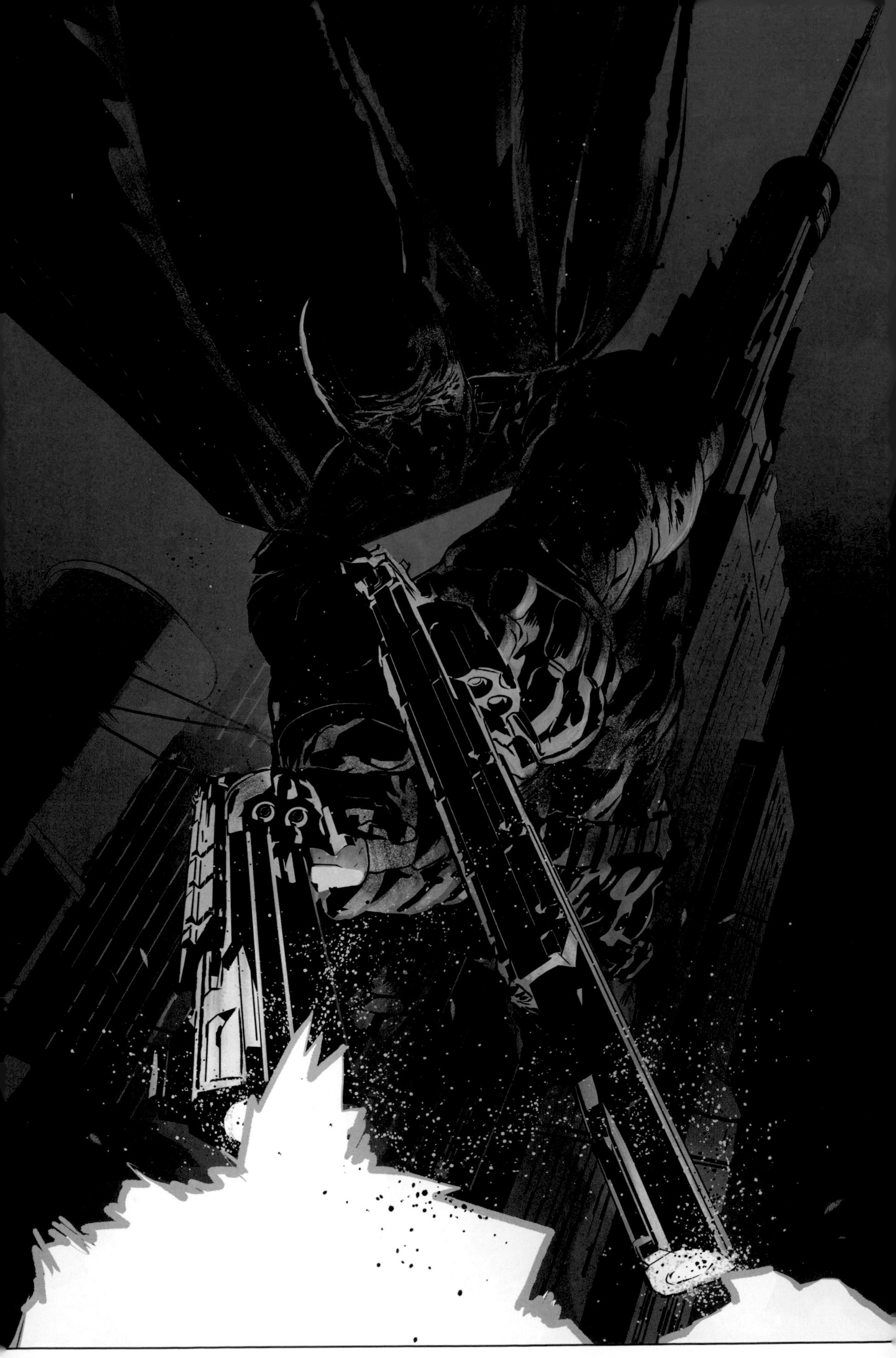

COVER ART FROM *CLOAKED* #4

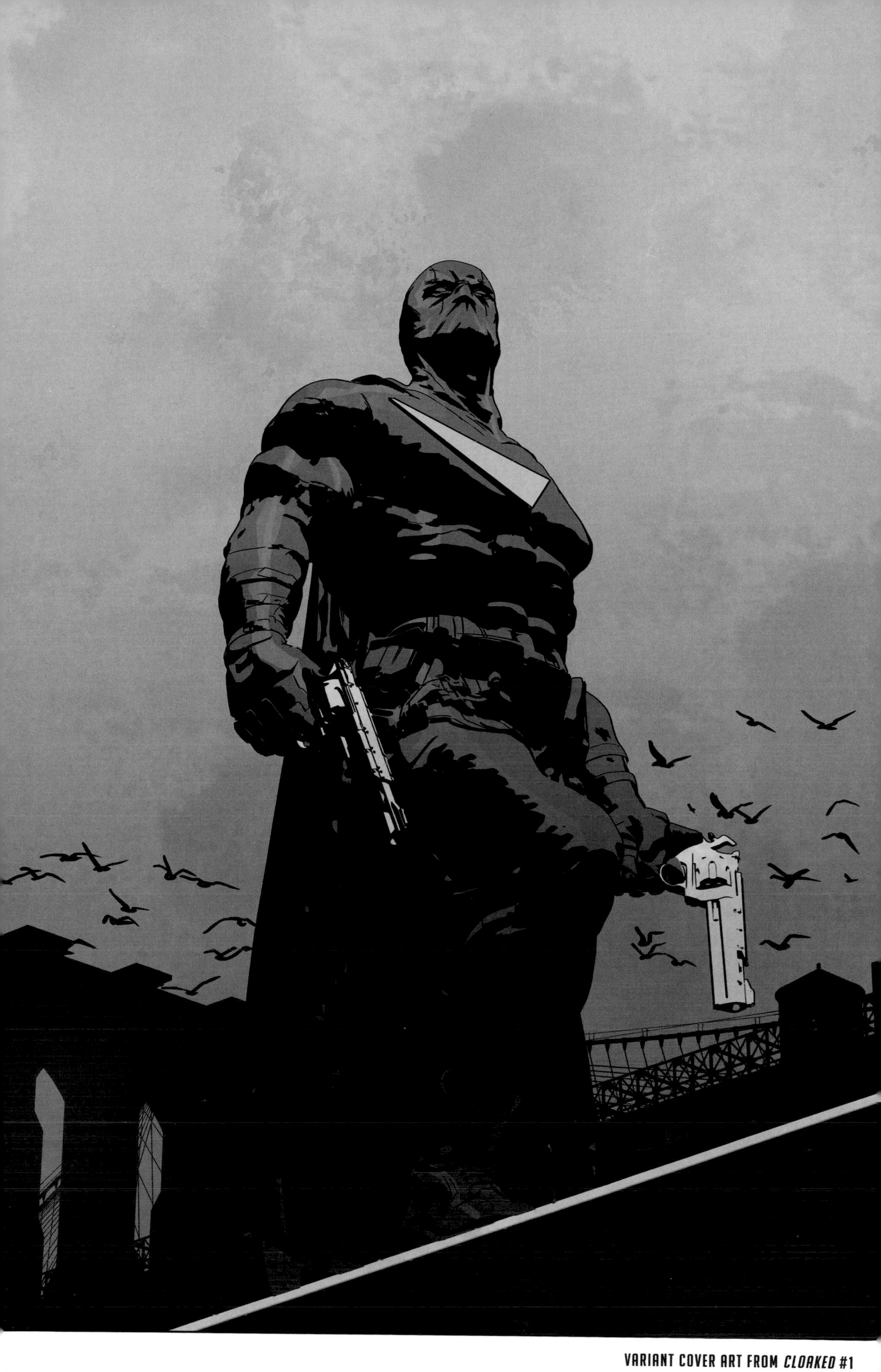

VARIANT COVER ART FROM *CLOAKED* #1

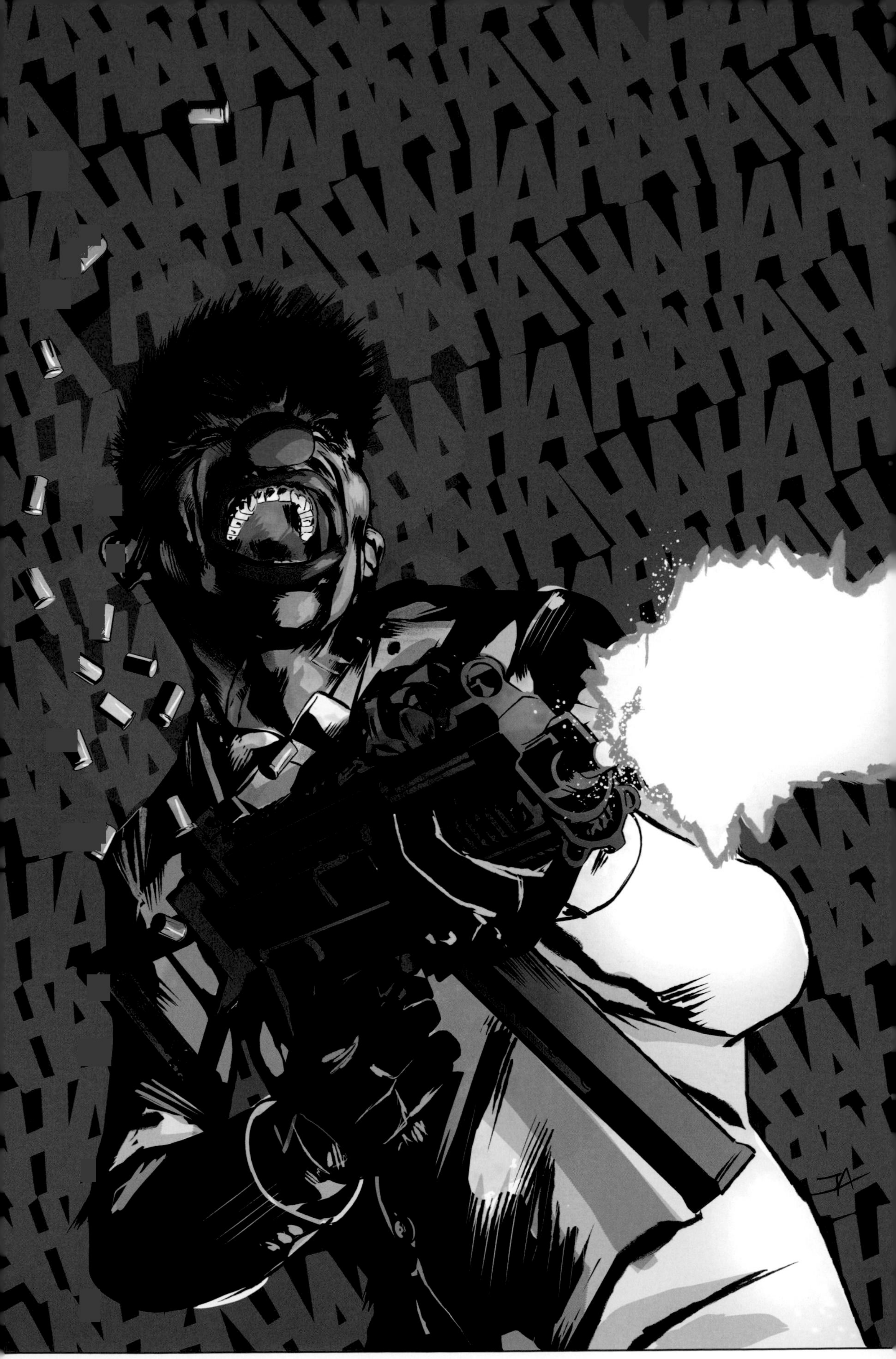

VARIANT COVER ART FROM *CLOAKED* #2

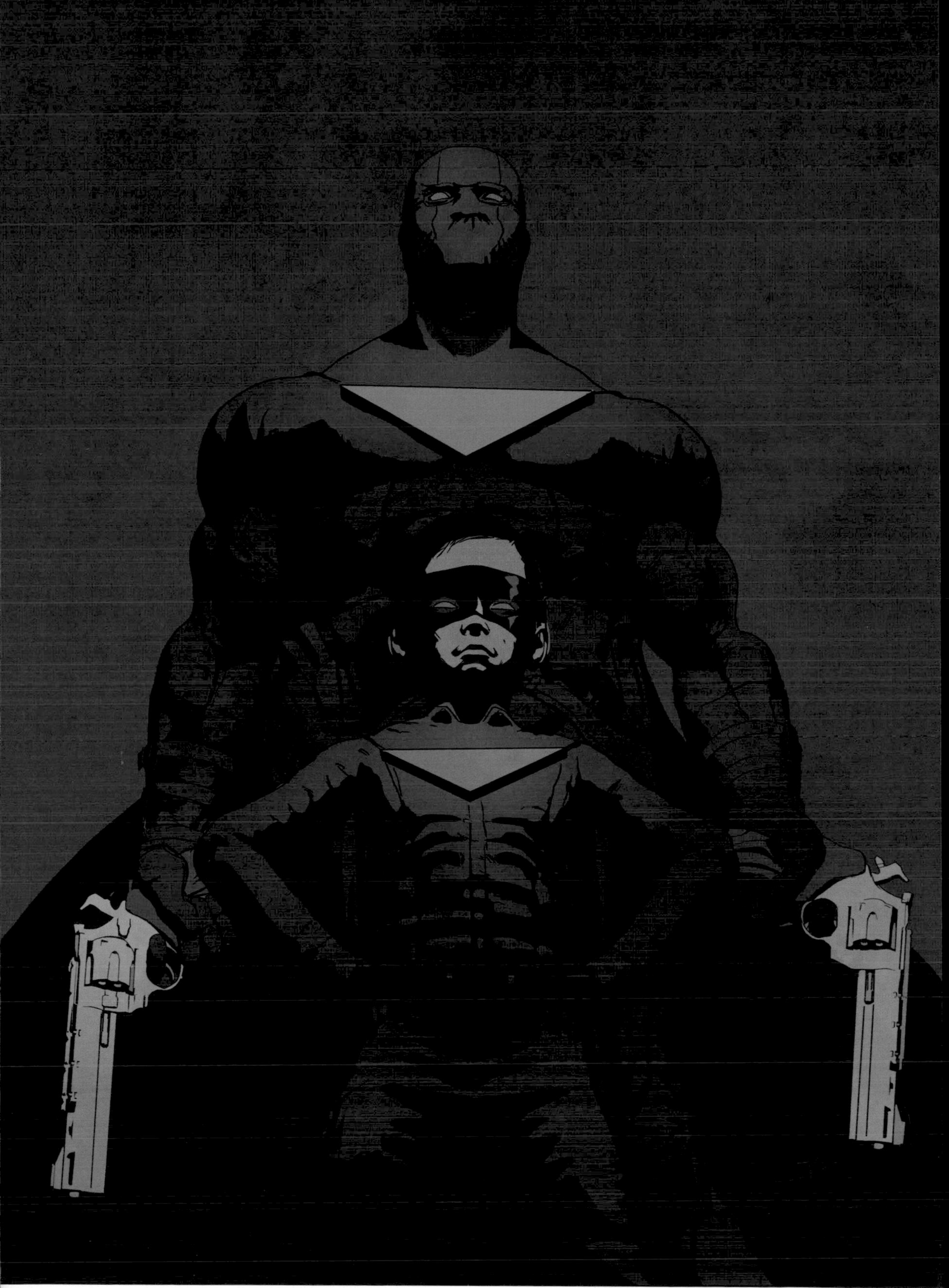

VARIANT COVER ART FROM *CLOAKED* #3

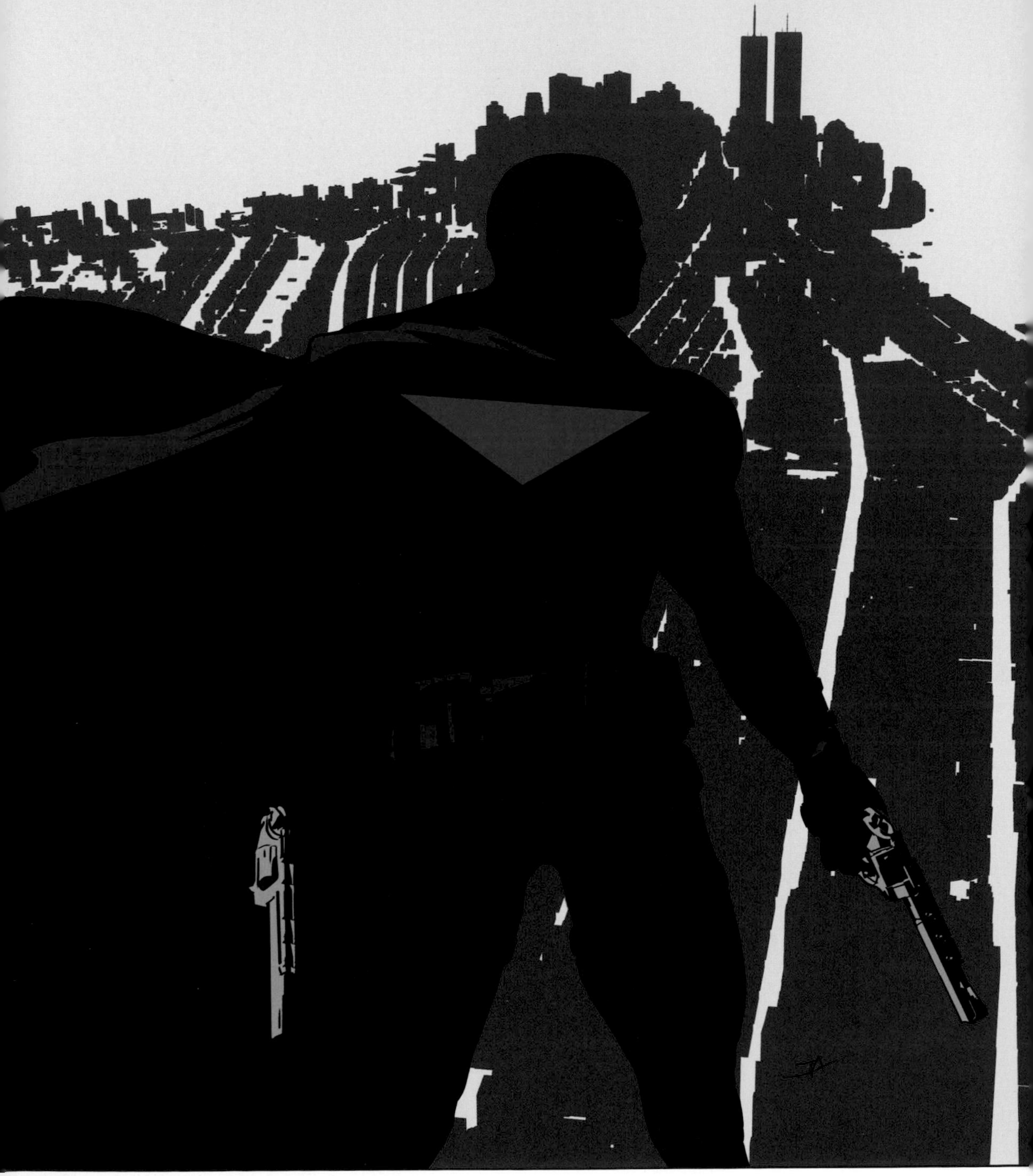

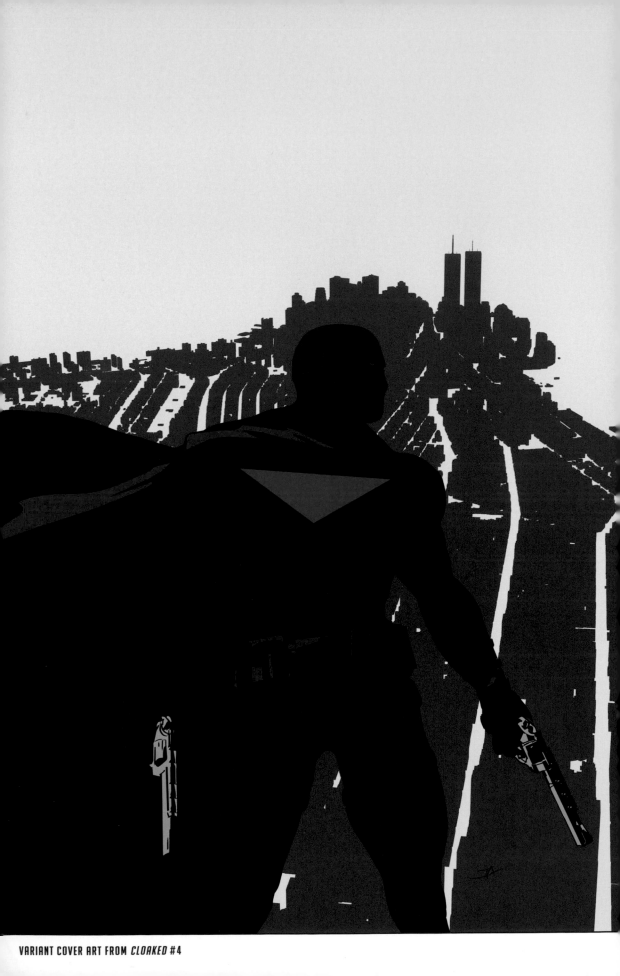

VARIANT COVER ART FROM *CLOAKED* #4

JORDI ARMENGOL'S DESIGN FOR THE SENTINEL/REAPER

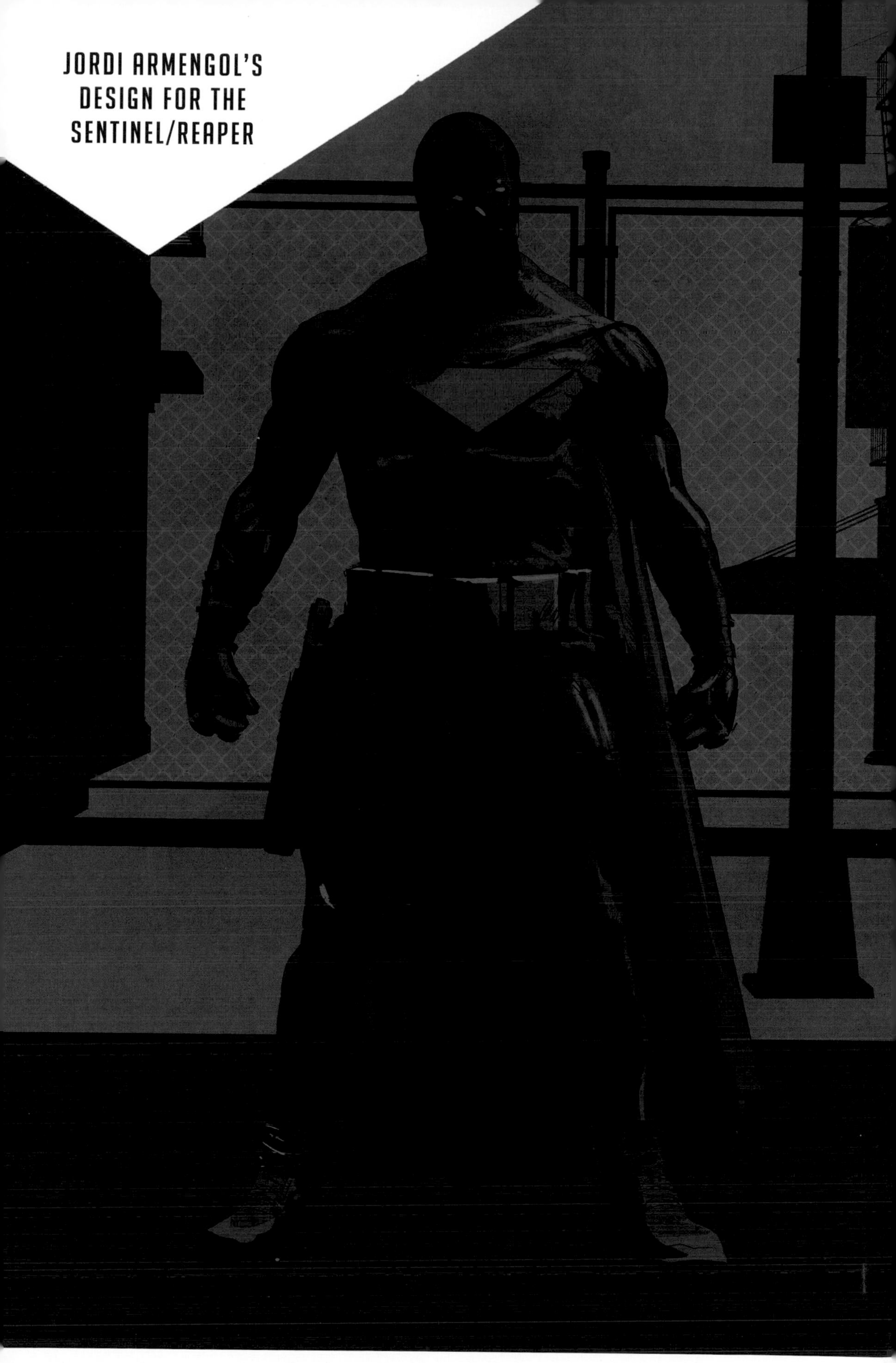

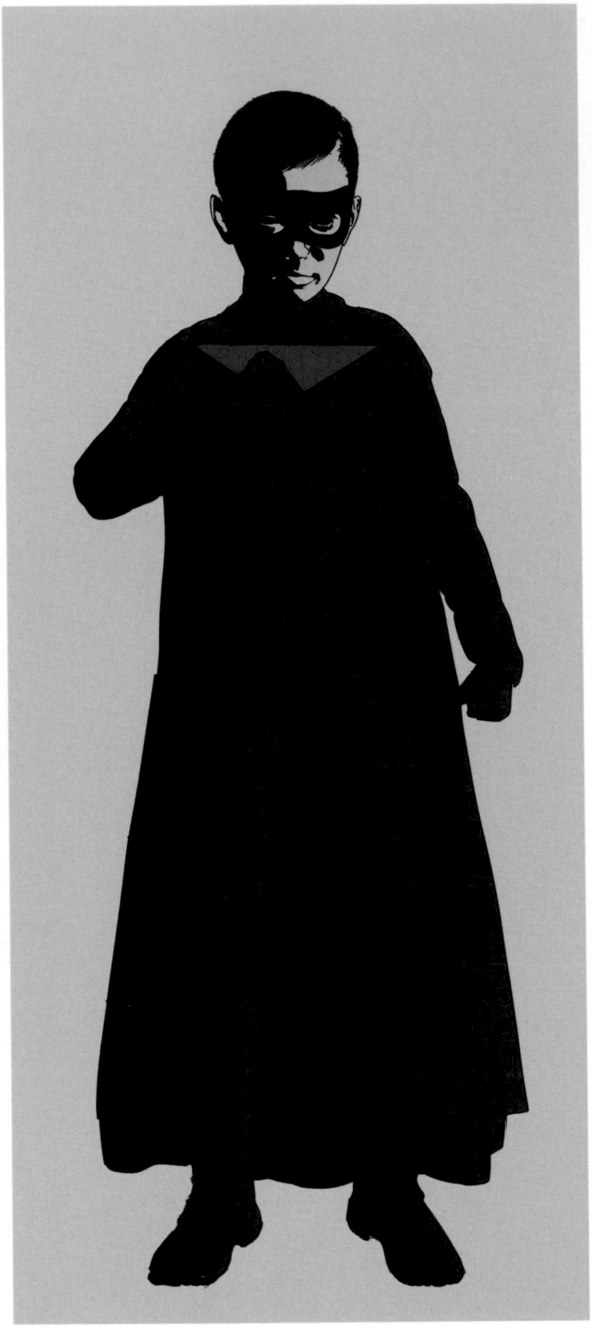

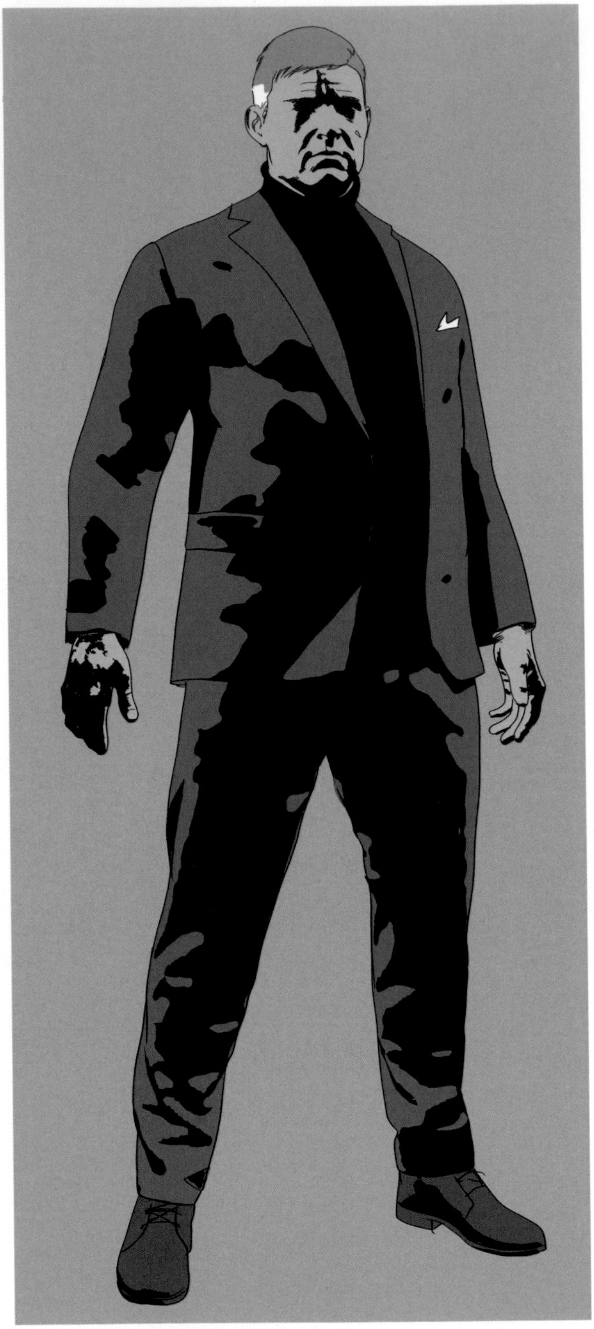

WONDER BOY AND BILLIONAIRE BYRON WEST.

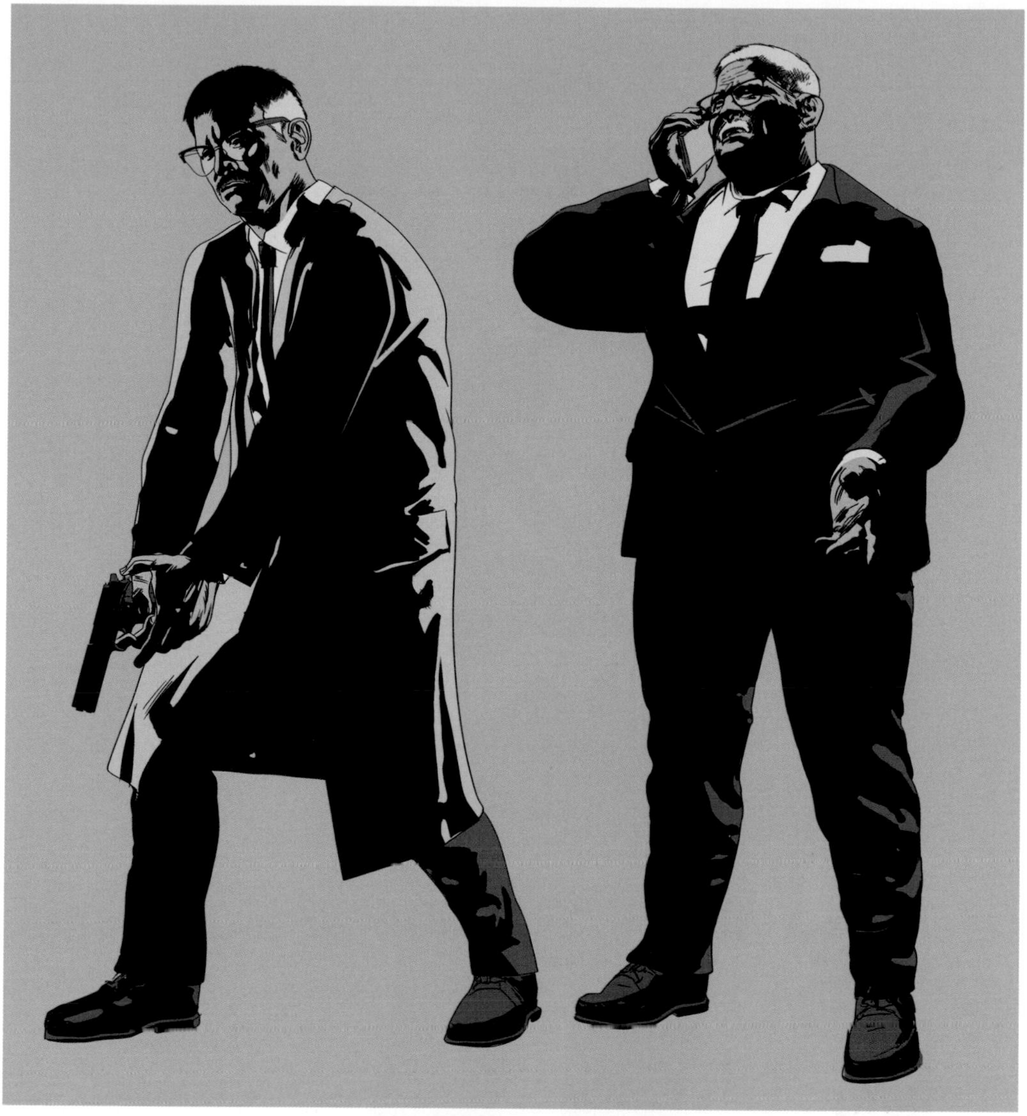

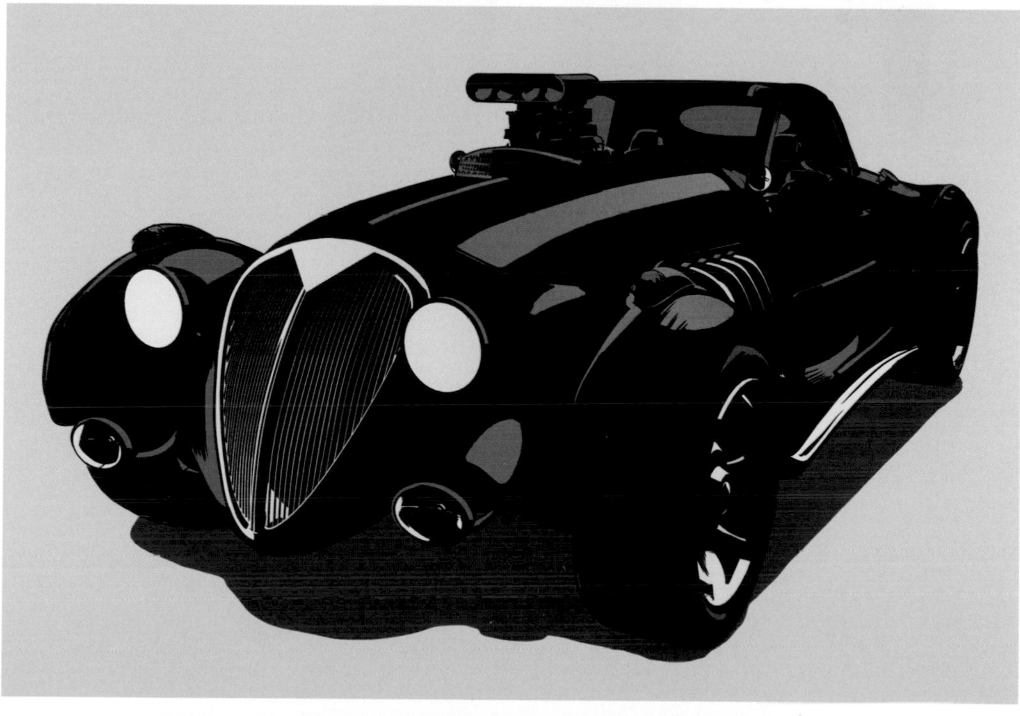

THE POLICE COMMISSIONER, THE GOVERNOR (WHO APPEARED ONLY IN A SINGLE PHOTO), AND THE SENTINEL/REAPER'S CAR.

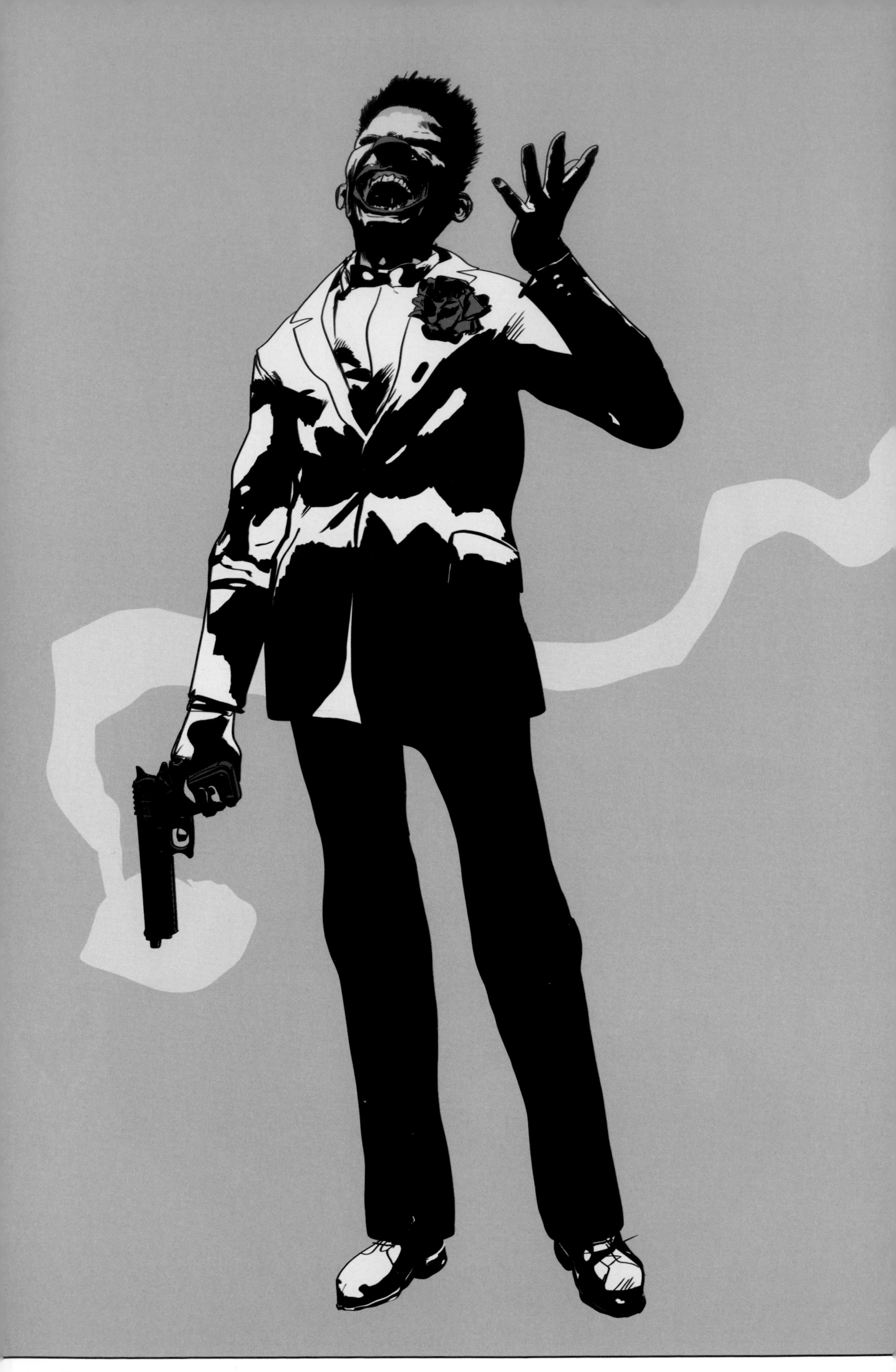

THE LUNATIC.

A VARIETY OF SENTINEL/REAPER STUDIES.

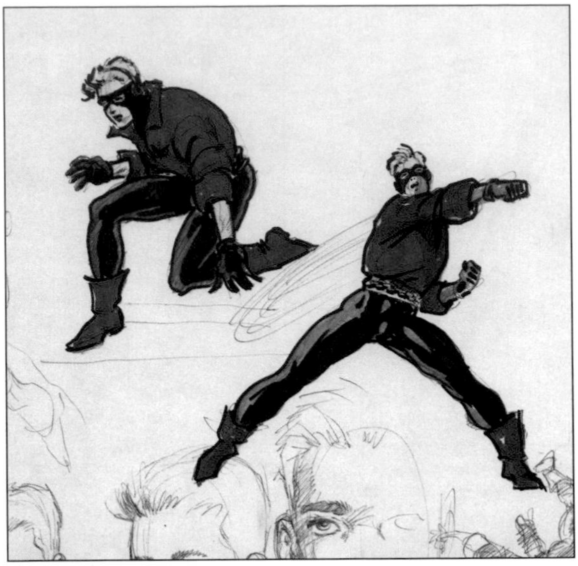

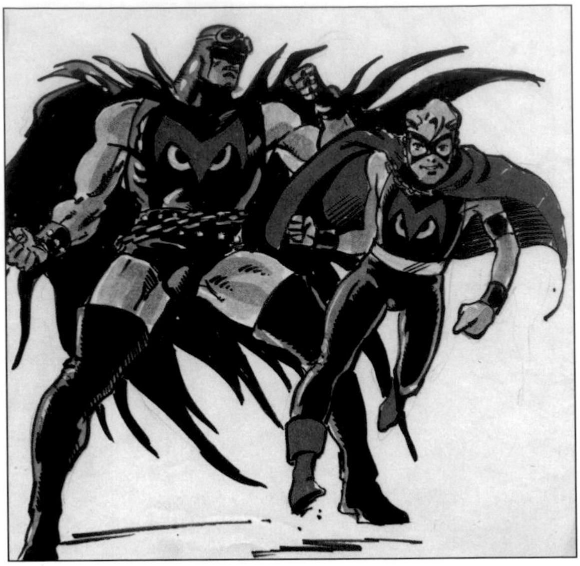

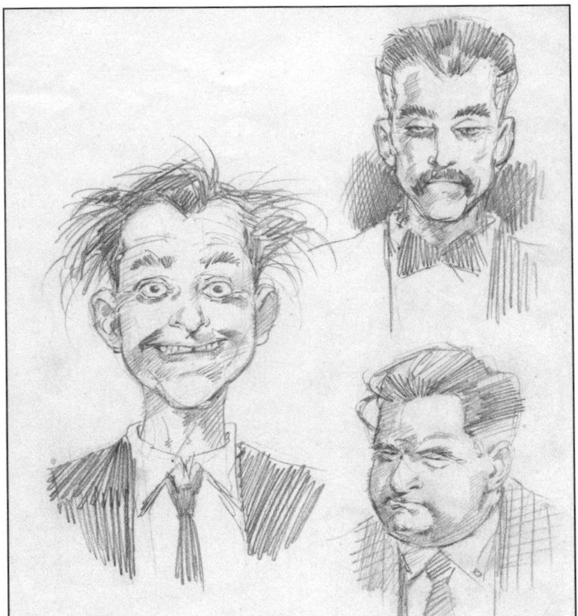

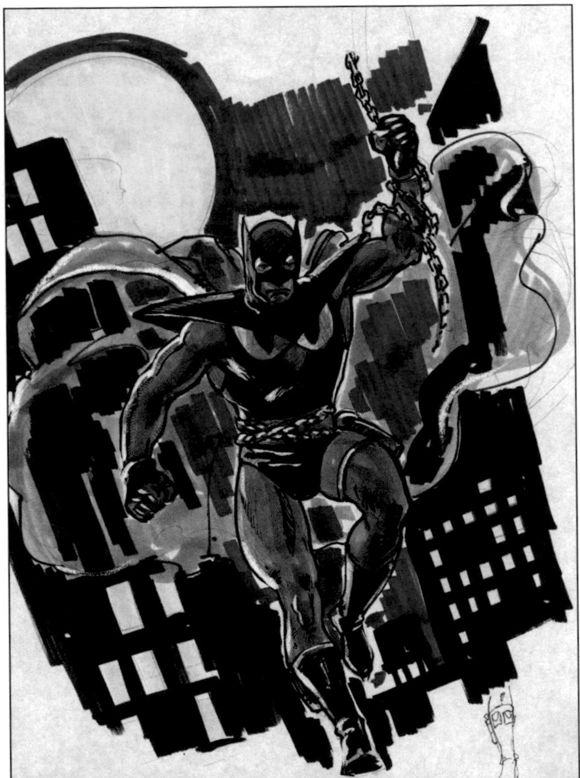

THE ORIGINAL CONCEPT FOR *CLOAKED* (ORIGINALLY TITLED *THE ICON*) WAS DEVELOPED IN THE LATE 1980S. THESE CHARACTER DESIGNS FROM 1989 WERE CREATED BY ARTIST GARY BARKER.

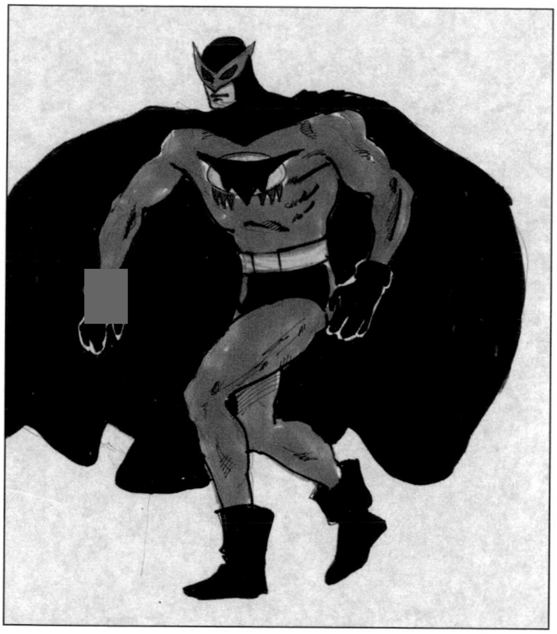
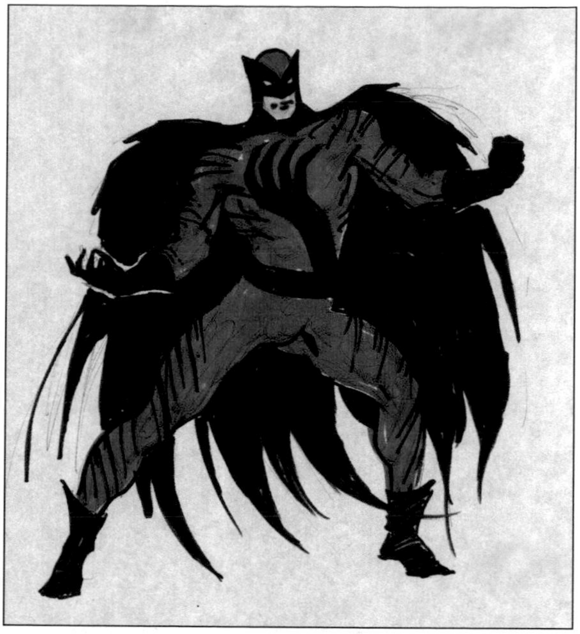
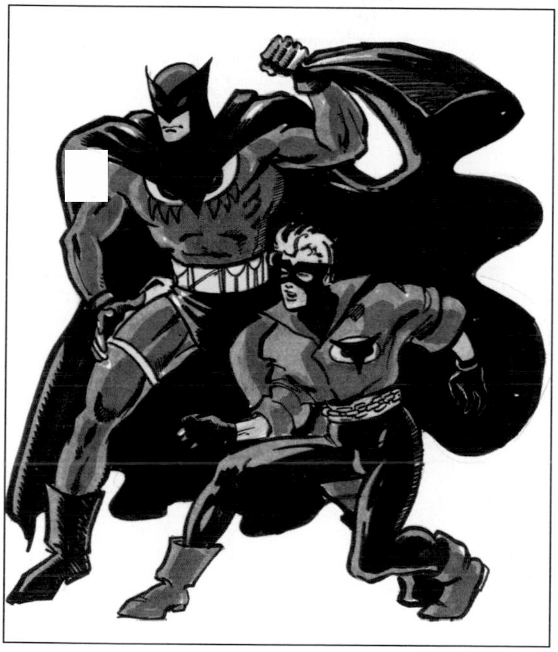
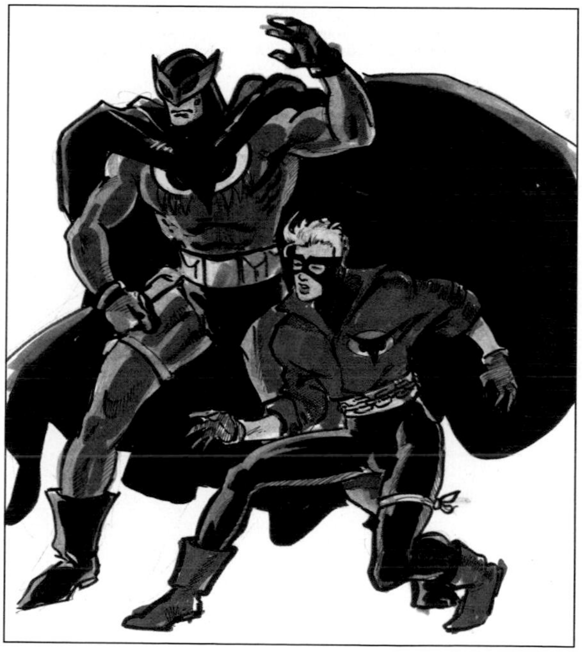

CREATOR BIOS

MIKE RICHARDSON is best known as the publisher, president, and founder of Dark Horse Comics and as a film and TV producer for *Hellboy*, *Mystery Men*, *The Umbrella Academy*, and many others. Mike has also written a number of acclaimed comics series and original graphic novels, including *Star Wars: Crimson Empire*, *47 Ronin*, and *Father's Day*. In addition, Mike has created an arsenal of unforgettable characters such as the Mask, Timecop, X, and the Atomic Legion. An avid collector and longtime owner of the Things From Another World comics-shop chain, Mike has an encyclopedic knowledge of comics and pop-culture history, featured in his contributions to the books *Comics: Between the Panels* and *Blast Off!: Rockets, Robots, Ray Guns, and Rarities from the Golden Age of Space Toys*.

JORDI ARMENGOL began his art career at age two with a huge graffitti in the hallway of his family's apartment (ask his mum) in Barcelona, Spain. With a passion for comics and science fiction, Jordi studied fine arts at Escola de la Llotja, then worked for sixteen years in corporate visual and graphic design while also creating fantasy and science-fiction book covers. In 2014 he joined Norma Editorial as a cover artist and writer, then entered the American comics market with *Rogues!* and *Offworlder* with writer Mike Baron. *Cloaked* is his first Dark Horse project, with more in the works. When Jordi isn't drawing, you'll find him reading Neil Gaiman or Cormac McCarthy or laughing with his beloved Laura.

NATE PIEKOS has created some of the industry's most popular fonts and has lettered comics for a broad array of American publishers, including Marvel, DC, Image, and Dark Horse. Nate's work has also been featured in product packaging, in video games, on television, and in feature films. His software has been licensed by Microsoft, Six Flags amusement parks, the *New Yorker* Magazine, the Gap, and many more corporate clients. 2021 saw the publication of his *The Essential Guide to Comic Book Lettering*, the definitive manual on digital lettering for comics.